The creeping shadow of the Great War and its bloody aftermath was yet to come as Tom Kealey played happily in the woods and hop gardens around his new home. The dark clouds of war gathered as a line of men marched out of the small Kentish village to join the thousands of others who were already dug deep into the clinging mud of the Somme.

As he grew into manhood, Tom's natural ability to handle a gun was honed in the woods where he was the gamekeeper. Little did he realise how it would be put to good use when together with his best friend, Tony Long, he enlisted into the 'gunners'. Soon, as the Second World War loomed, they would be sent to France as the German forces pushed the British towards the blood soaked beaches of Dunkirk.

The decision to stand and fight or to join the retreat was Tom's alone and the events which unfolded were only a prelude to what was to come.

Ito Sasaki was the brutal son of a Japanese peasant. On the other side of the world, Skip Krisner was dreaming of becoming a doctor in Phoenix, California. Both were unaware how their lives would soon become so violently entwined.

The enemy fought harder and were more vicious than anything Tom had experienced. Their cruelty was beyond belief and imagination.

Whilst vengeance and hatred burned deep in his heart, the welcoming flame of a candle flickered thousands of miles away in a cottage window in Kent.

After all, Tom had written to his mother to tell her he would be home for Christmas.

Acknowledgements

I wish to thank my family and the friends who gave their help and support which enabled me to bring this book to life.

I am also indebted to Peter Dunstan, a man I never met but whose letter to me helped to inspire this story. Its contents provided the details and authenticity only known to someone who has experienced the horror and suffering, some of which I have endeavoured to describe in the later chapters of the book.

The Long Journey Home

By Alan Vaughan

In memory of all the men who served and died whilst serving in the
85th Anti Tank Regiment 1939-1945

INDEX

Prologue   Christmas Eve 1939

PART ONE

1   Lavender Cottage 1913

2   The Witches Coven

3   Letters from the Somme

4   Dark Clouds darken a Blue Sky

PART TWO

5   Brothers in Arms

6   Flying Fish and Silver Pennies

7   To the Edge of Destiny 1942

8   A Warm Welcome Awaits You

9   Hell and High Water 1944

10   A Polished Boot on the Door Step

11   Journey's End

PROLOGUE

Christmas Eve-1945

He walked stealthily round the edge of the field. A crisp white frost was sparkling on the corn stubble like a million tiny stars but he moved on, silently, not making even the slightest of sounds. The biting wind was blowing light flurries of snow from the north-east and the hunter's lean face was pinched against the cold. His cupped ears were alert for the slightest of sounds and he could feel the tendons in his legs, taunt, occasionally twitching, ready should he need to run at a moment's notice. His finely honed shoulder muscles were as hard as the ground beneath his feet. He stopped for a while and looked up at the thin sliver of light coming from the new moon and saw it was lying on its back. More bad weather to come he judged and shivered in the chilling darkness when he thought of the warm bed he had just left. The crescent moon provided little light on this bleakest of nights but he could see well enough for what he had to do and he knew those he was hunting would probably be able to see him too. Yes, he would need all the stealth he possessed if he was going to make a killing. The lone hunter's instinct was telling him, he would have to be especially quiet tonight and keep close to the newly cut hawthorn and maple hedge which was growing round the edge of the field. It had become quiet now and the loud, heart stopping noises in the sky, that had sounded like a thousand shot guns and which turned night into day, had now ceased. The explosions on the ground had thrown the earth high into the sky, even higher than the tallest trees in the wood, had also stopped. He remembered how scared those explosions had made him. He had wanted to run and keep running but he went to earth, panting and shaking until the strange noises had stopped. Thankfully these things were in the past now and the hunter moved on knowing there would be some killing done tonight.

On the far side of the field he could see a light flickering in the window of the old cottage which stood alone on the edge of the woods. The snow was beginning to pile up on the roof whilst the winter's Arctic blast strafed the chimneys. Inside, slumped in a wooden chair and wrapped in a blanket was an old woman who was over seventy years old. She was quite frail with snow white hair. The deeply etched lines on her face betrayed her age and just clinging to the tip of her nose was a pair of wire rimmed spectacles.

The flameless fire in the room was hardly glowing for it had died down some hours ago and now the room was as cold as the night air the hunter could feel around him. The old lady was alone in the gloom of the soulless cottage but before she had fallen asleep, she had lit a candle in the bedroom window to welcome her son, Tom, back from the war. She had thought he would have arrived on Christmas Eve but never mind, she had said to herself before falling asleep, it will be lovely to have him home for Christmas Day. There were some Christmas cards on the mantelpiece, the old lady had put some holly round the mirror that hung over the useless fire and standing on the sideboard, were two bottles of Tom's favourite beer.

It was in the small hours of Christmas morning in 1945 when the old fox set out and the dreadful war was finally over. The starlit sky was at last clear of the Luftwaffe bomber planes and the doodlebug rockets which had caused such devastation to this small community and old Emily Kealey slept undisturbed, with only dreams of her son to keep her company.

The hunter had moved round the snow plastered fields to the place the villagers of this small Kentish village of Pentbury, called the Warren. Here he hoped to make his first kill, it would be quick and he would carry the still warm body back to his earth. The sly old dog fox knew this was the place to find a few juicy rabbits or at least it was, but since the deafening noises had started a number of winters back, the rabbits were harder to find. One day, in the heat of the summer sun when he was laying out in the lush shade of a whitethorn tree, he had noticed some humans carrying dead rabbits back into their houses. What did they do with them? Had the humans started to eat the rabbits, he wondered?

The fox sniffed the air greedily and licked his lips with a hungry intent as he started to work his way round the numerous rabbit holes which were dug in the sandy soil of the warren. Suddenly he felt more confident of getting a meal when he saw the small round droppings of the rabbits, were everywhere, but wait, he stopped and lifted his nose and smelt the cold night air. Yes, he was right. It was the smell of humans. He had learnt this scent when he was a cub, seven or eight summers ago but there was another scent which he could smell, was it a weasel or a stoat? No, it was different again. It was the scent of a polecat or as the humans called them, ferrets. The humans had been here again, taking his food! Where would he get food in a few moons time when he had found and mated with a vixen and there were cubs of his own in the earth?

He knew the chances of finding a sleeping bird were extremely slim and the frogs were still deep in the ponds, so he would have no luck there. Perhaps he would take a chance and go into the gardens where the humans kept their fowls, where sometimes he had managed to get into a hen or duck house and when he did, what fun he had. The old fox remembered the time with relish when he had killed every fear struck bird by biting off their heads and once done he had then made off with one of the warm bodies and had left the rest. The cunning fox licked his lips at the thought of it and wondered if times like that would ever return.

He had noticed that some of the humans had also started keeping tame rabbits in hutches in their gardens. Why, he thought, did they do this? Did the humans need the food, were they as hungry as him?

It was nearly daybreak when the old dog fox began making his way back to his earth. The black-coated rooks high up in the elm trees had already started their familiar raucous calls of *"caw, caw, caw"*. This was a sure signal the protective cloak of darkness was soon to disappear.

As he walked under the high wires which criss-crossed the hop gardens, the fox noticed the humans had been stringing the hills of hops in preparation for the young green bines to climb their way up in the spring. The humans had tied long wooden stilts to their legs so they could reach the top of the tall wires onto which they tied the strings. The old fox was grateful the men on their stilts had broken up the frosty ground and now, at last, there may be a meal to be had. He knew exactly what to do, he had done it many times before when other food had been difficult to find.

 From their lofty perch high up in the tall elm trees, the bemused rooks watched the fox with growing amusement as he started dancing. He jumped high into the cold night air and then landed heavily on his front feet. He did it again and again before stopping and listening. The vibrations from the fox's dance were beginning to bring the worms to the surface. Suddenly, he plunged his long pointed muzzle into the frost encrusted soil and brought out two wriggling worms that were desperately trying to escape from the clutches of his mouth. Quickly, the fox thrust his head back and greedily swallowed them. The rooks continued to watch the dancing fox until he couldn't find any more of the creatures. Ruefully, the old fox concluded as he finished the last of the worms, that although they had been a meal, it was not as good as a rabbit would have been.

 On the way back from the hop garden he stopped to watch a group of badgers drag the bedding out of their sett and replace it with some dry bracken and long dry grass which was growing nearby. Why the badgers did this was a mystery to him, he had never known any fox do it, but then, he had always thought that badgers were strange creatures. Once, when chasing a young rabbit he had foolishly followed it into a badger's sett and he remembered how surprised he was on seeing it had been carpeted with freshly gathered moss. He had even seen an old sow badger clean her clay covered feet by scraping them on low lying branches before she entered her sett. The fox shook his head at such a thought.

As he was trotting back across the field, the wily fox noticed the sky was turning the colour of amber as the sun began to rise in the east but his hungry belly still ached. Tasty as worms may be, he thought, they would not be enough to keep him alive in the long days which were to come. His long legs broke into a trot. He must hurry and find his earth and perhaps tomorrow, he would have better luck. He glanced across his shoulder at the old cottage he had seen when he had set out some hours ago and as he looked, he could see the flickering flame of a candle was still burning brightly in the window.

PART ONE

Life and summer are fleeting, sang the bird. Snow and dark and winter comes, nothing remains the same.

Elyne Mitchell

1

Lavender Cottage-1913

It was a wonderful spring morning which lifted Edwin Kealey's spirit filling him with optimism for what lay ahead. He was leaving the small village of Chartham where his family had lived for generations and was taking his wife Emily and their four young children to start a new position in the village of Pentbury, some twenty miles away. As the small group left the coach house which had been their home for the past twelve years, Edwin was in a cheerful mood. Partly it was relief that the long, dark days of winter were over but more especially it was because he was looking forward to better things to come. He had enjoyed being the coachman at the rambling old Grange, but the world had changed. The coaches and traps had been sold and his beloved horses were seeing out their remaining days frolicking and rolling in the freedom of the lush green water meadows, which would soon be strewn with buttercups and white and yellow faced daisies. Cheerful as Edwin was, he knew he would miss their home which had been next to the stables and the warm smell of the horses. He would miss his weekly routine of cleaning and shining the horse harnesses with their brass attachments and the coaches which had been kept in the coach shed. The days when the wealthy were driven about in their horse drawn carriages and attended to by liveried coachmen were over. The day of the automobile had arrived and Edwin had secured the position of chauffeur to Major Bentley-Ward at Parkington Hall in Pentbury.

Old Ben Turner, the village carrier had loaded the family's belongings onto his cart at daybreak, just as the birds had started to sing their daily morning chorus and was now well on his way following the

Pilgrims Way to Pentbury. It was along this narrow road hoards of pilgrims had trudged for hundreds of years to pay homage to the shrine of Thomas a Becket in Canterbury Cathedral but now the old carrier and his trusty Welsh Cob, securely harnessed between the shafts of the cart, were slowly heading in the opposite direction. Ben was delighting in the stillness of the early morning as he passed a meadow where a herd of brown and white cows were waiting patiently for the cowman to call them for their morning milking. They stopped chewing the cud to stare curiously at the carrier's horse, which despite Bens urging, had slowed his steady pace to stare back at the gaping creatures. The sun was still hanging low over the dew soaked hedgerows as Ben flicked the reins of his travelling companion.

"Gee up, gee up boy", he said, as he shifted his backside on the hard wooden seat of the cart piled high with the Kealeys' belongings, not least, with a crate of Emily Kealey's white chickens precariously perched on the top.

The cart bounced heartily as one of its wheels found another of the lane's potholes causing Ben to think, as he had for so many times in the past, how he wished the carpenter could have fitted some springs when he made the cart in his village workshop. He smiled wistfully at the thought as he flicked the leather reins. It wasn't necessary as Ben always let the Welsh Cob make its own pace. The journey to Pentbury would take about four hours, give or take some. He wasn't in a hurry. The old horse could still manage about five miles in an hour and Ben was happy it was a bright, dry morning and he hadn't needed to fit the tilt cover over the cart for the long journey.

Meanwhile the small family group had walked past the old farm house, appropriately named, Stour Farm, as it stood on the banks of the crystal clear River Stour. It was in this house, thirty five years earlier Edwin had been born. He looked towards the river as it meandered its way to the city of Canterbury. The tall reeds were bending in the margins as they yielded to the river's fast flowing current and Edwin wondered if the coots and moorhens had started nesting in them yet. Unknowingly, he licked his lips. He could almost taste the fried breakfasts of moorhens' eggs he had enjoyed when he lived in the farmhouse as a child. Sometimes, when he had walked across the fields to the village school, he would pick the horse mushrooms which grew as big as tea plates in the lush meadows and his mother would fry them with the little eggs the next morning.

Before Edwin pushed his childhood memories to the back of his mind, he bent down and picked a solitary primrose he had seen growing in the grass and threaded it through the button-hole sewn into the lapel of his jacket. A memento, he thought, and then for the final time, he looked across at the river knowing that soon the brown trout would be rising. He could see the flies were already swarming over the silver river and being greedily taken by the newly arrived swallows and house martins as they swooped and skimmed overhead.

The memories which were racing through Edwin's mind had briefly swept away his thoughts of the new beginnings for himself and his family at Pentbury. Perhaps in his own way he was closing one chapter of his life in preparation for the next one to open. He looked at the five acre field next to the old farm house and saw the dark green shoots of wheat emerging through the winter's cold bare earth. How many times, he thought had he sat on the grassy bank and watched his father, John Kealey, plough the field with his team of horses, Clover and Gold. Edwin smiled as he remembered the names of his father's shire horses and thought, when as a child he would lead them up the lane to the forge where his Uncle Jess was the village blacksmith and how he would watch the sparks fly as the two lumbering horses were shod.

Horses had always been part of Edwin's life. Even as a very young child, he had helped his father harness the horses to the plough and the hay carts and again in later years, when he had been responsible for the horses at the Grange. Yes, he thought, in the months and years ahead of him, one thing was certain, he would miss the horses.

Edwin was a quiet man, slightly built with a serious and thoughtful manner, qualities that had been honed by his many years of service to the gentry at the big house. On the other hand his father, John Kealey had been a man of the soil. He too, had not been a tall man and had been in his later years quite stout but with strong, muscular arms and broad shoulders. His time-weathered face had been framed by white mutton-chop side burns which had reached down to his pure white beard. He had been a jovial man, who despite the hard life on the farm, always had a smile on his face and a twinkle in his bright green eyes. The folk in the village who still remembered the old man's smile and laughing eyes had often remarked how much little Tom was like his grandfather in that respect.

One of those was the old carrier, Ben Turner, who had known the Kealeys for all of his life and as he made his way to Pentbury with all their worldly goods, he thought what good people they were and how much he was going to miss them.

The hedgerows were thick with sweet-smelling May blossom, as white as the winters snow and a cock chaffinch was singing his throat out in an attempt to out-sing an old thrush which was perched on the topmost branch of a willow tree. Edwin looked at the trees growing by the river and noticed they were resplendent in their livery of buds. Some, like the fat treacle-brown sticky buds of the horse chestnut tree were already starting to burst into life whilst others, like the ash, waited patiently for the warmer weather to arrive before they followed suit.

The place didn't hold the same memories for Emily Kealey. She had come to the Grange in service as a kitchen maid, when she had left her family home in Uxbridge at the tender age of fourteen. She had first met Edwin when he too was in service there as a houseboy. It seemed so many years ago and now although she was feeling slightly apprehensive about their move from Chartham, she was looking forward to seeing the cottage at Pentbury which would become their new home.

Emily and Edwin's two older sons, Harry and Fred ran ahead of the rest of the group, eager to get to the village station and watch the trains. The boys were dressed in their Sunday best. Tweed Norfolk jackets, with the three buttons at the front, neatly buttoned with matching knickerbockers trousers, whilst the large Eton collars of their white shirts spilled over the outside of their jackets. Their sister, Glad, with two new pink ribbons tied gaily in her hair, held her fathers' hand as she walked more sedately along, bag in hand, to the station. The youngest of the small group was four year old Tom. Although his name was Edwin, just like his father, since the day he had been born everybody knew him as Tom and the little lad held his mother's hand, skipping happily by her side.

"Nearly there darling", Emily said, looking down at her son, who the good Lord had blessed with a perpetual smile on his pale face. It was the kind of smile which enticed happiness whenever people saw it. His dark olive green eyes were the colour of the river when the sun darted on its surface and his hair was the shade of golden toast. It was no wonder that everybody adored little Tom, especially his mother.

"Mother", whispered Tom, "is this the start of our long journey?"

"Yes darling".

Emily smiled at her little son's innocence and added "it's the start of the longest journey of your life".

Above the square flint tower of the old Norman church, narrow winged swifts wheeled high in the sky as the family made their way to bid their farewells to the old crossing gate-keeper before stepping onto the platform at the train station.

The older children had been to the station many times before, when they would sit on the white-painted crossing gate and talk to Joseph Oliver who was the gate-keeper and watch the billowing steam from the locomotives as they chugged into the station. The children's growing excitement of the impending train ride was suddenly tinged with sorrow when they realised that they may not see the old man again. Old Joe, as the children called him, bent down and lovingly wiped away the tears which were streaming down Glad's cheeks with his spotted red handkerchief before he turned his head away and lifted the damp cloth towards his own wet eyes.

Emily, who was anxious to move on, said quickly to her little son, "Look that way and soon you will see the locomotive coming".

The boy gripped his mothers' hand as they stood on the edge of the platform and watched a porter, resplendent in a blue and rather tight fitting long sleeved waistcoat, as he pushed a long-handled barrow past them. Emily pulled Tom closer to her noticing the man's barrow was loaded so high with trunks and boxes he could hardly see over the top of them.

"Good morning, Mrs Kealey".

Tom looked round to see who had spoken to his mother. It was a portly man with a snow white beard. Firmly fixed on the man's head was a black coloured cap with gold braid round its peak and wrapped around him was an unbuttoned frock coat, the colour of a mid-summer sky, with each side not quite making it to the middle. Tom, who had his eyes transfixed on the man's enormous girth, looked at a gold watch chain which was disappearing into the pocket of the man's protruding waistcoat.

"Good morning, station master", Emily replied politely.

"I heard that you and your husband were leaving today. Off to Pentbury, is it?" the genial man enquired.

Tom, who was not particularly interested in what his mother was saying to the fat man, turned away and continued to watch for the arrival of the steam locomotive.

"HERE IT COMES, here it comes", the little boy shouted excitedly, interrupting his mother's conversation with the station master.

In the distance, snaking between the trees, some newly clothed in their fresh green leaves and the fields of the emerging shoots of corn were the puffs of white smoke, signalling the arrival of the locomotive.

Tom shouted out, "I CAN SEE IT", when he saw the smoke billowing from the locomotive.

It seemed like a living thing to the wide eyed boy. Just like a strange, unknown creature which was alive with power and threat. From its huge black head it was breathing out smoke and steam that rose high in the sky. The two, red painted round buffers looked liked blood dripping from the creature's mouth and as it raced round a bend in the track, Tom could see its long green body snaking back into the distance. He stood with his little feet fixed firmly to the platform as if he was made of stone and then began to shake with fright as he squeezed his mother's hand, tightly, not intending to let go. The huge black and green dragon which had come out of its lair was heading straight towards him.

Towering above the young boy, the huge locomotive slowly came into the station with its brakes squealing as it came to a halt just past where the family were standing. Tom covered his ears with his small hands as jets of steam started hissing from the pistons which were connected to three of the train's largest steel wheels by huge metal rods. The station platform filled with smoke and steam and Tom could see the burning coal in the engine's firebox. As more steam, this time gushing with spurts of boiling water from a large copper pipe under the belly of the hot engine gradually enveloped the small group of travellers, Tom's young nostrils delighted in its sweet smell. Although he never realised it at the time, for the rest of his life the delicious smell of the hot oil and coal dust held unseen in the clouds of wet, clammy steam would never be erased from his memory.

Edwin Kealey walked quickly towards the waiting train heading for the door of the nearest third class carriage and with a degree of urgency, turned the brass door handle which had been polished as bright as a shiny new penny by the countless hands which had already gripped it. He had never travelled in the second class carriages because of the expense and he knew that only the landed gentry together with the very rich would ever travel first class. Taking a step back, Edwin ushered his family on board the train.

"Quick Fred", Harry shouted to his brother, as the two eldest boys clambered up the step into the train's corridor and ran down it to find an empty carriage and *bag* the window seats.

In the locomotive's cab, the coal blackened fireman, his face streaked with rivers of sweat and glowing red from the heat of the fire, picked up his shovel and threw more coal, from the tender, into the roaring flames raging in the engine's firebox. The driver was already leaning out of the cab, watching for the guard on the platform to raise his green flag and then, upon seeing the man's signal, he blew the train's whistle with a long, deafening hoot. With his huge hands, the driver wrapped an oily rag round the handle of the brake lever and slowly released the brakes that were locked onto the huge wheels of the locomotive and then, with a loud hiss of steam escaping from the regulator, the lumbering train gradually started to heave itself slowly forward.

Meanwhile the children had bunched themselves round the carriage windows and with their faces pressed hard against the cold glass they waited for their journey to begin, making patterns on the misted windows with their flattened noses. Suddenly, on hearing the shrill sound of the train's whistle, they stopped their artistic creations and watched as white clouds of steam floated slowly past the windows.

"We're moving, we're moving.... the train's moving", shouted Tom excitedly, as he bounced up and down on the springs which were coiled deep in the richly upholstered seat he was sitting on.

"Look out the window and see what you can see, my dears", Emily said, smiling as she watched her excited children.

She reached out and took her husband's hand and tenderly lifted it to her moist lips and softly kissed it. Edwin put his arm round his attractive wife's shoulder and together they let their bodies sink together into the comfort of the fat sprung seat and with Emily's head resting on his shoulder. Edwin closed his eyes and fell fast asleep.

As the loaded train moved off laboriously, the children started to wave at the people who were standing on the platform and shouted with whoops of joy when the people waved back.

"Mother, Father, quickly...look out the window", shouted Glad urgently.

Together, Emily and Edwin, who had been awoken from his brief slumber, quickly wiped the misted window and looked out. They were just in time to see Joseph Oliver, the old crossing gate-keeper and the rotund station master standing side by side on the platform, waving their goodbyes and no doubt wishing the family well in the new life ahead of them. Edwin noticed both men had removed their hats as a sign of respect and he nodded his head in appreciation and breathed deeply.

The life he had known in Chartham was being quickly left behind.

"*Clickety clack, clickety clack, clickety clack*", Tom mimicked the sound the train as it sped over the gaps in the iron rails.

The young boy began to notice how the rhythm changed as the speed of the train grew faster and how the telegraph poles at the side of the track zoomed past the window in harmony.

"Clickety clack.. clickety.... clickety clack.. clickety...clickety clack..clickety", he repeated, deciding that he loved train journeys. How exciting they were, he thought.

After a while, Harry, who could be quite a fidgety child at times, grew bored of watching the countryside speeding past and upon realising his mother and father were now both asleep, quietly released the brown leather strap which held the window tightly shut and let it drop down with a thud. The noise and the force of the air rushing into carriage frightened Tom and made his eyes water and he quickly snuggled against his mother's warm body. The little boy could smell the smoke of the train in the carriage and he edged even closer to his mother for safety. Harry stood up and poked his head out of the open window. His eyes traced along the line of snaking carriages and up in front of them he could see the engine. There was black smoke pouring out of its smoke stack and squirts of steam were coming from every seam and joint around its wheels. As the train curved round a bend in the track, he could see, just ahead, the dark shape of a tunnel which had been cut into the chalk hillside. It was the loud blast of the train's whistle as it entered the tunnel which awoke Edwin from his sleep.

"SHUT THE WINDOW", he shouted at his son, "and come away from that door at once".

Trying not to look into his father's angry eyes, the chastened boy sat down, rubbing his eyes in a vain attempt to remove a small piece of gritty soot which had been blown from the engine's smoke stack.

In the hedgerow, the cow parsley was coming into bloom and orange bellied bumble bees searched for pollen amongst its early lace-like flowers as the family slowly made their way up the narrow lane towards the village of Pentbury. It had been a long walk from the station in the market town of Maidstone and everybody was feeling tired. The children felt as if their boots were filled with lead as they trudged slowly up the unfamiliar lane with its unknown number of twists and turns.

"Father, *how* much further is it"? each one of the children groaned in succession, as they stopped and looked up the never ending lane.

"Come on children, catch up", Emily said, as she lifted little Tom in her arms before pausing to wait for her other three dawdling offspring.

"There it is, that's the cottage", Edwin, who had been walking ahead, said, looking back at the others.

Tired and aching legs were instantly forgotten as the children ran up the lane, bordered as it was with bright yellow celandines, the colour of newly patted butter and little clumps of purple and white dog violets, hiding amongst the tussocks of grass.

The four children, each anxious to be the first to reach their new home, raced each other up the narrow lane.

"Edwin, it looks lovely", Emily said breathlessly, as she gazed at the cottage. Its creamy white stone walls glistened as they bathed in warm glow of the spring sunshine. "It looks like a dolls house, Edwin, it's so pretty", she gushed as she looked at the dainty blue gingham curtains fluttering in the small windows positioned either side of the brightly painted red front door.

Emily could not believe her eyes. A brick path, worn smooth over the years by the feet of previous tenants, led from the gate by the lane to the front door, bordered either side with brightly coloured pansies, their yellow and blue faces nodding gently in the warm breeze, whilst their rich perfume filled the air.

"Oh Edwin, we are going to be so happy here", she said, taking her husband's hand, "look at the sign over the front porch, Lavender Cottage, it's so perfect my dear".

Emily could not contain her excitement at seeing their new home. It was everything she had hoped for and with curiosity getting the better of her she set off with Glad to explore the inside of the cottage. In the meantime, the boys were already out in the sun dappled garden at the back of the house.

Fred's eyes lit up on seeing a water pump which was fixed to the wall and he could not resist lifting its long handle up and down until cold clear water gushed into an old galvanised bucket which was hanging from its wide spout. Meanwhile Harry had already begun to cautiously open the door of the red brick wash house, when Fred suddenly shouted out a warning, "LOOK OUT HARRY, I CAN SEE ITS YELLOW EYES".

Instantly, Harry slammed the door shut and quickly retreated backwards, almost falling over as he did so. With Fred's mocking laughter ringing in his ears he realised he had been tricked and quickly looked around in the hope of finding a stone to throw at his cackling sibling. He had slammed the door so hard some of its peeling white paint now lay in thick curls on the doorstep, revealing patches of the dark blue paint which had been its original colour many years before. When Harry started to slowly open the door again, there was a painful squeak suggesting it had been a long time since its creaking hinges had seen any oil. Peeping inside the dark building, Harry spotted the remains of a fire lying forlornly underneath the deep bowl of a copper whilst nearby was a pile of unused sticks, ready to stoke the fire into life when hot water was needed. Gradually, as Harry's eyes became accustomed to the gloom of the wash-house, he could see there was a grey tin bath hanging on a large rusty nail hammered into the white-washed wall and as he looked around, there was a dust covered mangle standing in the corner. Harry knew his mother always did the washing on Monday mornings at Chartham and once she had got the steaming washing out of the water boiling in the copper, she would turn the handle on the side of the mangle and squeeze the water out of the dripping washing as it was squashed between its wooden rollers. Yes, the boy thought, mother will be pleased finding there's a copper and a mangle here.

With the exploration of their new home completed, Emily and Glad joined Edwin and the boys in the back garden. Edwin's face broke into a broad smile when he spotted a few parsnips growing in soft black soil alongside a row of white stemmed leeks. Black and red currant bushes were growing in the corner with their small green fruit hanging down, waiting for the summer's sun to turn them into clusters of black and ruby-red coloured pearls.

"Plenty of room for the hens", Edwin said with a nod of satisfaction as he joined the boys and turned to inspect a dilapidated chicken house which was surrounded by a wire netting run.

"The netting is high enough to stop the foxes getting in but the hen house needs some work done to it".

His words were directed towards his two eldest sons who were standing next to him, their hostilities forgotten. Edwin had already thought this was a place where foxes could easily flourish in the woods and fields around the cottage.

"Look Edwin, rhubarb", Emily cried out, as she admired a clump of red crowns beginning to burst through the ground at the bottom of the garden by the small brick privy. She smiled demurely to herself as she recalled that rhubarb was always planted next to a privy.

The reluctant door of the small building was stiff when Edwin tried to open it. A large black spider made a hasty retreat as he shoved the door open with his shoulder, breaking the creature's web which it had carefully spun during the time the important little structure had been unoccupied and un-cared for. Under the long wooden seat was a large and slightly soiled wide-mouthed bucket and looking up, Edwin was amused to see impaled on a nail which had been driven into the wall by a previous occupant, there remained a few neatly cut squares of yellowing newspaper. At night, the only light would have to come from the stub of a drooping white candle which had been secured in a pool of its own wax onto a small dusty shelf. Edwin grunted with considerable satisfaction as he finally surveyed the privy for one last time, noting the height of the wooden door finished just above eye level, that's good for the ventilation, he thought to himself.

Meanwhile, the three boys had already climbed over the chestnut spile fence which divided the bottom of the garden from the woods beyond and Edwin and Emily smiled with contentment when they heard the shouts and laughter coming from the young explorers confirming they to, would be happy living at Lavender Cottage.

"Anybody at home?" shouted a familiar voice, coming from the front of the cottage.

"We're round the back, Ben", Edwin replied, as he walked round to meet the carrier. "You have made good time".

The genial old man, whose weather-beaten face was wrinkled like a sun-dried plum, said as a way of an explanation. "We started out before the cock crowed and for most of the journey the sun was on our backs and with luck *we* shall get home before *he* needs the light of the moon to find his way back".

Edwin shook Ben's calloused hand warmly, grinning at how the old carrier always referred to himself and his horse, as *we* and *us* and *our*. The pair of them had worked together for so many years and as Ben seldom carried passengers on the cart, preferring to work alone with his horse, the animal and the man had become mutual friends, genuinely enjoying each other's company.

"Fred, cut some kindling wood and light a fire in the range, so your mother can get the kettle on and Harry and Glad, come and give a hand to unload the cart", ordered Edwin sternly to the three eldest children, conscious that Ben would want to start for home as soon as he had something to eat and drink.

Whilst he waited for the cart to be unloaded, the brown and white Welsh Cob stood patiently between the shafts, eating oats from a hessian nose bag which Ben had fashioned from an old potato sack. Occasionally, the horse flicked the persistent bluebottles which tried to land on his back with his long tail. Harry jumped up on the cart and handed the crate of white leghorns to his sister who was eager to show them their new home.

"Glad, my dear", said Ben, as he turned to look at his horse as if to get its agreement to what he was about to say, "Give 'em", he said, nodding his head towards the agitated chicken, "some of them oats that are in the sack 'anging off the back of the cart. Those birds will start laying all the more quickly with some of them oats inside 'em after the shaking up they've 'ad".

Soon the cart was unloaded. The pots and pans were lined up on the shelves in the scullery with its stone slab floor and white marble shelves. Bedsteads and their horse-hair mattresses had been pushed and dragged up the narrow staircase and put into the appropriate bedrooms whilst Emily went from one to another with blankets and sheets and goose down pillows. Tom had carefully carried the heavy white chamber pots up the creaking stairs and into the bedrooms placing one under each bed, ready, should nature call during the night. Edwin and the two older boys unloaded the heavy pieces of furniture and carried them into the two rooms which were either side of the small hallway in the front of the cottage.

The Welsh Cob, having been released from the restricting shafts of the cart, was grazing contentedly in the large field in the front of the house until the time came for Ben to harness him and they would start to make the long journey home. Emily laid a pink cotton tablecloth on the living room table which had been left outside the back door and put out her best china. A large teapot of freshly brewed tea stood steaming on the table alongside a large crusty loaf and two glass jars of pickles, when Emily called out tea was ready.

Edwin and Ben Turner sat at the table chatting quietly, resting their aching muscles whilst they waited for the children to finish washing their hands under the pump in the back yard. Emily quietly watched some honey bees foraging for pollen in a lavender bush and listened in delight to the cacophony of the evening bird song until the sweet sound was shattered by the children's noisy arrival at the table.

"Most grateful to you Mrs Kealey", said the carrier as he reached across and helped himself to a large slab of cheddar cheese before cutting a doorstep sized slice of bread and digging two spoonfuls of plum chutney out of the jar standing next to the pickles.

"You're most welcome Mr Turner, after all, you brought it all here on your cart", smiled Emily as she watched the old man swirl his tongue round his mouth to savour the tang of the chutney before washing it down with a cup of sweetened tea. Without being asked, the old man reached across the table to take another plateful of the cheese and pickled beetroot and slice another doorstep off the loaf.

"Can I offer you a slice of fruit cake?" Emily asked the old man, already knowing with considerable certainty what his reply would be.

Unable to speak, due his mouth being full of the pickles, but concerned he would not be offered again, the old man nodded his head up and down so vigorously, he shook out a piece of pickled beetroot from his overfull mouth, which landed, much to Emily's alarm, on her clean tablecloth. The children started to giggle at the flying vegetable until their father told them to stop and mind their manners.

The family stood together outside their new home whilst Ben tucked a bottle of cold tea and the remains of the fruit cake which Emily had given to him for his journey home, safely under the seat of the cart. She could see there was sadness in the old man's eyes as he bent down to kiss Glad on her forehead. The little girl had always been his favourite and he put his hand into his pocket and with a wink of his eye, he gave her a penny.

"Thank you Mr Turner", she said politely as he smiled and walked along the line the three boys had formed. The old Carrier fondly ruffled each of the boy's hair in turn with a gnarled and calloused hand and then, when he reached Emily he touched his forelock and said, glancing back at the children, "Goodbye my dear, take good care of them........I'm going to miss them".

Emily took his hand and said softly, "Goodbye Mr Turner and you take care of yourself".

Finally, before he turned to go, he took Edwin's outstretched hand and gripped it tightly. Then with a wide grin spreading across his lined face, he said, "Edwin, when you go racing down those lanes in that 'orseless carriage, you remember that me and my old 'orse may be round one of them corners".

Edwin smiled and held onto Ben's hand saying, "Goodbye my dear friend".

With that said, the carrier slowly pulled himself onto his cart and with a final look over his shoulder, he shook the reins and as he felt his horse lean into its harness, he began to make his way back along the bumpy lane to Chartham.

Edwin licked his thumb and forefinger, something he had done for most of his thirty five years, before pinching out the flame of the candle which had been burning on the mantle shelf over the small cast iron fireplace in the bedroom. The children were fast asleep and he could see that Emily was already lying snugly, tucked up in bed. Her head had sunk deep into the marsh-mellow softness of the goose down pillow as she watched her husband walk towards the small window which overlooked the large field in front of their new home.

He pulled back the thin floral curtains and stood looking up as the passing clouds unveiled a starlit sky. Edwin liked to see the constellations and his eyes probed the coal black sky as they searched for familiar shapes. "There they are", he murmured softly with evident satisfaction, as he recognised some of the brightest of the stars twinkling in the night sky. "Orion's Belt, the hunter and there are the seven stars of the Plough. He felt content that they at least had not changed. His eyes followed the shape until they reached the bottom two stars which formed the plough's blade. He smiled as he remembered his father calling these stars, the pointers, because by following their direction, you could find the North Star, the brightest star in the sky.

Emily had been watching her husband and she whispered, "A penny for your thoughts, Edwin".

"I don't know what it is, my dear, but I've a feeling that we are going to be very happy here", he replied as he started to draw the curtains together.

"Leave them open tonight", Emily replied contentedly, "and let the moonlight shine in on us".

Edwin looked back at his wife and saw, not for the first time, that she had lost none of her youthful beauty. Her cornflower blue eyes still sparkled and her skin was as smooth as it was when she was seventeen and as Edwin admired his wife's slim figure and golden yellow hair, he realised how fortunate he was. After a few moments, he climbed into their bed and held Emily in a lover's embrace. After some moments of tenderness, they fell asleep, entwined in each other's arms.

On the other side of the world an old man was bent almost double as he returned home after twelve hours of labour in the paddy field.

His back ached as it did on every day and his feet were red and sore after spending a lifetime ankle-deep in the water-filled fields. The hours spent plunging the small rice plants through the water into the rich, stinking mud below had made his bony hands puffy and wrinkled. On his head he was wearing a conical hat his wife had made from rice straw and across one of his bony shoulders he balanced a bamboo pole with a woven basket dangling from each end. In the shallow baskets were a few small fish he had caught in the muddy water of the rice field and some vegetables he had grown in the patch of land allocated to him.

There was no happiness on the man's face. Life was hard and unforgiving. Sometimes he dreamt he had been born to become a farmer or a fisherman or even a metal worker. Then he would have been somebody who would be entitled to be shown some respect in society. But a peasant! He was not even entitled to eat all the rice and vegetables he grew as half the crop was taken in rent. Why couldn't he have been a *Shogun* or a *Dalmyo* with his own army of *Samurai* warriors or even an *Ashigaru*, a foot soldier to a *Samurai*. Now those years had passed long ago and instead he was a Japanese peasant with an unloving wife and an unwanted son they had named Ito. He sighed and shifted the weight of the bamboo pole to his other scawny shoulder.

Ito Sasaki hated being the unwanted son of the peasant. He hated his crooked-backed father and he hated the dirt village where they lived.

Despite the family's meagre diet, he was the fattest child in the village and ever since he had been born, the rest of the children who lived there had made fun of him. They used to bully and tease him but no more. Those days had passed. Although he had not yet reached his tenth birthday, the very same people were now scared of him and his violent fits of anger; scared of his flying fists and his vicious boots. His father rejected him. The teachers who taught in the Commoners school had rejected him. The village rejected him. The short, fat boy with the vicious temper didn't fit in.

Ito Sasaki's eyelids slowly closed over the cold, black pupils in his slanted eyes as he dreamt of the day when he would reach his twenty-third birthday and would be conscripted into the Imperial Japanese Army for seven years. He would pledge his loyalty to the Emperor and learn obedience, courage and sacrifice and the spirit of *bushido*. He would become like a *Samurai* warrior of old, prepared to fight to the end and if he showed the qualities required of a Japanese soldier, he might even be given a place at the Officers school.

There was a vicious smile on his young face as he brought his fist down on a brightly coloured butterfly which had landed innocently on the straw mat in front of him.

2

The Witches Coven

"Well I never did", the cook exclaimed when the butler informed her that the Bradley-Wards would be entertaining four guests for dinner that evening and the mistress would be discussing the menu with her later.

The cook was the kind of person who got flustered at even the smallest change to her well ordered routine. "I hope the mistress doesn't leave it too long. Meals like the ones she has been asking for lately don't just happen at the drop of a hat", she said, wiping her hands on her apron. "That's the fourth evening this week", she exclaimed not attempting to hide her exasperation. Huffing and puffing, she briefly turned away from the man standing in front of her to scold the young kitchen maid who had stopped washing the breakfast dishes to listen to the conversation.

Albert Fish stood and nodded his head in agreement but as the butler, discretion was his byword and he wouldn't dream of criticising his employer's domestic arrangements, at least, not in front of the kitchen staff. He had worked for the Major and Mrs Bradley-Ward at Parkington Hall for over twenty years and he knew, perhaps more than anyone else below stairs, how much more entertaining the Bradley-Wards had been doing during the past few months. The house had suddenly become alive with house guests staying there most weekends. Maids scurried to and fro along the narrow corridors carrying fresh linen and fluffy pillows. Picnic hampers had to be arranged for the trips in the countryside and once, when the master and his wife took two of their friends to Folkestone races for the day. "For the day indeed" he said quietly to himself, at the thought of it.

"It's that motor car", the old butler suddenly said absentmindedly, forgetting the cook and the kitchen staff could hear.

"I know it is, I know it is", responded the cook with zeal, making the most of the butler's lapse. She turned to face the unfortunate man. "I saw the thing going along the drive the other day", she continued with growing venom in her voice. "The noise it was making Mr Fish.......and the smoke, I thought the thing was on fire, I really did........and the smell of it, give me those lovely 'orses any day of the week.......oh it's a shame Mr Fish, they say all the lovely coaches and carriages are gathering dust now up in the old coach shed by the farmyard......oh it's such a shame Mr Fish".

The ill-fated butler nodded his head slightly. It was just enough to show that he had heard her but not enough to indicate that he agreed with the red-faced woman's views.

"I cannot think why on earth anyone would want to ride in that thing, can you Mr Fish?....dirty smelly thing, I say give me those lovely 'orses any day", the cook continued without hardly drawing breath as she started to wipe her hands again on her apron, only more furiously this time. "And another thing Mr Fish, what about all the extra work it's causing....all those people who are coming here to see the thing and to ride in it......I've never known anything like it in the kitchen.....all that food they want....it's not simple food either Mr Fish.....I never did Mr Fish, I never did. I'll tell you one thing Mr Fish, you won't ever catch me riding in a thing like that........give me the 'orses any day".

The butler gave the cook a thin smile and as he departed for the sanctity of the upstairs, he heard the opinionated woman continuing her tirade against his master's new form of transportation to the helpless kitchen maid.

With the butler gone, the cook once again turned her attention to the maid, "Do you remember what Percy Wright told us? Over three hundred guineas, he said". Her voice rose even higher and growing with indignation, she spluttered, "Three hundred guineas, that's what the head gardener said the thing had cost".

Edwin Kealey loved the motor car from the first moment he saw it standing in the now redundant carriage yard outside one of the newly vacated stables.

The sun was leaving broad shadows across the cobbled yard and the motor car was gleaming in the late spring sunshine as Edwin took a well-earned rest from polishing it. He stood back and admired the car, marvelling at its size and complexity. Edwin folded his damp polishing cloth to form a pad and gently smeared it into the tin of wax polish he was holding, before using it to achieve a final lustre on the royal blue paintwork of the motor car's long body and doors. At first, he had found it difficult to drive the car and even more difficult to understand how all the various parts worked. It seemed so different from the life he had left behind at Chartham but Major Bradley-Ward had assured him that he would soon be driving the motor car with the same skill as he used to drive the coach and horses.

"Kealey", the major shouted, as he walked with his familiar limp across the yard with his two bull mastiff dogs at his heel. "Mr and Mrs Ridley at Manor Hall have very kindly agreed to allow their chauffeur, Cecil Harris to spend some time with you...at least when he isn't needed", the major added as an after-thought. "He will explain some of the intricacies of a motor car to you", he continued, before finally saying, curtly, "tomorrow would be convenient".

Edwin pinched the peak of his cap with his thumb and fore-finger and said deferentially, "Thank you sir", as the two large dogs bounded off across the park for their morning's exercise. He had seen Cecil Harris from a distance, a few days earlier when had been out for a walk with Emily when the old chauffeur was polishing the Ridley's car, outside the centuries old manor house on the other side of the village.

Edwin was relieved with what the major had just told him and whistled joyfully whilst he finished polishing the car with the same care and attention as he had lavished on the coaches. The car had been made by the Rover Motor Cycle Company who grandly called it a Landaulet. It positively gleamed in the soft spring sunlight as Edwin finished shining its sweeping black mudguards and running boards until he could see the reflection of his face in the paintwork. By jove, he thought, how fortunate I am to secure a position like this.

The next morning, Edwin carefully drove the Rover up the long gravelled drive towards the Elizabethan Manor and as he approached, he could see clusters of mellow, red brick chimney stacks rising from the manor's pan tiled roof, twisting and towering in the sky like giant corkscrews. Driving through the central arch and on to the paved court yard, Edwin marvelled at the rows of mullion windows, each made with a multitude of small panes of glass, lining the Virginia creeper-clad walls of the ancient building. This certainly is a grand house, he thought, but secretly he felt quite smug that the house was neither as large nor as impressive as Parkington Hall.

"Why do you think it is called a Landaulet? " Cecil Harris questioned Edwin, as the two men walked round the parked car.

Edwin thought for a moment before replying to the fellow chauffeur, "Is it because it looks similar to a landau carriage?" Then, as the proverbial penny dropped, he threw his head back and laughed a good belly laugh, saying, "Of course, that's why motor cars are called horseless carriages".

"Precisely", said Cecil, with the air of elderly school master as he continued with his instruction. "Instead of the large wooden spokes in the wheels of a carriage, this has smaller metal ones with rubber tyres in place of iron hoops".

Edwin had immediately liked Cecil Harris. He was older than Edwin, perhaps forty five or fifty and like his pupil, he too had been a coachman before the Ridley's had purchased their car. Edwin watched as Cecil walked round to the side of the car and started to caress the leather hood at the back of the vehicle, with his gloved hand. "You will have already discovered Edwin, this folds down just like the hood on a landau, so when the weather is clement, the master and mistress can take the air".

Edwin smiled at Cecil's comparisons but said nothing as the old chauffeur continued unabated, "Obviously, the driver sits outside of the passengers, just like a carriage driver". Cecil's explanation of the Rover continued in such detail it crossed Edwin's mind, the well-meaning man may have forgotten he had already learnt to drive the car and what he really wanted to know was how everything worked and what all the strange looking things under the folding panels of the bonnet were called.

"Thank you, Cecil, I appreciate the help you have given me", Edwin said, as his shook the older chauffeur's hand at the end of the instruction but as he did so, he could not help wondering if he would remember everything the kindly man had just told him.

The following day Edwin was enjoying the short walk from the cottage to Parkington Hall. It was the drone of a bee searching out the nectar in the white flowers of the early blackberries which made him realise that summer was just round the corner and soon the sun would be higher in the sky and bring with it, the warmer weather. As he walked briskly towards the old stable where the Landaulet was kept, he was thinking what a joy it will be when he could drive down the leafy lanes of Pentbury with the sun breaking through the low hanging oak boughs overhead. Upon arriving at the old stable, Edwin slid the metal locking bar across and opened the small wicket door to let some light in. He sighed with disappointment when, as the sun's rays flooded into the stable, he saw the car was covered in dust. I must get rid of all the old hay up there, it won't be needed now, he thought, as he looked at the offending particles floating down from the hay loft above. Edwin lost no time in flicking the dust off his beloved car and as he did so he tried to remember what Cecil had said about its three speed gearbox and massive engine. He pushed any concerns he had to the back of his mind, safe in the knowledge that he could always ask his new friend again if need be. In his mind, Edwin recalled how astonished he had been when the old chauffeur had explained the car's engine had the power of twelve horses. Twelve horses, he thought. Cecil had also said something about sparking plugs and something else he had called a belt-driven magneto, which was connected to something else called a propeller shaft. Edwin remembered he had thought at the time, it was strange for a motor car to have a propeller and as he continued to clean off the dust, he reflected he would probably need to speak to the Ridley's chauffeur again.

He had been instructed to collect the major and his wife at the front entrance of the Hall at ten-thirty that morning and to drive them to the nearby Grange and to stay there until they were ready to leave. He was pleased they wanted him to wait because he had got to know their friendly cook and she would be sure to give him a bite to eat.

Plenty of time to make sure the Landaulet is perfect for its short journey, he pondered as he swung open the grey painted stable doors. Before attempting to start the car, he walked to driver's side and leaning inside, he slid the small brass slow-running speed lever, which was fixed to the centre of the steering wheel, to its forward position. Edwin had already learnt that this little lever would increase the revolutions of the engine when the car was started. Next he went to the tool box fixed to the car's long running board to find the crank handle needed to start the car. Edwin inserted the end of the crank handle into the keyhole slot under the radiator and before he turned the handle he remembered the dire warning Cecil had given him. "Make sure you cup the crank handle in the palm of your hand, if wrap you your hand around it and it kicks back, it will break your thumb".

Slowly, Edwin cranked the handle round a couple of turns to prime the engine with petrol, before giving it a quick half turn. With a roar and a cloud of smoke, the two cylinder engine burst into life. Edwin replaced the starting handle back in its box and moved smartly round to the right hand side of the car and slid across the bench seat from the passenger side until he was sitting behind the steering wheel. The door on the driver's side was designed not to open because the hand brake and gear change levers were fixed on the inside of its side panel, with the spare wheel and the polished brass horn held securely on the outside.

Although Edwin had been driving the car for two months, including a long journey to Folkestone, he was still quite cautious whenever he drove the car out of the stable. Slowly, he released brake lever and gently pushed his foot down on the clutch pedal and engaged first gear by pushing the gear lever through the gate change. He gradually increased the acceleration and slipped the clutch until the one ton car started to move gracefully out of the fume filled building.

With the car safely parked Edwin pulled his father's silver watch from his waistcoat pocket. "Ten minutes past ten, soon be time to get moving", he said to himself, as he snapped the hinged cover of the watch shut with a resounding click.

He took his grey serge jacket with its blue ribbon edging off the rich leather upholstery of the back seat where he had put it before he had started to dust the car and put it on. Next, he reached for his matching peaked cap and lowered it carefully onto his head before finally checking that his long, brown boots were unblemished. It was only when he was absolutely sure his own appearance was as immaculate as that of his beloved car, did he drive it to the front of the house. As he brought the car gracefully to a halt alongside the wide steps of the Hall, the thought struck him that only a few months earlier, a coach and a pair of fine strutting horses, would have been doing exactly the same thing.

"Good Morning, Mrs Bradley-Ward", Edwin said respectfully, as he held the door of the landaulet open with a gloved hand, whilst he proffered his other hand to her, in case she needed it for balance as she stepped onto the cars long running board.

"It's such a lovely morning, I'm so pleased you have the hood down", Mrs Bradley-Ward said, with a smile warm as the summers sun, as she carefully sat down on the plump leather seat.

"Thank you, ma'am", Edwin replied, before promptly walking round the back of the car to open the other door for the major, who was already waiting.

"Good day Kealey", the major said, not unkindly. Edwin could detect there was still with a military tone in his master's voice, although it had been many years since the major had served in the army. "Northdown Grange if you please".

Edwin touched his cap before replying respectfully, "Yes sir", as he hurried back to carefully place a tartan rug over Mrs Bradley-Ward's knees. Once again, her face lit up with her warm smile.

With the rug smoothed out, Edwin repeated the earlier procedure by pushing the brass slide forward on the steering wheel before cranking the car's engine into life. Quickly he replaced the crank handle into the long tool-box on the running board before opening the passenger door and sliding across the smooth leather seat to the driver's side.

With the large engine purring under the Landaulet's bonnet, Edwin pulled the goggles, which had been hanging round his neck, over his eyes, before releasing the handbrake and then, with the car engaged into gear, it gracefully moved off down the tree lined drive and onto the narrow lane.

Motor cars were a rare sight on the narrow lanes and roads around Pentbury and Edwin smiled when he spotted one of the women from the village on the grass verge in front of him as she stopped to gape at the car as it sped by. She had been alerted by the strange sound of the oncoming machine and watched in amazement, whilst her two children politely waved at the Bradley-Wards before chasing alongside the car in a vain attempt to out-run it.

The roar of the car's engine changed, sounding more like a throaty cough. Edwin eased his foot off the brass button of the accelerator, squeezed between the clutch and the brake pedals as he approached a horse drawn cart, loaded high with newly mown hay. He was particularly cautious whenever he passed horses knowing the skittish creatures invariably reacted badly at the unaccustomed noise and sight of the horseless carriage.

Edwin glanced down at the small odometer gauge which was fixed to the side of the car. The car had a top speed of forty-five miles per hour although he always drove it with extreme care and rarely exceeded thirty miles per hour. Sitting upright in his seat, Edwin's eyes darted from side to side of the badly rutted road. He was alert for any of the many pot holes which would be deep enough to break the semi-elliptical springs of the car and for any cast off horse-shoe nails, which would puncture its inflated tyres.

As the journey continued the smile of contentment spread wider across Edwin's face. This is certainly more comfortable than driving a carriage, he reflected, as he increased the speed of the car.

"Father", said little Tom on one balmy evening in July, just after the family had finished their tea, "mother said Harry and Fred could go nesting, could I go with them?"

"And me", shouted Glad, anxious not to be left out, "mother said I could go as well".

Edwin smiled as his little son shook his head up and down so vigorously in anticipation of the answer he was hoping for his mop of flopping hair reminded his father of slender stalks of ripe barley being blown in the wind.

Edwin thought for a moment, remembering Tom was not yet five years of age and then turned to his eldest son and said sternly, "Harry, make sure you keep an eye on the nipper and you're all to be back before it gets dark".

"Thank you father, thank you", Tom said, as he ran to grab his father's leg and give it a hug.

The four children immediately went out into the woods to look for the birds' nests and the eggs they contained. Both Harry and Fred collected birds eggs, which was a popular hobby for most of the boys in the village and the two boys were extremely proud of their small collection of the speckled treasures.

Harry led the way with the air of an African explorer. His eyes were darting to and fro, from the occasional tussock of grass on the ground, to the top of the tallest trees, scanning for any sign of a nest. When he reached a part of the woods he hadn't been to before, he stopped in front of a dense thicket of blackthorn. Cautiously, he peered into it before shouting impatiently to the others, "Come on, catch up".

When Glad and Tom had caught up, the children, with little Tom following at the rear, crawled on their hands and knees under a low tunnel which Harry had discovered made by the arching branches of the blackthorn. The long, vicious thorns of the trees tore into the children's soft skin and clothing as they pushed their way deeper through the tangle of thorns. By the time Harry reached the centre of the thicket, the needle-sharp thorns had already made a small three cornered tear in Glad's thin summer dress and all of the children were bleeding from the cuts and scratches on their bare arms and legs. "Nobody has been in here before", Harry declared, as he stood up in the middle of the secret place where the roof of branches was much higher and looked around. The others were still crawling through the tunnel when suddenly Glad let out a scream which was so loud, it made Tom, who was following her jump out of his skin.

"What's the matter?" Harry shouted.

"My knees have just touched something wet and slimy".

Fred, who had nearly reached the spot where Harry was standing, turned round and crawled back and began to investigate with noticeable caution. At first, he just poked the *thing* with a stick and then after closer inspection, he grabbed a corner of the *thing* which was protruding from the ground and tugged it.

"It's just an old black cloth", Fred said dismissively, as the soft earth released its grip on the *thing* and then with some extra effort, he started to pull it back along the tunnel for Harry to inspect his find.

Harry studied the muddy length of cloth carefully and realised somebody had been in the thicket before them! He screwed up his face and said, as he threw the disgusting cloth to the ground and kicked it deep into the thicket, "Come on, let's start looking for nests".

Glad held Tom's hand tightly as she pretended to search the thicket for bird's nests, having come to the conclusion that nesting was something she would not be doing again. She had no intention of getting scratched again by the spiteful thorns and was worried what her mother would say about her torn dress. Instead, the two youngest siblings watched as the older boys pulled the branches from side to side, intent on finding a nest. Fred had somehow managed to get deeper into the thicket without becoming entangled in its branches, when he shouted in alarm, "Harry, Harry, look at this".

Harry turned and when he looked over his brother's shoulder he could not believe what his eyes were seeing. Above the boys' heads was a row of dead creatures. Each small corpse had been carefully impaled separately onto the long spikes of the blackthorn. There were at least three large May bugs and a small, sad looking blue tit, with a thorn piercing its tiny throat. A chill ran down Harry's spine when he saw there were also a large moth and a wood mouse which had fresh blood running down the soft white fur on its belly.

It was Glad, who had been standing behind Harry who spoke first, "Let's get out here" she said, "I feel scared, it's creepy. Come on, let's go home".

None of the others argued with her and they all came out of the thicket much more quickly than they had gone in. Once they were

30

safely outside, they sat on the soft damp earth with a mixture of fear and wonderment.

Her voice was shaking when Glad exclaimed, "This is a place where witches meet". Harry and Fred laughed somewhat nervously at her suggestion.

"Yes", Glad said, with growing authority, "they use the bodies of those creatures to make their spells and the black cloth we found was a witch's cloak".

Harry shrugged his shoulders, as his sister continued, "They call a place like this a witch's coven. I've read about it in a story book". Tom, looked up nervously at his sister and held tightly onto her hand, as she said finally, "We shouldn't be here, it will be dark soon, let's go home before the witches come back".

None of the children said much on the way back to the house and with their mother's scolding ringing in their ears, they washed the mud off their hands and knees and without saying a word of what they had found, they went to bed. The three boys slept together in a large old brass bedstead and once Tom had gone to sleep, Harry and Fred, who laid either side of their little brother, decided the blackthorn thicket was probably the place where witches secretly carried out their sinister craft, just as their sister had said.

It was Fred who heard the noise first. It was as black as pitch in the bedroom as he lay listening to strange noises which were coming from deep in the woods. At first, it was just one single *churring* and then, as he listened, the *churring* became louder and was now coming from different parts of the woods. His chest rose up and down and his breathing quickened when he realised the witches were calling to each other, probably because their coven had been discovered. He knew it was not the sound the foxes made when they were calling and it was nothing like the cries the owls made when they were hunting. No, he decided, it was the witches who were making the noises.

"Harry wake up, I'm scared, there are noises in the wood", Fred whispered breathlessly, as he reached across to wake his brother.

Both boys listened together. At first they heard nothing and then, there it was again. *Churr, churr* but then it was followed by a loud *errr*. Neither boy actually said the word, *witches* but despite their silence, they were both thinking it.

Several days had past and the strange noises in the night had stopped, when the two older boys decided it was safe to go back into the woods and find the witches coven again. One day after school and without telling anyone, they found themselves crawling back into the blackthorn thicket. Once they had crawled through the tunnel of branches, they raised their heads and looked at each other with relief. The creatures which had been impaled on the thorns had gone. Harry was just about to say whoever had been using this place wasn't there now, when, as he looked round, he saw to his horror there were more bodies impaled on a different branch of the tree. This time they were caterpillars. Three fat green ones and four striped, hairy ones, which the boys recognised as the kind they found on the yellow ragwort plants growing by the side of the field.

"Glad was right", Fred said quietly, "it really is a witches' coven!"

The boys knew the blackthorn tree was different from other trees. It was always the first tree to blossom in the spring. Its snow white flowers were in bloom a long time before other trees were even in leaf and it was at this time of year when they would see the bright yellow brimstone butterflies seeking out its pollen.

"Perhaps", Harry concluded, "it is a special tree the witches use".

In the autumn, when the trees were loaded with hard purple fruit called sloes, the old woodman, Jim Colegate, picked them and took them to a woman in the village who made sloe gin and in return, she would give him a bottle of the purple elixir she had made the previous year, reminding the old man, "It was for Christmas" but knowing full well, it wouldn't last that long.

"That's it", Harry said decisively, "We'll go and find Jim Coalgate and ask him about the witches coven".

It was the next day when the children had finished their tea and had listened solemnly to their mother giving a dire warning of what would happen to them if they came back with their clothes dirty and torn again, they ran down the lane towards the church with its wooden shingle-clad spire and to the part of the woods where they knew old Jim would be working.

Jim was a thickset man with huge wiry hands, invariably covered in a criss-cross of scratches. He was over seventy years old and his ruddy complexion was almost hidden by an expanse of the white whiskers which covered his face. Leather gaiters wrapped around his legs protected them from the ever present tangle of undergrowth around him. As did the hob-nailed boots on his feet and despite the midges that swarmed around him, the sleeves on his dirty brown shirt were rolled tightly up his swarthy arms. The old countryman had worked in the woods since he was twelve and he knew them and everything which lived in them, better than anyone else in the village.

He was coppicing the wood when the children arrived. With four swings of his broad-bladed axe, he was cutting down each of the chestnut trees ready to turn them into fence posts and the larger ones into hop poles. He put his axe down and wiped his brow when he saw the children, grateful for a rest. Then, sitting on one of the felled trees, he listened with amusement whilst they told him breathlessly, what they had found in the blackthorn thicket.

"Tha'll beent no witches coven", he laughed, revealing a couple of yellow teeth and an expanse of brown gums, "wat tha found is thay larder of yon butcher bird".

"A butcher bird", Harry repeated the words, "what's that?"

"Well", said Jim, patiently, "thay buggers come over 'ere in May and they bugger off back whence they came in thay autumn. Thay name folks now use is yon shrike. Thay buggers stores thay food on thay thorns in thay same way a jay-pie stores acorns in thay ground. "Thay creature's yoos saw stuck on thay thorns were its food, that's all".

Little Tom looked mystified at what the man had said but the other three smiled at the old man's broad Kentish accent and the way he always used the names of the birds he had been taught as a child.

"If tha young uns are nesting, thay shrikes nestie will be 'igh up agin to its larder. 'Igher than the places yoos boys find the nesties of the blackies and the throstles but not as 'igh as thay agisters".

He means blackbirds and thrushes and magpies, Harry whispered quietly to Fred, as he translated the ancient names.

"But what about the churring noises we heard in the wood at night", Fred said, remembering the sounds they had heard when they were in bed. "We thought it might be witches using their secret language".

Jim threw his head back and raised his huge eyebrows. "Thay beent thay sound of witches, thay was the call of the night crow", said old Jim laughing. "These-a-days folks now call it a nightjar. When I was a lad some folk called it a goatsucker, cos thay say at night, it sucked the milk out of thay goat's tits".

The children laughed when the old Jim said the word tits and as they ran off , he shouted to Tom, who was only four and not very tall, "Tiddy little thing, you keep yon eyes about you or thay butcher bird, thay shrike, will lift you up and stick you on one of thay sharp spikes".

The little boy shuddered and ran quickly to catch up with the others.

It was Saturday morning when Harry and Fred went off to try and find the butcher bird's nest in the blackthorn thicket. Harry had already told Fred he never believed there was such a thing as a witches coven and this time the two boys crawled into the sea of thorns much more boldly than they had before.

With their eyes looking skywards they soon found the nest, just where old Jim said it would be, high up in the top-most branches. It was a large nest for the size of the bird, which Jim had said was smaller than a thrush and standing on his brother's shoulders, Fred cautiously reached out for the nest.

Confident the bird was not there, he put his hand inside the roughly built nest of twigs and green plants and felt it was softly lined with horse hair and dried grass and then, very carefully, took out one of the brown and white speckled eggs. Putting his other hand into his pocket, he took out a matchbox and carefully laid the precious egg onto a soft bed of cotton wool he had put inside it.

What a find, he thought.

3

Letters from the Somme

It was a bitterly cold December evening when Edwin returned from work. The frost had stayed on the fields for days and looking up at the low lying clouds he noticed they had a yellow look about them. There's snow on the way, he thought, as he quickened his pace home.

Emily had already made sure there was a fire burning in the grate, small as was, it warmed the little room and provided comfort to her husband as he lowered himself into the Windsor chair close to the glowing coals.

"That's a good Kentish fire, my dear", Edwin said, smiling, as he warmed his hands.

"Edwin", said Emily, "you've a grin on your face as wide as a Cheshire cat".

The grin on her husband's face grew even wider as he put his hand into his jacket pocket and pulled out a crisp white envelope and then without saying a word, he handed it to her. Intrigued, Emily slipped a small white card from the envelope and looking at the embossed gold print, she read out, *"Major and Mrs E H Bradley- Ward request the pleasure of Mr and Mrs E Kealey to attend a Christmas party to be held at Parkington Hall on the 20th December 1913"*.

Emily gasped and stood quite still before she let out a scream of delight. "Edwin, Edwin", she shouted, as she danced up and down with joy, before pulling her husband to his feet and spinning him round and then saying excitedly, "Is it really true Edwin, an invitation for us to go to a party at the big house. Oh Edwin"

"Yes my dear, the Bradley-Wards are inviting all of the indoor and outdoor staff to the Hall this year, as well as some of the staff from the Manor House and Northdown Grange".

Edwin's face was beaming and although he didn't say it, he was as excited as Emily at the prospect of attending the party. "The Major is a good man", Edwin said, "He told me everyone is to go to the front door when they arrive, not the servant's entrance. Can you imagine that Emily, all the servants going into the Hall by the front door".

Emily felt as if she was walking on air as she held the small gold-edged card in her shaking hand and almost in disbelief, read it aloud, time and time again until she suddenly gasped, only this time, it was not excitement that Edwin heard in his wife's voice, it was despair.

"Oh Edwin", she said despondently.

The look of joy drained from Edwin's face and he took Emily in his arms and said with evident concern, "My darling, what on earth is the matter?"

"Oh Edwin", Emily repeated, "I haven't got a dress to wear".

"Have you ever been inside the house?" Emily asked nervously, as she walked arm in arm with her husband along the winding drive, flanked on either side by a row of towering lime trees and towards the house.

Other couples were also making their way to the party along the leaf-strewn drive. Emily smiled when she recognised the gamekeeper and under-keeper with their wives and noticed the men were attired in their tweed jackets, flat caps and plus fours. As she smiled into her husband's eyes, she was secretly pleased he was not in his grey chauffeur's uniform, smart as it was and thought how handsome he looked in his black suit and white shirt with its stiff, starched rounded collar.

"I've never been in the main part", Edwin replied, "usually, I'm required to park the car outside the front door, or if I'm not needed, I wait in the kitchen, either there or in the buttery at the back of the house".

 There was a knowing smile on his face as he continued, "The kitchen is best, cook always gets the kitchen maid to make me a cup of tea. It's warm in there and always smells of food. Outside in the passage leading to the pantry is the row of the servant's bells, so if the major rings for me, I can hear my bell from the kitchen. Once or twice I've had to go up the back stairs to the servants' rooms with their trunks and suitcases, but that's as far as I've been".

"Edwin, this is the grandest house I've ever seen", Emily said, clearly very impressed with her first sight of the imposing Parkington Hall.

Either side of the huge, double oak doors, were four massive stone pillars, standing like towering sentinels and around each of their bases was a pile of rusty iron cannon balls arranged to form small, decorative pyramids. The stone pillars supported a huge stone canopy which protruded over the wide entrance steps and carved on its facia was the imposing crest of arms of the Bradley-Ward family. Emily stood enthralled at the huge house and looking up into the moonlight she saw an ornate, stone balustrade running along the length of the roof for as far as her eyes could see. Beyond, rising from the lead covered roof was a square turret with a cupola top, looking like a giant finger pointing upwards at the stars in the night sky.

Emily gripped Edwin's arm as they made their way up the wide stone steps. She could feel her heart beating under her long violet coloured dress with its lace overlay, Edwin had bought for her in the ladies outfitters shop which stood by the river in Maidstone. As the couple entered the outer hall they saw other guests giving their hats and coats to Mr Fish who was carefully hanging the garments on a row of highly varnished coat stands and with the precision of a surgeon, placing the assorted hats carefully on white marble-topped tables which lined the side of the long hall. Emily glanced around, almost too frightened to look and shuddered when she noticed the legs of the tables had probably once belonged to the fallow deer whose heads and antlers, now ordained the walls above them.

Continuing on, the line of servants and their wives made their way nervously into the warmth of the equally long inner hall with its floor of black and white marble tiles looking like a never ending chequer board. Emily quickly looked down at her feet, hoping they were not leaving any muddy footprints on the shining floor. As she looked up, she saw on the walls were not the remains of dead creatures as there had been in the outer hall but huge portraits of the Bentley-Wards from ages past, staring down menacingly at the servants who had dared to enter the house by the front door.

 Edwin put his arm round his wife's slim waist and pulled her closer to him, whispering into her ear, "That's Major Bentley-Ward and his wife".

There just ahead of them at the entrance to the main hall, stood the elderly couple who were greeting their guests like old friends, rather than the master and servants which indeed they were. The Major was wearing a black evening suit and a white bow tie. His snow white hair and bushy moustache appeared to shine in the glowing yellow light of the gas lamps lining the walls. Emily noticed the old man was leaning heavily on a stout walking stick with a stag horn handle. She remembered Edwin had told her the Major had been badly wounded by a Russian bayonet charge during the battle of Alma, when, as a young officer he had served with the Royal Welch Fusiliers in the Crimean War, as had his father and grandfather before him. By the major's side stood his wife, who despite her advancing years, glowed with radiance. She was wearing a long, elegant blue dress, the colour of the cornflowers which sometimes grew in the wheat field in front of the cottage. Round the elderly women's, slender neck, were three rows of creamy white pearls which matched the colour of her hair. On her face was a smile, so warm, Emily thought it would melt even the coldest of hearts.

"Kealey and Mrs Kealey, you are both welcome. Please come in and enjoy yourselves at this most festive of times", Major Bentley-Ward greeted them warmly as Edwin instinctively touched his forelock and said rather stiffly, "Thank you sir".

Emily felt the Major's firm grip as she took his outstretched hand. "I'm pleased to meet you sir, thank you for inviting us", she said breathlessly.

Next she took Mrs Bradley-Wards soft, gentle hand and said in a voice which betrayed her nerves, "You've a lovely house, ma'am", before giving the lady a slightly out of place curtsy.

"Thank you my dear, if you would like to, I could show you some more of it after tea", smiled Mrs Bradley-Ward.

Emily blushed with embarrassment, realising she had been perhaps indiscreet with the wife of her husband's employer and stuttered nervously, "I'm sorry ma'am, I didn't mean..."

"My dear", Mrs Bentley-Ward reached out and took Emily's hands into her own. "I would love to show you the interior of the house. I shall come and find you after tea", she said, as though that was the end of the matter.

As Edwin and Emily made their way further into the main hall, Emily gasped when she saw towering in front of them was the most magnificent Christmas tree she had ever seen in her life. It was at least thirty feet tall and lit with hundreds of twinkling candles. Large as it was, the hall was filled with the perfume of burning wax. "It looks like fairyland", Emily whispered to her husband as she looked in awe at the bedecked tree.

A garland of pine and holly was draped over a roaring log fire crackling in a large stone fireplace, sending showers of golden sparks racing up the wide, soot blackened chimney before releasing them into the cold night air. Freshly picked mistletoe hung over the high door arch hoping to witness a kiss or two under its white berries. Edwin and Emily walked across the polished wooden floor to greet Cecil Harris, the chauffeur at Manor Hall and his wife when they saw Mr Fish was preparing to make an announcement to the assembled guests. Emily noticed the elderly butler was the only servant who worked in the house who was allowed to wear a wing collar and a bib-fronted waistcoat which denoted his rank and importance and smiled respectfully at him.

"Ladies and gentlemen", the butler announced in a somewhat shaky voice.

The man coughed and then noisily cleared his throat before continuing, "Will you please make your way through to the housekeeper's room where tea is about to be served".

The room was huge and Emily wondered why such a cavernous room was called the housekeeper's room as they sat at one of the small round tables, each covered with crisp, white tablecloths. Her hand reached secretly under the table to feel the starched freshness of the linen before Mr and Mrs Harris, together with the butler at Manor Hall and his wife joined them. In front of the six nervous guests were dainty porcelain plates which had been equally placed round the table. Balanced on larger plates were huge piles of neatly cut, triangular ham and tongue sandwiches and to the astonishment of the seated servants, on each of the tables was a large Christmas cake smooth with royal white icing and decorated with small sprigs of imitation holly.

Rows of red, yellow and blue Chinese lanterns, each glowing with a candle inside their paper concertinas, hung from the high ceiling above the guest's heads.

Edwin pointed at the shimmering gas lights around the walls and said quietly to Emily, "Better than the candles and oil lamps in the cottage. The whole of the downstairs of the house is lit with acetylene gas", he explained to his wide-eyed wife. "It's generated on the estate from something they call carbide, which looks like lumps of grey coal. Percy Wright told me it's made by mixing coke and lime together". Edwin drew Emily close to him and whispered with a loving smile, "Therefore, tonight my darling, you really are in the limelight".

Emily looked into her husband's eyes and returned his smile but remained silent. What could she say? Never in her thirty five years had she ever seen a house as grand as this.

With tea over, the sound of a small band specially hired for the occasion resonated around the main hall. Gardeners danced with kitchen maids. The normally dour cowman and his spouse came to an abrupt stop during a quickstep after they had collided with the carpenter and his portly wife, both couples hooting with laughter as a result. Emily smiled as she watched a youthful Mrs Bradley-Ward dancing an impressive "Dashing White Sergeant" with one of the gamekeepers on one side and the young footman on the other, then demanding an encore when the reel had finished. Edwin was aware that some of the men's shoulders turned and their heads swivelled as he took his beautiful wife's hand to lead her onto the dance floor and out of the corner of his eye he noticed the major sitting on a highly polished leather chair, close to the Christmas tree, laughing and clapping as he watched the servants enjoying themselves on the dance floor. "Marvellous", he shouted paternally. "Bravo, bravo".

Never in her life had Emily experienced such happiness.

"Mrs Kealey". Mrs Bradley-Ward touched Emily's shoulder which made her jump, not realising the old lady had returned from the dance floor.

"I need to take a rest from the dancing, can I show you the house. Do you mind if I call you Emily, it's such a pretty name?"

"Oh no ma'am, I mean yes, of course ma'am, I'd love to", a flustered Emily stammered in reply.

Taking Emily's hand into her own, Mrs Bradley-Ward led her into the drawing room which was the most sumptuous room Emily had ever seen in her life. Even in the penny picture books she had never seen such a room. Heavy brocade curtains, the colour of burnished gold were draped from the inlaid plaster ceiling down to the polished oak planks of the floor. Oil paintings hung from the Chinese silk lined walls. Two crimson velvet chairs stood in front of yet another fireplace with more huge logs blazing in the grate, whilst a large Bull Mastiff dog which was dozing in front of the fire caught Emily's attention.

"That's Prince", Mrs Bradley-Ward informed and at the sound of his name, the sandy coloured dog lazily opened one eye and not bothering to open the other one, went back to his slumbers.

Emily could not resist taking one final look over her shoulder at the elegant room before Mrs Bradley-Ward closed the huge oak door behind them and walked down the seemingly, never ending corridor to the next set of doors. The old lady turned the ornate brass door handle and pushed the doors open, before moving to one side to allow Emily to peer into the gloomy room.

"Oh", Emily said in surprise. Had it not been for the moon shining its pale light through the huge windows which stretched round two walls of the huge room, it would have been in total darkness. There were no gas lamps on the walls and as far as she could see, there were no candles to light either. Emily's eyes gradually became accustomed to the gloom. On the far side of the room, standing grandly under a huge, curved topped mirror was a large white marble fireplace with an unlit fire laying in its cold, black grate. Cautiously, she took a couple of steps into the room. Under her feet she could feel the thick pile of a large rug and as her eyes darted round the room, she could just about make out the dark shapes of various sofas and large armchairs. Then, as her eyes alighted on a very ornate desk which was standing in the corner of the dark room, she heard Mrs Bradley-Ward laugh and say, as a way of an explanation", This is the morning room Emily, we only use it during the day", and then, still laughing at Emily's quizzical expression, she added quickly, "It's lovely in here when the morning sun is shining".

Emily laughed with pleasure as she continued to be whisked from one room to another. Next to be visited was a small study followed by the billiard room with its panelled walls of tropical mahogany, the colour of old bronze coins. The only light in the darkened room came from a rectangular light, covered with a green silk tasselled shade which was hanging low over the green baize of the billiard table. Emily quickly glanced around and noticing the smell of wood smoke, she saw there was a small fireplace at either end of the long room but only one of them had been lit. Clustered around the burning fire was a number of green leather, high button-backed chairs which were placed around a small polished table. She recognised the smell of stale cigar smoke which lingered in the room and saw on one of the tables were two brandy balloons and a cut glass decanter which sparkled diamond-like as the light from the long gas lamp caught it. This, thought Emily, is the room where the major entertains his gentlemen friends.

"Come on, Emily", laughed Mrs Bentley-Ward, "there's more to see", as she took the wide-eyed woman's hand and led her down a dark corridor and into the library.

Emily's eyes fell on the hundreds of books stacked soldier-like along the rows of shelves lining the walls. Never in her life had she seen so many books, "Does the major read all of these?" she asked in amazement.

"No my dear, he comes here quite often and reads some of them but to tell the truth, the major's not much of a book worm these days and regrettably, most of these dusty old tomes haven't been read for years".

Emily was dragged down more corridors and into more large rooms and some smaller ones until Mrs Bentley-Ward entered a large glass conservatory.

"It's hot in here", the young woman said, as she wiped the perspiration which was already forming on her brow, with a small white lace handkerchief, tucked up in one of the long sleeves of her dress.

Mrs Bentley-Ward pointed towards some large rusty pipes which ran along the base of the low brick wall, explaining, "It's coming from the hot water pipes, all the way from the boiler house in the kitchen garden".

Emily looked in wonder at the array of clay pots filled with different ferns and shook her head in disbelief when she glanced upon some trees with glossy green leaves growing in enormous pots standing on the damp floor. "Oranges and lemons", she gasped in disbelief.

Like a mother and daughter exploring an unfamiliar house, the two women crept down another long, gloomy oak-panelled passage which seemed to Emily to have no end. They had nearly reached the kitchens when old lady stopped and unlocked an anonymous looking door. In front of them, neatly stacked on the dusty shelves and shining like mirrors, were silver objects of every description, plates, jugs, teapots, goblets, candlesticks and cutlery. Emily stood in the doorway not saying a word as Mrs Bentley-Ward explained to her, rather unnecessarily, "This is the silver pantry, Emily".

Holding her finger up to her mouth and whispering, *shh,* indicating she was about to let Emily into a secret, the old lady opened the door to the adjoining room. She smiled and said in a hushed voice, "This one is called the butler's pantry, it's where Fish cleans the silver".

Emily could not resist walking into the small room to take a closer look at the strange looking sink in front of her, with two tall brass taps rising from it. The major's wife smiled as she watched the young woman run her hand along its surface, obviously unsure what it was made of, or indeed, what its purpose was.

"It's lined with lead", the old lady explained in a very matter of fact way, "If it was a stone sink, it would scratch the silver and the crystal glasses".

Hand in hand and grinning like mischievous scamps, the women returned to the main hall just as the dancing was coming to an end.

Immediately Mrs Bradley-Ward joined the happy thong and clapping her hands together, she called out excitedly, "Everybody, gather round the Christmas tree for carols. There's plenty of room to sit on the stairs. Come on. Everybody must join in".

With a gracious bend of her thin wrist she beckoned towards the huge oak staircase which branched out at the top onto a wide landing encircling the hall below.

"Emily, come and join me. We will sit on the stairs and watch the candles twinkling on the Christmas tree whilst we sing the carols together".

The piano suddenly burst into life.

Dum Dum...der. dum... dum, dum,dum, dum......

Mrs Bradley-Ward reached out and took Emily's hand. "It's my favourite carol", she whispered. "Do you know it?"

Slightly embarrassed, Emily shook her head.

"It's called, "I heard the bells on Christmas day"". "The words are by Henry Longfellow", gushed the excited woman.

The other instruments in the band joined the piano which prompted Mrs Bradley-Ward to burst into song long before being joined in unison by the assembled servants.

I heard the bells on Christmas day,

Their old familiar carols play,

And wild and sweet the words repeat,

Of peace on earth, good will to men.

44

"Kealey", Major Bradley-Ward said as he approached Edwin, who had just spotted his missing wife sitting on the highly polished stairs and was about to walk over to her. "Will you join me in the billiard room?"

As the two men left the hall, the major smiled as he heard his wife's voice rising above those of everybody else in the large hall.

I thought how, as the day had come,

The belfries of all Christendom,

Had rolled along, the unbroken song,

Of peace on earth, good will to men.

"You don't know how much I envy the energy of the people on the dance floor", the Major confided to Edwin as he lightly tapped his walking stick against his gammy leg. He smiled as he continued, "Before this, I would have been the first one on the floor".

A slight nod of the head and a sympathetic smile indicated Edwin had understood but he did begin to wonder what his employer really wanted to talk to him about.

The Major ushered Edwin into the billiard room and patted the back of the leather chair which was in front of the burning fire, indicating for Edwin to sit down. The old man picked up the decanter of brandy from the small table in front of them and poured two generous glasses. Edwin was surprised at the informality but he knew the position of chauffeur carried a senior ranking amongst the other staff and wondered if this treatment was in recognition of it.

"Happy Christmas", the Major said, as he handed Edwin a large balloon glass of the golden liquid.

Edwin raised the glass slightly and returned his employer's seasonal greeting", noticing the Major's mood was changing.

"Kealey". The major briefly wrapped his brandy glass in his cupped hands warming the liquid inside to release its aroma, before swirling the glass and raising it slowly to his lips. "This time next year I fear we will be at war with Germany and therefore we must all enjoy ourselves now and hope to God that I am wrong", he said seriously.

"At war sir?" questioned Edwin, who was taken aback at hearing the word. He knew nothing about a war and as he was recovering from the shock of what the major had said, he could hear the happy sound of the carols being sung around the Christmas tree.

"A war sir, surely not".

"Yes, I fear so. The Balkan countries are squabbling over their boundaries. Soon things will get messy there and not forgetting the Kaiser would dearly love to march into France and the Lord only knows what that would lead to".

The Major stopped and looked reflectively at the diminishing brandy swirling around in his glass.

Edwin remained silent. He did not even know where the Balkans were and he looked at the old man in front of him who had experienced war before and who clearly feared it was about to engulf him again.

Edwin drained the shallow pool of spirit which remained in the bottom of his glass. "With respect sir, we can only hope you are wrong", he said glumly.

"That's it. Good man. Yes, drink up Kealey. Yes, you're right and let's hope I'm wrong".

The Major's mood lifted. "Goodness knows it wouldn't be the first time in my life that I've been wrong. Let's go and join the others".

Emily's head was swimming with everything she had seen and done and she chattered non-stop as they walked back to the cottage under a star-studded sky. "You're quiet my dear", Emily said, when she realised her husband had hardly said a word since they had left the party. "That was the happiest night of my life", she continued, without waiting for her husband's reply. "Edwin", she said, not noticing that her husband was deep in thought, "we are so lucky to be living here".

As the New Year was welcomed in by the people of Pentbury, Emily, like the majority of the villagers, was unaware of the imminence of war. Edwin had said nothing to her of what Major Bradley-Ward had said at the Christmas party because she was so happy and he continued to hope the Major had been wrong.

The winter whimpered into spring, which in turn gave way to a hot, dry summer. Eight months had passed since Christmas and whilst Edwin had seen the odd mention about the unrest in some of the Balkan countries in the newspapers the major occasionally left on the back seat of the car, he had seen nothing which suggested the country would be going to war with Germany.

"You mark my words", said Percy Wright, who was the head gardener at Parkington Hall, when he brought the days supply of vegetables into the kitchen. "This business with Russia and Germany is a pretty kettle of fish".

Although Edwin was sitting at the table waiting for the servant's bell to ring for him to take the car to the front door, Percy appeared to be directing his comments to the cook. Edwin didn't raise his head and sat staring at the thin wisps of steam rising from the cup of tea the cook had made for him. Instead he listened with some amusement as she admonished the gardener for bringing mud into her kitchen on the soles of his knee high leather boots. Edwin knew, given the woman's nature, it was something she did on a regular basis and as he did on most days, Edwin ignored what she was saying and carried on looking into his tea cup.

"It was in the paper yesterday. Saw it myself, front page it was. Russia has mobilised its army, we'll be next, you'll see". Percy continued to give his views, unabated.

The red faced woman stood with her back to the opinionated man, as she finished rolling out some short crust pastry for the beef pie she was making. "Stuff and nonsense", she said dismissively, as she wiped the sticky remains of the pastry from her hands onto her otherwise, spotlessly clean apron. "What about the poor woman who was arrested outside of Buckingham Palace who wanted votes for us women?" the cook said, as she turned around to face the gardener.

Edwin could see she was searching her mind for something.

"Emily   Pankhurst,   that's   who   it   was.   No.   No.   Not Emily.........Emmeline, she said, somewhat triumphantly and after a few moments of deep thought, she continued to say, "bit more important than what's happening in Russia, that's what I say". "Florence", the cook snapped as she turned to the kitchen maid, who wasn't in the least bit interested in what was being said, "put that pie in the oven, times getting on".

The young maid was used to hearing Percy Wright pontificate on every subject under the sun and as far as she was concerned this morning was no different from any other morning.

"If you ask me", the gardener proclaimed loudly, not waiting to hear if anybody would actually ask him, as he trudged through the kitchen to deposit the wooden trug full of mud-covered vegetables into the sink in the so-called dirty room where they would be washed and prepared by the young scullery maid.

"Yes", he continued, on returning back to the kitchen with his empty boat-shaped basket, "The die is cast now. If the Huns march into Belgium to get to the French, we'll be at war the very next day".

Edwin continued to sit silently at the table sipping his tea. He had no wish to get involved in conversation with the opinionated gardener but he knew the man was right. If the Germans did invade Belgium, the country would declare a state of war on them and the joy of this particular summer would be shattered and it probably would be for many summers to come.

Pentbury was only a small village, sheltered as it was by the steep folds of the North Downs. There was not many more than fifty houses in the village itself, most of which were clustered along the Street which was the rather imposing name given to the lane that wound its way through the village and past the farm buildings belonging to Alfred Day before continuing down to an old stone bridge. On one side of the lane was a pasture grazed by a herd of Shorthorn cattle, much favoured by the village butcher, and on the other side were fields of ripening corn. At the bridge, it crossed a river called the Len which was in fact little more than a fast flowing stream but with a current strong enough to turn the water wheel of the old white boarded mill which had stood on its grassy bank for a hundred years. The lane then meandered upwards for two miles on its way towards the white chalk faces of the Downs in the distance. Yet it was from the small group of black and white half-timbered houses and stone cottages with their red, peg-tiled roofs, that sixty-eight, able-bodied men immediately volunteered to serve King and Country. Fathers and sons, brothers and cousins, uncles and nephews and to a man, they all stepped forward to the call of arms. Hubert Day, the fresh faced nineteen year old son of farmer Day was amongst them and so was thirty-eight year old Edwin Kealey.

Emily's life had developed into a regular routine during the seven long months her husband had been in France, keeping herself busy about the house, cooking and sewing and with the daily visit to the village shops, searching the shelves for the ever dwindling supply of food. Despite this, Emily never left the house until the postman had either called to deliver the mail or she had seen him walk past the window, empty handed. The light spring winds and the warmth of the April sunshine had dried the garden soil sufficiently for Emily to start sowing the vegetable seeds and she was dropping the seed potatoes in the holes Fred was making in the rich black earth, when she heard the clock on the mantelpiece indoors strike ten. "Fred", she said, "it's ten o'clock. I must go and watch for the postman, I'll come back to help once I've seen him". It was at this time every morning when Emily would stop whatever she was doing and watch the lane, just in case the post man stopped. She knew there was hardly a house in the village where exactly the same thing wasn't being done.

"There he is", she said to herself upon seeing the postman walking up the lane.

The postman stopped and holding her breath, Emily ran to the door and unlike the other times, this time the man was holding a letter from France in his hand. Emily's heart was in her mouth as she quickly reached out to take it from his grasp.

"Morning, Mrs Kealey", he said with a smile. He was older than Edwin, which was hardly surprising as nearly all the young postmen had already enlisted in the Post Office Rifle Battalion and were now fighting in the trenches of Flanders. "I hope its good news", the genial man said as he handed her the blue envelope.

Emily gave him a weak smile and closed the door. The children had seen the postman stop, came indoors and gathered round to see who the letter was from, that was apart from Harry, who was working as a gardener's boy for the Ridleys at Manor Hall.

49

"Children", Emily said, "I'll read your father's letter to you when Harry is here".

She held the letter tightly to her pounding breast and could not help noticing that her hand was shaking. Fred, Glad and Tom knew their mother always read their father's letters when they were all there and ran back to the garden to wait for their mother to continue to plant the seed potatoes.

After tea, which was earlier than normal and with all her children around her, Emily sat down and opened the letter, noticing as always, it was written in pencil.

"My dear Emily" she read. *"Your most welcome letter is at hand. Thank you for the spoon".*

Emily looked at the children and could see they did not understand their father's reference to the spoon.

"Children", she explained, "do you remember when we received the last card from your father and he said he needed a spoon to eat his meat stew". The older children smiled as they remembered what their father had written.

"Thank you for the spoon", Emily repeated, *"and the parcel containing the socks and the razor. You said you hoped I would have many a soothing morsel with the spoon, unfortunately that is my greatest trouble, we do not have enough to eat".*

Poor man, sighed Emily, "Your father is hungry", she told the children.

"Should like to have a free hand at a good old loaf, some cheese, beetroot and pickled onions, what ho".

Everyone laughed. Good old dad.

"The weather is rotten here, snow and rain and plenty of mud, mud and more mud. They are nearly killing us here with training. Going up and down makeshift ladders, running, marching, then quick marching and of course, rifle practice. Can you imagine it, Emily?"

"Poor father", Gladys said with evident sadness in her voice.

"Spotted fever has broken out in the barracks and we all have to gargle every day", Emily read.

"What's gargle?" asked little Tom.

"Shhh", his mother scolded, as she carried on reading the letter.

"Glad to hear all at Parkington Hall are well. Have not had the letter you speak of regarding the good news of George. Bravo, Bravo. I do hope it's true".

"That's Uncle George, your fathers' brother", Emily whispered to the children.

"I am so glad you are all in good health. I will hold you all in my arms when I come home, by Jove I wish it was tomorrow. Tell the boys to keep the garden well stocked and look after the chicken, good food is important and I think that Gladys should be helping you a bit too. We are off to *church parade at 9.30. It seems a strange Good Friday to me.*

A happy Easter to you Emily and to the children,

God bless you all

Your ever loving husband,

Edwin"

"Children", said Emily quietly, as she quickly read the letter again and then looking up, she said "it was good news, wasn't it, your father is well and he sends us his love".

Once his mother had finished reading the letter, Harry got up from the old wooden chair and went to the pump in the backyard to wash the Ridley's garden dirt from his hands. Nobody had noticed the serious look which had come over the boy's face.

Emily folded the letter with as much care as if it was a priceless document written on wafer thin parchment, before putting back into its envelope. I will read it again later when the children are in bed, she thought.

The light from the oil lamp, hanging from the low ceiling of the cottage was casting shadows on the living room wall when Emily sat in gloomy solitude to read Edwin's letter. She held the pages with the same tenderness as she had held him the night before he had sailed to France. She felt close to him at times like this, when the heart wrenching distance which was between them somehow didn't seem quite so far. Emily's face broke into a smile when, as she closed her eyes, she could almost hear her husband's saying, "Should like to have a free hand at a good loaf and some cheese".

That's Edwin, she thought lovingly.

Her eyes were racing up and down the letter, searching out each of the precious words her husband had written.

"Thank God", she said to herself, when she realised what the words were saying.

Her husband was not in the trenches.

She knew he had been in some of the terrible fighting that had taken place before Christmas, when tens of thousands of men had been killed in the first few weeks of the war, including some of the village men who had marched with Edwin a few months before. Edwin never wrote of the fighting he had experienced, his fears or the horrors that he had seen. Instead he chose to tell her about the weather or the food, in fact, anything that might lessen the worry he knew his beloved wife would be feeling. As Emily tenderly stroked the envelope she remembered what the butcher had told her. He had said that Field Marshall French had ordered Schools of Instruction to be established behind the front lines where training was to be given in fighting skills such as marksmanship, gunnery and signalling.

"That's where he is", she exclaimed and sighing with relief, she reached up to turn down the wick of the smoking oil light.

"He's safe in a School of Instruction".

A few weeks passed and Emily, and her young son, were just leaving one of the village shops when Emily heard a familiar voice calling her.

"Mrs Kealey, Mrs Kealey". Emily turned round and saw it was the head gardener's wife, Florence Wright. Although the two women had known each other for over two years, as was the custom, always addressed each other by their surnames.

"Good morning Mrs Kealey", said the somewhat flustered Florence, "Oh Mrs Kealey, it's dreadful.....the postman has just told me.... three more of our men have been killed.......that makes seven from the village now. It's dreadful. When will it all stop?"

Emily's blood froze and clearing her throat, she spluttered, "Who! Do you know who they are? Panic raced through her body.

Florence Wright continued unaware of the suffering she was causing, "One was Lawrence Day, Mr Days' nephew... poor man. He will worry all the more now about his own son, Hubert. They are so young, little more than just children. I was so shocked, I didn't think to ask the names of the other two".

It was then the woman noticed that Emily's face had turned ashen white. "I'm sorry my dear, so sorry, It quite slipped my mind about your Edwin, I'm sure he is safe", she added quickly.

Emily had already turned for home.

"I must get back for the post" she whispered and holding Tom's hand tightly, she hurried back up the lane almost dragging the young boy along, totally unaware Florence Wright was endeavouring to catch them up.

Florence was a portly woman aged about sixty who lived in one of the Lodge Cottages with her husband. Red faced and out of breath and as she tried to catch up with Emily she was thinking how fortunate she was that Percy was too old for the dreadful war raging in France.

Emily quickly opened the front door and instantly her eyes alighted on a solitary letter which was lying on the bristle doormat. "He's been early", she gasped, "the postman has come early".

Holding her breath as she ripped the envelope open, she was frantically thinking, was it....was it?

"No", the distraught woman whispered as a surge of relief flooded through her body. The letter was from George, her husband's brother, saying he was now back home recovering from his injuries.

She fell to her knees and started to sob, "It's not Edwin, he was not one of those who have been killed", she whispered with relief.

Tom had his arms round his mother's neck when a red-faced, Florence Wright came in. "Sit down", she said breathlessly, as she helped Emily to the chair, "I'll make a pot of tea. That's what we need...a good cup of tea".

As they sat at the table drinking the soothing brew, Mrs Wright said thoughtlessly again, "Yes dear, this war is certainly dreadful. My hubby was telling me just yesterday, every train which is going down to Folkestone harbour is full of troops all heading for the front line. He said they seem to be getting younger by the day and when the trains come back, they are full of the wounded. Our lads, gassed, blinded, swathed in bandages...missing arms and legs some of them. There, there dear, don't cry and drink your tea".

Emily was not listening. Thank God, not this time, she was thinking.

It was only a few weeks later when the *bolt from the blue* happened. Emily had put young Tom to bed and Harry and Fred had come in after weeding the vegetable garden and were washing their hands at the red earthenware sink when Harry turned to Emily and blurted out, "Mother, I've something to tell you .... I've enlisted".

Emily froze. Her mouth dropped open and her eyes glared at her son, as much in shock as in anger.

"What! ...you will do no such thing Harry", she shouted. "You're not old enough. I can hardly cope with your father away in those terrible trenches".

Mother and son stood staring into each other's eyes. Harry had never seen such anger in his mother before and it shocked him into silence. After a few moments, Emily regained her composure and was determined to finish the conversation.

"That's enough", she said breathlessly, "I will hear no more of it".

Harry opened his mouth to speak.

"Just hold your noise Harry", she retorted with a raised voice, as she turned her back on her son.

Harry finished wiping his hands and walked round to face his mother once more and said defiantly, "Mother, I have enlisted...... I've got to report to the Maidstone Reception Centre next week for a medical and then it will be two weeks training before I leave for France".

With a look of disbelief flooding her face Emily looked directly into her son's eyes and screamed, "Then you can go and un-enlist". You're only just seventeen, you're not old enough and that's an end to it".

Harry started to speak but Emily interrupted him, "Do not answer me back, Harry...do you hear me", her face was flushed and red with anger. "I will not have you disobeying me, you are not joining the army and that's an end to it".

Harry waited for a few moments and then said calmly, "Mother, I've been thinking about it for a long time, I know what it's like over there but it's my duty to serve King and Country. It's something I want to do........ I told them that I'm eighteen..... I'm going into the West Kents".

Nobody said a word and a deep unsettling silence suddenly enveloped the room until Emily said despairingly, "Oh Harry, what have you done, what would your father say?"

She sunk into a chair by the table as if all the strength had been drained from her body. With her head in her hands and knowing she was defeated, she could taste the bitter tears which were rolling down her white cheeks. Fred and Glad were standing in the doorway leading to the garden. They had never heard Harry answer their mother back before and felt shocked at what had just happened.

"Don't worry", said Harry, smiling at his mother as he played his winning card, "I'll be alright, in any case, if I don't go this year, the War Office will call me up next year".

"I hope to God it will be over by then", snapped his mother, as she realised that all was lost.

Some weeks later Tom was standing on a chair and looking out of the window when he spotted the postman. Jumping down, he grabbed the postcard from the man's out-stretched hand and ran into the room with it. Emily took the card from the excited boy and smiled when she realised it was from Edwin. It was so pretty and she could tell at once it was not bad news. One side the card was edged in white lace and embroidered in gold silk, with the words saying, *"I'm thinking of you"*.

With a shaking hand, Emily turned it over. *"Dearest one, I am sending this postcard to wish you a belated happy birthday. I am sorry it will arrive past the day but rest assured you were in my thoughts"*

"Mother, what does it say?" Tom said impatiently

"It's from father. Let me read it.... It's pretty isn't it?"

She continued reading the small writing. *"I hope you are all well. Thank you for the parcel, your knitted socks are always welcome as was the tin of peppermints. Oh how they reminded me of home sweet home. My dearest, what a shock I had when I read your letter regarding Harry. How proud I was that he wanted to serve but like you, I hope he keeps himself safe. Myself, I am safe and well"*.

Emily sighed and realised that her husband was probably far more worried about Harry, than he had written.

"We are back from the Front having a thoroughly deserved rest in what was once a small village. I have been de-loused and have had a bath and issued with clean clothes. Oh what joy, those lice are real blighters.

Give my love to the children

Your affectionate husband, Edwin"

A cold shiver ran down Emily's spine. He's fighting at the front again, she thought.

The months and seasons crawled by slowly and there was a cold north-easterly wind blowing when Emily saw the postman making his way up the narrow lane. He was hunched up against the chilling blast which was blowing directly into his red face from the North Downs. She could see he was not the usual man, this one was much older. Perhaps he too has been conscripted now, what a pity, she reflected sadly. As the man got closer, Emily could see there were three stripes sewn onto his blue jacket with its edges piped in red trim. The jacket had seen better days and the stripes on his arm meant he displayed a good attitude to work and was a good time keeper. On his head he was wearing a tall peaked cap. Emily recalled her husband once referring to them as shakos. She shuddered at the thought of her husband and wondered if the postman would be bringing the letter she was expecting from him. Edwin was good at writing to her, unlike Harry.

Emily shivered as he cold wind gripped her thin body and she drew her woollen shawl round her shoulders as she opened the door to wait for the old postman.

"Morning missus", he said with a smile, "hope everything is well over there. It's a cold morning. ...winter is on its way" and with that the man touched the peak of his shako and left Emily holding the letter. He had learnt it was best not to make idle chit chat when delivering letters from the front. He knew full well the women folk who had been anxiously waiting for a letter from their loved ones, would want to open it quickly, rather than passing the time of day with him and in any case, if the letter contained bad news, they would want to be alone with their grief.

Emily closed the door quickly and retreated to the warmth of the living room. She looked down at the handwriting on the envelope and recognised it at once.

She sighed with relief. At last, she had received a letter from her son. Although she sent regular parcels to Harry containing a few things she thought would make his life more bearable, cigarettes, sweets and some knitted woollen socks and gloves, he seldom wrote. At first, when she wrote to him she had scolded him about it but she knew it was *just Harry* and as long as he came home safely, it was all she asked.

Dear Mother

I hope you are well and not worrying about me.

I certainly am, thought Emily.

I am sorry I have not written before but I am receiving your letters and parcels which are most welcome. Mr and Mrs Ridley sent me a box which contained 2 ounces of tobacco, some chocolate and a thick woollen sweater. I can tell you it was most welcome. I hope father is safe and well. I have not heard anything about the Buffs. I heard they were further up the line. Where we are now must be the wettest place on earth, the dugouts are full of water and it is as high as the fire steps in the trenches. It never stops raining. The worst thing is our clothes are thick with mud. It is weeks since I had a change and a good wash. It's now getting colder and last week we had some frost. The barrage never stops. The noise of the shells the Boche are sending over is deafening. We were sent out on patrol 3 times last week, sometimes when they see us all hell breaks loose. We lost some men but we gave the Boche a good hiding. Mostly we have to wait around and snatch sleep when they let us. We brew tea when we can but it always tastes of petrol from the cans they bring the water in. How I long for a nice cup of tea in your best cups and poured from a china teapot with a large slice of your fruit cake. Could you send me a pencil and some more sheets of paper. I think of you all and father every day. Do not worry about me. I will come home safe and sound and soon I hope.

Your loving son,

Harry.

Emily carefully folded the letter and put it back in the envelope and with a love that only a mother knows, she kissed it. Slowly she took off her wire rimmed spectacles and wiped away the tears which were running down her cheeks.

The rain was dropping from the heavens like stair-rods as Emily made her daily journey to the butcher's shop to buy whatever meat was available. It had been a long winter. Mercifully not too cold but remorselessly wet and dreary and the stream which normally trickled its silent way alongside the lane was now a torrent, racing to reach the river beyond.

"If this war doesn't finish soon, we will all starve to death", a woman standing in front of Emily, said gruffly.

Emily just smiled politely at the rain-soaked woman and looked at the water running off her sodden coat and forming a large puddle on the butcher's sawdust strewn floor.

"Everywhere is the same", continued the woman, "the shops are empty. What's the point of rationing meat and butter when there isn't any to be had anyway"?

"It does seem a long time since we saw sides of pork and beef hanging in here and the cuts of lamb and chicken", Emily replied, as she looked down at the few pigs trotters and some pale looking sausages which were lying on the white, marble counter.

"Goodness knows how I am going to get these clothes dry without a decent fire. The coalman hasn't had any coal since November and the house is so damp and cold with all this rain. It makes you wonder if the winter will ever end", the woman complained forlornly.

Emily listened sympathetically. She knew she had been more fortunate than most. Mrs Bentley-Ward had given her a small joint of beef and a sack of coal at Christmas so the family could have some festive cheer without the company of Edwin and Harry. Fred had also brought back and cut up some fallen branches from the woods so she had at least kept the cottage reasonably warm and dry during the winter.

"Let's hope the war will finish soon and we can all get on with our lives again. Anyway, bad as it is here, it's a lot worse for our men-folk out there", Emily said ruefully to the woman whom she hadn't seen in the village before, as the rain continued to lash against the shop's window panes.

The March wind was gusting against the old weather-beaten sign hanging from an iron bracket over the door of the White Horse. As the sign swung to and fro, its melodic creaking appeared to be beckoning Percy Wright to come inside the ancient pub for his nightly pint and to sit by the fire burning in the smoke-blackened inglenook. Percy glanced up at the image of the creature which had been painted on the sign, long ago by some itinerant artist. It portrayed a horse rearing up on long, heavily muscled legs with its wind- blown mane looking as if the windy night had brought it to life. The creature's large, brooding eyes had kept sentry on every living soul who had stepped over the time-worn threshold of the ale house. The old pub had stood at the crossroads where White Horse Lane met the Street, long before good Queen Bess was crowned and it was the place where the men of the village congregated. Tonight was to be no exception. The black window frames stood out starkly against the white painted clap-boards fixed to the upper half of the old building. Either side of the small entrance door were two dilapidated bench seats, occupied by piles of rotting leaves blown there some months ago from the towering beech trees overhead.

Percy Wright displayed many years of practice as he lowered his head and pushed open the low oak door and entered the pubs narrow corridor with its flagstone floor. On one side of the passage was a brown painted door leading to a small but cosy snug, with its low beamed ceiling and hard, wooden settles. The snug was not used by Pentburys working class. Not just because they had to go back into the tap room to fetch their beer but more importantly for the men of the village, a pint of beer in the snug cost a ha'penny a pint more than in the larger bar and Percy, as he always did, ignored the door. A buzz of noise came from inside as the gardener pushed his thumb down on the iron latch and pushed open the door leading to the tap room. Through the smoke haze, he could see a group of farm labourers standing in front of the fire. Their voices were raised in anger and one of the men was stamping one of his hobnailed boots, depositing clods of Kentish loam looking like small molehills rising from the stone clad floor.

"Evening, Percy, it's a wild and woolly night". The publican did not wait for an answer and had already taken the old gardener's pewter tankard off a hook over the bar and was heading towards the row of barrels lined up on a cobweb strewn wooden rack, to draw off a pint of the chestnut brown beer.

Jack Gosling had been the proprietor of the pub for over twenty years, ever since he had taken over the licence from his father back in 1897. He was a thickset man with a pallid complexion betraying the fact he had spent most of his sixty years deep inside the tavern's thick brick walls. Here, he had been hidden from the sun's rays amongst the smell of stale beer and the yellow smoke from the labourer's clay pipes.

"Thre'pence if you please, Percy". The genial publican smiled as he placed the over-flowing tankard down, slightly more heavily than he meant to, spilling some of its contents onto the beer stained counter.

"I trust you won't be doing that when you start to charge me another penny", Percy grumbled. His face had a look which would have curdled the morning's milk as the publican reached for a cloth under the bar. The earlier smile had also drained from Jack Gosling's face, as with a sweep of one of his large hands, he began to wipe away the small puddle which had formed on the counter.

"It's the war Percy", he explained glumly. "It's all part of the government's emergency measures. At first, they started telling me when I could and when I couldn't sell my beer. Now it's the increase in the excise duty that's putting the extra penny on a pint and there's even talk now that the country is running out of malted barley to make the stuff".

Percy slowly raised the tankard to his mouth and with brown froth from the warm beer dripping from his lips, he said "A penny a pint, Jack, I ask you, it's nothing short of day-light robbery. I'll tell you one thing. Just wait till when the lads come back from the war, they won't be standing for it".

The farm men standing by the fire had been joined by four others, who had been sitting on the wooden settles in the far corner of the bar playing dominos and were now beginning to shout at the older men in the group.

Jack Gosling turned towards the men and leaning over the bar, called out in a stern and controlled voice, "Gentlemen, let's have some order if you please. That kind of behaviour is for outside".

Some of the younger men in the group continued the argument but with lowered voices.

61

"I will not be asking you again", the publican said firmly, as he started to wipe the top of the polished bar again.

He did not have to say any more. He had a reputation for keeping an orderly house and the men knew it. In the close knit community of Pentbury, everybody knew being barred from the White Horse by Jack Gosling would result in a social stigma which could last for years. Even worse, it was not unknown for the local farmers to refuse to hire any man who they judged to be a drunk or troublemaker and none of the men Jack was addressing wanted that to happen to them.

Jack Gosling turned back to Percy Wright, who had no intention of letting the dispute by the fireplace stop him from continuing to complain to the publican about the price of beer.

"A penny a pint more, Jack", the irate gardener ranted, "I'll tell you one thing. With the way things are going, beer will soon be a shilling a pint, a shilling a pint, mind you. What with the shorter licensing hours and now another penny added to a pint.....my old father would be turning in his grave if he knew a pint of mild will soon be costing four pence".

The two men had been friends since childhood and had developed a mutual respect for each other over the years and the publican shrugged his shoulders and said with a conciliatory tone in his voice, "There's one thing for certain, Percy. If the price of a pint does go up to a shilling, it will be the ruin of me, that's for sure. It just makes me wonder when this war will end".

Percy pushed his tankard across the counter for a refill and nodded his head towards the few remaining men by the fireplace that it seemed had put their differences behind them and were now laughing and joking. "What was that all about, Jack?" he asked.

Jack Gosling gave a short laugh, as he placed the brimming tankard on the bar with more care than he had displayed with his friends first pint. "They've just heard one of those Land Army girls has been recruited on the farm and they don't like it".

"I'm not surprised, none of us like it", Percy said reflectively, as he stared at the froth which was quickly disappearing from the top of his beer. "It can't be right, can it, employing women to do a man's job but I think we will just have to accept it, at least until the war is over".

"The problem is", Jack reflected, "with all the young men away serving at the front, there aren't enough men left to work on the farm and those that are left are like us Percy, they are all getting on in years now".

Percy Wright nodded his head noncommittally and surprisingly said nothing.

"They said the cows down by the river weren't milked yesterday", the publican continued. "There are still some fields waiting to be ploughed before they can get the seed corn in and that's not to mention how they will get the apples and hops picked and thence it's the harvest to get in". Jack Gosling, stopped when he realised he had said enough on the subject and walked away to serve two of the men who had been by the fireplace and who were now waiting patiently for their tankards to be re-filled.

There was a glint in publican's eye when he returned to his old friend. He winked at Percy and said with a beaming smile, "The truth of the matter is that it is not so much that the men are fearful of losing their jobs, it's all the trouble it's causing at home. When my missus was in the baker's shop the other day, she overheard Wally Arnold's wife say, if there was a young woman working on the farm, it would be putting too big of a temptation in the way of her husband".

Percy drained the last drops of his beer from his tankard and turning away from the bar, said with a grin spreading across his un-shaven face, "She probably remembered that poor old Wally's fire had gone out years ago and she didn't want any young filly to be lighting it up again".

"Goodnight, Percy". Jack was now laughing like a naughty schoolboy and just as the old gardener was about to push the door open and leave the pub, he raised his voice and said, "Do you know what Percy, there may be hope for you and me yet. I'm already thinking of having an early night".

He was still chuckling as he heard the sound of laughter echoing down the corridor as Percy walked out into the chilly night air.

Emily was daydreaming as she looked out of her window at a kestrel hovering over the hawthorn hedge growing round the edge the field. From a distance, the small bird looked liked a large butterfly as it fluttered over leafless branches, hoping a vole or maybe a field mouse would run out from the safety of their hiding place. As she watched the bird it suddenly wheeled backwards up into cloudless blue sky and effortlessly flew off to find a more productive hedge to hover over. Emily was smiling with pleasure at seeing the kestrel when she heard the loud whinny of a horse. Turning her gaze away she saw somebody leading a pair of shire horses across the field towards her. It was the way the person was dressed that caught Emily's attention. They were wearing a long white smock which was fastened at the front with a long line of buttons and drawn up at the waist with a cloth belt. As they got closer, Emily realised the person who was holding the naffles of the two heavy horses was a young woman whom Emily guessed was not much older than twenty. She was wearing a wide brimmed hat and a green arm band with a red crown embroidered on it. "Women's Land Army", Emily said to herself upon recognising the young woman's uniform, as she walked out of the cottage to greet her.

"Whoa boys", the young woman said softly to the horses towering over her, as Emily walked towards them. "Steady now, steady now". The huge horses came to a halt but tugged at the shiny steel bits in their mouths as they tossed their heads up in unison as if they were annoyed at being stopped.

"Hello", the young woman said brightly. "Are you Mrs Kealey? The men on the farm told me you live here. My name is Mary Wheeler. I've come to work on the farm whilst the war is on".

Emily started to put her hand out to shake the girl's hand but realised just in time that the poor girl didn't have one free as she struggled to hold onto the pair of restless horses standing either side of her. Instead, Emily reached up to pat each of the horse's massive heads as they stood with their heads and manes bobbing at one end of their long bodies whilst their tails swished at the other.

"I think they are anxious to be harnessed to the plough", the girl said, stepping back, as one of the beasts started to stamp one of its huge, feathered hooves on the ground perilously close to her feet. "Goodbye Mrs Kealey", Mary Wheeler said brightly, as she tugged the horse's leather bridle, "see you again, no doubt".

Emily watched them go and realised beneath the long smock the girl was wearing a pair of thick corded trousers and as the young woman made her way across the field Emily stared at her in disbelief. She had never seen a woman wearing trousers before.

Turning to go across the lane to make her way back into the cottage, Emily saw the familiar shako of the old postman bobbing above the hedge. Quickly she made her way back to the cottage to meet the man.

"Good morning Mrs Kealey", the man touched the peak of his hat and said with his usual smile on his face as he handed Emily a letter, "I hope everything is alright over there.....good day to you" and with that, he continued quickly on his way.

Emily's blood froze as she looked at the unfamiliar envelope. It was from France but the handwriting was neither that of Edwin nor Harry. She ran through the open door of the cottage and taking a knife from the sideboard drawer she quickly slit open the brown envelope. Fearfully and with her heart pounding through her cotton blouse, she began to read the unfamiliar writing.

Dear Mrs Kealey   *25th March 1917*

I am sorry to inform you that your husband has been injured during a recent offensive and is being treated for his wounds at the 58th casualty clearing station. He was in good spirits when I saw him this morning and asked if I could inform you of his circumstances..With the Grace of God I am praying for his speedy recovery

Yours sincerely, Reverend Henry Meadows (Chaplain)

Emily stared down at the letter with desolate eyes.

"Oh no", she whispered "it's Edwin".

Her hand was shaking so much now she had difficulty in reading the letter again, hoping somehow the words it contained would be different.

Her eyes had filled with tears and her voice was quaking with a mixture of fear and emotion as she read out the words, "treated for his wounds".

She felt numb inside but gradually as she read and re-read the letter, her sobbing stopped as the words gradually began to make some meaning to her.

He is alive, she thought, and in good spirits.

"Thank God", she said softly.

There was a sense of relief in her voice as she realised the letter did not contain the news she had dreaded. Her heart was still beating quickly as she walked up the narrow staircase and into her bedroom to put the letter under her pillow, amongst the others she had already received from both her beloved husband and son.

Emily decided not to say anything about it to the children and hoped in her heart everything would be alright and their father would recover from his wounds. Perhaps he may even be sent home.

Each day seemed an eternity as she waited anxiously at the window to see if the postman called. She prayed to God, if there was a letter, it would contain the news she was waiting for. That was, Edwin was alive and returning to full health.

She hardly left the house and every day the old postman passed by without anything, other than a cheerful smile and a wave of his wrinkled hand. Apart from the day when the man was earlier than normal and the first Emily knew of the letter she had been so desperately waiting for, was when she saw it, laying forlornly on the door-mat.

Emily stared at it at first, leaving it where it lay. She did not want to touch it, let alone open it, fearful of what it may contain. It was little Tom, who had been standing at his mother's side, who picked it up and innocently handed it to her.

Dear Mrs Kealey   28th March 1917

It is with deep regret that I have to inform you that your husband, Edwin, died of his wounds three days ago. I sat with him and offered what comfort I could. He was a brave man in battle and met his end in the same manner.

The trenches had been under unusually severe artillery fire since the early hours on the 22nd March and our gallant soldiers repulsed no fewer than eight German attacks during the day. During these engagements casualties had been high and a number of Edwin's comrades had been killed and wounded in a forward dug out.

Towards the end of the day, the enemy machine gun fire which had been raking the ground between the trenches during most of the day had finally ceased .Your husband was one of the volunteer stretcher bearers who went out to retrieve the poor souls who had lain dreadfully injured in the shell craters. On returning back to the trench, Edwin and his fellow bearer were hit by gun-fire from a German sniper. Despite the wounds he suffered, his thoughts to the end were of you and the children.

Your husband was of good bearing and set a splendid example to the rest of the men. He met his death in the noblest of fashion and I hope the courage Edwin displayed in helping his fellow men will be of comfort to you.

Please accept my most sincere sympathy. May God be your strength at this very sad time.

Reverend Henry Meadows (Chaplain)

"We have lost him. Oh my God, we have lost him", Emily gasped.

She sank to the floor and buried her face in the crumpled letter, but it could not stop the tears which were flooding down her cheeks. Tom was frightened and knelt by her side, wrapping his little arms round his mother's narrow waist in an attempt to comfort her. He needed to be close to her and to feel the warmth of her body.

"Your father has died" she wept, "my darling Edwin....... ".

The mother and child hugged each other and cried together for a brave man who was now lying buried in the mud of France. Emily's heart was broken and pierced with grief.

"He was such a gentle man, a good loving man and such a good father. Why dear God? Why?" Emily wailed in the misery which had overwhelmed her.

The waning moon had broken through the dense black clouds which were hanging low over the cottage and through the gloom the moon was casting its icy light into the bedroom where Emily lay. Her bloodshot eyes were wide open and staring at the roughly plastered ceiling. Her face was drawn and white and even her lips looked colourless. They were mouthing Edwin's name but not making even the slightest of sound. Her frail body was shaking, convulsed in grief as memories of Edwin continued to race through her mind. She was in turmoil. She knew she would never be able to see him again or hear his laughter. Feel his warm body against hers or to share their dreams for a future together. Emily started sobbing again as she thought of the finality of her husband's death. She turned over, alone in their bed and buried her face in the tear soaked pillow in the vain hope the dreadful thoughts would stop and disappear from her troubled mind. But despite everything, the wet coat of despondency still clung to her. Emily turned on her side and saw the moon shining into the bedroom. Its light was casting shadows which danced on the wall of the small, cold bedroom each time the iron bedstead was moved by Emily's restlessness. It was nearly daybreak when the thoughts which had been racing through her mind began to slow and as she lay there, Emily heard in the distance, an owl calling. There comes a time when everybody has to die, she thought as she tried to come to terms with her dreadful loss. Although it didn't give her the comfort her tortured mind demanded, she gradually began to realise every living thing has a lifespan, even the old owl and the tree he's calling from will die one day, she thought. Then, just before her tired body and restless mind drifted into the comforting embrace of sleep, she looked at the white face of the moon and thought that perhaps the moon itself would die one day.

The black veil of grief which had descended over Emily slowly began to lift in the weeks and months which followed Edwin's death but it was only to be replaced by a feeling of dreadful loneliness which wouldn't leave her. She knew she would never see Edwin again, nor would she ever again feel his body next to hers. He was her husband and her friend and as she cried in her bed, she wondered if everybody felt like this when they lost a loved one.

Then, as the weeks slowly passed, her thoughts turned increasingly to Harry who was still fighting in the trenches, dug deep in the fields and woods of the Somme. "Please God", she wept, "Please keep him safe. Please God, keep my son safe".

Emily stopped to watch some blackbirds as they hungrily stripped the blood-red berries off the old holly tree which stood alongside the lych gate of the ancient village church. The birds were used to the clanging of the bells ringing high up in the belfry and continued with their feast, knowing their lives in the cold winter ahead depended on it. The hungry birds didn't even bother to cock their heads to see what was making the noise knowing it wasn't a threat to them, the way God's creatures do. As Emily watched them, a cold breeze stirred the tree's branches, causing two or three of the birds to flutter off and find new and sturdier boughs to feed from.

She shivered and pulled her black woollen shawl tightly around her thin shoulders and walked slowly towards the open door of the church. Her once youthful beauty had begun to desert her and lines had formed round her once, blue eyes. Even these, showed the sadness she still felt.

The stooped figure of the vicar was just far enough inside the church to protect him from the chill December wind. The elderly cleric had a thin, gaunt face and his sunken eyes were surrounded by dark purple shadows matching the colour of the Advent vestments he was wearing. His white clerical collar seemed to be several sizes too large for the scrawny neck protruding from it, which, together with his bald head, gave the appearance of a reptile coming out of its shell. The man had been in the midst of the suffering caused by the never ending war and he needed the comforting arm of the Lord to be wrapped around him just as much as the grieving womenfolk in the village he attended to.

The Reverend Lamb solemnly welcomed Emily to the Christmas service. He knew that she, like the other black-coated women who were already sitting on the hard unforgiving pews of the ancient village church, would be praying for the soul of her dead husband whilst others would be asking God to return their sons or husbands safely back to them once the dreadful war was over. The bleak faced cleric had seen so much sadness in the village and knew there would be others in his flock, who like Emily, would be praying for both. Emily found an empty pew near the back of the church. She had no need for company today. The church was bleak and dark, devoid of any seasonal happiness. She listened as the vicar started the service by preaching about the meaning of the four white candles which were burning for hope, peace, love and joy. Her thoughts were elsewhere as the man's sombre voice started the Advent reading and then, when he had finished, she heard the organist as he began to play the first carol.

It was then, Emily's eyes misted over.

Dum Dum...der. dum... dum, dum, dum, dum......

It was the carol which the band had played at the Christmas party at Parkington Hall.

Emily remembered it had been Mrs Bentley-Wards favourite carol when, without warning, a torrent of memories suddenly came flooding back into her mind.

Oh Edwin, she thought, as congregation burst into song.

I heard the bells on Christmas day,

Their old familiar carols play,

And wild and sweet the words repeat,

Of peace on earth, good will to men.

Emily couldn't remember the words and as the singing of the carol echoed around the cold, stone church walls, her mind drifted back to the servant's party at Parkington Hall and how happy she and her dear

Edwin had been that night. It had been a happiness she thought would last forever and never end.

The carol was in the closing verses when Emily sensed its tone had changed and once again she listened to the words which were being sung.

And in despair I bowed my head,

There is no peace on earth, I said,

For hate is strong and mocks the song,

Of peace on earth: of good, it will despair.

Emily stood motionless on the cold slabs of the church floor, pondering the bleak words which were going round and round in her head. A chill ran down her spine and she couldn't hold back the bitter tears any longer as they began to run down her cheeks.

"Surely not", she said aloud as a pain of disbelief stabbed at her heart. She could not stop the words which were tumbling from her quivering lips, "A million men died for nothing. No, surely not".

She started sobbing and her sobbing grew louder and turned into a mournful wail as she ran from the church with her head in her hands and into the cold December air.

Harry had been back from the trenches of the Somme for two months but would not say a word about it, other than he once said the mud had been so deep that men drowned in it.

The weather was exceptionally mild during the following January when Tom, who was now nine years old, sat one evening with his elder brother on the back door step.

"Harry", Tom said, "I was so sad when father was killed and I am so pleased you came back from the war".

"Are you? " Harry asked gently, as he put a protective arm round his young brother's shoulder.

Harry knew even at the mention of the word, *war,* the memories, those terrible memories he had so desperately tried to erase from his mind would come flooding back. He could feel his hand shaking as it searched frantically in his trouser pocket for his cigarettes. Apart from his tormented mind and the ever recurring nightmares, the only thing he brought back from France was his love, no not love, need, yes need, he thought, of a cigarette. He took one of the white sticks of comfort out of the packet and lit it.

Tom had noticed his brother's hand was shaking and asked with childlike innocence, "Harry, are you alright?"

Harry held the cigarette between his fingers, stained yellow with nicotine and inhaled its smoke deeply into his lungs. After a few moments he slowly exhaled, anxious to smell its mind numbing smoke. It was now the putrid smell of rotting flesh which filled his nostrils and he shook his head in a vain attempt to get rid of it.

Muted images were beginning to form in his head. At first they were just black shapes and then, quite slowly they started to merge into human forms. He tried to rebut them from his mind but they continued to form into more black shadows and human shapes. The terrible sights of war had returned. His hand gripped the cigarette packet and crushed it. He could see the human debris of war littering the water-filled shell holes. Out-stretched arms with beckoning fingers were asking for help and rose up from the glutinous, black mud. Fat brown rats were scurrying from the bloated bodies laying there. The rats' long slithering tails were leaving lines in the mud and one of the repulsive creatures stopped to look at Harry. He could see the rat's razor sharp teeth beneath its switching nose.

"Yes", Tom continued brightly, unaware of the torment which was tearing his brother's mind apart, "I'm glad you're back because you're my best friend.......... Harry, did you have a best friend in France?" the innocent young boy probed.

Harry could feel his chest pounding but it was the sound of Tom's voice he could now hear and it was the smoke of his cigarette which filled his nostrils. The images and the smell of the war had gone, but he knew that they would return. They always did.

"What did you say?" he asked his young brother, absent-mindedly.

"Did you have a best friend when you were in France?" Tom repeated, impatient at his brother's lack of attention.

Harry continued, not hearing the question. "They told us that our artillery bombardment would destroy everything the Germans had. They said it would destroy their trenches and cut through the barbed wire entanglements, all their defences, everything they had. For eight days we sent the shells over. The noise was deafening but the Boche had moved their men into the safety of their deep dug-outs. When our shelling stopped we were given the order to climb the assault ladders and go over the top but they were waiting for us with their bloody machine guns ".

The sounds Harry began to hear in his head were distant at first. Then, as the dark shapes of men began to form again, the noises became louder. It was the raking sound of machine guns he could hear and he could feel his boots sticking in the glutinous mud as he ran blindly forward. The sound of the gunfire was growing louder. On either side of him, men were screaming as they fell to the ground. He had reached the entanglements. Men were hanging from the barbed wire like fish trapped in a net. He forced his way through the deadly never-ending tangle. Behind him whistles were blowing, more lads were following. He could hear the splash of water as he jumped down into the end of a German trench. He was wading through the filthy oozing mud and he could hear the squelching underfoot as he desperately tried to keep his balance. Suddenly there were men running towards him and the hand to hand fighting was beginning. He could hear the sickening thuds and fearsome screams as skulls were being smashed with the wooden clubs his chums were carrying, He could see himself running further down the trench. There he was, a Hun, a wide eyed Hun. Harry lunged forward with his bayonet and drove it into the man's soft belly. He could hear the last rattling gasp of the dying man before he saw the red liquid spurt from his belly. It was him or me, he told himself. The straw dummies which had hung on the wooden stands during training didn't scream when they had bayonets jabbed in them. They didn't bleed or have their guts hanging out.

"Harry, Harry, did you hear what I said. Did you have a friend over there?" Tom was asking him for the third time.

It was the sound of Tom's voice which once again brought Harry back from the bloody trenches and he took out another cigarette from the crumpled packet he was gripping.

There was a long silence before he started to answer his brother's question.

"It was near to a town called Albert. It was quite a big town but it had been shelled to bits".

Every word seemed to be an effort for Harry. It was almost as though he was deep in thought between each of the words he uttered.

"The houses and the trees around the town had been blasted to bits. The fields were just seas of mud with shell craters everywhere. In most of them were broken carts, field guns, dead horses, men, flies ....." his voice trailed off. "New drafts were being marched across the wooden duckboards towards the front lines..... Wounded men were being helped or carried to the field hospitals. The dead, at least the ones we found, were buried just behind the lines. We were in the trenches and at the sound of the whistle, over the top we went. The lads were mown down like wooden skittles, sometimes they pushed us back and at other times we pushed them back into their own trenches and things............"

 Lighting the cigarette, Harry once again drew the smoke down deep into his lungs.

"Well, things got bad. Sometimes we would take over their trenches. Reverse things. Dig the fire steps on the other side of the trench and then the lads with the Lewis guns would dig in and we would wait for the Boche to attack........right across the battlefield you could hear the moans of the wounded...crying out for help...screaming......."

Tom listened, almost spell-bound. In his young, innocent mind, it all seemed quite exciting.

Harry sat there, white-faced and shaking. Once again he wrapped a protective arm around his young brother.

"But your friend, Harry, tell me about your friend", the young boy urged again.

"Yes", Harry said, deep in thought as he returned to the question. His voice was not much more than a whisper now. "His name was Bill... Bill Busbridge. He enlisted with me in Maidstone. We both went into the West Kents.....he was a good artist....liked doing oil paintings", he said absentmindedly.

"Did he die?" Tom prompted.

"He had two brothers out there as well", Harry said, not having heard a word his younger sibling had said and deep in thought, he continued, "One of them was in Flanders ... I think he was killed there, I don't know what happened to the other one.... dead probably". His voice trailed off.

"It was in a place we called Stump Road on the way to Pozières. Bodies began to pile up in no-man's land. In the distance I heard three blasts from an officer's whistle...more of our lads were being ordered over the top. The Germans were firing and sniping at the poor sods who were still alive and trying to take refuge in the shell holes. Bill and I were in a telephone dugout with three other chaps when the communication trench was hit by a shell sent over by the Boche. It was on the 8th October, 1917. I'll never forget it". Harry stopped. In his head he was hearing the dreadful noises again and was struggling to find the words

"What happened to you?" Tom asked impatiently, as he noticed his brother's hands were shaking again.

Harry remained silent, collecting his thoughts.

"It was near to a town called Albert," Harry said, not realising he was repeating himself. "It was quite big town but it had been shelled to bits". Every word seemed to be an effort for him, almost as though he was looking at the destruction in the French town again.

"The houses and the trees around the town had been blasted to pieces, the fields.... The shelling was dreadful....all around us....the noise was indescribable.... the ground was vibrating beneath our feet".

Harry paused again, he could feel the damp-cold of the trenches invading his body again and there was a croak of anguish in his voice.

"There was a bright flash and a Christ Almighty bang.....the ground heaved up in front of me. It happened so quickly, I did not even realise it was a German shell. The blast lifted me up and threw me backwards... earth was showering down on me like pouring rain, hitting me, hurting me. I couldn't hear anything... silence as thick as night. They laid me on a stretcher, I tried to say I was alright but I couldn't hear my voice. What about the others I was shouting at them, what about the others?".

Tom was taking in every detail. "What about the others?" he asked.

"The others were ahead", Harry continued, "There was a bend in the dugout...they took the blast...... red hot shrapnel ...huge shards of wood, all four men were mown down. One of them had blood streaming from his tunic. I could see a large piece of the shrapnel had hit him. They said he had been calling for his mother. He was still writhing in the bottom of the trench as they lifted me out". "A lot of men, when they had been badly injured, called for their mothers... I suppose they knew they were going to die.........they wanted their mothers to comfort them. Perhaps they just wanted their mothers to know what had happened to them....how they died, where they were. Who knows?"

"I was fortunate to escape without too much damage but I was taken to the casualty clearing station along with the others. Bill was so plucky. His left leg had a gaping wound above the knee. It was clearly smashed. I could see the white bone. One of his arms was hanging lifeless, he was covered in blood".

"Did he die?" Tom asked. His voice was muffled.

Harry's throat was dry, he coughed. It was more like a choke and then after a few more moments of thought, he carried on. "He was so cheerful all the time. I'll always remember his courage. He seemed so well. When I left him the doctor was very hopeful his life would be spared. I suppose he died of shock.... loss of blood, infection. One of the others died too. I don't know what happened to the other chaps. Just one of the thousands of the poor sods ...he was always so bright.....buried where he fell amongst the shattered trees. A place we called Stump Road" he repeated......

Harry's voice had become just a whisper. His cigarette had gone out and he flicked it away before lighting another one and drawing the tobacco smoke deep into his lungs, he walked off.

He had released the memories of war and as his tormented mind cleared, he vowed he would never speak of them again.

Although he had returned safely from the war and the thick yellow clay of the Somme had fallen from his boots, the images he had brought back from the blood-soaked trenches were irrevocably etched into his subconscious and he knew they would never go away. They never did, they never would.

4

Black Clouds Darken a Blue Sky

It was the familiar sound of the horses' iron-clad hooves and the rhythmic squeak from the carts' wheel hubs which caused Emily to look out of the window. There was a soft early morning mist floating over the field as the horse and cart passed by the cottage. The man leading the horse touched his cap on seeing her at the window and even without looking at the load stacked on the cart, Emily knew from the dust covered man he had come from the quarry. The slabs of Kentish ragstone had been carefully shaped by the hammers and chisels of the men who worked deep in the quarry close to Bell Woods. Now the stone was being taken to a corner on the village green where it would be painstakingly put together by the local mason. Although the long brutal war had been over for nearly a year, the sight of the stone brought the memories flooding back to Emily. The cold, grey stone was being used to build a war memorial to honour the men of Pentbury who did not return from the blood-filled trenches of France and Flanders. Hard as times were, everybody in the village had contributed towards the cost of the memorial and soon there would be a tall stone cross standing proud on the village green with the names of the men who died in the bloody war carved on it's octagonal base. Emily watched as the cart trundled off in the distance and after a few minutes of silent thought, she called up the stairs to her son who had not yet come down for his breakfast.

"Tom...hurry up, we must leave in ten minutes".

The long warm days of the summer were yielding reluctantly to the mellow fruitfulness of autumn as Emily and Tom walked across the stubble field to the hop gardens. She knew the low hanging mist of the September morning would soon lift and with the strengthening warmth of the sun which was already rising, the day would eventually become bright and sunny.

"It's a lovely hopping morning", Emily said brightly, referring to the phrase the locals had used for generations to describe the early mornings during the hop picking season, when the mist hung heavy over the meadows before the heat of the rising sun burnt it off.

"I'm cold", her son replied grumpily.

It was just after six in the morning, he was tired and not looking forward to spending the next four or five weeks picking hops.

"It isn't any good sulking, Tom", his mother said patiently, "you know full well the school closes at this time of year so the village children can help to pick the hops".

"Do I have to help you every day?" the boy enquired sheepishly, with the faintest glimmer of hope in his voice.

Emily looked at her young son in reproach before saying disapprovingly, "You're thirteen years old now Tom and with your father dead, we need the money to keep us clothed and fed". She fell silent and thought for a moment or two before offering a compromise, "If you help me to pick ten bushels a day, you needn't come with me at the weekends".

"Thank you mother", the boy replied gratefully.

Emily smiled, knowing that Tom didn't have the slightest idea what ten bushels of hops looked like or how long they would take to pick.

Tom brightened up immediately and was already thinking what he would do at the weekend as he ran ahead to chase a covey of grey partridges he had seen hiding in the corn stubble. The birds saw him and pushed their bodies, fat with the grains of wheat which had fallen in the field during the harvest, flat into the stubble. Then, after realising at the last moment the boy was nearly on them, they took off with a loud flapping of their short wings.

Emily watched her son's antics as she made her way towards the hop garden. An apple never falls far the tree, she thought and smiled as she realised how much Tom reminded her of her dear, departed husband. She walked slowly behind the young boy, who was now some way ahead, taking her time to admire the beauty of the hedgerow. The dogwoods and the spindle bushes were the first of the trees in the hedgerow beginning to show their autumn hues of reds and gold. Countless spiders' webs still wet with the dawn mist, sparkled like strands of glistening jewels were strung amongst the rosehips and blackberries which were ready to be gathered. Bright yellow honeysuckle flowers occasionally added to autumnal splendour but their sweet scent was now disappearing as quickly as the long, lingering days of summer and was no longer able to tempt the visiting bumble bees to feast its sweet nectar.

Tom ran on amongst the rows of towering, dark green hop bines which had grown up the strings during the summer and had now reached the top of the wire-work which criss-crossed the field. The hop garden, heavy with its distinctive smell was already full of people waiting around their bins for the sound of the measurer's whistle which would be the sign for them to start work.

"Tom we'll pick in this bin", said his mother, as she walked towards a pale faced lady who was about the same age as Emily, but looked as fragile as the spider's webs in the hedgerow.

The woman was sitting on one side of the large, box-like bin which was made of strong hessian sacking, strung like a hammock between two long wooden rails which were supported at each end with a cross frame. The bin was about seven feet long and fixed to the cross frames at each end were two wooden handles so it could be lifted up the alleys as the hops were picked and new bines pulled down.

"Good morning Mrs Spartell, said Emily, "do you mind if we share your bin?"

"Not at all my dear, I'll be glad of your company", said the woman pleasantly.

Tom smiled at Mrs Spartell, noticing she was wearing a long black dress which was almost completely covered by a dark brown apron. A black woollen shawl was draped around the thin woman's bony shoulders and fixed firmly on her head, was a large hat with a floppy brim. Tom knew that since the end of the Great War, all the women in the village who had lost their men-folk had taken to wearing black clothes. His mother was one of them.

The bin had been divided into two with a piece of sacking so Emily and Tom could pick into one half and Mrs Spartell could pick her hops into the other. With the shrill sound of the measurer's whistle, the frenzy began with the pickers starting to pull down the hop bines. Tom grabbed the bottom of a bine and gave it a hard tug to break the string which was holding it to the wire-work above. The bine was nearly twelve feet high and heavy with green hops wet from the morning mist and as Tom tugged, it crashed down on the unsuspecting boy, showering him with water and the sticky yellow pollen of the hops. Before the day was out, Tom knew he would have to do this many times over, both for his mother and Mrs Spartell. Emily perched herself on the side of the bin and laid the fallen bine across her apron-covered lap then together with her Tom, begun to quickly pluck the fat hops from it. Once a bine had been stripped of its hops, Tom pulled another one down, then another and another, until slowly, their half of the bin began to fill up with the sweet scented hops, gloriously smelling like a heady mix of roasted herbs and pine needles.

"He's coming, he's on his way", a cry went up from an alley further down the hop garden.

"The tallyman will be here soon, the tallyman will soon be here", chanted some very young ragamuffin children who had stopped playing their game and were now waiting excitedly at their mother's bin for the man's arrival.

Emily turned to Tom, saying "Come on; let's finish picking this last bine before he gets here".

After a few minutes of frantic activity, they heard the tallyman shouting, "HOPS READY, HOPS READY".

It was mid-morning and the tallyman and the measurer were making their rounds to record the number of bushels of hops which had been picked into the large bins before bagging them up and taking them away.

"Morning Mrs Kealey, Mrs Spartell....nice to see you both again", the tallyman greeted the ladies warmly, "and you young Tom, I hope there's no leaves in there" the genial, weather- beaten man said, peering down into the bin.

On his head he had an old felt hat and the dirty jacket he was wearing was tied round his portly waist with an odd length of coconut hop string. Below his knees the legs of his hop stained trousers were tucked into his tightly buckled leather gaiters and on his feet was a pair hobnailed boots. In one of his hop stained hands he was holding his tally book which he always referred to as the bookings whilst in the other hand, he was gripping a thick black pencil, held at the ready for the measurer to shout out the numbers.

The measurer, a thin man, who instead of wearing gaiters had tied his trousers round his legs with two lengths of brown, hop string, plunged his bushel basket into the freshly picked hops and scooped them out. Tom watched as each basket brimming with hops was counted and then tipped into a large hession sack, which the men called a poke.

"THREE", the measurer shouted.

"Three, Mrs Kealey", repeated the tallyman, as he carefully recorded the number of bushels Emily and Tom had picked in the bookings, before the two men moved to the other end of the bin to measure out the hops Mrs Spartell's had picked.

Tom was secretly pleased when the men returned at midday to repeat the procedure, because it meant it was time to stop for lunch. The smell of wood smoke was already wafting across the field from the small fires which had been lit around the edges of the field to boil water and brew tea in smoke-blackened kettles. The sun was shining in a cloudless blue sky when Emily and Tom sat down. With their backs resting against the bin, it was time to eat their bread and cheese sandwiches together with the bread pudding Emily had made before the old cockerel in the back garden had signalled the arrival of daybreak.

As the heat of the sun of midday was being replaced with the cool air of the autumn afternoon, Tom continued to pull more bines and strip more hops from them, in addition to helping his mother and Mrs

Spartell move the heavy bin up the alley. His back was aching and his fingers were becoming sore when he heard the shout, "NO MORE BINES, NO MORE BINES". At last, he thought, on hearing the tallyman's command, the first day of hop picking had finished.

It was some days later when he first saw her.

He had been helping the tallyman to carry a poke to the bottom of the hop garden where the waggoner was waiting with his horse and cart, ready to take the bulging pokes to the oast house where the hops would be dried. She was standing close to the wagon and Tom could not take his eyes off the young girl. She was about his age, perhaps a little younger and her sun-bleached, straw coloured hair, tumbled like a cascade down to her narrow shoulders.

When her sparkling blue eyes saw Tom looking at her, she grinned and said in a very soft voice, "Hello".

"Hello", Tom said shyly. He felt his face flushing as he plucked up the courage to ask the girl, "What's your name?"

"Lucy", said the young girl demurely "What's yours?"

"Tom", he replied, slightly more boldly this time.

"TOM, TOM, WHERE ARE YOU?"

It was a few moments before Tom realised it was the sound of his mother's agitated voice he could hear in the distance and with an anguished look on his young face, he turned to run back to her.

"Goodbye", Lucy said, when she realised she was about to lose her newly found friend and as Tom stopped and looked forlornly at her, a smile flashed across her young face like a ray of sunshine on a summer daisy.

"Bye", he said reluctantly over his shoulder, as he started running up the alley where his mother and Mrs Spartell were picking the hops.

"TOM", his mother said sternly, "please do not run away again. I need you to pull some more bines down for me and Mrs Spartell".

Tom looked at the thin woman and could see that she had a smile on her face. It was not an unkind smile. It was one more of amusement, for a reason Tom did not understand.

He could only think of one thing as he pulled down the bines and stripped off the plump hops stubbornly clinging to them. Lucy. Where did she come from, he thought? She wasn't a village girl and she certainly wasn't a hop picker. Her clothes and her hands were much too clean for that .As Tom pondered the matter, he decided the next time the tallyman came round to take the hop pokes to the wagon, he would ask his mother if he could help the man again......just for a few minutes, that's all he would be.

It seemed like hours before the tallyman came round again and he grinned when Tom asked him if he could help carry the poke to the cart. The red- faced old man knew the beginnings of young love when he saw it but he said nothing as he winked at the two women.

"Where is she?" Tom asked the waggoner despondently, on seeing no sign of Lucy.

"Who's she?" said the man, who was more interested in getting his wagon loaded and back to the oast, than to waste time talking to the young boy.

"Lucy", replied Tom.

"Oh hers", said the waggoner, as he climbed back up onto the cart with a groan. "Gone back home with her mother, I would wonder".

Tom was now running alongside the cart as it trundled back to the oast with its load of hop pokes towering above the boy.

"Where does she live?" he shouted to the waggoner who was contentedly sucking on a battered briar pipe.

"'ampshire, Shropshire, somewhere down that way", declared the waggoner, as he took the pipe from his mouth to spit out a strand of tobacco. "You keep clear of them wheels now or you'll get yerself run over".

The week was coming to an end and there had been some drizzle in the air since midday, not too much but enough to make everything and everybody soaking wet. Tom was cold and much to his relief, there were only a few more bines to pull before the tallyman would do his final count of the week and he could go home. His hands were black and sore from stripping the hops from the bines and his golden brown wavy hair was wet and matted as the last of the heavy bines fell on him. He wasn't sure now if he even preferred hop picking than going to school.

"Hello Tom", a familiar voice said.

Startled, he looked up.

There she was looking very clean and pretty.

"Hello Lucy", he stuttered in surprise at seeing her again, "I thought you had gone home" and then suddenly, for the first time in his young life, he became aware of how scruffy he must look.

"Oh no", she said, smiling sweetly at her embarrassed friend. "I'm staying with my aunt and uncle during hop picking. He's the drierman in the oast house", the bright-eyed girl explained.

"Mr Taylor!" said Tom, almost in disbelief, wondering how such a rough looking man could have such a pretty looking niece. He knew Bert Taylor was responsible to see that all the picked hops were dried properly in the oast and therefore had to be shown the utmost respect.

Lucy nodded, "Can you play tomorrow?" she asked. She hesitated before adding in almost a whisper, "or do you have to work?"

Tom held his breath as he looked quickly towards his mother, desperately hoping for her approval. Emily laughed, "No, Tom", she said lovingly, "you don't have to work tomorrow, we've picked over fifty bushels this week". Tom was so pleased he hardly heard his mother say, "But you have to work on Monday".

The little girl jumped up and down with joy as she turned to Emily and said excitedly, "Thank you, thank you very much". "Meet me at the oast house at ten o'clock", she said to Tom and with that, she was off, skipping as she went.

Saturday morning dawned and as Tom ran across the stubble field he had no intention of stopping to chase any partridges today or anything else for that matter. Through the hop gardens he ran, not even stopping to say hello to his mother and Mrs Spartell, who were already sitting on their bin and busy picking the hops.

"TOM", CAN YOU PULL SOME BINES DOWN", Emily shouted in vain to her quickly disappearing son, as he raced through the hop garden and onto the track with the deep cart ruts which led towards the oast house.

On reaching the huge building, his heart sank. She wasn't there. Whilst he waited anxiously for his new-found friend to arrive, Tom watched some swallows swooping low over the farm yard with their tiny beaks wide open, to accommodate any insect which was foolish enough to fly in front of them. Some of the birds were already collecting together on the weather vane protruding from the conical white cowl of the oast. Tom, alerted by the constant twittering of the birds, looked up and realised they would soon be flying away to find somewhere warmer to spend the winter months.

"Hello Tom", shouted Lucy, as she skipped across the farmyard, carefully avoiding a muddy puddle close to where Tom was standing, so she didn't get her freshly laundered, white ankle socks dirty.

A smile spread across Tom's face, as he greeted the bright eyed young girl, saying rather breathlessly, "Hello Lucy, I'm pleased you came". Casually he kicked a stone across the yard, the way boys do and without looking up, asked, "What do you want to do today?"

"Let's go and see my Uncle Bert in the oast house", she replied.

Without waiting for his answer, she grabbed Tom's hand and explained, "He stays in the oast all the time during hopping, so the only time I see him is in there".

Tom felt the warmth of her small hand which was as soft as an angel's touch. He had only ever held his mother's hand before and that of his sisters and they didn't feel like Lucy's, he thought, as he held the small hand so tenderly, as if it might break.

The main part of the oast house was a huge, round building appropriately called the roundel. It was built of red bricks with a distinctive conical, clay-tiled roof and adjoined to it, was a weather-boarded barn. The two children paused to watch some sparrows taking tiny beaks full of straw through a hole in the roundel's roof to build a late nest in the cavernous space inside. Perched precariously on top of the tiled roof was a white painted, wooden cowl and when Lucy saw Tom was looking up at it, she asked, "Do you see the carving of a horse fixed to the weather vane, it's the Invicta horse?.

Tom nodded his head.

"The vane makes the cowl turn in the wind, so the damp air which comes from the hops when they are being dried, doesn't get blown back into the oast", Lucy explained, with a remarkable degree of knowledge.

"How do you know that?" Tom asked in amazement.

Lucy laughed. "My uncle told me", she said, in a very matter of fact manner. Have you ever been inside the oast house Tom? They call the inside of the roundel, the kiln", she added as an after-thought, anxious to show off her knowledge of the building and its complicated workings.

"No", Tom lied, knowing he had been inside the building twice before. It was only used for about five or six weeks during hop picking. The rest of the year it stood empty and once he had climbed through a broken window with Harry and Fred when they were out nesting and looking for a barn owl's nest they hoped was inside. The other time he had crept in through an open door, was to scrump some apples which were being stored there during the fruit picking season.

"Come on, I'll show you", Lucy said, dragging him inside. "It'll be fun".

It was quite dark inside the building and the high, small windows were thick with dirt and cobwebs, stopping any light they might have captured. Giving some illumination were two dusty paraffin lamps tied precariously to a wooden beam just above the children's heads and as

Tom's eyes slowly adjusted to the gloomy interior, he could just about see the figure of a man who was sitting on an old apple box by the glowing embers of a large coal fire.

"Hello Uncle Bert", said Lucy in her usual bright manner and looking at Tom, added, "this is my friend, Tom".

In the half-light, Tom could just about see that the man was eating from a roughly opened tin of sardines and had tomato sauce running down the side of his mouth which was disappearing into his thick grey beard. By his side was a mattress stuffed with straw and a coarsely woven blanket half covering a dirty old pillow. Tom noticed some of the goose feather stuffing was poking out from a large hole in one of its corners.

This is where he sleeps, Tom thought, as he looked rather nervously at the rough looking man in front of him and remembered what Lucy had told him, that her uncle never left the oast during hop picking.

The drierman was the most important man on the farm at this time of year, as it was only him who knew the mysteries of drying and cooling of the hops which had to continue both day and night. It meant he had to live in the gloom, amongst the hops and cobwebs until the hopping had finished for another year.

Bert Taylor wiped the side of his mouth on his shirt sleeve. "Hello young lady", he said, obviously very pleased to see his niece. "And you, Tom", he added, as he narrowed his eyes and looked the boy up and down, somewhat suspiciously. "What are you two youngsters up to?"

"I've come to show Tom the oast", Lucy said, as her uncle bent down to kiss her on the forehead.

"You'll soon know more about drying hops than I do", said the old man, smiling at the young girl. "Be sure not to get into any mischief now and don't get in the way of the men working up there", he said gruffly. Then, winking his eye at his young niece, he said, "When you've finished make sure you come and say goodbye to me". He stood up and put some more coal on the fire which was burning in the brick built hearth and noticing Tom was watching him, he said, pointing at the fire, "It dries the hops upstairs and the old sheet of corrugated iron I've hung over the top of it, helps to spread out the heat".

Tom nodded his head to show he understood.

"Come on Tom, first we'll go outside and watch the hop pokes being winched up to the top floor", Lucy said, already on her way.

The two children ran round to the side of the roundel and sat on the grassy bank to wait for the waggoner to arrive with another cart-load of the large sacks. Lying side by side in the long grass they watched the swallows swirling in circles overhead until the man and his horse arrived. High up, fixed on the outside of the roundel was a large iron bracket with a pulley wheel hanging from it and as Tom and Lucy watched, one of the men who was standing on a wooden landing beneath it, threaded a rope around the pulley and let both ends drop to the ground below. When the waggoner arrived, he stopped his cart under the pulley and unhitched the horse from the shafts of the cart.

"He's going to tie one end of the rope to the top of one of the hop pokes and tether the other end to the horse's collar", Lucy explained to Tom, who was looking at what was happening with growing fascination.

The pair watched as the waggoner took hold of the horse's bridle and led it along the track, pulling the poke high up to the landing where the men were waiting to swing it into the oast.

"They call the bracket with the pulley on it, the gallows bracket", Lucy whispered nervously into Tom's ear, as if, even by saying the word, *gallows*, it would set free all the spirits of those from centuries past who had met their end in such a manner.

Tom didn't answer but he took the opportunity to hold Lucy's hand again.

"Come on, let's go up there and see the hops being dried", Lucy said, as she let go of Tom's reluctant hand and raced up the wooden steps which were fixed to the outside of the roundel and onto the rickety landing.

Tom cautiously followed his high-spirited friend up the steps, but much more slowly. It was his turn to be nervous as he had never been so high up in his life and by the time he had reached the landing, Lucy had already gone through the door and into the top floor of the oast house.

"Hello Miss Lucy", said a man, standing knee-deep in a thick green carpet of hops which were spread on the drying floor, as he stopped what he was doing to greet the young girl with a jovial smile.

Tom's heart was pounding as he stepped with growing trepidation onto the hops which covered the horse hair and wooden slatted floor. It felt to him as if it would give way at any moment and they would fall to the bottom of the building and straight into Uncle Bert's fire, some twenty feet below.

"Hello Mr Crouch, I'm showing Tom round the oast but my uncle said I mustn't stop you from working", Lucy said, with a child-like innocence.

The man gave an understanding nod of his head and straightened his back. As did so, the other men, who had been turning the hops over with large wooden shovels, took the opportunity to stop and rest their aching muscles. Despite the air being hot and humid, the men were all wearing black waistcoats and stiff brimmed hats and they roared with laughter when Tom started coughing as the overpowering smell of the drying hops and the sulphur laden fumes got down his throat.

"I'm sure Mr Taylor wouldn't begrudge us a minute or two to talk to his pretty young niece". Mr Crouch laughed as he took off his hat and reached into his pocket for a hop-stained handkerchief to wipe away the rivers of sweat which were running down his face.

"Are you two youngsters off to see the hops in the cooling room now?" he said, putting his hat back on his sweating head.

"Yes", said Lucy with a smile. "Goodbye Mr Crouch" and with that, she took Tom's hand and led him across the warm carpet of hops across to the other side of the drying floor.

The children walked through another small doorway and down some rickety, age-worn wooden steps and into the attached barn. Tom knew where he was. It was the place where he and his two brothers had climbed through the broken window to look for the owls nest.

"Hello", Lucy said. Her eyes brightened on seeing her uncle who was scooping up a handful of hops from the cooling room floor.

"Hello bright eyes", the grubby looking man replied, as his face broke into the same smile it always did whenever he saw his pretty young niece.

The two children watched as Bert Taylor rubbed the cooled hops between the palms of his hands. With a studied expression on his dirty face, he looked down at the crumbled remains for a few moments of careful consideration and then breaking off the stalk from one of the dried hops , he muttered to himself, "Brittle enough".

"Those are ready to be scuppeted into the press", the old drierman exclaimed, nodding his head, satisfied that the hops were neither too moist nor too dry.

Some other men, who Lucy and Tom hadn't seen before were standing in the now golden yellow coloured hops watching the drierman and nodded their heads with satisfaction of his verdict.

Turning towards the waiting men, Bert said simply, "Those can be scuppeted now".

They immediately picked up their large wooden scuppets and started shovelling the hops down a hole in the floor and into a strange looking machine with a large turning handle on the side.

"That's the hop press, the men are shovelling the hops through that hole in the floor so they fall into the long sack we call a pocket", Bert Taylor patiently explained.

Tom watched as one of the men turned the handle of the press. He could see the man's grimaced face was distorted by the effort of squashing the dried hops into a solid lump in the rapidly filling hop pocket below.

"When the pocket is full of the pressed hops", Lucy, who was annoyed her uncle had taken over from her in explaining the workings of the hop press, said quickly to Tom, much to the amusement of the old man......... "he will sew it up and let it drop to the stowage floor below, ready to be taken to the hop market in London", she concluded somewhat decisively.

"There you are Tom", the old man chuckled, "now you know how it's all done you can be the drierman when you're a bit bigger".

The next day, with the bells of the village church ringing in the distance, the pair ran into the part of a hop garden where the Londoners were picking hops. Lucy had often wondered why they never picked in the same part of the hop garden as the villagers and the gypsies but she knew farmer Day would never let them all pick together.

"'ello cocker", said a large man with red cheeks and a handkerchief of a matching colour tied round his neck.

Tom nervously replied, with a faint "Hello", noticing the man was part of a large group of people who were all picking into the same bin.

He had never seen so many people picking hops together and thought they must all be the same family, probably grandparents, aunts, uncles, mothers and fathers and their assorted children and as he looked around, he saw it was the same at every other bin.

"'ere nipper", the man had turned his attention to Lucy. "Ain't you the one 'oose wiv the old geezer wiv the 'orse an cart, who comes up 'ere to pick up the 'ops?"

Lucy, who had never heard such strange language before just smiled and said rather meekly, "Yes".

The man with the red cheeks turned round and said something to the women who were stripping off hops in the next bin, which made them scream with laughter and they told him to stop it. Lucy didn't understand what the man had said to the women, but she thought it was something to do with the waggoner's horse.

"Come on, Tom", Lucy said as she grabbed his hand and as they ran off, they could hear the jovial Londoners laughing their heads off. Stopping to sit on the fence, Lucy said earnestly, "Tom, don't tell my uncle we went to see the Londoners. I've been told to keep away from them. My aunt said they are all uncouth with loose morals".

He wasn't sure what loose morals meant but he knew there was always a lot of singing and dancing at the tin-roofed hopper huts in the wood, where the Londoners lived during hopping. He had heard that some of the men got drunk on Friday nights at the White Horse and finished up fighting in the lane.

Some days, Lucy would come and find Tom and his mother in the hop garden when she would sit on Mrs Spartell's end of the bin and help her to pick the hops. Tom knew the poor woman, who had lost not only her husband in the war but also her only son, Michael, was grateful of the help and that his mother enjoyed listening to Lucy's non-stop chatter.

On the following Saturday the pair explored the woods behind the Lavender Cottage and Tom showed his young friend the place where his sister thought she had found the witch's coven. Although he didn't say anything to her, Tom always felt quite nervous when he was in this part of the woods and was quite pleased when Lucy said that she didn't like it there either.

The next day, Tom took the stub of an old candle he had found in the privy and a box of vestas borrowed from the scullery and together the children walked to the disused quarries to find the caves his older brothers sometimes went to. The entrance was almost hidden, overgrown with trees and the twisted bines of the old man's beard which grew in abundance. This was a secret place, only known to the bats which roosted there and a few of the local children. Nervously the intrepid explorers crept inside the dark mouth of the caves where many years previously, the quarrymen had hacked out the soft ragstone from the rock face. As Tom led the way, with just the flickering light of the candle to show the way, they explored every nook and cranny in the dark, damp tunnels until they realised it was time to run home.

It was by looking forward to the weekends and Lucy's company, which made the monotonous task of pulling the fat green hops from the bines bearable for Tom. One Saturday, when the autumn wind moaned in the tall beech trees on the edge of the field and the first golden leaves danced down, Tom and Lucy suddenly stopped the leaf fight they were having when a swarthy looking gypsy walked past them. Covered in the autumn gold, they brushed the leaves from their hair and watched as the man walked slowly across the field with his eyes fixed to the ground. The children could see the man's jet black hair glinting in the weak autumn sunshine as he took off the black hat he was wearing and stooped to the ground.

"What's he looking for?" Lucy asked.

"Mushrooms", Tom said, knowing his brothers often brought back the horse mushrooms which were often the size of dinner plates from the field. He suddenly felt quite sad when, quite unexpectedly, memories of his father came flooding back into his young mind as he remembered how much his father had enjoyed eating them for breakfast, together with three fresh eggs from the chicken in the back garden.

"I know", Lucy said excitedly, as she watched the man putting the mushrooms into his hat, "let's go down to the gypsy camp and watch the gypsies".

Tom's mood lightened and he didn't need any more encouragement. He liked the gypsies who came to the village every spring time to twist the young hop shoots around the strings. When the hop training was over they stayed for the summer to pick the cherries and apples and then in the autumn, they would pick the hops. Once hop picking was over, the olive skinned people would disappear again, just like the swallows which swooped over the oast house, coming back again when spring returned. The gypsies knew the countryside better than anyone. They knew where to gather the wild cherry plums and they knew the platts where the cob nuts grew. They knew the fields where the peewits laid their eggs and the secret places where brown trout could be tickled from the chalk streams.

Tom and Lucy sat under one of the old gnarled apple trees in the orchard next to the gypsy camp and watched a blackbird as it turned over a rotten apple which had been hidden in the long grass, in the hope of finding a worm hiding underneath. Unbeknown to the children, the sharp-eyed gipsies knew that they were there and were watching them but they ignored the pair and carried on with their lives as normal.

"Look at the different colours of the caravans", Lucy whispered. "I like the big red one with the yellow wheels best. Which one do you like, Tom?"

Tom looked across the field at the long row of caravans. There were about twenty of them, all different shapes and sizes. Some were taller than the others, with flat roofs, whilst the shorter ones had hoop shaped roofs. Between some of the caravans were tents the gypsies had fashioned from chestnut poles and some old green canvas they had probably taken from the farm.

"Tom", Lucy tugged Tom's shirt sleeve. "Look at the yellow caravan with flowers painted all over the front of it, isn't it pretty, and look Tom", the excited girl tugged at Tom's sleeve again, "even the sides of the wooden steps going up to the door have flowers painted on them".

As Tom gazed at the gaily painted caravan, he noticed coming out of a small stack pipe in the caravan's roof was a wisp of smoke curling skywards, carrying with it, the smell of burning wood which hung heavily in the still autumn air.

"Come on", he urged Lucy, "let's go to the end of the orchard and get a closer look".

Lucy nodded and the two children moved stealthily from tree to tree, hoping the gypsies wouldn't see them and chase them away. From a new vantage point they could clearly see a crackling fire in front of one of the flat-roofed caravans. It was burning brightly and hanging over it, from a hook shaped metal rod, driven into the ground, was a large black pot. The children could hear the throaty voices of the group of women who were sitting round the fire warming their hands. They were all wearing bonnets, tied with wide ribbons under their leathery chins and brightly coloured blouses and pretty skirts which stopped short of their ankles. Unlike mother's, Tom thought.

"Lucy" he whispered cautiously, "look at the old lady who is plucking a chicken".

He heard Lucy trying to stifle a laugh as she looked towards the cloud of white feathers which were swirling around the woman like snowflakes blowing in the wind. "Tom, she's smoking a pipe", the girl spluttered, before succumbing to a prolonged fit of the giggles.

Beyond the women, on the far side of the field, Tom's eyes rested on four of the dark skinned men who were running round in a large circle with their piebald horses. He watched enthralled as each man ran with a horse on either side of them, hanging on their rope bridles to stop the thundering beasts from galloping off. As the horses raced round the field, the long flowing manes and the wispy feathers swirling around the magnificent creatures hooves looked as if they had taken to the air, just like the mythical creatures Tom had seen in one of the story books at school.

Suddenly out of the corner of his eye, Tom saw a group of dirty-faced gypsy boys running towards them and grabbing Lucy's hand, he shouted urgently, "Come on".

The two friends ran hand in hand, back to the farm yard as quickly as their young legs would carry them.

The hop garden had begun to strike a desolate chord as the bines stripped of their precious hops lay lifelessly on the rich brown soil of the hop garden. Gone were the towering green hop bines which had hung on either side of the alleys and all that remained now were the lines of the chestnut poles standing like rows of soldiers. Some odd clumps of hops which had broken free as the bines had been pulled down, fluttered in the autumn breeze, marooned and clinging desperately to the wires overhead.

"In a day or two, there will be no more hops to pick and then it will be back to school for you, young man", Emily said to her son, as they walked alongside the hedgerow one morning on their way to the hop garden.

Tom didn't answer his mother. His thoughts were about Lucy and somehow, the thought of going back to school didn't seem as bad as not being able to seeing Lucy for another year.

"I've come to say goodbye Tom", Lucy said glumly, "we are going back home today and I've been told I have only got five minutes". Her usual bright manner had disappeared as she looked at her young friend with her head bowed and tears running down her soft, rose-pink cheeks.

On hearing what the girl had said, Emily looked at her downcast son. Words had failed to come from his mouth and as he put down the hop bine he was stripping, he just stood there, forlornly, looking like a lost soul.

Eventually, with his head bowed, he mumbled sadly, "Bye Lucy".

Then, as he quickly kissed her cheek, he tasted for the first time in his life, the bitter taste of the tears of good-bye on his quivering lips.

Emily knew only too well what it was like to lose a soul-mate and knew that Tom's young heart would soon be mended, whilst her own would remain broken for the rest of her life. Looking at Tom, she realised for the first time he was no longer a child but somebody who was rapidly growing into a young man. A shiver ran down her spine when the thought suddenly struck her, that one day she might lose him too.

It was some months later when Tom was on his way to the baker's shop in the village to buy a cottage loaf for his mother when he heard the church bell tolling in the distance. He stopped and listened to the sound which was blowing in on the chill wind. He knew by the slow clanging of the bell it was sounding the death knell and the verger was ringing the bell once for each year of the dead person's life. Although he tried, the adolescent boy soon lost count of the number of times the mournful sound had been rung. He guessed from the length of ringing, it must have been an old person who had died. Tom hurried on his way, anxious to get out of the cold and into the warmth of the shop and to enjoy its lingering smell of freshly baked bread. The small brass bell fixed to a spring on the back of the door rang wildly as he entered the shop, startling the two women who were waiting for the baker to pull out a fresh batch of loaves from the blackened doors of the bread oven which was built into the thick back wall of the shop.

"Sorry", Tom said politely, aware he had pushed the door a bit too enthusiastically.

The women ignored him and carried on with their conversation.

"He will be missed on the farm, I know that much", one of the women was saying in a hushed voice, "may God rest his soul".

"I expect Sid Crouch will be the drierman at the oast next year", the other one replied, "now that he's gone".

As he waited for the baker to pull the loaves from the oven, Tom suddenly realised that the death knell he heard had been for Bert Taylor. I must remember to tell mother Mr Taylor has died, he thought to himself, as he watched the hot bread tumble off the baker's wooden shovel and onto the floured surface of the old pine table.

It wasn't until he was on his way home with the hot loaf safely tucked under his arm when Tom realised with a horror which ran down his young spine that Lucy may not come for hop picking next year now her uncle was dead.

Nor did she, and as the days and months ticked by and Tom became older, his love of the countryside continued to flourish.

Since he had arrived in Pentbury, ten years earlier, he had learnt the ways of the animals and birds in the woods and fields around his home and when the time came for him to leave school, it was no surprise to his mother when he said he wanted to work in the woods and not in the big houses like his sister and brothers.

For the past two years, Tom had sometimes made a shilling a day during the winter months, beating for George Saunders, who was the gamekeeper at Bell Woods. Tom had enjoyed walking through the woods in line with six or seven other boys from the village, shouting and wildly beating the undergrowth with their sticks. It was in the tumbled mass of brambles and rotting wood where the pheasants had hidden and the noise of the beaters caused them to take to flight with a loud flapping of their wings. As the birds clumsily rose into the air they flew blindly unaware of the line of men dressed in tweed suits who, with guns raised, were waiting for them. At midday the beaters would sit inside a small brick hut which had been built in the middle of the woods. They would sit on the dirt floor in front of a roaring fire enjoying their simple lunch of bread and cheese, washed down with bottles of Fremlins Elephant brown ale, whilst the guns enjoyed a more substantial meal at the big house supplemented with bottles of rich burgundy from the copious cellars.

The morning was bright and sunny when Tom, who had just turned fourteen, walked down the lane for his first day as apprentice keeper to George Saunders. The pink and white May blossom was resplendent in the hedgerows and the sweet scent of the cow parsley hung heavy in the air. In the distance a cuckoo was calling and bird song filled the cloudless blue sky overhead. Tom stopped for a moment to watch two orange tip butterflies seeking out the milk maid plants, desperate to feast on the honey sweet nectar which lay hidden in their delicate lavender blue flowers. What a day to start work, he thought as he walked on.

Within five minutes he crossed over the narrow road that wound its way to the small fishing town of Hastings and passed a little pub on his right as he continued his way towards the cottage, where the gamekeeper lived. He grinned as he noticed the newly painted door of the little pub and wondered why it had been painted red when the pub sign left passers-by in no doubt the pub was called the Blue Door and he was still smiling at the thought of it when he arrived at Bell Cottage. The cottage was tucked in the wood, just off the road and perched on its roof was a small wooden turret with an old brass bell hanging from its centre. Years ago, the cottage would have been the home of a farmer and the bell would have rung to call the men in from the fields when their meals were ready. Now it hung lifeless, patiently waiting for the occasional winter gale to ring it.

George had already been in the woods since sunrise and had returned for his eight o'clock mug of cocoa and a wedge of his wife's fruit cake. He was sitting in the scullery when Tom arrived and he rose to greet the young man with a warm smile and a firm handshake but as Tom observed, no offer of a slice of cake or even a cup of the steaming cocoa was forthcoming.

The would-be apprentice could not help noticing the wisps of ginger hair escaping from the sides of the cap fixed firmly on the gamekeeper's head. The man's face, weathered by the fifty years he had spent in the woods, had the texture of old Moroccan leather. His jacket, the same tweed as his cap was hung over the back of his chair. A white shirt with a starched, rounded collar was pulled tight around his neck by a plain brown tie and buttoned across his broad chest was a waistcoat of a similar colour to his tie. The burdocks and the cleavers clinging to his heavy trousers showed evidence of his early mornings work. Thick leather gaiters protected legs from the beds of nettles and tangled brambles which grew in profusion in the woods and on his feet was a pair of stout, muddy boots. As George Saunders continued to eat his cake Tom looked at the clods of mud which had dropped off the man's boots onto the scullery floor and wondered what his house-proud mother would have said.

"Tom, why don't you walk round to the back and see the dogs whilst I finish my snap" the gamekeeper suggested to the wide-eyed youth who was standing in front of him licking his lips.

Tom had been to the cottage a few times in the past and on his way to the kennels he paused to look at the gruesome evidence of George's work which had been nailed in neat rows to the shed door. Tom recognised the grey fluff of squirrels' tails and next to them he noticed the dried skins of the rats and weasels which George had caught in his traps. Looking at the exhibits further down the door, Tom was secretly pleased to see the russet brown pelts of three stoats remembering the time when he went into his mother's chicken house only to find all the hens had been killed by a stoat. Killing machines, they love killing for the sake of it, just like foxes, he thought grimly. Walking on to find the dogs at the bottom of the garden he noticed hanging on the chestnut spile fence which divided garden from the woods was the vermin line as George called it. Dangling from it were the remains of some crows, jays and magpies some with their black beaks wide open as if they had been uttering their last raucous cries before they had been shot. Tom didn't linger, he knew George didn't keep the remains of the egg thieves as trophies but as proof to his employer that he was doing his job, preserving the game in the woods and was therefore, well worth his meagre pay.

The three dogs were barking their hellos as Tom approached. The two black, Flat Coated Retrievers named Jack and Woody were running up and down in their run whilst Maggie, the Cocker Spaniel, was literally jumping in the air, delighted at seeing Tom once again.

Tom entered the run and as he rubbed the little dog's belly, he recalled once asking George how he had chosen the dogs' names and what the old man had said, "Well Tom, I have always named my dogs after the birds in the wood, Jack, for jack snipe, Woody for the woodcock and Maggie?".........

George had waited for Tom's response and Tom recalled the pleasure he had felt when he had thought, "Maggie... Maggie ...before finally bursting out, MAGPIE"

Hanging on the side of the kennels was a bundle of gin traps. Tom knew these were tools of George's trade he used in his constant battle to eliminate the predators which roamed the woods and which were a constant and deadly threat to the precious pheasants.

Walking past the kennels to a stand of tall ash trees, Tom came to the pens where the young pheasants were being kept in relative safety before being released, deep in the woods. George called this place the rearing field and in two of the pens, Tom noticed some broody hens poking their heads through the rails of the home-made coops. Some of the mother hens were sitting on pheasant eggs, whilst others were keeping a watchful eye on the little birds they had successfully hatched. Tom knew once the chicks had grown their tail feathers and could fend for themselves, George would transfer them to the poult's pen deeper in the woods before their final release.

The old gamekeeper came out of the cottage, wiping his mouth with the back of his hand as he walked the length of his garden to find his new assistant and without further ado, said evenly, "Lad, I've a job for you".

"Take that old galvanised pail hanging under the pump in the yard and fill it up with ants' eggs". George continued with his instructions, "You'll find plenty of 'em on the south bank of the quarry and take a spade from shed with you to dig 'em out".

Tom knew exactly where he would find the ants' eggs because when he had been beating, he would stand on the bank and watch the guns shoot the ducks rising from the marshy ground around the quarry margins, but what on earth did George want the ants' eggs for?, he thought with a quizzical look on his face.

Making his way through the woods, already brightened by the shafts of sunlight breaking through the thick canopy of leaves overhead, Tom heard the familiar screech of a jay. The secretive bird's call was unmistakable and Tom, who knew of the bird's voracious appetite for pheasants' eggs, made a mental note to tell George of the birds unwelcome presence when he got back. Arriving at the south bank and looking down into the quarry, he paused to watch a grey heron standing motionless in the green-blue shallows at the water's edge, waiting to stab any unsuspecting fish or frog which might come within striking distance of its sharp, pointed beak.

A cloud of gnats were swarming over Tom's head when he found a place where the grass was thin and the sandy soil was dry and dusty and then, much to his relief he saw the nests of the wood ants. The nests were huge, three or four feet at their base, with each one reaching up to Tom's knee. All around the brown ants were scurrying to and fro, frantic in their task to build the nests even bigger with the broken-down bracken and small twigs they were carrying. Tom plunged the spade into the nearest nest and revealed its cache of eggs, each one looking like a fat grain of white rice. The ants reacted immediately to the unwelcome intrusion and sped into action, trying to remove their precious eggs and secrete them into a deeper place of protection away from Tom's marauding spade.

The pail which Tom had taken off the pump was more than half full of the sticky eggs as he carried it back to where he had left George. Some of the panic stricken ants which had been mixed up with the eggs were desperately trying to escape from their metal prison and were running up the handle of the pail and onto the bare skin of Tom's wrist. He had no intention of letting any of the little blighters sting him and he quickly dropped the spade to brush them back whence they came.

Tom was triumphant with the successful completion of his first task and upon his return he found George boiling up some rabbit's flesh in an old iron pot. Tom's young and unaccustomed nose flinched at the obnoxious smell coming from the stew bubbling in the pot. The old gamekeeper chuckled at his apprentices discomfort as he wandered off to the back of the poult's pen before returning with two buckets, both considerably larger than the pail Tom was holding. Tom watched George with growing interest as the gamekeeper tipped the rabbit's flesh in one of the buckets.

George saw the puzzled look on Tom's face and turning to him, he said with a smile, "Put half of 'em ant's eggs in this bucket and the other half in the other one".

George then went into the house and came out carrying a large saucepan of hard-boiled pheasant eggs which were still in their shells.

"Erm be addled", he said, by way of explanation. "No need to use good uns", he added, as he tipped the olive brown eggs into the bucket which didn't have the boiled rabbit's flesh in it.

"What are you doing?" ventured Tom, anxious to learn the mysterious ways of a game keeper.

George grinned and winking at Tom, said, "I'm making up my own food mixture. The bucket with the 'addled eggs, is for 'em chicks and the one with the rabbit flesh is for the poults. I give the ant's eggs to both the chicks and the poults cos it builds 'em up. Ant's eggs are bloody good things for putting some fat on their bodies".

Tom listened in awe.

The old man then carefully measured three saucepans full of white biscuit meal into each of the buckets before passing Tom a smooth, round stick which in a previous life had been a broom handle, saying, "ere, young Tom, mix both of 'em thoroughly .... Thoroughly mind you".

Under George's watchful eye, Tom mixed the contents of the buckets as he was instructed and once this had been done to the gamekeeper's satisfaction, the master and his boy went off to feed the young birds.

"Mr Saunders", Tom asked, as he poured the contents of a bucket into a feed trough, "Why do ants always follow the same narrow line through the wood?"

The gamekeeper smiled at the inquisitive nature of the boy.

He thought for a moment before saying, "Well Tom, my old dad once told me that when one of 'em finds some food and returns back to the nest with it, it rubs its belly along the ground leaving a trail for the others to follow and when they come across it, they follow it all the way back to the nest".

Tom's brow furrowed before asking, "How do they know which way to go?"

"Bugger me, Tom, you do ask the most difficult questions". George laughed as he pushed his cap back to scratch his head. After a few moments of thought he said, "I've often wondered about that myself but I think they must lay down two different types of scent. One tells 'em which way to go to the nest and the other tells 'em where the food is...... clever little sods, ain't they?"

Later, when Tom was by the water pump washing out the mixing pails, George walked up to him after feeding the dogs and said, with a smile on his face, "Well, my young Tom, "we'll make a game keeper out of you yet. Mind you, it'll take a year or two but you've got the makings in you".

The apprentice gamekeeper looked up with a grin which spread across his face from ear to ear and said politely, "Thank you Mr Saunders, I've enjoyed working with you today".

"Tomorrow, we'll walk through all the woods and take a look at the traps and with luck, we should find some early eggs which we can bring back and put under the broody 'ens".

Tom stood by the pump, listening with growing pleasure to what his mentor was saying, whilst wiping his wet hands on the back of his trousers.

"Make sure you wear some heavy boots tomorrow", the gamekeeper continued, "and later this week I think we better see what kind of shot you are with my old twelve bore".

"Thank you Mr Saunders", Tom repeated, almost speechless with the excited anticipation of being able to handle a shot gun.

George nodded, saying, "That's enough for today Tom, off you go home now and I'll see you tomorrow .....and Tom", he said, with a grin on his leathery face, "Seeing that we'll be working together now, you better start calling me George".

"Thank you Mr Saunders", Tom replied, unwittingly.

"Well Tom, how did it go?"

Emily had been waiting anxiously for her son to return from his first day at work with George Saunders. Although he was fourteen years old, she still worried about him, particularly, as he was the only one of her children who was at home now. Harry and Fred were living away and were working as garden boys and Glad was in service as a kitchen maid, at a big house in Sussex.

"Mother, George." Tom corrected himself. "I mean Mr Saunders; he said he would teach me to shoot his shot gun".

Emily smiled and looked fondly at her son. It didn't seem long ago when he was a baby in her arms and there he stood, taller than her now and talking excitedly about his first day at work. How proud Edwin would have been of him, she thought ruefully.

The thin light of the early morning sun shone through the trees making dappled patterns on the track as George and Tom made their way through Popes Wood, each with a gun tucked under their arms. It held the prospect of being a fine day for Tom's first lesson in shooting a twelve bore shotgun.

"We'll make our way up to the four wents and then go through Wents Wood and find that stand of tall black poplars", George explained.

Tom already knew the names of the different parts of the wood and he knew that four wents was the place where two of the paths crossed and although he nodded his head in understanding, he wondered why they needed to find the stand of poplar trees in Wents Wood before he could fire the gun.

"Look up there", the gamekeeper said, as they reached the group of towering trees, that's what you're going to shoot down".

"Mistletoe! Tom exclaimed, with a hint of disappointment in his voice, as he looked up and saw the huge clumps of the parasitic plant growing in the topmost branches of the poplars.

"That's it, Tom, shame it's not Christmas. The missus always likes to 'ang some sprigs of the stuff over the doors.....Didn't think I would let you wander round the woods shooting every living thing in sight 'til I knew you were up to it.....did you?" The old keeper chuckled at the thought of it.

Tom watched as George broke open the gun he was holding and pushed two cream coloured Sanders cartridges into the barrels.

"They're number six shot..... I always use 'em", George explained as he closed the barrels with a resounding click. "There's a choke on the left hand barrel which restricts the spread of the shot", the gamekeeper said mysteriously to his apprentice before handing the gun back to the lad. "Bring the stock up to your shoulder and find a comfortable place for it to nestle", he continued.

Tom nervously lifted his gun and followed the old man's instruction.

"Let the gun become part of you and when it feels right, look down the barrel and sight it up to the big clump of the stuff that's growing at the top of the middle tree...... That's it....don't be impatient...........take your time".

Tom squinted as he looked down the guns' barrels towards the small bead at the end and swivelled his body round as he swept the gun from side to side before lining it up to the clump of mistletoe George had pointed to.

"That's it, now curl your finger round the trigger and before you squeeze it make sure you keep the stock firmly against your shoulder, otherwise when the gun fires, it will kick back and break your shoulder. That's it..... good, now remember, gently squeeze...."

Tom saw the bunch of mistletoe explode through the small cloud of smoke which was coming out of the barrel, almost before he had heard the booming sound of the gun.

"Remember Tom", George's head nodded with satisfaction as he continued his instruction, "if speed is the only thing on your mind, you will jerk the gun and miss the target and then the woods will be full of bloody vermin and we'll have no bloody pheasants left".

As Tom continued to load and fire the gun and the mistletoe fell from the trees like confetti, a contented grin spread across the old gamekeeper's face. There's a young man who certainly knows how to handle a gun...no mistaking it, he's a natural, he thought proudly, as he continued to watch his young prodigy.

"If it was a moving target you would keep your gun moving when you fire", George concluded his instruction as Tom brought the gun up once again, "never check its swing on a moving target ....follow through...follow through".

During the weeks and months that followed the spring morning in May when Tom had started his job in the woods, he became a model pupil and every minute he spent with George Saunders, he showed him how eager he was to learn the ancient craft of game keeping. George liked the energy which Tom showed and taught him everything he himself had learnt, many years before. The old gamekeeper stressed time and time again on his young apprentice that the most important thing to remember was the care and well being of the pheasants and that meant raising and feeding them and killing any creatures in the wood which would threaten either them or their eggs.

The control and extermination of vermin was George's main pre-occupation. "Number one on my list", he once confided to Tom, "is that cunning bloody thing called a fox".

He then went on to list the others, "stoats, weasels, squirrels, magpies, crows, jays, hawks and last but not least", the old man's eyes narrowed, as he said, "the two legged kind, bloody poachers".

The following spring brought with it Toms' favourite task which required him to search in the woods fields and surrounding hedgerow for the pheasants' nests and collect their eggs. The nests were little more than hollow scrapes in the ground, containing ten to twelve olive coloured eggs and every day, with eager eyes, Tom would walk round looking for nests. Then, with the eggs safely laid on a straw bed in the wooden trug tucked under his arm, he would return to the rearing pens and place them under the broody hens in the coops.

Over time, Tom had grown from the once gangly apprentice to a muscular young man who was more than capable of taking care of himself and when George was satisfied that he had become a proficient shot with the twelve bore, he allowed Tom to do some night watching. Tom enjoyed patrolling the woods to deter any poachers who might be lurking in the shadows with the deadly intention to bag as many of the precious pheasants as they could. He would vary the pattern of the times when he set out to do the night watching but usually, when he had finished his evening meal with his mother, he would return back to Bell Cottage to collect Maggie, before starting his patrol. Tom enjoyed watching the small dog working the woods. She had known them ever since George Saunders had brought her here as a puppy and was constantly alert for any strange sounds she heard. Every so often, the dog would stop and look into the blackness which stretched out in front of her to see if anything was moving. She would lift her head to sniff the breeze which blew softly through the trees, alert for any alien smell that might be out there. Tom despised poachers, not just because of their thieving ways but because he saw them as cowards who would shrink back into the shadows like frightened rabbits, if they thought there was a keeper about. Whilst Tom disliked the poachers with intensity, George on the other hand, hated them. "Thieving bastards", he called them, "first bloody cousins to the fox", he would often say, before spitting a throat-full of green phlegm onto the ground, as though the very words were poison in his mouth.

It was around midnight on a cold night in November when the wind was rising and the clouds were scudding across the face of an icy moon. Tom stood and listened to a pair of tawny owls calling to each other when in the distance he heard whispered voices coming from deep in the Long Copse. Maggie had heard them too and was making off towards them through the tangle of brambles and undergrowth.

"Heel", Tom ordered in a whispered voice.

The silence of the woods was suddenly broken by the noisy flight of a pheasant. POACHERS, the word flashed across Tom's mind, as he realised the birds never flew at night unless they were disturbed.

Maggie had the scent and started to skirt round the brambles towards the oak plantation where the ground was clear of undergrowth. Tom could feel his heart beating against chest as he knelt down and in a low voice, told the dog to stay. Maggie raised her head as if to ask the reason why and then she lay down with a sad, disappointed look in her large, amber eyes. Tom slipped the safety catch off his gun and could feel the soft mulch of the rotting oak leaves beneath his feet as he began moving from tree to tree towards the voices. He was breathing so hard now he paused behind the trunk of one of the larger trees to catch his breath and looked towards a thicket of thorn bushes where he knew was a roosting place for pheasants. If there were poachers in the wood, it was likely they would be in there trying to grab the sleeping birds by their feet before wringing their necks and stuffing them into the large inner pockets of their coats.

There was a glimpse of movement to Tom's left and as a ribbon of cloud passed over the moon he suddenly saw a sullen faced man looking towards him. Although the man had his head hung down as if in the admission of guilt, there was sufficient light for Tom to see the cold, malice in the poacher's furtive eyes.

Tom's body was trembling as he slowly raised his gun.

Another shape suddenly loomed out of the darkness and before Tom had time to react, he felt a heavy, crashing blow to the back of his neck which sent him sprawling before the blackness of the night descended over him.

It was Maggie's wet tongue licking his face which Tom felt as he slowly opened his eyes. His head was hurting and as his senses slowly returned, he could feel the pain coursing through the rest of his prone body. Then, a feeling of panic suddenly overwhelmed him and he hauled himself onto his knees. "The gun!" he groaned, as he frantically groped around in the wet leaf mould for the precious weapon.

"There it is", he said to himself, as the strength drained from his body and he sank back to the ground in relief. At least they didn't take the gun, he thought as he fought off the dizziness he was feeling and staggered to his feet and slowly made his way home.

"Vicious bastards", George Saunders said ominously the following morning, as he examined the egg-sized lump on the back of Tom's head. "You came across a couple of bad 'uns last night lad, no mistaking it", he understated to the young keeper.

George watched as Tom rubbed his head and walked towards a group of beaters who had already gathered for the days shooting and thought what a plucky young man he was... no mistaking it.

"No mistaking it", he said to himself.

Tom would have spent more hours in the woods than the day gave him and as the months rolled into years, he became an accomplished gamekeeper used to living and working by the rhythm of the seasons. Of them all, he loved the coming of the spring best. It was the time of year when the woods were awoken from their winter slumber by the deafening dawn chorus of the song birds and it was when the brown buds on the trees, which had secretly been growing under the winter's cloak, would once more begin to burst into leaf. Tom's spirit always lifted when the signs of life were around him and when the solitary cock pheasants, in their magnificent new plumage were strutting through the woods like Georgian dandies on the lookout for the plainer looking, speckled hens.

Eventually, the simmering heat of summer would see Tom roaming through the woods with his eyes as keen as a hawk, on constant lookout for any predator which would threaten the precious game that was in his care, not least, the hundreds of pheasant chicks which were hatching out under the broodies.

Autumn would come with its cool winds and mellow colours and would bring with it the most important day in the life of a gamekeeper. It was when the gentry would press the hand-carved, walnut stocks of their expensive shotguns against the padded shoulders of their tweed jackets to enjoy the fruits of Tom's labour. It was on this long awaited day, the first day of the shooting season, Tom would look as resplendent as any cock pheasant and would walk in the line of beaters with Maggie running amongst the undergrowth with her wet nose pressed to the ground, getting the birds to break cover and fly towards the guns. George, with Woody and Jack, would be with the guns, standing ready at their pegs with guns raised, pointing in anticipation towards the sky. Walking behind the beaters was another group of men, who George called the pickers up. It was these men with their barking dogs, who would retrieve the pheasants as they fell to the ground with dull, lifeless thuds. The sounds of the beaters thrashing through the undergrowth and the echo of the guns would reverberate like thunder around the village for twelve weeks during the cold, bleak days of the shooting season.

When the shooting parties had left the woods for another year a stillness descended on this empty world, like a silent feather falling from the grey sky. The wet dew of the winter's nights froze on the bare branches of the trees, signalling the arrival of the crisp hoar frosts. It was when the ice on the puddles crunched under Tom's feet telling him it was time to carry out repairs to the rearing pens behind George's cottage, in preparation for another year with its four seasons to start again.

It was Tom who found George Saunders body. George had not come back at midday as was his usual habit and at mid afternoon, his wife who found Tom repairing one of the empty poult pens and told him of her concern. Her voice was tense and Tom set off immediately with Maggie snapping at his heels to find George. It had been an exceptionally wet winter, all the ditches were full of water and earlier, George had referred to the month as *February full dyke* when the two men had noticed the water in the quarry spilling out over the marshes which bordered it.

"GEORGE, GEORGE", Tom shouted, as he started looking for his friend, walking immediately at a brisk pace. A chill breeze was moaning through the leafless branches in the spinney as if evil forces were at work. As Tom entered Popes Wood, Maggie ran ahead, sniffing the air searching for the familiar smell of her master, occasionally stopping to absorb any sound or movement that would help her find the old man. Tom had been searching the different woods for over two hours and was walking along one of the muddy tracks which criss-crossed the wood towards four wents when he heard Maggie ahead of him, yapping excitedly. It was as he walked over the brow when Tom saw George in the distance, lying on his back in the puddled mud in front of the old wooden style. One of the old man's arms was outstretched, grasping the style's bottom rail whilst his other arm was by his side. Tom could feel his heart pounding under his jacket and his throat went dry as he realised something awful had happened to the game keeper. "George, George", he croaked, as he started racing towards the motionless body.

At first, Tom thought the old man had fallen from the style but as he approached the prone body, he saw a sight that would haunt him for the rest of his life. The left hand side of George's face had been shot away and what was left of the poor man's mouth was wide open, as if it was still in the throes of making one last scream. As Tom got closer he could see that one side of Georges tweed jacket had also been blasted away, revealing the bloody mess of what had once been the dead man's broad shoulder.

"Christ", screamed Tom, "no....no....George.... no.....BLOODY HELL, NO".

Maggie had reached the lifeless body before Tom and was faithfully licking the blood from her master's face in a fruitless attempt to revive him. Tears were already welling in Tom's eyes as he bent down and roughly pulled the dog away by its collar, wincing at the awful sight in front of him. Shock overwhelmed him and he could taste the bitter yellow bile which was rising from his stomach and he retched when he looked down and saw more closely what remained of the old man's face. It was black with gun smoke and Tom could smell the unmistakable smell of a discharged cartridge on the dead man's jacket and realised whoever had killed his old friend, had shot him at close range.

He was now crying inconsolably.

Tom glanced down at his dead friend.

"What bastard did this?" he gasped, as his lungs fought for breath. "No...no", he howled, as his shaking legs suddenly gave way and as he fell on his knees, with his head resting on his dead friends still warm chest, he started sobbing again.

Tom still had a restraining hand on Maggie's collar, when something George had said to him, soon after they had started working together, raced into his mind.

"First bloody cousins to the fox", he heard his friend's voice saying.

"BASTARDS", Tom shouted, as he realised who had killed George. "Poachers... I'll kill the bastards", he vowed, in a low threatening voice and for the first time in his life, his eyes burned with hate and an uncontrollable anger surged inside him.

Dusk was falling in the woods and Tom's hands were trembling as he frantically searched his pockets for his cigarettes. He watched in silence as the village constable lifted the coat which Tom had placed over George Saunders shattered face to begin the investigation into the man's tragic death. Standing behind him was a police inspector with a cold, emotionless expression set hard on his face. Tom felt sick and raised a cigarette to his quivering lips.

He desperately sucked on it, getting the flame from his lighter to bend closer to the tip and then, once the cigarette was lit, he gratefully drew the nicotine-infused smoke deep into his yearning lungs. Tom turned his head away, unable to watch, as the inspector, who until that point had only observed the scene from a distance, knelt down alongside the constable and peered at the lifeless remains of the game keeper. The emotionless man had hardly said half a dozen words since he had arrived but as Tom glanced across, he noticed the inspector's eyes were as restless as the cold breeze which started blowing through the trees. The man walked up and down, occasionally stopping to look back at the grim scene in front of him, first from one direction before he shifted his position a few yards, to look from the other.

Tom had seen enough. He turned and strode away, holding his temper in check with a huge effort. He was angry. He wanted to tell the man to stop walking around and do something positive. What good was he doing, what was the point of it all? Instead of showing such little respect for the motionless body, why couldn't he let the poor man rest in peace and start rounding up all the local poachers? After all, everybody in the village knew who they were.

Tom was sitting in the kitchen in the gamekeeper's cottage some days later and sharing a consoling mug of cocoa with the old man's grieving widow, when the police inspector gave a perfunctory knock on the back door and walked straight in.

Tom and Mrs Saunders sat and listened in disbelief as the cold-eyed man did his usual and paced up and down. He told them he had finished his investigation and had concluded that George's death was the result of a tragic accident. Tom's face paled and he quickly swallowed the remnants of the cocoa in his mouth as he tried to grasp what he had just heard. No, surely not, he thought in disbelief, as he quickly looked towards the distraught Mrs Saunders.

In the minutes which followed, the grim faced inspector outlined his findings by starting to say it had became clear to him that George, like all gamekeepers, never walked with the barrels of his gun broken and always kept them full cocked, with the hammers back and the muzzle pointing skywards. Tom unconsciously nodded his head in agreement to the inspector's assumption of his friends working practice which was readiness should any vermin cross his path. The man pressed on to say in his monotone voice that George had been found lying on one side of the stile whilst his gun, with one of its barrels discharged, lay on the other. The slimy mark in the wet mud on the bottom step-board of the stile, showed where the unfortunate man's foot had slipped. As a result, the gun had fallen from his grasp and as its wooden stock hit the step-board on the other side of the stile, it had fired.

Tom's mind went numb as he stared anxiously across the kitchen table at Mrs Saunders, who was now silently weeping inconsolably into a tear-soaked handkerchief. He reached across the table and tenderly took the distraught woman's hand. It felt cold and Tom could feel it was shaking as she came to terms with what the policeman had just said. Her beloved husband of over forty years had fallen victim of his own gun.

A few months after the old gamekeepers wasteful death, Tom was walking towards the beaters hut in Horish Wood when a sudden burst of bird song jolted him from his daydream. As he looked up to see if he could see the songster, a cock pheasant waddled out from a bed of nettles in front of him. Tom stopped and watched the bird.

"What a proud thing you are", he said quietly to the bird.

The pheasant was holding its head high and on either side of its curved beak, hung blood-red wattles. The bird stopped as if it was issuing a challenge to Tom and stared arrogantly at him with bright yellow eyes. Tom had always loved the colours of cock pheasants and had often thought that their sapphire-blue neck plumage with the ring of white neck feathers made them look like country rectors. The biscuit-brown and orange feathers with their ink-black tips shone in the weak spring sunshine like enamelled icons on the bird's puffed-up chest. The pheasant was proudly holding its long tail feathers clear of the ground as it strutted past the gamekeeper with a certain deliberation as if it didn't have a care in the world, before finally disappearing into the spinney.

Tom suddenly felt depressed when he thought how different these lovely creatures looked after they had been shot and were hanging limp and lifeless from the picker-up's belts with their once bright amber eyes shrouded by the black hoods of death. Tom knew he had always had mixed feelings when he shot these lovely birds and although he had often felt disappointed when had missed a shot, he equally had to hide the shame he felt every time he had brought one of these fine birds crashing down to earth. Instantly, Tom made up his mind. He would stay on as the gamekeeper for a few months until a replacement keeper could be found. His heart was no longer in the job and he would seek employment elsewhere.

Not only had he lost a fine friend and a good gamekeeper, he had also lost a man who had become like a father to him, filling the gaping hole the Great War had bestowed on him.

Yes, his mind was made up as he decided he had seen enough of death in these woods.

PART TWO

These men knew moments you have never known,

Nor ever will

David Kennedy Raikes

5

Brothers in Arms-1939

Although Emily had wrapped herself in her warmest clothes, she was hunched up with the cold as light flurries of powdery snow swirled like whirlwinds as they were blown across the field already frozen hard by the biting north wind. She pulled her thick woollen scarf tightly around her head as she quickened her pace home after buying some neck of mutton from the butchers shop by the green.

 Entering the cottage, Emily sighed with relief when she saw the small fire in the range had kept in and there were still some red embers smouldering in its grate.

"Thank goodness", she said, thankful she would not have to re-lay the fire with her dwindling supply of kindling wood and light it again. Not even bothering to shake off the dusting of snow which had settled on her coat, she hurried across the room to make up the fire whilst there was still some life left in it. Bending down, she scooped a small shovelful of coal from the brass scuttle on the hearth and carefully let a few knobs drop on the glowing embers. Her hands were stinging from the cold and she was grateful of what little heat there was to warm them.

There were still four days before it was twelfth night when she would take down the Christmas decorations and as the fire burst into life, dancing flames reflected on the coloured glass baubles hanging from the small Christmas tree which stood in the corner of the room. Emily pulled the Windsor chair closer to the fire and looked around the room. She had always loved Christmas. Of course it had been different

119

this year, with just Tom to enjoy the Christmas dinner and then afterwards, as they had sat by the fire in the best room listening to the wireless, sipping a glass of sherry and enjoying some of her freshly baked mince pies.

Reluctantly, Emily left the comfort of her chair and made her way into the scullery to prepare the evening meal. She glanced at the little silver Victorian three-penny pieces she had put in the Christmas pudding which were still laying on the table waiting to be put away for another year. A soft smile spread across her lined face as she remembered how frantically the children used to search through their helpings of pudding in the hope of finding one of the lucky little coins inside.

This year on Christmas Eve, when she had been in the midst of rolling out the pastry for the sausage rolls and mince pies, three children from the village arrived and had sung carols, whilst they huddled against the cold at the front door. The youngsters had brought such joy to Emily she gave each of them a sixpence.

Strands of silver tinsel threaded through the branches of holly still bedecked the top of the mirror and twinkled in the firelight. She closed her eyes as she recalled it had been on a cold December day when Edwin had told her they had been invited to the Christmas party at Parkington Hall. Her mind drifted back to that evening so long ago and the dancing and the laughter which had echoed around the hall. She sighed. How happy they had been. Oh, she thought, what lovely Christmases there had been when Edwin was alive.

When Tom walked in from work the house was filled with the delicious aroma of the rich brown gravy of the stew bubbling in a large white enamelled saucepan on top of the range.

"That smells good", he said flatly, as he stood with his back to the fire relishing its warmth but without the usual sparkle in his voice.

Emily finished laying the table and as she placed two plates of steaming stew on the table, she said, "I thought it would warm you, it's neck of mutton, with suet dumplings and parsnips. I had such a job digging up the parsnips with the ground being so frozen".

Tom didn't reply. His thoughts were elsewhere.

"You're quiet tonight, dear", Emily said, as she watched Tom push one of the mutton bones aimlessly round his plate.

Tom was always good company when they had their evening meal together. He would usually ask his mother what she had been doing during the day or tell her about the things which had happened at the engineering works but tonight it was different and Emily sensed there was something troubling him. She had raised four children and it was a mother's intuition which was telling her something was wrong.

Tom had been putting this moment off for months. He had agreed with Tony Long they would wait until after Christmas before they said anything to their families. They had both felt there was no point in spoiling Christmas. He took a deep breath and several minutes passed before he felt ready to speak. His eyes focused on the uneaten food on his plate, it saved having to look at his mother's reaction to what he was about to tell her.

"Mother", he said so solemnly it startled Emily and instinctively confirmed to her something was wrong.

"What is it, Tom?"

He swallowed hard and waited for the words to form in his mouth, words which he had been rehearsing for weeks. Christ, this is going to be difficult, he thought, without lifting his eyes to confront his mother.

"Tony and I have decided to join the army", he blurted out.

Emily's knife and fork fell to her plate with a crash. Her hands went up to clutch her face with the shock of the words her son had just uttered. The clatter of the cutlery startled Tom and he quickly looked up at his mother. She just sat there, speechless, with her mouth agape. Her hands were shaking as they cradled her head and the tears which filled her eyes were spilling down her flushed cheeks. Tom felt rotten. He hadn't meant to hurt his mother, it was the last thing in the world he wanted to happen. He had dreaded this moment ever since his friend, Tony Long had suggested they should enlist in the Royal Artillery. Tom knew his mother wouldn't approve, particularly as his father had been killed in the Great War but he was twenty seven years old and there was a life to live beyond Pentbury.

Tom's felt his face flush. "Mother", he ventured, anxious to explain.

Emily held up her hand to silence him.

"No Tom, please Tom not that". The words tumbled from her trembling lips and her eyes were pleading with him to change his mind as she wiped away the bitter tasting tears.

Tom got up and walked to the window and looked out. He could hear his mother weeping and he realised how much he had hurt her. Snowflakes, driven by the freshening wind were hitting the glass panes and the sky had turned dark. Behind him he heard his mother say quietly, "I wish you had never met Tony Long". In her heart Emily knew that Tom was a grown man and would have been more than a willing partner in the decision to join the army. She had always been pleased that Tom had found such a good friend in Tony Long but she was in shock at what her son had said and she desperately needed somebody or something else to blame.

An icy silence had enveloped the room, broken only when Tom heard his mother's footsteps going slowly up the stairs. Tom didn't know what he could say to mend the hurt and as the snowflakes melted against the warm glass and turned to water, his mind drifted back to the place where he had first met Tony Long.

It was seven years previously when he had cycled over Maidstone Bridge on his way to the engineering works. He remembered noticing a group of swans bobbing about in the muddy brown waters of the River Medway as it flowed sluggishly under the arches of the old stone bridge. Various industries flourished along the banks of the wide river and on that particular morning the air was heavy with the smell of malted barley and dried hops coming from the breweries which lined the rivers eastern bank. On the opposite side, the deliciously sweet smells wafting from the cherry brandy distillery and the rambling Sharps toffee factory, mixed incongruously with the acrid fumes seeping silently from the electricity generation station and the coke burners in the nearby gas works.

In the thinning shrouds of the early mist which hung over the murky river that morning, Tom recalled being amongst an army of flat-capped men who were cycling five and six abreast towards their various places of employment. He was pedalling his old black bicycle more quickly than the rest as he didn't want to be late for his first day of work at the Bridge Engineering Works which stood next to the toffee factory on the other side of the river. As he crossed the wide bridge, Tom remembered seeing the barges up-river, full of coal and moored side by side against the stone wharf. In the distance there was another barge in full sail, its ruddy-brown heavy canvas foresail, flip-flapping in the light wind as it slowly made its way to the distant corn merchant's wharf. Once he was over the bridge, Tom turned towards the engineering works. On one side of the narrow road was the old church of St Peter with its walls scarred by centuries of time whilst opposite, were the round storage tanks of the gas works which gazed down contemptuously on their ancient neighbour. As he cycled past the toffee factory, Tom could not resist smiling at the lines of girls who were making their way through its huge iron gates. He had arrived with time to spare at the parking yard of the engineering works where dozens of bicycles were already hanging by their front wheels in purpose-built racks, looking like the black crows dangling on old George Saunders vermin line.

The sound of his mother coming downstairs jolted Tom back to the present and that evening, neither he, nor his mother spoke of the matter again. Emily sat quietly. Terrible thoughts were flooding through her mind. If there was another war, as some people were saying, would she lose him too? If she did, she would be alone and even if there wasn't a war, she would still be left in the cottage alone. The memories of all the joy and happiness there had been over the years came flooding back and the tears of fear, both for herself and her beloved son started to flow again. Suddenly, Emily began to feel quite old. She knew she must not try to stop Tom but in her mind there was a dreadful foreboding and it was telling her that she could not cope with another heart-break.

It was the melodious, low pitched warble of a lone blackbird which distracted Tom's attention from what the gunnery instructor was saying. He gazed out through the bars of the small window in the Nissan hut and watched the bird as it sung its sweet song perched on a lichen covered branch of an ancient oak tree. In the distance Tom could hear the rasping voice of a Drill Sergeant barking out his orders to the latest squad of recruits who were being introduced to the delights of six weeks of square bashing on the parade ground.

"Stand to attention", the voice was shouting. Tom could hear the sound of dozens of new army boots stamping on the tarmac.

"You sloppy pile of shit, when I shout halt, I bloody well mean halt, you poor bloody excuse for humanity", the Drill Sergeant screamed at one of the hapless recruits.

"Don't you know your left foot from your bloody right"? Tom smiled as the tirade in the distance continued.

Barely two months had passed since Tom and Tony Long had been on that parade ground and the sound of their drill sergeant screaming out orders was still ringing in Tom's ears. Tom looked across at Tony, kitted out in his army battledress and his mind drifted back through the years to the time they had first met at the Bridge Engineering Works.

"Tom Kealey reporting for work", Tom remembered saying to the bespectacled man sitting in the small, single story, brick building on one side of the parking yard. The time-keeper's office was dwarfed by the massive three story building of the engineering works standing on the other side with its rows of dirty, steel framed windows and towering, smoke spewing chimneys.

Tom watched as the diminutive time-keeper took a sheet of paper from a tray on his cluttered desk and began to run his pencil thin finger down the list of names typed on it. Other men were coming into the office to take one of the long, buff coloured cards from the slotted racks on the wall and then, after inserting the card into a slot under the face of a large clock, each man pulled down a brass handle with a resounding clonk, stamping their arrival time on the card.

This is going to be different to the solitude in the woods, Tom thought apprehensively as he tried to keep out of the way of the stream of good humoured men. Tom noticed with a grin the men were coming into the office much faster to clock on, than they reluctantly left it, to start their days work.

"Here you are", said the pale faced time-keeper with a sense of satisfaction as he found Tom's name, "You're to report to Alf Ashdown in the metal stores", he added as his skinny finger reached the last name on the list.

"Arthur". The man turned to speak to a young lad who had been loitering in the background and handed him a clock card with Tom's name and clock number already written on it. "Show Tom how to clock on and then take him up to the metal stores", he said. Tom looked at the lanky youth who was now strolling towards him with a grin on his spotty, adolescent face.

The time-keeper was already striking a line through Tom's name on his sheet of paper when he paused and looked up and said, "Best of luck, Tom". Then, sensing Tom was feeling nervous about the strange world he was about to enter, added in a kindly manner, "Alf's a good sort, you'll be alright".

"Three minutes late is all you're allowed, then you're docked quarter of an hour...three times late in a week and you're in for a bollocking", the spotty faced youngster said with a sense of self importance in his voice, as he ushered Tom through the door.

Tom followed the young lad across a yard where rows of neatly parked lorries were lined up waiting for delivery. He knew the company built them and it had also been building buses since before the Great War but this was the first time in his life he had seen so many of the vehicles standing together. Arthur stopped so Tom could get a closer look at them, before saying, "It's some sight to see. We build diesel engines as well as these, but they crate most of those up and store them separately in the despatch department".

"In here is the assembly line", Arthur explained, as Tom ducked his head and went through a small, wicket door which allowed pedestrian access through huge, tightly-closed sliding doors and into the cavernous factory. He stopped in amazement at the new world he had entered, looking at a long line of vehicles in various stages of completion. Those nearest to him were virtually fully built and had sign writers putting the finishing brush strokes to the newly painted green cabs. Down at the other end, at the start of the assembly line, skeletal looking vehicle frames swung on chains from the overhead cranes, like spiders hanging from webs. Further up the line men in blue overalls were beginning to fit huge wheels onto one of the swinging chassis. Soon the lifeless beasts would have their engines started and have a life of their own breathed into them, Tom thought.

"The bogs are outside", Arthur said in a blunt matter of fact way, suddenly realising Tom would want them at some time. He paused, waiting to see if his companion needed them before saying, "Okey dokey, we'll have to go upstairs and walk through the fitting and machine shops before we get to the metal stores".

Tom followed the young man up two flights of wide concrete steps and into a cathedral-sized workshop, looking left and right and wondering if he would remember the way out when he finished for the day.

"Morning Mr Lock, this is Tom Kealey, he starts in the metal stores this morning", Arthur said brightly to a middle-aged man who was wearing the only white coloured coat Tom had seen that morning.

"Mr Lock is the foreman of the fitting shop", Arthur explained, as the grey haired man with a large hook nose acknowledged Tom with perfunctory nod of his head whilst he remained seated on a long-legged stool in front of an even taller desk. Walking away and on seeing the quizzical look on Tom's face, Arthur explained, "It's so he can see right down to the far end of the workshop", before adding with a grin, "to make sure the buggers up that end aren't bloody skiving".

Reaching the end of the fitting shop, Arthur led Tom through a wide battered door into another large workshop which was considerably darker than the previous ones. Tom peered around and saw the only light coming into the place was from a double row of long, filthy windows at each end and from a few skylights in the roof, which were covered in decades of dirt and bird's droppings.

Christ, this is grim, Tom thought., as he blinked, adjusting his eyes to the dim light, amazed at the rows of lathes in front of him. He guessed there were over fifty of the whirring machines. All different shapes and sizes and hunched over each their rotating chucks was a grey-coated turner, their faces distorted by the flickering light of the electric lamps which were fixed to the top of each machine.

"This is the machine shop", Arthur shouted rather obviously over the incessant din. "This is where all the bits and bobs for the engines are made".

Tom did not attempt to make himself heard and instead just nodded his head and stopped to look at a man who was operating the grey painted lathe along him. He watched as the man slowly moved the lathes sharp cutting tool into a spinning bar of metal which was gripped securely in the huge jaws of the machine's chuck. Tom looked at Arthur and could see this was nothing new to him and continued to watch with growing fascination as spirals of razor sharp steel turnings snaked away from the cutting tool and tried to wind themselves round the arms of the turner.

Eventually, as the two men walked through the lines of lathes, Tom could see the spinning chucks were being driven by wide, flat belts which went up and wrapped around dozens of pulleys fixed high up in the machine shops dark ceiling. Tom's ears were ringing with the relentless noise of the flapping belts and the array of different tools, cutting and boring their way through the unyielding metal bars spinning round in the machines.

How different to the peace and quiet of the woods, he thought wistfully.

"Alf, this is Tom Kealey", said Arthur, as they walked down a wooden staircase from the machine shop and entered, what Tom could see was the metal stores.

The man in front of them remained seated on a small box with faded black stencilled lettering on its side indicating it had once contained a dozen Whites lemonade bottles. Its top had been padded with an old hessian sack for comfort. Tom looked cautiously at the gaunt man and guessed he was probably over sixty. The button-less jacket he was wearing had seen better days and was tied together with string. Perched on the back of the un-shaven man's head, with its peak pointing skywards, was an oil-stained flat cap. Tom extended his hand to greet the stern-faced man who was still sitting on the box.

The old storekeeper put down the bottle of cold tea he was drinking from to take Tom's hand. "Nice to meet you, Tom", he said cordially. The friendly tone of his voice did not match his grim demeanour.

"As soon as I've finished my snap, I'll show you how things are done around here".

The man had no intention of hurrying and as Tom waited, he looked around at his new place of employment and at all the various shapes and sizes of metal bars which were kept there. Eventually, Alf slowly rose from his seat informing Tom his daily routine was to search through the racks of metal and find and cut precisely what had been requisitioned for the turners and then deliver it to whichever of the men who had requested it.

Tom cautiously nodded his understanding.

"Make sure the requisition forms have been signed by Fred Lock before you take anything out of here", Alf instructed his newly arrived workmate. "Most of those buggers out there are thieving sods. If I didn't keep my eyes open, they'd empty this place in a bloody week", he said with a wink of his eye.

Tom sensed the stern looking man in front of him, protected the metal in his stores with as much zeal as George Saunders had protected the pheasants in the woods.

Arthur had hung around in the background, clearly in no hurry to get back to his duties in the time-keepers office as Alf Ashdown continued to tell Tom. "Once you have delivered the metal to them up there", the old man nodded his head towards the wooden steps going up to the machine shop, "you'll have to collect all the bits they've finished and take them to either the bench fitters who assemble the engines or if they're not needed there, you'll take them to the main stores where they'll be booked in and collected when they're needed".

"I'm sure I'll get the hang of it", Tom replied, not at all convinced that he would.

In the weeks that followed, as Tom trundled his four-wheeled barrow with its squeaking wheels between the various points of collection and delivery, he soon became a popular and a well liked newcomer with his friendly nature and good humour.

At first, the men in the machine shop and the main stores would tease him because he couldn't tell the difference between all the different types and grades of metals, but in time and with Alf's guidance he gradually became quite skilled.

It was as Tom went from machine to machine he became friendly with Tony Long who everyone knew as *Chopper*. Like Tom, Chopper's father had been killed in the Great War but unlike Tom, his mother had died some years later and since her death, Chopper had lived with his sister Joy and her husband and their two children, in the small village of Farleigh, which nestled beside the river, just west of Maidstone.

Chopper had worked as a turner at the engineering works for eight years, ever since he had left school at fourteen, almost as long as Tom had worked in the woods. Now at twenty-five, Chopper was a similar age to Tom and they both enjoyed the same interests, darts, beer and an eye for a pretty girl. Chopper was a good looking man with a mass of dark wavy hair and broad shoulders, matched with a cheerful laugh. It was always this laugh Tom would hear as he wheeled his trolley to and fro the stores and it was this happy disposition, together with their similar appearances, which meant that Chopper and Tom could have been mistaken for being brothers.

Tom's daydreaming was brought to an abrupt end as the booming voice of the gunnery instructor echoed like thunder round the corrugated-tin walls of the black-painted Nisson hut.

"Mr Chamberlain, God bless him, has spared no expense in the training you lot are about to be given and as a result of our dear Prime Minister's bountiful bloody generosity, I'm about to show you one of the things you will be able to stop with a single shot from your anti-tank guns".

Tom watched the instructor as he slowly turned a page on a large flip chart revealing an image of an alarmingly large German tank. Tom's eyes roved at the other 85th Anti-Tank recruits in the training room as they stared at the picture in front of them. This is it, Tom thought. No more square-bashing and rifle practice. No more night marches. This is going to be for bloody real.

He detected a snarl of intimidation in the instructor's voice as the man started to turn over the next page of the flip chart.

"And this is what you're going to stop that bloody big tank with and when you've stopped that one", the man paused before saying, "you'll have to stop a lot more of the buggers".

Slowly, like a strip tease artist unveiling her hidden delights, he turned over the page to disclose a picture of an alarmingly small artillery gun mounted on a two wheeled carriage.

Nobody in the hut said a word. Tom turned to look at Chopper. Surely this was just the prelude to some further instruction that was to come when they would be using larger weapons that would be more suited for stopping tanks, he thought wistfully.

"This gentlemen, is the QF two-pounder anti tank gun. QF stands for quick fire".

Tom noticed that the instructor's voice was becoming more serious.

"Small it may, but with accurate fire this little pop-gun with highly trained men behind it, is more than a match for Jerries's Panzer tanks and by the time I have finished with you, that's exactly what you lot will be doing. It's got a range of five-thousand yards... however", the man paused slightly, "for every bloody tank you hit at that distance, you will miss another ninety-nine of the sods which means you'll probably get yourselves killed.... BUT", he raised his voice somewhat dramatically, "if you reduce the range to one-thousand yards, you've got a ninety per cent chance of hitting Jerry with your first shot, What that means gentlemen is that this insignificant looking gun is a close combat weapon. However", the instructor paused again before continuing with a more sarcastic tone in his voice, "if you soppy lot want to see your mummies and daddies again, you'll have to learn how to shoot this weapon at a range of no more than five-hundred yards gentlemen...five-hundred yards".

Tom heard somebody express the view that five-hundred yards was too close to be to a German tank.

"Any closer than that and we'll be able to shake hands with the bloody driver", the man who was sitting at the very back of the hut boldly interjected.

The instructor ignored the laughter and reached under his desk to produce a sharp-nosed shell, about the size of a policeman's truncheon which he placed on his desk with a resounding bang. The men who were sitting close to the desk flinched, expecting to be blown to kingdom come, quickly sliding their chairs back on the concrete floor with an orchestrated scraping, causing goose pimples to rise on the back of Tom's neck. He stared at the shell, surprised to see how small it was.

The instructor saw the look on Tom's face and looking directly at him, said, "Small as these little buggers may be, they will be very effective against the hardened skins on the Jerry tanks". The hint of sarcasm returned to the gunnery instructor's voice, "These things weigh two pounds and if you stupid sods haven't worked it out yet, that's why the gun is called a two-pounder. These little fuckers leave the barrel of the gun at over two thousand five hundred feet per second and as you can see, if you can keep your bloody eyes open, they are about one and a half inches in diameter". The man's eyes looked round the room, pausing briefly to look at each of the fledgling gunners in turn, "This, gentlemen", he continued, "is about the size of my cock and is fitted with an armour piercing tip with an explosive charge at its base".

"Sir, did you mean the shell or is your cock fitted with an armour piercing tip and an explosive charge?", asked a reckless recruit who was sitting in the row in front of Tom.

"You'll find out when I stick it up your bloody arse", the instructor responded, smiling slightly. A wave of laughter resonated around the hut.

 "I will continue if I may" and looking directly at the mouthy recruit, he said sarcastically, "By the time we have finished on the ranges, you'll be able to achieve a rate of fire of more than twenty rounds a bloody minute....blindfolded, if not Sonny Jim, you will have one of these things shoved so far up your arse it will make your nose bleed and you will run back home crying your bloody eyes out".

A grin spread across the instructor's face. He had outsmarted the cocky little sod with the mop of ginger hair. Job done, he thought with a degree of satisfaction.

Perhaps it was the Instructors use of the word *arse* which caused the smile to spread across Tom's face as he recalled an incident which happened soon after he had first met Chopper at Bridge Works.

Chopper was a man of habit. At ten o'clock every morning, with the Daily Sketch newspaper tucked under his arm, he would walk down to the lavatories which were situated outside the back door of the factory in the loading yard. Although in the winter they could be as cold, as Chopper had once remarked, as a nun's passion, the *bogs* provided him with a place to sit down in relative peace and quiet to study the football pages. He was an avid reader of anything that would help him to complete a winning line of match draws on his Littlewoods Pools coupon. His dream was to get the magical row of eight score draws and the rich prize money that would come with it. The building which housed the *bogs* was quite spacious. At the front, under a line of dirty windows, were long stone sinks with three equally spaced cold water taps curved over them. On the grimy window ledge was a small cardboard box of coarse sand the men would use to clean the ingrained grease and oil off their calloused hands, once they had lathered them with the blocks of red soap which were left on the sinks. To one side of the bogs was a glazed pottery urinal with the obligatory fag ends floating in the lagoon of dubious looking liquid and at the back was a row of fourteen individual cubicles the men called the traps. It was in one of these traps Chopper would sit and study his paper on the seat-less pan, which by its state had yearned for many months to be cleaned. On the odd occasion, Chopper would even surprise himself and actually use the traps for the purpose they were intended. Once, when Tom had asked him if he had any luck when he had checked his pools coupon on the Saturday night, Chopper reminded his friend that it required skill and knowledge to choose the draw games and that required time to study.

One particular morning, when he was sitting reading his newspaper in trap five, which was his favourite, Chopper's concentration was disturbed by the grunts and groans coming from the occupant next door. Chopper heard the lavatory flush as the person pulled the chain and let the water rush into the grimy pan from one of the rusty old cisterns fixed high above their head. When Chopper was satisfied he had gleaned every bit of football information he needed, he pulled the chain, just as a precaution, in case the foreman was in there using the urinal and started to make his way back to the machine shop but not before he casually looked into trap six to see what had been going on.

"Jesus Christ" he exclaimed in shock at the sight in front of him. "Jesus bloody Christ".

Urgently racing up the stairs into the machine shop, Chopper saw his friend on the far side.

"Tom, Tom" he shouted breathlessly.

Concerned something was wrong, Tom hurried over to his friend.

"Tom, get down to the bogs as quickly as you can and have a look in trap six. There's the biggest turd in there you have ever seen in your life. Hurry, a queue's forming already to take a look at it"

Tom swiftly made his way down the concrete stairs and saw just as Chopper had told him. At least a dozen men were waiting patiently to see the eighth wonder of the modern world which had been deposited in trap number six by a person unknown. The queue moved slowly foward, as men, amazed by the sight they had seen, left to return back to work, whilst all the time the queue was getting longer.

"Never seen one that big" said one of the turners, "It looked like a dead rat!"

"I've never seen a rat that bloody big", replied his mate, anxious to correct the record.

Tom, who had been patiently waiting in the ever increasing queue, recognised one of the tinsmiths who had viewed the sight.

"Bloody unbelievable", the man said, turning to Tom. "It goes right round the bend with at least six inches sticking out the water. We'll soon know who did it. His bloody eyes will be watering for at least a week".

At last, it was Tom's turn to view the beast. Yes, Chopper was right. It is the biggest one of its kind I've ever seen in my life, he thought, with a broad grin on his face

The queue had grown even longer. Word had obviously got around and the whole factory was being emptied of its workforce. Nobody wanted to miss this once in a lifetime opportunity.

At the back of the queue was an embarrassed looking apprentice holding a broom handle on which he had tied a long, metal hacksaw blade.

"What's that for?" Tom asked him, as he started to make his way back to the shop floor.

"Mr Lock has told me to cut it up and flush it away. He said enough's time has been wasted on the bloody thing already", said the down-trodden apprentice.

As he turned to go up the stairs, Tom noticed some latecomers were pushing in front of the lad before he could do his surgical work on the offending item. Tom smiled all the way back to the metal stores.

"Well, you said you wanted some excitement in your life", Chopper said, as he sat on Tom's bunk in the barrack room discussing the day's gunnery training. A grin spread across his face as he waited for his friend to respond.

Tom laughed and replied, "I knew we would need to get close to the enemy but not that bloody close. At five hundred yards it's not just their tanks we'll have to worry about. We will be sitting ducks for their infantry, if our own boys ever let them get that close".

"That's not all", ventured a familiar sounding voice from the other side of the barrack room.

Tom looked round and saw it was the man who had made the comment about the instructor's lower appendage and whose bunk was opposite Chopper's. He was younger than Tom and Chopper, probably no more than twenty or so. He was a lean, lanky individual with a mop of curly flame coloured hair, brilliant blue eyes and a constant smile on his freckled face. Tom studied him and immediately liked the skinny youngster with the infectious smile and the shock of red hair.

Chopper shot a curious glance at the man, "What do you mean Lenny?" he asked earnestly.

"My brother is an infantryman in the Dorsets", continued Lenny Thomsett. "He told me that the infantry thinks it will be silly sods like us who will be out there in front, protecting his lot from the enemy's tanks". "In any case, with our stationary guns, the Panzers will easily out-flank us, that is if they haven't already blown us to kingdom bloody come", he said, somewhat too knowingly for Tom's liking.

Chopper laughed, "Cheer up Lenny", he said, "I'd rather face the German tanks any day of the week than having Sergeant Bowden's cock shoved up my jacksey".

In the days which followed the men learnt the theory that lay behind the need for all the various battle tactics they would need to employ. Once, when the instructor was telling them of the importance of good concealment, it had reminded Tom how the pheasants concealed themselves amongst the golden autumn bracken when they were hiding from the guns. Had he now switched roles with the pheasants and it was him who was about to become the one who would be shot, he thought grimly? As the instruction progressed, the men listened in silence as they were told about the different stages of readiness they would face in battle. All of a sudden it was all becoming very real to them. Finally, to make sure they had understood the commands which would be used in action, Sergeant Bowden made the men shout out the answers, when he called out the three stages of readiness.

"NORMAL", he bawled out.

"Tank attack not expected, sir", the men replied in unison.

"PREPARE FOR TANKS".

"An attack is possible and observers will need to be posted and the ammunition prepared, sir"

"TANK ALERT".

There was an immediate response from the gunners.

"ATTACK IMMINENT, THE GUN NEEDS TO BE LOADED, SIR".

There was no doubt now that the men knew exactly what to do if and when the final command was given.

Tom breathed in the fresh early morning air as he heaved himself over the tailboard and climbed into the back of the Morris truck which was taking them from the barracks to the firing range. The weeks of square bashing, rifle drills and the twenty-five mile route marches were over. The tactical training in the classroom had been completed and it was now time to fire the two-pounders for the first time. The men had learnt how to obey orders without question and how to react instinctively to a single word of command. Now they were all ready for the final phase of training. The sun had already risen and was peeping out from the streaks of clouds overhead when the five trucks passed out of the camp gates and meandered down the narrow Hampshire lanes. April was Tom's favourite month of the year. Mother Nature had at last shaken off her drab cloak of winter and life was bursting forth once more. He relished the invigorating air of the early morning and looked with pleasure at the signs of spring he could see from the back of the bouncing truck. The noise of the trucks had alerted some new born lambs which had been gambolling by a newly trimmed hedgerow and they ran away on hearing their mother's bleating cry calling them to safety. Tom smiled at their antics and looked up at the wide expanse of sky which was already changing colour from the grey of the early morning to one that was full of fluffy cumulus clouds being chased across the bright blue sky by the brisk breeze.

"It's going to be dry", Tom said optimistically to Chopper, as the trucks slowed and drove through the already opened barrier of the firing range.

"Come on lads, jump to it, it's time to get your hands dirty. No more pretty pictures to look at". It was the familiar sound of Sergeant Bowden's voice Tom could hear, as one by one, the men quickly swung down the rope hanging from the back of the truck and began to rub some life into the flesh of their deadened backsides.

"Form up into two lines behind the gun", he shouted, as the last man jumped from the furthest truck.

The sixty embryonic gunners ran at the double and with a click of their heels, stood to attention behind the wheel mounted, QF anti-tank gun.

"At ease", the Sergeant ordered.

"It's bigger than I thought it would be", Chopper whispered to Tom.

There was a sense of relief in his voice as they looked at the green painted gun for the first time. Protruding from a large, square metal shield was the long barrel of the gun. Chopper judged that the length of the barrel was about seven feet. Behind the shield was a small seat where the gunner sat. To one side of the seat, at eye level, was the range finder whilst on the other side was the breech loading mechanism and the ammunition storage box. Sergeant Bowden was now standing in front of the gun and Chopper observed that the overall height of it was no more than five feet whilst its length, including the long tow-bar, was probably about that of a small motor car.

"Gentlemen", the Sergeant gave the black rubber tyre on one of the guns two wheels a meaningful kick with his highly polished boot. Then, with one arm wrapped around the barrel, as if in a lovers embrace, he said, rather obviously, "The purpose of this little beauty is to kill tanks. "Not many years ago", he continued. "The only way to stop a tank was with a rifle or a grenade or even a mine. Now we have these things to do the job but....."

He hesitated, "You need to remember that tanks are moving targets and that means we have to engage them with direct fire".

The instructor walked away from the gun and towards Tom who was at one end of the front line, and starting with Tom, he started counting as he moved up the line of men, "One, two, three, four, and five" he stopped and said, "You five men stay with me. The others", he nodded towards the spot where a group of other instructors were waiting, "go over there and they will split you up into individual gun crews".

The five men looked at each other, all wondering what would happen next. There was Tom and Chopper, Lenny Thomsett, a pleasant looking man with a country look about him, called Percy Gorringe and a short Welsh man who everybody called Taff, but whose name, as Tom was to learn later, was ironically, Doug Scott.

"Gather round the gun and let's get the show on the road", the Sergeant said to the would-be gun crew

Tom noticed the man was more visibly relaxed than he had been before and sensed it was because he liked working with the men on the ranges, rather than spouting theory to them in the Nissan hut back at the camp.

137

Sergeant Bowden casually sat down on the tow bar of the gun and said, "You will be with me for the next two weeks and by the time I have finished with you, this will be the best bloody gun crew in the battery. You may well ask me why it is I intend to turn you into the best crew ever to come through that barrier", he nodded towards the entrance to the range. "It is to bloody well keep you alive".

Tom noticed the man's attitude change as he said solemnly, "Once the war begins and Mr Hitler is doing his best to ensure it does, each gun crew will need to operate independently. In the middle of a battle you won't be able to wander across and ask your friendly instructor what you've got to do next". His voice was raised, "You will have to select your own targets. Judge the range and then engage the enemy without anybody to help you. Screw it up and you will all be fucking dead".

The five men looked nervously at each other. This man certainly knew how to spell it out.

It was Lenny who broke the silence which followed, "I wish you had told me that earlier, Sarge, I would have joined the bloody navy".

"Don't worry lad". Sergeant Bowden had enjoyed the joke and countered, "If you get yourself killed, you can always come back and complain".

"Right", he said briskly, anxious to get on, "let's get started to turn you into a gun crew. The detachment for one of these guns is five men, but if need be, they can be operated with just two or three of you".

"That's if the rest of us get killed", Lenny interrupted, with a joke which fell as flat as a pancake.

"Kealey", the Sergeant reached out and grabbed Tom's arm and pulled him forward until he was a few paces in front of the rest of the group. "I hear that you were a gamekeeper", he said.

"Yes, Sergeant",

"You will be the Number One on the gun. Your job will be to judge the range and the speed of the approaching tanks, so you can give orders to your Number Three".

"Number Three, Sergeant?" Tom questioned.

"I'll come to that later", snapped the Instructor, annoyed at Tom's interruption. "You will have to prioritize the targets and judge the moment to fire. Your job is what the eyes and brain are to an infantryman. Have you got that?" Tom nodded as the responsibility of the Number One's role was beginning to dawn on him.

The Sergeant studied the remaining four men for a few moments before saying, "Long, you're Number Two. You will load the gun as if your life depends upon it, which of course, it bloody well will"

Chopper nodded.

"By the time I've finished, you will be pushing those two pound shells into the gun's breech at a rate of twenty-five to the minute. As good as the Number One may be at judging the range and the speed of the tank heading towards you and then giving the orders to fire, the gun will be no bloody good if it hasn't got a shell in the spout".

"God help me", the Sergeant exclaimed in mock humour as he turned his attention to Lenny Thomsett. "Ginger, you will be Number Three. You will need to have the co-ordination of the eye and the hand of a rifleman. Your job is to sit on that little seat", he cocked his head towards the gun, "and keep the point of the gun aimed on the tank and keep it there until Kealey gives you the order to fire".

"How will I do that?" asked Lenny, with an unusual seriousness in his voice.

"You will lay the gun onto the target by looking through the telescopic range finder and traverse the gun accordingly."

"Gorringe and Scott", Sergeant Bowden looked at the last two men left in the line.

"Gorringe, you will be Number Four and Scott, you will be Number Five".

The two men waited apprehensively to hear what roles they would have as part of the gun's crew.

"You two useless bloody specimens will make sure that the ammo boxes are kept supplied with shells so that the guns Number Two", the Sergeant looked towards Chopper, "can keep pushing the shells in the breech at the rate required".

On hearing their cushy roles, Percy Gorringe and Taff Scott had grins on their faces like two cats that had just got the cream.

"You two buggers won't be smiling when all hell has broken loose and you are running between the gun and the truck where the ammo will be stored and you're being sprayed with machine gun fire, courtesy of the bloody Jerries".

Tom noticed there was the familiar savage grin on Sergeant Bowden's face and that Percy and Taff had stopped smiling.

Specks of dust danced in a rare shaft of sunlight shining into the room as Emily took the gleaming bronze medallion off the mantelpiece over the fireplace. The lines around her weak eyes were beginning to betray her age and she held the disc close to her face so she could read its faint inscription. She had been polishing the plaque every week for over twenty years and the name which had been so carefully engraved upon it all those years ago, had all but disappeared. Emily adjusted the spectacles resting on tip of her nose and tears filled her eyes as she read out the precious name engraved on the shining bronze disc. There was hurt in her voice as she murmured softly, "Edwin Kealey".

Her hands were shaking as she read the words cast round the outside of the large, coin-like object, "He died for freedom and honour", she said with sadness in her voice.

She remembered the words which on the letter she had received from the King, when the plaque had arrived on her doormat all those years ago, *"I join with my grateful people in sending you this memorial of a brave life given for others in the Great War"* but Emily had never forgotten what Harry had said when the plaque had arrived on that bitterly cold January day in 1919.

"Dead man's penny, not much for the life that was sacrificed for nothing", he had scoffed so dismissively.

She remembered thinking at the time, Harry more than most, knew what it had been like for the men who had died in that dreadful war and he had every right to feel bitter when he had seen such a small, insignificant object, given for the loss of such a fine man.

Emily carefully put the plaque back to its resting place and re-read the letter she had received in the mornings post. There was going to be another war and her precious son, Tom was going off to fight and of all places, he was going to fight in France just like his father.

Her eyes closed as she took a deep breath. "God, please keep him safe", she said quietly. It was not for the first time in her life she had uttered those heart-felt words and Emily's face was becoming wet with tears as she repeated, "Please God, keep my son safe".

Every part of the French landscape was carpeted with lush green foliage and brightly coloured spring flowers. The sweet songs of the birds were confirming summer had thrown open her doors and winter had retreated at long last. Long legged crickets were calling amorously to their mates as the sun warmed the air and their passion.

It had been particularly cold, wet and miserable since the men had arrived as part of the British Expeditionary Force. They were now taking advantage, fleeting as it was, of the peace and tranquillity of the morning and the opportunity to bask in the warm sunshine. For over three months, their lives in this foreign land had been trapped in idleness, only broken occasionally by moving from one farm billet to another, first digging latrines and then firing their anti-tank two-pounders in never ending practice sessions.

Tom had propped himself up against the sun-warmed tyre of one the trucks parked in the farmyard. He was idly watching the clouds overhead as they floated by, undisturbed in the bright blue sky and driven only by the balmy summer breeze gently singing in the trees. He could feel the heat from the rubber on his back as he looked towards the farmhouse to watch a drowsy bumble bee which was moving amongst the mops of red clover and the yellow buttercups gilding the uncut lawn. The air was heavy with the scent of a nearby lilac tree as Tom closed his eyes and relished the calm beauty of the May morning.

It had only been a few weeks earlier, when they had been billeted in farm close to the Belgium border Tom and the rest of the troop had heard heavy anti–aircraft fire coming from the direction of the Ardennes forest. Their sleep during that night had been disturbed by the unmistakable sound of distant gunfire and the sky had been illuminated by the ordnance of the enemy. Although the French forces had stiffened their defences, the Germans continued to sweep into Belgium and the men knew the time was coming for them to break free from the never-ending routine of training and to prepare for action. For the past three weeks or so, the troop of gunners were moved from one position to another, the roads had become choked with the milling masses of refugees desperate to escape from the war erupting around them. Even a journey of only a few miles took hours as the trucks became ensnared with the numbers of people blocking the roads. During the hours of daylight, large formations of German aircraft began to dominate the sky and the men were in no doubt that very soon, they would be called to action.

"Tom, eyes up".

It was the sound of Chopper's voice which stirred Tom from his doze. He could hear the barking of the two farm dogs as they ran from their wooden kennel, fashioned from a large wine barrel, and chased after the NCO's who were running into the farmhouse where the Commissioned Officers were billeted.

"It looks as if the balloon's gone up", Chopper said grimly.

Lenny, who had been talking to Percy and Taff joined them and said, "Taff reckons we are going to be ordered to fire off all the remaining ammo and destroy the guns, then head towards the coast".

Chopper sucked his bottom lip and nodded his head.

The men knew that orders had already been given for the main body of the troops to pull back and make their way to a place called Dunkirk from where they would be evacuated.

"This is a complete and utter cock-up", Chopper said, as he wiped beads of sweat from his forehead.

The men's eyes were fixed on the weather beaten door of the farmhouse when one of the Sergeants emerged from the gloom of its interior and barked out, "Prepare to move".

"We're off lads", Lenny said happily, "Taff was right, it's back to Blighty for us".

Tom remained silent. He was already thinking the NCO had said nothing about destroying the guns.

Clouds of dust swirled by the spring breeze, blew across the farmyard as the truck drivers jumped into their cabs and, with their guns hitched up and engines racing, formed up in a row, ready to hit the road. The drivers then jumped down from their vehicles and formed up with the rest of the men who were already falling in line to await final orders.

"Men", the bright blue eyes of the young officer raked up and down the line of the assembled men, "we are to advance towards the Belgian border". He ignored the groan of astonishment which came from some of the men and continued to say, "A moving column of Panzers has been spotted, which our intelligence believe is heading towards Dunkirk. As you may be aware, the general order has been given for our forces to pull back towards the port, from where they will be evacuated".

Chopper gave Tom a knowing look as if to say, at least Taff had been right about that.

Lieutenant Moss was continuing unabated, "Soon we will have over one hundred and fifty-thousand men on those beaches and if the Jerry tanks get through, God knows what damage they will do to the men who are trapped there".

Tom looked at the man and admired the spirit in his clipped voice. They were of similar age and Tom suddenly became conscious that neither of them had faced enemy action before.

"If we can get through in time", the officer paused, as if he was in some doubt and then added as an afterthought, "with all these wretched people on the roads. We'll dig in at a village on the other side of the border called Veurne. We are to break up the leading wave of their tanks ....."

He paused again.

The men watched the officer as he seemed to be collecting his thoughts before continuing, "Destroy them or scatter them, anything we can do to stop or delay the buggers from reaching Dunkirk". Lieutenant Moss looked towards his NCO's and then turned back to face the line of grim faced men, "Any questions?" he didn't wait for any. "Good, best of luck men", and with that said, he hauled himself up into the passenger seat of the leading truck.

Chopper was already in the driving seat of the truck as Tom and Lenny reached it. Lenny sat alongside him whilst they waited for Tom to heave himself in.

"Wait", Tom shouted, as he ran back to chase after a large sheet of paper which had been whipped off the briefing table by a sudden gust of wind and was being blown waywardly across the farmyard.

"Come on Tom", Chopper shouted impatiently, as he half turned the ignition key in readiness to start the truck's engine.

Lenny grinned as he said, "It's a bloody fine time to go on a paper chase.

The two men watched in growing amusement as their Number One tried to capture the fluttering square of paper. Every time it appeared to be in his grasp it was swept along in a dozen different directions in gusts of wind. Suddenly the wind eased and paper floated lifelessly to the ground, no more than an arms-length away from the increasingly frustrated man. Lenny let out a cheer as Tom finally grabbed it and started running back to the waiting truck.

"What is it, Tom .... a bloody big five pound note? Chopper enquired sarcastically, as he gave the ignition key a final twist and pushed his boot down on the Morris's accelerator pedal as the engine burst into life.

"It's a map", Tom said triumphantly, as he squeezed his body onto the narrow bench seat beside Lenny, before slamming the door shut. "In their panic to get moving, they must have left it on the table", he said, as he caught his breath and pushed the map deep into one of the breast pockets of his khaki coloured battle tunic.

A rising cloud of dust covered convoy of trucks with thirty eight men on-board as it drove out of the farmyard and onto the road that would lead them away from Dunkirk towards the Belgium border and the oncoming German army. Lieutenant Moss and the seven Sergeants were in the first three trucks together with fifteen of the gunners. Tom, Chopper and Lenny were in the fourth truck and behind them were another two trucks, each carrying four gunners and following up at the rear was the final truck carrying Percy and Taff and two more gunners. Through the dust, the column of trucks, with their guns bouncing behind them, raced along the rough ground of the farm track before turning onto the road, heading east.

"Bloody hell", Chopper exclaimed, as the leading trucks suddenly slowed down to such an extent that he nearly slammed into the truck in front of them.

The road was clogged with fleeing refugees, young and old, men, women, children and babes in arms, stretching back as far as the men in the truck could see. Tom looked at the faces as they streamed past and saw they were distorted with horror.

"Look", said Lenny, on seeing mixed amongst the civilians, were French and British soldiers and the strain that was clearly etched on their weary faces. Lenny looked at Chopper with evident alarm and remembering what their officer had told them, said, "I don't know about our lot falling back to Dunkirk, it looks more like a bloody headlong retreat to me".

Gradually as the trucks pushed their way through the desperate sea of humanity, Tom looked through the grime covered window and saw, beyond the avenue of thin trees, the ditches were filled with piles of belongings which had been jettisoned by the fleeing people. His eyes focused on some army short-range wireless sets which looked as though they had been smashed with a blow from a rifle butt or by the rapid descent of a size ten boot, strewn amongst numerous pots and pans. All of a sudden the weight of his steel helmet felt very heavy on Tom's head. As the truck drove on, he continued to look at the never ending piles of abandoned household objects and realised their owners had come to the conclusion nothing was more precious and worth saving than their own lives.

"What now?" Chopper said in exasperation, as the trucks slowed from a snail's pace to a grinding halt.

Tom wound his window down and called over to a group of soldiers who were rolling out strands of barbed wire along the roadside. "What's the hold-up?"

"We're putting in a second line of defence. Mind you, the way things are going up there", a grim-faced soldier motioned his head towards the direction the gunners' trucks were heading, "it's only a matter of time before we will become the bloody front line of defence".

None of the men in the truck spoke, sensing the spine tingling reality in what the man had just said.

Slowly the convoy moved on again, driving past the lines of infantry who had already dug in, prepared for the inevitable onslaught which was to come. They had been travelling for over two hours when a voice rang out, "Hey.... gunners".

Tom turned round to see who was shouting at them. It was a soldier who was hanging his head out from under the canvas tilt of a battered truck which had drawn up alongside them and was trying to push its way through the stream of refugees. "You're wasting your time with those things", the man's eyes were fixed on the anti-tank guns the trucks were towing .... the only way you're going to stop one of their bloody Panzer tanks with those things, is to fire a shell up the bloody arse of the Jerry who's driving the fucking thing".

"Bloody idiot", Lenny spat out the words at the grinning soldier.

Normally, Tom enjoyed the banter and good humoured insults which he learnt were the bread and butter of army life but this time he ignored the grinning man and watched as Chopper held his hand on the trucks horn as he gradually forced his way through the tidal wave of desperate people and drove on to confront the enemy.

Tom cursed as he looked anxiously at the gap developing between them and the three leading trucks. "If we're not careful, we'll lose sight of them soon", he warned.

It had become unbearably hot in the truck and Chopper grunted his frustration at the situation. He knew as soon as the front trucks had pushed a path through the hordes of people and vehicles blocking the road, they all quickly returned and he would have to force his way through them again.

Tom swivelled round in his seat and looked back at the trucks following them, "At least the others are close behind us", he said, hoping it would give his friend some consolation.

It was Tom's keen eyes that first saw the planes as they descended from the sky, not dissimilar to the way the sparrow hawks swooped down on the unsuspecting pheasant chicks back in the woods at Pentbury.

"CHOPPER....STUKAS.... GET OFF THE ROAD", Tom shouted. There was no mistaking the urgency in his voice.

Instinctively and without the need for any explanation, Chopper wrenched the steering wheel hard round. Instantly the truck hit the adjoining grass bank with a glancing blow before ricocheting off, sending clumps of mud and grass in all directions. Tom and Lenny gripped the thin cushion on the bench seat helplessly as Chopper struggled to keep control of the truck as it careered along the water filled ditch until he managed to bring it and the bouncing gun behind, to a sliding halt.

Tom looked anxiously towards the leading trucks and watched in horror on seeing they were continuing along the road, quite unaware of the screaming terror which was about to strike them. Instinctively, he glanced back and saw the three trucks behind had followed Chopper's example were now similarly splattered with mud with plumes of white steam rising from where the ditch water had been thrown up onto their hot exhaust pipes.

The three men could now hear the blood curdling screams of the Stukas sirens and watched awe-stuck as the planes dived down. One after another, the birds of death were coming in with their deadly forward-facing machine guns firing and tearing through anything which was still on the road.

The speed of the attack was so swift it was difficult for the watching men to take it in. Bullets ripped through the leading trucks with lightning speed. Tom could see their canvas tilts being torn apart as if by huge unseen hands. Without warning the lead truck suddenly burst into a massive ball of flames. As Tom and the others watched helplessly, the intensity of the fire quickly spread to the next truck and they could see through the inferno of hell, men jumping from the vehicles, ablaze like burning torches. Choking, thick black smoke billowed into the air, driven by the intensity of the fire which had engulfed the three trucks.

"OUT, OUT, OUT", Tom screamed, "THERE ARE AMMO MAGAZINES IN THOSE TRUCKS".

Chopper pushed open his door and jumped clear of the truck, with Tom and Lenny jumping from other side close behind and the three crouched as low as they could in the stagnant smelling ditch water as the pressure wave of the explosions hit them. The chaotic scene in front was now a blazing mass and splinters of red hot shrapnel were being thrown in all directions as one by one the burning trucks was torn apart by the deafening explosions.

Unhurt and gasping for breath, Tom got to his feet and looking through the acrid smelling smoke could see the plane's deadly burst of bullets had cut a bloody path through the throng of fleeing refugees who had been herded together on the road. Their panic- filled screams were of such intensity Tom could hear them over the disappearing howl of the Stukas. Their deadly work done, it was now time to hunt for more unsuspecting targets.

"Jesus", Chopper uttered, almost frozen to the spot, as he stared in disbelief at the scene of the devastation in front of them.

The planes had not discriminated between young and old, male or female and blood-stained bodies lay in the grotesque shapes ordained by the manner of their deaths. Some of the survivors had huddled together silent as mutes, their faces ashen white with the shock of what they had just witnessed. Others screamed with a mixture of terror and grief, as they searched for their loved ones amongst the bloody carnage the planes had left behind.

"CHOPPER, CHOPPER", are you alright". It was the sound of Tom's voice the stunned man heard. "I'm going to see if anybody got out the trucks alive. Go back and make sure everybody is alright in the other trucks behind".

Shaking and still in a state of shock, Tom raced up the road towards the blazing inferno, which just minutes before had been twenty-three men, together with their trucks and guns. Already some of the refugees who had survived the attack were fleeing from the scene, carrying what pathetic bundles of belongings they had been able to find amongst the piles of the hastily discarded suitcases and overturned carts littering the road. A once, proud cart horse still harnessed between the shafts of the cart it had been pulling lay whimpering amongst the wreckage with its belly ripped open.. The smell of burning flesh pervaded Tom's nostrils and unable to contain the bile which was rising in a surging wave from his stomach, he gagged, doubled up and threw up.

Wiping off a dribble of the bitter tasting slime running down his chin, Tom pushed his way through the groups of refugees who were aimlessly wandering around, too shocked to know what to do or where to go. Although Tom could see their mouths were moving, his ears were still deaf from the blast of the explosions to hear their cries. Cautiously, he approached the burning trucks, aware each one had been carrying at least ninety-eight rounds of the high explosive shells together with the fourteen rounds stacked in the guns' magazines. Ignoring the risk and the skin blistering heat, he started to search for anybody who may have escaped from the trucks. Nothing.........He gulped the foul, hot air and ran quickly round to the front of what would have been the leading truck in a frantic search to find anyone who was still alive. His stomach knotted with the fear of what he would find and a feeling of panic was beginning to grip him....... There was nothing, other than scattered, blackened bodies and the acrid smell of the burning flesh. The poor bastards were thrown out of the trucks by the force of the explosions, he thought grimly. Anger, which had begun to replace the panic and shock he felt, surged at the sight in front of him.

"My God", he muttered, as he realised that everyone who had been in the three trucks had perished.

Tom gagged again and as he straightened his back, he peered through the smoke and there, some way in front of him and strewn across the road, was, what had been moments earlier, a line of soldiers marching towards the beaches of Dunkirk and possible safety.

Tom left the burning trucks and ran towards them.

"Is there anything I can do?" he anxiously asked a Corporal who was hunched over an injured soldier lying moaning on the road with blood streaming from an open leg wound.

"It looks like we've got three dead and half a dozen wounded", croaked the shocked man, glancing round at the mayhem around him.

The soldier's voice was hardly audible. He gulped air into his scorched throat. Tom could see the man was still clearly dazed by the speed of the attack and was hardly coherent. Looking at the man more closely, he saw the rearing Invicta horse on his cap badge. West Kents, Tom thought, and judging by the man's appearance, he had seen quite a lot of action already.

Tom spat the acrid taste of burning rubber from his mouth and asked the Corporal once again if there was anything he could do.

"No, it looks as though there's about thirty of us who are alright so we can manage to sort things out here and then try to get back to Dunkirk the best we can.... What about your lot?" the man muttered.

"All dead in the leading trucks", replied Tom, "the rest of us are alright".

"Fucking hell", the Corporal exclaimed, wide-eyed, pausing slightly as he continued dressing the injured man's wound. He raised his head and looking directly at Tom, said grimly, "Those bastards in the Stukas work ahead of their ground infantry. They hunt as they please and they do this for target practice".

"Why would they do it?" Tom asked, his voice breaking with emotion.

"Apart from the fun of it, they are trying to keep the roads clear so their tanks can stream through". The man looked down again at the injured soldier before adding, "what will you lot do now?"

Tom shrugged his shoulders noncommittally, ignoring the infantryman's question. "Best of luck", he said quietly as he started to race back to find Chopper and the others, only pausing briefly to look for one last time at the burning trucks and the guns they had been towing.

He found Chopper and Lenny had been joined by the men from the other three trucks. Nobody was talking and it appeared to Tom, they were all waiting for him to say something.

"Everybody alright", he said breathlessly. His mind was muddled and incapable of thought.

Chopper erupted. "Best we can be" he replied angrily, making the point that they were not alright after what had happened and what they had seen. "What now?" he demanded. The hate he suddenly felt towards the attackers was ablaze and burning deep inside him.

Tom could feel his body shaking and all he could say was, "All dead, officers, sergeants.....everybody.......all dead". There was nothing else he could say.

"What now?", Chopper repeated.

It was Lenny who broke the deafening silence which followed. "We've still got four trucks left, together with their guns and ammo. That's more than enough to stop a few tanks----".

Tom, who had already decided that all they could do now was to turn round and head back to Dunkirk, looked in amazement as the young man continued unabated,.

"Look Tom, if we can find that village, we should be able to do something to delay the Jerries and give all those poor sods a better chance of escape", the ginger haired man said, as he looked through the clearing smoke towards towards the group of soldiers scattered across the road.

Tom looked at the men gathered around him and saw they were looking at him, waiting for a decision. He did a quick head count, "Fourteen plus me", he murmured, "and four guns".

His eyes scanned the small group looking for signs of dissent.

"We'll go on", he said decisively, "you're right Lenny, we can't go back, the orders were to go forward".

Tom suddenly remembered the map he had retrieved from the farmyard. Frantically he plunged his hands into his trouser pockets. Nothing! The other hand was simultaneously searching the pockets of his tunic. The relief on his pale face was visible, as he pulled the crumpled map from his tunic. Quickly, with the foul smelling smoke from the burning lorries swirling around him, he wiped off the lumps of mud which had been thrown up onto the truck's bonnet and spread the map out. The men crowded round the improvised table and watched as Tom's finger traced a line on the map until it stopped and drew an imaginary circle around the place his eyes had been searching for.

"Veurne! That's where they were heading for", he said with obvious relief, "if we are lucky, we can still reach it before nightfall and find somewhere to dig in". He paused, before saying thoughtfully, "Lenny's right, if the murderous bastards sweep through unopposed, the men on the beaches won't stand a chance, we've just seen what the Jerries are capable of. If we could just delay them…"

"You're right", Chopper said, as if he was confirming the rest of the groups agreement to Tom's decision, "Let's get moving". The men had started to run back to their trucks when Chopper turned to Tom and said abruptly, "We'll lead the way. I'll drive".

Tom didn't say anything. He was hoping for all their sakes he had made the right decision.

The German blitzkrieg seemed unstoppable as the small convoy of Morris trucks with their two-pounders bouncing behind them, weaved their way through the narrow crowded roads towards the village which was snuggled close to the Belgian border. The Germans had the initiative but Tom guessed the infantry together with that of the French, had probably received orders to hold the ground to allow the forces behind them time to withdraw back to the beaches of Dunkirk. He knew that it was not only going to be a race to get to the village before the advancing enemy forces reached it but also, to try to find a well concealed position to set up the guns before the impending black curtain of darkness fell.

Tom peered through the truck's mud splattered windscreen and realised, what days ago had been a trickle of refugees was now a flood of humanity as wave after wave of the frightened refugees continued to flee from the German onslaught behind them. It was not the first time that Chopper banged his fist against the vehicle's door and shouted out his frustration, as he tried to force a path through the desperate wall of people in front of him, as he tried desperately to keep the truck moving.

Despite the incessant bouncing of the truck and Chopper's oaths of frustration, Tom managed to study the map before finally saying, "That crossroads ahead looks promising, I think the village we've been looking for is a probably a few miles beyond it".

Chopper reacted immediately by bringing the Morris to a sudden halt and as he wrenched up the handbrake's ratchet, he checked in the mirror that the other three trucks had caught up and were still behind him.

With his nose almost pressing against the windscreen Tom peered through the grime and said, "If the Jerry tanks come up from the village and reach the crossroads, it will give them the opportunity to open up their flanks. That is", he added pessimistically, "if they haven't already broken through the French infantry. I think we better forget about reaching the village and stop here to give us time to get into a defensive position".

"The trees in those woods are big enough to stop the tanks crashing through which means, if they come this way, they'll all have to come down the lane in front of us", Chopper replied, as he turned off the truck's engine, confirming Tom's assessment of the situation

Tom looked at the trees. Oaks he thought. Their young leaves were still a bright green, it would be another month or two before they turned to their darker summer colour. A full moon was beginning to rise triumphantly in the sky like a newly minted coin and in the distance Tom could hear two owls beginning to call to each other with their familiar hoots as the light began to drain from the sky.

Chopper had heard them too, "They won't be here much longer", he said grimly.

Tom's head nodded in agreement and he pointed at the moon, saying, "If the tanks come, that will help us get a sight on them". "That's it then", he said, "We'll try to stop the tanks before they reach the crossroads. We can use the trucks to get the guns in position the best we can and load the magazines and then unhitch and ditch them further back in the woods so the Jerries can't see them".

 With the lack of an Artillery Officer, Tom was taking control. He could feel his heart racing and his throat felt as dry as an old boot as he started to shout orders to his two man gun crew.

 "Lenny, jump out and tell the lads in the other trucks what we're doing", he shouted, breathlessly.

Tom rattled out his orders, "I want two guns on the other side of the lane. We'll stay on this side together with Percy and Taff's gun ......Oh, keep one of the trucks on the road facing the way we came just in case we need to make a run for it.......tell Percy to get one of his men to keep a guard on it, there's a lot of desperate people about".

Lenny looked surprised at Tom's quick thinking, "Christ", he exclaimed, "I hadn't thought about that".

It was then the three men realised if they survived the battle which seemed inevitable, there would only be one way for them to go. A spike of fear ran down Lenny's spine.

"And Lenny", Tom's mind was racing as he continued barking out his orders. "Remind them that the guns need to be placed in a defensive position, fifty yards apart, so we have one leading gun each side of the lane, with each of the other guns placed behind them, so we can concentrate our fire....... and Len, don't forget, well concealed positions and make sure they remember to judge their range correctly. No one is to open fire too soon". Tom knew that by positioning the guns that way, the two outer guns could turn their fire if an enemy flank developed.

Lenny leapt from the truck's cab and started running towards the other trucks behind them. He heard Tom shouting at him and he stopped so he could hear what he was saying.

"Lenny, tell them that nobody is to fire until the target is at five hundred yards range". Tom's shouting got even louder, "No more than five hundred yards, Lenny....FIVE HUNDRED YARDS........TELL THEM THAT ONCE THE FIRST GUN FIRES, WE WILL ALL BE BLOODY COMMITTED".

Tom was relieved to see that almost unnoticed, the darkness had now descended on them. It meant concealing the guns would now be a lot easier but he knew that when each of the two-pounders loosed off their first rounds, the cordite flashes and the smoke coming from them would make it easy for the Jerries to get a fix on their positions.

Chopper was already reversing the truck and gun carriage into the woods when Len returned.

"I doubt whether we will be troubled by any of their tanks coming in from the flanks but if their escorting infantry break through and come in that way, we're going to find ourselves in the fucking brown stuff", Len added grimly.

Tom didn't reply, he had already thought of that and knew if the enemy's infantry did come up with the tanks, they would have no protection and would be finished. He ran from gun to gun, which were now all unhitched from the trucks and the men were already manhandling them into their stationary positions in the woods. Muscles strained as the crews pushed and pulled each of the three quarters of a ton of British steel through the layers of leaf mould that had lain undisturbed for decades in a thick blanket on the forest floor. Once they were satisfied with the placement of their gun, the crews knocked off the heavy cast steel brackets which held the wheels onto each side of the carriages, with frantic blows of heavy hammers.

Beads of sweat were running down Tom's face as he helped the crew of the leading gun on the other side of the lane, who had knocked off the wheels but were now struggling to open the arms of the gun's split carriage assembly which would form the flat tripod to support the weapon on the soft ground. Tom pushed his boot into the ground. It was spongy under foot. Christ, he thought, I hope this will keep the gun stable when we start firing..,too late now. One by one, the rubber tyred wheels were released from their axles and pushed out of sight into the woods. Now the four guns were static and without their wheels, every man knew they could not be repositioned again.

Tom continued to run amongst the guns making sure everyone was ready and they had understood his instructions. Despite the screaming of a lone Stuka somewhere overhead and the constant shelling in the distance, he thought he could hear the faint but unmistakable sound of the high revving engines of tanks on the move. He stopped and listened again. Then, through the thick leather soles of his boots he felt vibrations in the road. "

Bloody hell", he said, as the numbing realisation dawned on him.

There was no mistaking it. He could clearly hear the clanking and squeaking of the tank's heavy metal tracks on the macadam surfaced lane. Tom looked towards the village where the noise was coming from and glanced at the grass verges of the lane strewn with a jumble of debris discarded by fleeing refugees. What had once been a treasured item, much valued by the person who had dumped it, had been transformed in a blink of an eye or a throw of the hand, into the rubbish of war. A young girl's favourite doll had been crushed by an upturned oak table which Tom guessed had probably been thrown from a horse-drawn cart, piled high with a terrified family's household effects. Tom thought about the family who by now probably had nothing left other than the clothes they were wearing. Who were they? Where would they go in their desperation to escape the terror which had so swiftly descended upon them?

Then it struck him... the lane was empty. There were no refugees and no retreating soldiers.

"THE LANE'S EMPTY, LOOK........ THE LANES EMPTY....THEY'RE COMING", he bellowed in a cracked, breathless voice.

Haupsturmfuhrer Ernst Albers felt confident in the turret of the *Panzerkampfwagen* as it clanked its way across the Belgian border and onto the narrow roads of France. Together with the other Panzers following him, he continued to push the defeated British army back towards the beaches of Dunkirk where, within days, their destruction would be complete. He was sure the resistance from the French infantry would be of little consequence against the superior German forces and the *Panzerkommandeur* and his crew were comfortable in the knowledge that the blitzkrieg was progressing according plan.

There was a relaxed and confident mood onboard the Panzer. Ernst Albers knew there wasn't any need to issue any directions to his driver who was entombed in the hull of the tank alongside the radio operator. The speed of the tank was constant and although night was falling fast, the driver could see the road well enough and in any case, it would probably be some hours before they would see any serious action.

"*Heuptsturmfuhrer*, this is not going to be much of a war", joked the gunner, "if the Tommies keep running away, we will all be back in the *Mutterland* by Christmas".

"I suppose you would like the war to continue until after Christmas, so you don't have to buy your wife a present, you tight bugger", the driver of the tank joined in with the banter.

The *Kommandeur* had left the inter-coms on in the tank and all the men laughed together at the jokes as the panzerkampfwagen rumbled along the empty lane towards Dunkirk and the rest of France beyond.

Tom was standing in the middle of the lane between the two groups of guns. "TANK ALERT", he shouted, "TANK ALERT".

Tom's training was kicking in.

"Jump to it lads, the Panzers are on their way.......remember, no gun is to be fired until the range is five hundred yards......best of luck".

Before he ran back to join Chopper and Lenny at his own gun, Tom looked around at the other three guns to make one last final check. The Number Twos were climbing onto their metal seats behind the armoured shields. Some of them were checking the traverse of their guns, whilst others were already looking through the eye level, sighting devices.

Tom quickly eased himself into the seat of the gun. All of a sudden, the weight of his steel helmet seemed very heavy on his head but instinctively he pulled the chin strap tighter. His legs were squeezed between the vertical column of the gun's elevation control and with his left hand, he turned the small hand-wheel on the column to the left and right, watching with satisfaction as the barrel of the gun rose and fell. At the same time his other hand was already turning the traversing hand-wheel which was tight against his right leg. His foot found the firing pedal and he leaned forward in his seat. He was now ready for the action that was to come. His stomach churned but for some reason he did not feel any fear, on the contrary, he was almost looking forward to what was about to happen.

"Tom, you may need rapid traverse if the tanks come through at speed. I'll stand at your side just in case I need to push the gun round", Len, who was now acting as the gun's Number One, reminded him.

Tom knew exactly what Lenny was saying. If the gun needed to be swivelled quickly, rather than laboriously turning the-hand wheel, he could throw out the clutch by pushing his right foot down on the pedal and Lenny could then move the gun round on its pedestal, just by pushing on Tom's shoulder.

As the barrel of the gun started slowly turning towards the lane, Tom looked through the sighting telescope. "Shit", he cursed, "I can't see the bloody cross hairs".

It was as black as pitch amongst the trees now that darkness had fallen and Tom could have kicked himself for not thinking of it earlier. Although the moon had struggled free of the clouds, its light was not enough for him to see the gun's sights.

He turned to Chopper and said, "I'll have to aim with open sights".

Chopper nodded as he opened the door of the magazine storage locker. He knew that if they had any chance at all of stopping the Panzers he would have to reload the single shot gun every three or four seconds and even quicker if a second tank broke through.

"I'm going to fold down the top part of the shield to get a better view", Tom said as he looked down to Chopper who was crouched to his right, ready at the magazine. Tom quickly looked to Lenny, standing to his left, who would judge the range and traverse the gun rapidly if necessary. Both men realised the implication of what Tom had said. With the top part of the shield down, they all would all be exposed to enemy gunfire and with almost indiscernible movements of their heads, each of the two men signalled their agreement.

"With the trees so close to the road there's not enough room for them to be two abreast, so they'll be in single file", Tom shouted to his crew. He knew that once the tanks arrived all hell would break loose and there would be no time to talk tactics to them. "We'll concentrate our fire on the lead tank and try and knock it out. Even if we can't do that, we may get it to stop and withdraw.......and if we can do that, it will block the others from coming through and hopefully slow things down for all those poor sods we passed on the road".

The men could now clearly hear the throaty roar of the powerful twelve-cylinder *Maybach* engines and the clanking of the tracks cutting through the night air.

Lenny looked at Tom and said in a low voice, "Sounds like more than one, probably three or four".

Chopper, who was kneeling by the breech of the gun, looked up at Lenny and replied grimly, "The bastards always operate in groups.......they sound like big buggers, I don't think we are going to miss them when they appear", he added optimistically.

The tanks were now moving quickly towards them. Tom cocked his ear and judged their speed to be about ten to fifteen miles per hour. "Panzer Three's", he said under his breath as the dark grey shape of the first tank appeared in view, Tom's eyes narrowed as he saw the large black cross which was painted on its turret.

"Lenny, I'll shout if I need the rapid traverse once I've let off the first round", Tom said to his number one, without taking his eyes off the open sights of the gun. Without the use of the telescopic sights, he would have to aim it in a similar way as he had aimed his gun in the woods. Tom's concentration wavered briefly as he remembered the number of times he had gauged the distance of the foxes in the woods at Pentbury as he had looked down the barrels of his twelve bore gun towards the small bead at the end, before squeezing the trigger.

He cleared his throat with a cough as he saw the turret of the tank turn. Its huge gun was now directly facing them.

"Twelve hundred yards and still coming", Len shouted, "are you layed on it Tom?"

Tom's reply was lost in the sudden explosion which came from the leading gun on the opposite side of the lane as it fired at the tank. In the corner of his eye, Tom saw a flash of light coming from the two pounder's muzzle and he watched in horror as the shell it had fired, bounced harmlessly off the tanks armoured side plates.

"Christ, they've fired too bloody early, the stupid fuckers". Choppers voice was a mixture of anger and astonishment at the other gun crew's stupidity. He had hardly finished the sentence when the gun positioned behind followed suit and also fired off another innocuous round at the tank. "Jesus wept", Chopper's despairing voice was lost in the explosion of another wasted shell hitting the tank's side.

The *Haupsturmfuhrer's* thoughts had drifted back to his family and their home in his beloved Bavaria when he saw the flash of the guns which had fired at his tank.

He had been deep in thought of the last Christmas they had spent together. How the children had laughed when they played in the snow in the little village that nestled against the Bavarian Alps. He remembered how his wife *Tilda* would make the *Advents wreath* four weeks before the *eve of Christmas*. He smiled to himself as he thought how she would create the wreath with such loving care out of small branches of fir and four equally spaced bright red candles. The children would light the first of the candles on the first Sunday and on the following Sundays they would light the second one, then the third and finally on the Sunday before Christmas, all the candles would be lit and would be burning brightly in the window of their wooden house. The *Kommandeur* closed his eyes and breathed deeply through his nose. Instead of the smell of hot oil and diesel fuel of the tank, all he could smell was the sweet scent of freshly picked pine branches and the warm aroma of burning candles. He knew if he was still fighting this war next Christmas, the candles would be flickering in the window. If only I was there, he thought and imagined as the *eve of Christmas* approached, Tilda, his lovely *Tilda*, with her blue eyes and flaxen coloured hair would tell his two young sons that *Christkind* would come down from heaven to bring peace and joy. Then, if the boys had been good, the *Christkind* would also bring a brightly decorated Christmas tree and of course, presents. Albers sighed as he remembered how the family sat down after all the presents had been opened to a meal of *bockwurst und kartoffelsalat*. They would then walk through the deep crisp snow to the small church on the hillside and sing Christmas carols. He started to sing quietly, *"Stille naght, Heilige Nacht, all is calm, all is bright.* How long ago it seemed and how far away he felt from his family.

It was the muzzle flash from the enemy's gun that wrenched the thoughts of his family from his mind and brought him back with a jolt to the matters in hand.

He cursed, *"Mein Gott"*. How stupid he had been to let his attention drift to matters of such little importance at a time like this, he thought.

"FEUERN SIE DIE GEWEHR AM LIGCHT AB", Ernst shouted into his throat microphone to the tank's gunner.

His gunner had already seen the two flashes of light and had heard the metallic sound of the shells hitting the side of the *kampfwagen* and immediately followed the *Hauptsturmfuhrer's* urgent command and turned the turret to the position where the light had come from. He started firing the tank's heavy machine guns even before he saw the shadowy figures of the English gunners who were attempting to escape from their still smoking anti- tank gun. Then, without waiting for further orders, he fired the tank's main gun twice in quick succession and smiled with satisfaction as he saw the enemy's guns disappear in an explosion of fire and smoke, in front of him.

"Gut, gut", said Ernst Albers with a degree of satisfaction. He had recognised the guns as the small anti-tank guns used by the British army. He smiled when he thought how desperate the Tommies must be, to be using such pea-shooters of a weapon against the mighty German forces.

Never the less, he thought, it was foolish of him to have been so complacent, he would not let such a thing happen again.

As soon as he heard the first gun fire, Tom had jumped from his seat and started to run across the lane, bellowing in a cracked and breathless voice, "STOP FIRING, STOP BLOODY FIRING....YOU'RE GIVING YOUR POSITIONS AWAY TO EARLY........THEY ARE OUT OF RANGE". Before he could say anymore, he had seen the turret of the Panzer begin to turn towards the guns positions. "RUN", he shouted desperately to the crews of the two guns, "RUN". Desperately, Tom turned and under the protective cover of the night ran back across the lane to his own position, just as the tank's thirty-seven millimetre machine guns burst into rapid fire again, cutting down the helpless men on the other side of the lane as they tried to run from their guns.

Tom reached Percy Gorringe's gun crew who were positioned behind his own gun. "I don't think they've seen us on this side of the lane yet, fire after me, I repeat, after me. Aim for the track's drive links and fire off as many as you can", he shouted breathlessly.

Percy Gorringe's expression was set hard as stone, as he nodded his understanding

The tank was still slowly moving forward as Tom clambered back into the seat of his gun.

"LEN", he shouted, as he quickly positioned himself on the seat and hovered his right foot over the firing pedal. Leaning forward in his seat he lined up the sights and quickly shouted to Len again, "I'M GOING FOR THE TRACK LINKS TO TRY TO STOP IT".

"CHOPPER, RELOAD AS QUICK AS YOU CAN".

"FOUR HUNDRED YARDS", Len shouted back quickly.

Tom screamed, "FIRING".

The flash and smoke from the gun was immediately followed by Percy's gun as his crew copied Tom's example. Chopper was already loading a second round into the gun's breech as the armour piercing shells from the two guns smashed in quick succession into the front of the Panzer's tracks. Everything was happening so quickly and as Tom was about to shout, FIRING again, the night sky was lit up by the blast of a tank shell exploding to his right. He heard Chopper shout as the force of the explosion knocked him backwards. The gun shook on its carriage at the same time as Tom felt the debris thrown up from the blast hit them.

His eyes whipped across the lane. "Christ", he shouted, as he realised the Panzer had knocked out the other gun. Without hesitation, he turned back and checked his aim. Frantically adjusting the traverse and elevation hand wheels he pushed his foot hard down on the firing pedal.

"FIRING", he screamed once more.

With the second shell away, Tom watched with horror as the turret of the huge tank started slewing round across the lane towards his gun.

A flash of light illuminated the sky.

Chopper spat the taste of burnt cordite from his mouth and shouted hoarsely, "IT'S A HIT, YOU'VE HIT IT".

Tom looked through the smoke and at first thought he had missed the tank's drive links but then realised he had scored a direct hit on the tank's tumbler drive sprocket. Burning wreckage flared into the night sky as he looked quickly across to the other side of the lane where the other guns had been. "God", he groaned when he saw that the Panzer had scored a direct hit on the forward gun. He peered quickly through the drifting smoke of the explosion but could not see anything which was left of the one behind.

Things were happening too quickly for him to comprehend.

Tom's second round was immediately followed by one from Percy's gun which also slammed into track's of the tank. Tom watched with satisfaction as the disabled tank slewed round and came to rest, blocking the narrow lane.

"WE'VE GOT IT", Chopper screamed, "THEY CAN'T STEER THE FUCKING THING".

The words had hardly left his mouth when without warning, flashes of light from the tank's machine gun spat through the darkness as it burst into fire again, only this time the murderous fire was being directed at Tom and Percy's guns. Once again, the position of the guns had been given away by the flashes of light from their barrels.

"TOM, TOM", Chopper was screaming at him as he grabbed Tom by his collar and hauled him backwards off the seat of the gun, as if he was pulling a terrier dog from a rabbit.

"WE'VE GOT TO GET OUT OF HERE".

Tom never heard the burst of machine gun fire which hit the two-pounder as he was pulled from his seat and thrown to the ground. Nor did he hear Len's dying cry as the tank's deadly bullets cut through his unprotected body.

"FALL BACK TO THE TRUCK".

Chopper was shouting to the men from Percy's gun as he half carried and half dragged his friend through the woods towards the waiting truck.

"RUN, RUN".

Chopper was screaming at the four men who were behind him.

It was only when Tom attempted to climb over the truck's tailboard did they notice the blood running down his right arm and dripping off his fingers, forming a small crimson puddle on the road.

"Christ Tom, you've been hit" said Chopper, alarmed at the sight of Tom's blood soaked tunic. "Quick, get him into the back", he ordered.

Chopper realised it was probably only minutes before the disabled tank was pushed clear by the others which were following and the road would be opened for the enemy's forces to pour through and pursue them. He knew there wasn't any time to spare. They had to get moving now if they were to have any chance of escape.

"FOR CHRIST'S SAKE GET A MOVE ON", he shouted, almost in panic, as Tom was being hauled up the back of the tall truck, "and let's bloody get out of here. Tom, give me the map", Chopper demanded, and without waiting for an answer, he snatched the map from Tom's pocket as he was being pulled head first, over the tail board and onto the truck's steel floor. Chopper heard Tom groan as he flicked his cigarette lighter into life with a well practised thumb and urgently studied the map by its flickering flame. "If we stay on this lane we're as good as dead. I'll try and get to this small road by going through the trees", his finger was tracing a line on the map, "then head towards Dunkirk by avoiding the main roads, that's going to be our best chance".

He looked up for acknowledgement of his plan but there was nobody there, those that had survived the Panzer attack had realised the need to get moving and had already clambered into the back of the truck. Without a second glance, Chopper screwed up the map and stuffing it unceremoniously into his pocket ran round to the driver's door. Snatching the handle of the open door, he hauled himself up into the cab and swung his body into the drivers' seat. Frantically in the darkness he began to fish about for the ignition key. Please God let it be there. He was praying harder than he had ever prayed in his life, as he slid his hand along the dashboard desperately searching for the elusive key.

"Thank Christ", he exclaimed with relief as his fingers found it. He rapidly turned it and heard the starter motor turn. "Come on, you bastard", Chopper drastically urged the lifeless engine, as he felt the panic rising from the pit of his stomach. He turned the key again and then, in quick succession, a third time and a fourth time. He could feel his hand shaking in frustration, as he turned the key once more before thumping his fist hard down on the steering wheel.

His throat was dry. "Come on, come on", he pleaded and then, just as he was beginning to think all was lost, the engine caught and barked into life. Choppers sigh was audible as he quickly let off the hand brake and slammed the truck into gear. He could hear the engine roar when he pushed his foot hard down on the accelerator pedal and yanking the wheel round, he manoeuvred the truck off the road and surged into what was left of the comforting darkness in the forest.

Instantly, Chopper had to fight the steering wheel as the truck hit the rough ground with a spine breaking thump and lurched into the gloom which enveloped it, not unlike a fist being pushed into a glove. Automatically, he took his hand from the steering wheel and reached for the headlight switch, "No", he said, spitting the word out from his mouth as if it was poison, suddenly remembering the need to keep hidden from the enemy who by now were probably close on their heels. He quickly returned his grip to the steering wheel and with both hands he struggled to keep control as the truck's front wheels defiantly tried to follow the rutted forest floor. His wrists ached and his fingers and thumbs were starting to go numb from having to grip the wheel so tightly. "I can't see a bloody thing", he said, as if he was speaking to an unseen passenger as he started to lean so far forward in his seat his breath was condensing on the Morris's windscreen. Frantically he attempted to weave a path through the trees which appeared as black shadows as they hurtled towards him. Chopper's eyes darted from side to side as he increased the speed of the truck, looking for any fallen trees and gullies which would stop their escape. "Shit", he shouted, as one of the silhouetted trees suddenly appeared in front of him. He wrenched the steering wheel hard round to the left and automatically stamped on the brake pedal in a desperate attempt to avoid the tree. The truck jerked and the tree loomed. The Morris skidded sideways and with a sickening bang hit another unseen tree with its flank. The door bulged inwards and Chopper felt himself being sprayed with shards of glass. He gasped as the breath was knocked out of him as his chest was thrown against the steering wheel by the impact. His heart was beating hard and adrenaline raced through his body as he wrenched the steering wheel to the right, in a frenzied attempt to regain control.

The truck was now like a charging bull, blind of the consequences. Immediately Chopper slammed on the brakes in a desperate attempt to stop the truck's front wheels plunging into a dried-up stream bed which had suddenly appeared from nowhere. The truck skidded on the soft soil of the forest and it came to an abrupt halt when its front wheels dropped into the gully. Without time to take any evasive action, Chopper was suddenly thrown from his seat as the rear wheels raised up and his head hit the screen with a sickening crunch. Everything went black and he never heard the shouts of the men who had been sliding about in the back as the vehicle bounced and skidded on its journey through the woods. Now, with the impact of the crash, they had been tossed like rag dolls from the floor of the truck and had been sent crashing into its bulkhead in a jumble of humanity.

"What the fuck are you doing?" One of the surviving gunners, whose name was Dusty Miller, spat the words out, as he jumped from the back of the motionless truck and ran round to the driver's door. Still in shock, his outrage was evident. "You nearly bloody killed all of us in the back, you crazy sod", he continued spitting venom as he tried to force the door open. The window was missing and he saw Chopper's prone body as he desperately tugged to open the caved-in door.

"Christ, Chopper, are you alright?" he exclaimed. It was when he saw Chopper slumped forward in his seat the anger in his voice abated. There was a trickle of blood slowly making its way down his forehead and there was a cobweb of cracks on the windscreen radiating from the point of Chopper's impact.

"We've got to keep going", Chopper murmured. Although he was dazed and his head was spinning like a top, he was still aware of the danger they were in and said again in a shaking voice, "we must keep going".

"Chopper, Chopper", Dusty Miller continued saying, trying to get some sense from the man, "Are you alright?"

Chopper shook his head violently, as if to bring some coherence back into it. "I'll live", he replied grimly, as he wiped away the blood from his forehead with the back of his hand. "Sorry about that, I forgot about you lot in the back", he mumbled, "how's Tom?"

"Same as you.... He'll live", the young gunner replied ruefully.

"Let's hope I can get this bloody thing out of this bloody ditch", Chopper said, as he hurriedly turned the ignition key once more. This time, the stalled engine responded quickly and roared immediately into life, belching a plume of black smoke from its battered exhaust pipe and into the obscurity of the dark forest.

Dusty Miller stood and watched as Chopper slammed the gear lever into reverse and slowly eased the truck out of the stream bed and then before selecting a forward gear, he lifted his legs up onto the dashboard and with one hefty push, kicked out the remains of the shattered windscreen.

"Jump back in and tell them I think we have nearly reached the road that should take us along the coast to Dunkirk", he yelled out of the windowless door to Dusty. That is, he thought to himself, if I haven't been driving round in circles in this fucking forest.

His head was hurting like hell but all he could think about was to escape from the Germans and hope to God his quick glance at the map had been right and the lane would lead them to the coast. If I'm right, Chopper thought, the elusive lane is no more than a mile away. Once again, he increased the speed of the battered truck and raced between the endless stands of trees, desperately dodging the water filled ditches and rotting tree trunks which were strewn across the woodland floor.

Chopper was not the only soldier in the truck who breathed a sigh of relief as it broke from the oak forest and onto the comparative smooth surface of the narrow lane. He looked left and right and was grateful it was clear of refugees. Despite what had happened earlier, he turned towards the coast and continued to drive the truck as fast as he dared, knowing he had to take risks if they were to have any chance of keeping ahead of the enemy. The lane was dark and its twists and turns were difficult to see without the luxury of the truck's headlights. Chopper relaxed and eased himself into the seat, thankful it was now not nearly as bad as the drive through the woods had been. His fingers began to probe the egg-sized lump on his forehead, disturbing the congealed blood which had formed, causing it to start flowing again and as it mixed with the sweat, it began to run into his eyes.

Although they had escaped from the Panzers, Chopper knew the murderous Stukas still roamed the sky and a vehicle travelling at night would be an easy and tempting target for them. His foot pressed harder on the throttle and felt the glass from the broken window crunch beneath his foot.

"Christ, I'm bloody tired", he murmured to himself, as he tried to fight off the exhaustion which was beginning to overwhelm him like a thick, city fog.

He blinked his eyes quickly, as he strained to focus on the dark, winding lane, stretched out ahead of him, looking for a safe place to park up and to get the men out the back of the battered Morris.

"That will do", he said to himself, when after about ten minutes of searching through the gloom, he saw a spot where the branches of the trees were overhanging the lane, forming a dark tunnel.

Chopper slowed the vehicle and brought it to a halt. He breathed deeply and slowly as he climbed down from the cab. The chill of early morning air sent a shiver running through his shaking body as he ran to the back of the mud splattered truck. Silently, he watched as one by one, the men emerged from inside and slowly hauled their bruised and battered bodies over the tailboard and lowered themselves onto the road below. Nobody said a word. They were all overwhelmed by a mixture of shock, tiredness, hunger and thirst. The small group of men just stood there, not daring to move too far from the illusionary safety of the truck, believing it would give them some protection if there was a sudden attack. Somewhere, far in the distance, a lone dog had started barking and now, with the truck's engine as silent as the stars peeping through the leafy canopy above them, the men relished the feeling of tranquillity the place was giving them. It was something they had not known since they had driven out of the farmyard with the rest of the detachment.

Chopper was lighting a cigarette when Tom struggled out of the truck. His face grimaced with pain and exhaustion. "How's the arm, mate?" Chopper asked, as he passed the smoking cigarette to his friend.

"Could have been worse", Tom said. His breathing was heavy and he felt dizzy as he slumped against the side of the vehicle. "I think I must have been hit by some shrapnel when the Panzer got the guns".

"Christ", Chopper exclaimed, as he flicked his lighter into life to light another cigarette and to look at the men who were standing by the back of the truck, half hidden in the darkness of the trees. He suddenly realised in the dash to escape, he didn't know the extent of the casualties. "How many on board?" he enquired and not waiting for Tom's reply, he looked towards the rest of the men in a futile attempt to count the red glows of light which were coming from their cigarettes.

"Six, including you", Tom croaked, as he tried to clear his throat.

"Six....Christ.....that means"............ Chopper was stunned. His head was spinning. Everything had been happening so quickly he hadn't had time to think about the number of men who had been killed.

"Thirty two dead including those who were hit by the fucking Stuka", Tom said grimly, answering the question which was on his friend's lips

He could feel his arm throbbing through the field dressing the men had hastily applied in the back of the truck and although the flow of blood had been stemmed, it wasn't the pain that was tormenting his mind. It was the thought of Len.

"I killed him", he mumbled as his eyes misted over...."I folded the bloody shield down on the gun....if I'd left it up, he wouldn't have been hit".

Chopper looked compassionately at his friend but he knew as well as Tom did, the shield was only as thick as a pencil and whilst it would have stopped small arms fire, it would not have stopped the armour piercing bullets from the tank's machine guns. He said nothing, he knew that time would heal Tom's torment. He also knew that if Tom hadn't folded the shield down, he probably wouldn't have hit the tank and then they all would have been killed.

Eventually he broke the silence which followed. "We have to move on, there's only an hour or so before it starts getting light". He looked at men and on hearing no objection, he said firmly, "We'll keep going 'til then and ditch the truck and head out on foot towards Dunkirk. Get back into the truck and let's get on our bloody way".

Once more, the four-cylinder engine groaned into life and black smoke belched from its exhaust pipe. Chopper pushed his foot down on the throttle and drove along the dark, winding lane which he hoped would lead them towards Dunkirk and evacuation. How likely was it, he thought to himself that they would reach Dunkirk and even if they did, would they be in time to get off the beach? As he drove on, his eyes and ears strained as he looked and listened for anything which could threaten their desperate flight. He looked towards his rifle which somehow had remained propped up against the passenger seat like a mute travelling companion and suddenly he felt despondent about the situation they found themselves in.

Dawn was breaking as Chopper drove the truck off the road and parked it up with one last determined pull of the handbrake. Kicking open the damaged door, he jumped down onto the dew covered grass and threw the ignition key away with a throw so powerful that any bowler on a village cricket pitch would have been proud of.

The rose-pink clouds, trimmed with streaks of yellow and orange, gently rose above the slate-grey sky of the new day. The sight of the sunrise briefly lifted the men's hearts after the grim night they had just lived through. But it wasn't the sweet sound of the early birdsong which greeted them as they clambered out of the truck, it was the droning of enemy bombers which were sweeping in, lower and lower and were only minutes away from dropping their cargoes of death with impunity onto the Dunkirk beaches.

Tom's face was as pale as the fading moon when Chopper, with evident concern in his voice, asked "Are you sure you are alright?"

"I'll live". Tom had regained his composure. "What next?" he asked.

Chopper's hand was shaking as he lit another cigarette and after a couple of hefty drags to make sure it was alight, passed it across to Tom who took it eagerly. Chopper's thumb flicked his battered Ronson lighter into life once more as he lit another cigarette but this time it was for himself.

"Look what's happening over there", he blew a lung full of white cigarette smoke westwards.

Tom's eyes followed the wisps of the smoke and in the distance saw the plumes of black smoke rising hundreds of feet into the lightening sky.

"That lot's coming from the direction of Dunkirk. It looks as if they're bombing the bloody place to bits, so Christ knows what it is like for the poor buggers waiting to get off the beaches", Chopper said quietly.

Both men stood looking at the ominous columns of smoke as they grew taller and hung in black clouds over the beleaguered port. Words were not necessary as they both knew what it meant. It was the sound of more German bombers flying overhead which broke the silence. Tom looked at Chopper and said grimly, "If we aren't going to try to get down to Dunkirk and with the Jerry infantry closing in on us from the border, it means we've got to reach the coast from here and try to get across ".

"I think what it means is that we are well and truly fucked", Chopper said bluntly, as he flicked his cigarette butt into the undergrowth.

Tom ignored him and just as he had taken command after the Stuka attack, he looked towards the rest of the men before saying, "I think our best shot is to head towards the coast on foot and when it gets dark, we'll find a boat from somewhere but first we need to try and find some grub and get some rest if we can ",

The four men stared at him. Their mood was sombre but they nodded their heads in compliance. They could think more about how they would get home once they had found some food and had some sleep.

Tom knew he would have to use all the skills he had learnt in the woods if he was going to keep the men hidden from the enemy and have any chance of reaching the coast. He wondered if the others had the same doubts in their minds....how likely was it they would even find a boat, let alone get home, he thought grimly, as any confidence he had began to ebb away?.

"Which way now?" he pondered quietly to himself.

Chopper fished deep into his pocket and pulled out the increasingly crumpled map and handing it to Tom, he said with a grin, "I knew this would come in handy".

Tom grinned back at his friend and after staring at the map for a few moments, said, without looking up, "I think we are about here and this will be the quickest way to the sea". His blood-stained finger drew an imaginary line on the map. Without waiting for a reply, he said conclusively, "Come on, let's get moving" and as he hoisted his rifle onto his shoulder, he started to walk briskly away from the battered truck towards the coast. He knew the risks but felt more comfortable now he had made his decision.

When eventually the small group of men had left the relative safety of the woods, they walked along the water- filled ditches which edged the fields, keeping close to the hedgerows to give them such cover as they afforded across the open ground. The anxiety which showed on the mens grime-smeared faces revealed they knew if the German infantry had already reached this far and they were caught without cover, their chances of survival would be virtually nil.

The sun had been up for nearly two hours and the dew was already drying on the grass when in the distance Tom saw a group of farm buildings nestling in the folds of the rolling, emerald green fields. He held his hand up, motioning to the line of men following behind, to stop and then turning to look at them, he saw they were nearly dead on their feet. In the silence which followed he could hear some dogs barking and the sound of cows bellowing coming from the direction of the farm.

"We'll stop here and recce the place for ten minutes or so to see if there are any signs of life before we approach the house and try to get some food", Tom whispered. Not waiting for an answer, he added ominously, "We don't want to walk into the Jerries if they are already there".

Gratefully the men sank to the ground, thankful for the rest. After some minutes had passed it was Arthur Gold who broke the silence. Before his enlistment, he had worked on a dairy farm in Sussex and still had the weathered look of a countryman. Knowingly, he said, "From the racket those bloody cows are making, I'd say the poor sods need milking. I know the Froggies are funny buggers but they would milk their cows. I'd say the place is either deserted or it's full of Jerries who don't give a shit for the poor fucking creatures".

"That decides it", Tom said, suddenly, getting to his feet, "we'll get moving and take a look and hope to Christ the place isn't crawling with Jerry". Then, with him once again leading the way, the men slowly followed suit and began to make their way through an old apple orchard towards the back of the old house.

Taff plucked a small apple which was hanging from one of the gnarled trees and hungrily bit into it. Almost immediately his face screwed in disgust as he tasted the bitter fruit. "Bloody cookers", he said, spitting out a mouthful of the sour juice into the long grass.

Arthur Gold snorted out a laugh, as if to say any idiot would have known that.

"Quiet", Chopper, who was bringing up the rear, whispered angrily.

With the caution a country fox displays when approaching a hen house, the men made their way towards the back of the house and on reaching it, Tom turned and looking towards Chopper pointed towards the shuttered windows. Chopper looked at them, noticing the sheets of peeling yellow paint but more importantly, he could see the shutters were all firmly closed, even the ones on the ground floor. He understood at once what Tom had noticed and nodded his head in a gesture of understanding. Did this mean the house was empty, he thought? To their relief, the men reached the back door without mishap and Tom motioned to them to stand to one side whilst he slowly turned the huge knob and gently pushed against the door. Nothing, the door was locked. He looked back at the men and with a satisfied grin on his face, said quietly, "So far, so good. We'll spread out and go around the sides of the house to see if anybody is about before we try the front". Taking Taff and Dusty with him, he motioned to Chopper to take the other two round the other side of the old, seemingly deserted farmhouse. Tom beckoned to Taff and Dusty to keep low as they passed under the shuttered windows just in case they were flung open by the enemy, should they be inside.

The three men had nearly reached the front corner of the house when out of the corner of Tom's well trained eye, he saw something move across a small gap between two of the farm buildings to his right. Instinctively, he dropped onto one knee and aimed his rifle towards the gap. Taff and Dusty quickly followed suit.

"What was it?" Taff whispered.

"Don't know", Tom replied in a similar tone, "I'm going to cross the yard and take a look. Cover me".

Taff and Dusty knelt and pushed their backs against the farmhouse wall as they kept their guns levelled on the gap between the outbuildings. Taff gave the thumbs up sign to Tom, signalling they were ready to give him the covering fire he had asked for, should it be needed.

Dropping his rifle to his side, Tom began to run the short distance from the house to the buildings. He was keeping low and zig-zagged across the yard, the way they had practised so many times back at the camp in Hampshire. He had not reached the gap when Taff, whose eyes had been solely focused on the spot where Tom was heading, glimpsed to his left. It appeared to be a crouched figure as it suddenly appeared from behind a dilapidated chicken shed and began to race towards them. In the heat of the moment the word *Jerry* flashed across his mind.

"TOM", Taff screamed out the warning and in the split second it took for him to look across to Tom, he saw Tom throw himself to the ground and take cover.

Things were happening too fast for Taff. It had only taken an instant for him to glance across at Tom and shout his warning. Instinctively he twisted his head back to confront what was now racing towards him. Even before he could fully see the dark shape of the enemy, he squeezed the trigger of his Lee Enfield. The deafening noise of the gun shattered the peace of the sunny morning and a flock of jackdaws, startled by the sound of the gunfire rose noisily from a large tree behind a stone barn. Apart from the noise of the gunshot echoing round the farm yard all that could be heard were the birds calling out their harsh warning cries of "scraaaak, scraaaak", like a black cloud of screaming banshees.

No more than a second or two had elapsed, not even enough time for Taff to feel the beads of sweat which were streaming through the dirt on his face. His heart was heaving and his mouth gaped wide, when out of the corner of his eye, he glimpsed some movement coming round from the front of the house. Automatically he swung his rifle round and took aim. But this time, thankfully before he pulled the trigger, it was Chopper he saw in his gun-sight. Chopper had heard the shot and together with the other two men, had raced round the front of the house, unsure what they would find on the other side.

It was Dusty Miller who had been kneeling alongside Taff who broke the silence and spoke first.

"It's a pig. You've shot a bloody pig".

Taff was still breathing fast when he looked at the sight in front of him. There, flat on its belly, with its legs sprawled out on either side like a collapsed table, lay a large black pig with smoke coming from a neat bullet wound between its eyes. He pushed his steel helmet to the back of his head and exclaimed with a sense of amazement, "Where did that fucking thing come from?"

On the other side of the farmyard Tom picked up his rifle and walked back to join the others who were grouped together and joking at Taff's expense how easy it was to confuse a four-legged pig with a two-legged German infantryman.

"Next time", Percy advised solemnly," the German will be the one without the curly tail".

With the dead pig lying at their feet, the mood of the men had lifted and the events of the past few days had been briefly forgotten.

It was only Chopper who had maintained a serious look on his face. He glanced around nervously and said, "Let's get moving. The noise Taff made taking the squeak out of that bloodt pig was enough to awaken the dead".

Tom nodded and said, "At least we know the house is empty. Let's try to get inside and see if we can find some food before the bloody Jerries turn up".

With his eyes peeled, Tom continued making his way to the front of the house and feeling fairly certain there wasn't anyone else about, he paused to look carefully at the various pens and stables which were scattered on either side of the large, cobbled farmyard stretched out in front of him. In an instant something struck him as he looked from building to building.

Quickly, he turned round to speak to Chopper. "Look", he said, in a low voice, "the doors of the pens are open. They must have let the animals loose before they fled the place". Chopper looked and once again nodded his head in agreement and motioned to Tom to continue.

In front of the house was a small flower garden. The clumps of orange marigolds and white daisies looked as though they had been lovingly tended by the farmer's wife right up until she had been forced to flee from her home. Tom cautiously approached the front door and slowly eased it open with the barrel of his rifle. The ancient door hinges yielded reluctantly making a teeth grating squeal and, with a strange feeling of intrusion, Tom entered a large cluttered hall. On its flagstone floor lay a pair of boots with moist mud still clinging obstinately to their thick leather soles and alongside was an assortment of different sized wooden clogs. Two long handled pitchforks had been propped up in the corner against the roughly plastered wall. Tom studied them with curiosity and guessed they had probably been brought in straight from the hay field which indicated the haste of the family's retreat from their house. On the far side of the hall Tom saw a narrow oak staircase winding its way up to the floor above. The wood was black with age and the treads worn smooth by the generations of feet which had obviously used it. He could sense the other men were close behind him as he tip-toed across the hall to a half-closed door on the other side. They were all moving as quietly as church mice, desperate that their boots did not make a sound as they came into contact with the hard stone floor. Tom turned and held his finger up to his lips and mouthed *shh* as he raised his rifle and cautiously began to push the door open with his boot. As the door opened, he could see it led into a large kitchen and with the door fully opened Tom saw much to his relief, in the middle of the deserted room was a long pine table with some food still on it. Thank God, he thought.

One by one, the men made their way into the kitchen and as their mood lifted and the need for silence diminished, the men's hunger was evident as they grabbed what food they could from the table. Chopper squeezed a long, half eaten baguette which had been left on a wooden bread-board as if to test its freshness, before tearing off a chunk and stuffing it into his mouth.

"Poor buggers", he said, as he began to sniff a pot of red-coloured, glutinous looking jam. "They certainly left in a hurry", he scoffed, as he started to spoon the sticky substance into his mouth.

"If there are any Jerries about, they must have heard the shot Taff fired off", Tom said briskly, "which means they will soon be down on us like a ton of bloody bricks. We'll take what food we can and then find somewhere to get our heads down for a few hours before make for the coast".

"You're right mate", Chopper grunted, as he pushed off the wire clips on top of a cider bottle to release the stopper, before taking a quick swig. "The sooner we can get away from this place the better". Tom did not have to say any more. He could see the men were hurriedly pushing food into their mouths with one hand and filling their pockets with the other. They all know the need to get moving, he thought, as he grabbed a tin of peaches from a green painted cupboard, above a small stone sink.

Stuffing the tin into a pocket on his webbing belt and with an unceremonious sweep of his forearm, Tom cleared one end of the table and began to smooth out the precious map. The noise of the plates and cutlery crashing onto the rough stone floor had stopped the men in their tracks as they continued to forage for food and they crowded round the table to look at the map spread out in front of them.

"Look", said Tom urgently, as he stubbed his finger on the screwed-up paper, "this is where we are now and this...." The men watched intently as he slid his finger across the familiar map towards what they could clearly see was the coast. Tom bent over to take a closer look at the creased document. "This looks like an old quarry", he murmured to himself, oblivious to the men crowding round, all trying to see what he was looking at. "That's it", he said decisively, as he slowly straightened his aching back with a groan, "we'll find a place to hide there until dusk and then head for the coast".

"Let's get going then", Chopper said, as he hoisted his rifle on his shoulder and made his way towards the door. As he passed the remnants of food which remained on the far end of the table, he stuffed some strong smelling cheese into his pocket and then thinking better of it, threw it back whence it came."Christ" he spluttered, screwing up his nose and wiping some of the soft cheese which had stuck to his hand onto his trousers, "do they eat this bloody stuff?" With Tom leading the way, the group left the farm and walked briskly down the lane before cutting across country towards the quarry Tom had seen on the map. They had been walking for nearly an hour and were grateful the rain which had been threatening ever since they had left the farmhouse had not yet arrived. In the distance they could see another isolated farmhouse, once again with its shutters tightly closed and dotted across the lush, surrounding pastures was a large flock of sheep, silently grazing.

Tom kept his eyes scanned and he was the first spotted one of the exposed sand faces of the quarry showing through the vegetation which had grown over it since it was last worked, presumably, many years before.

Although the men had satisfied their craving for food and drink, the journey through weed-entangled ditches and bramble-covered hedgerows had sapped the remaining strength they had left in their weary bodies and they all needed a rest.

"That looks like a likely place to get our heads down and finish the food", Chopper said, as he peered over the rim of the quarry towards a rusty corrugated-iron shelter, half buried by a fresh fall of yellow sand.

The men immediately started sliding down the sloping quarry face towards the shelter, where no doubt, the previous occupants would have sheltered from inclement weather and where they would have eaten their cheese and baguettes and shared bottles of cider.

Chopper had been asleep, propped up in one corner of the shelter when he woke with a start as he heard Tom shout, "Look out here lads, look at the birds in the sky". The rest of the men rushed out and with blinking eyes, looked up into the early evening sky.

"Blimey, they're seagulls, they're bloody seagulls", whooped Percy with delight as the birds dipped and wheeled above him.

There it was - the sea. It was probably less than a mile away, foaming white in the twilight. Tom's face broke into a smile of relief. Some of the men cheered knowing they had nearly reached the sea, the good old English Channel. Now all they had to do was to find a boat.

On the horizon, the dying sun was already beginning to set in a blaze of burning red. It was so low in the darkening sky it appeared that drips of its molten core were falling into the sea like blobs of wax from a burning candle. Although it was pale and faint, Tom could see the thin outline of the moon rising from behind a belt of thickening cloud. The men, still weary as they were, quickened their pace as they left the shelter in the old quarry far behind them. First into a gentle trot and then they started to run, hopeful they would soon be on their way home and safe from the advancing German army.

Tom could begin to see huge sand dunes rising from the flat fields in front of them and the patches of the coarse sea grass which had sunk its roots deep into the windblown sand. He quickly looked to his left and then to the right. There were towering dunes as far as his eyes could see. Some of the men were already running through the gullies which had been cut through the dunes, no doubt by countless children and their trailing parents, all anxious to find the quickest route to the sea. Once, perhaps not long ago, the dunes had echoed with the sound of laughing children. Now all that could be heard were the plaintive cries of the seagulls wheeling in the brooding sky overhead and the sound of the sea as it crashed rhythmically on the yellow sand of the beach.

Chopper had been one of the first men to find his way through the labyrinth of gullies and Tom could see he was now heading back towards him and could tell by the expression on his friend's face, something was wrong.

"Nothing there", Chopper was shaking his head despondently. "No boats. No houses.... fuck all but miles of fucking sand".

Without saying a word, Tom pushed past Chopper and ran towards the beach. Although there was a stiff breeze blowing in from the sea, he could feel the sweat running down in beads from under his steel helmet and stinging his face. As he wiped it away with the back of his hand the searing pain in his arm returned. There it was, just as Chopper had said. The beach, just miles of sand for as far as he could see, but nothing else, no boats...nothing. He swore in loud and desperate tones. Suddenly fear gripped him like invisible chains. Had they reached this far only to be captured or worse still, to be killed by the Germans. He looked around him and could see the same fear in some of the other men's eyes. Tom sank to his knees and knelt on the soft, wet sand. He could feel the salty moisture seeping through the thick wool serge of his khaki trousers.

"It's no bloody good kneeling there saying your prayers. What the fuck are we going to do?", Chopper said acidly.

Tom looked up at Chopper and despite the situation they found themselves in, he managed a weak smile at his friend but deep down, there was a feeling of panic beginning to rise from the depths of his stomach. He knew the chances of escape were dwindling fast. Christ, he thought, what shall we do now?

The *Haupsturmfuhrer* cursed obscenities when the order came through. All tank commanders were to cease moving forward when they reached the defensive canal close to Dunkirk. "Stop before we reach Dunkirk", he fumed, "we should be driving into Dunkirk and pushing the retreating British and French forces into the sea".

He knew the *Panzer* spearhead had moved so fast it had now advanced too far in front of the German infantry which had already defeated the inferior armies of Poland, Holland and Belgium. All that was left now was to mop up the sorry remnants of the British and French forces cowering on the beaches of Dunkirk and then he would be home for Christmas. Ernst Albers heart briefly lifted when he thought once again of being in his beloved Bavaria at Christmas. He knew that hundreds of thousands of enemy forces were trapped at Dunkirk. He smiled at the thought of the thirteen British Infantry Divisions which were now caught between his own forces and the sea. He smiled that the Tommies had already abandoned most of their equipment in their rush to flee from his victorious army. The smile spread further across Ernst's face as he recounted in his mind the speed and success of his comrades in arms. The town of Dunkirk had been reduced to rubble and many ships of the British Royal Navy lay sunk in the harbour. His face suddenly grimaced as he said quietly to himself, "All this and I am ordered to stop before I can see the Tommies surrender".

The *Panzerkommandeur* composed himself as he prepared to speak to his crew. *"Achtung, achtung",* he shouted into his throat microphone and felt the pace of the tank gradually slowing as the driver listened to his commander's voice. "I have received orders that we are to stop at the canal before we reached the town of Dunkirk", Ernst Albers spoke in measured tones. He paused expecting a reaction from his tank crew. They are no fools he thought, they will see the stupidity of the order as well as I can.

"Stop *Haupsturmfuhrer!*". It was the exasperated voice of the driver, incredulous at what he had just heard.

"We stop when we reach the canal", repeated Albers calmly but firmly. "We have exceeded all expectations. We have moved quickly and now our *Panzers* need refuelling and servicing before we commence our next blitzkrieg through France".

Ernst Albers hoped his crew would be reassured by the logic of what he had said.

"But sir", it was the driver's voice again. "With our superior tank numbers we could surround the British at Dunkirk and hammer them until we force them to surrender. They would be humiliated. It would mean the end of the war".

Albers knew the man was right but he spoke calmly with a growing measure of assertiveness in his voice. *"Reichmarschell* Goring believes his aircraft are more than capable of destroying the enemy which are now trapped on the beaches, without placing our infantry at any unnecessary risk". Albers was not the only one who knew Goring wanted the personal glory of being the one whose strategy defeated the British army and that it was not a prize he intended to be shared amongst others. Albers hoped that his voice had not betrayed his dislike of Goring whom he considered to be a vain and self glorifying man.

"Sir", it was the driver's voice again.

Albers had heard enough, *"Stopp",* he commanded. It was now time to show his authority. "As I am speaking to you now, our *Junkers 87* dive bombers are pounding the beaches of Dunkirk. We will now be able to stop and rest for a few hours and let our infantry catch up before we move on. *"Heil Hitler"* but there was no mistaking of the sound of impatience in his voice.

There was a click as *Haupsturmfuhrer* Albers turned off the microphone attached to his chest.

"Fuck it", he cursed silently to himself.

Arthur and Taff were sitting on the wet sand with their heads resting on their knees, whilst Percy and Dusty were looking at Tom and Chopper, anxiously waiting for one of them to say what they would do now.

It was Tom's voice who broke the silence. "We'll wait here for a couple of hours until it gets completely dark. The dunes will give as some cover and then we'll make our way down the coast towards Dunkirk and somehow try to get over from there". He looked at the concern on Chopper's face. Chopper didn't say anything. Instead he turned his head and gestured towards the destruction which was clearly happening at Tom's intended destination just to make the point.

"I know it's not looking good but it's going to be the best chance we've got now", said Tom, desperately hoping his voice would not betray the despair he was feeling. "We'll set off when we've had some sleep", he said wearily, as he lay down on the soft, fine sand of the dunes and rested his head on the cold steel of his helmet.

The strain of the past few days was etched on Tom's blackened face. His tired, half-closed eyes had not yet surrendered to sleep whilst his restless body twisted and turned in the tussocks of goose grass and the clumps of pink sea thrift he had chosen for his bed. Despite the relentless noise of the constant shelling and bombing in the distance and the fear that the German infantry would appear at any moment, Tom had at last drifted into a deep, exhaustion induced sleep. His breathing was coming in short bursts and his tunic clad chest rose and fell as if it was in time with the foam topped waves of the restless sea.

Percy and his gun crew were sitting together sharing the last remaining packet of Wills Woodbines. The men were not in the mood for idle chit chat and just sat there, in the relative safety of the dunes, watching the thin wisps of their cigarette smoke curl their way into the evening sky, the red tips of the cigarettes glowing in the gloom. The small group were already feeling a sense of hopelessness.

Tom was half asleep, when, in his sub-conscious he could hear Chopper's voice shouting at him. They were in a strange dark, damp place and Chopper was saying. "Hey, over here, over here". Tom was trying to find him in the darkness and looked in vain to find his old friend but search as he did, he could not find him. "Hey, hey", Chopper was still calling.

"HEY... HEY...... HEY".

Tom was suddenly jolted from his sleep by the sound of Chopper's voice. A feeling of panic rose from his stomach and he started fighting for breath. A cold fear was surging through every nerve in his body and his lungs were demanding oxygen, the way they did when he was young and was woken with a start by a childish nightmare. Breathing hard, he forced himself to sit up and instantly jumped unsteadily to his feet.

"WHAT IS IT?" he shouted to Chopper, who he could see through his rapidly blinking eyes, was standing in the thin, white waves that were washing on the shore.

"It's a boat...it's a bloody boat.....hey.... HEY... OVER HERE".

Tom ran down to the water's edge. He rubbed his eyes, still blurred from sleep, but it didn't matter how much he strained them, all he could see were the white caps of the waves on the incoming tide. Eventually, he turned to Chopper and said dismissively, "There's nothing out there", his irritation showing.

The two men stared angrily at each other, with no give in either of them. There was a thick silence in the air as their anger boiled over and for a moment their friendship had been forgotten.

"IT **IS** A BOAT", Chopper started shouting at Tom in frustration, "LOOK, look. Look further out, it's a bloody boat".

Tom's eyes strained in desperation of seeing the boat, until in the fading light, he thought he could just make out a dark shape which could have been a boat.

"I think I saw it", he said with a discernible lack of conviction in his voice. "Have they seen us?" he tentatively asked Chopper, who was now frantically waving his tin hat in the direction where he thought he had seen their ticket to freedom.

Some of the men were standing in the sea with their eyes focused on what could have been their last hope of salvation. Further out and unaware the waves washing over his waist, Tom stood silently in the cold water.

Small, white crested waves were forming further out to sea before building up speed and strength and then rushing in, scattering small pebbles in front of them as they crashed onto the shore. Tom turned back and watched the waves pounding the small, helpless pebbles and thought how similar it was to their own position.

"Where...where is it?" Arthur demanded, as he and the rest of the men anxiously scanned their eyes seaward, each desperately hoping to see the elusive boat.

Tom turned back, all he could see were the lengthening shadows cast by the rising moon dancing their final dance of the day on the rapidly blackening sea.

"There's no bloody boat out there", Arthur said acidly, as he shrugged his shoulders and returned to sit with Taff, who had already given up and was crouched in the shelter of the sand dunes.

Tom watched the men with concern. They were soaked to the skin and shivering with the cold. Their heads were bowed and they kicked the sand in frustration. He knew they were on the verge of giving up, like the players of a football team who were losing twelve nil. He turned and looked questionably at Chopper. Chopper's eyes were still wide open with battle shock and once again they blazed with anger.

"There WAS something out there", he raged and then with a hint of doubt in his voice, he said despairingly, "I'm sure it was a bloody boat".

Their eyes met and neither man spoke. Each was hoping against hope it was a boat Chopper had seen but Tom doubted it and the sight of the despondent men sitting in the dunes made up his mind.

"COME ON", he retorted, "get your things together, we'll make our way further down the coast and find a boat there".

Percy Gorringe was already on his feet as Tom looked towards Chopper, who was still standing staring out to sea. Christ, Tom thought, there's nothing there. "Come on mate, let's get going before the bloody Jerries arrive", he shouted out in frustration.

An overwhelming sense of self doubt began to play on Chopper's mind whether he had actually seen anything at all, as he stood alone now, almost shoulder-deep in the freezing cold sea. Already the moon had broken through the clouds and he knew that with the light fading fast, the chances of seeing anything out at sea were now extremely slim. The wind-driven spray was hitting his face as he narrowed his eyes against the remaining patches of light which were shimmering on the sea and surveyed the horizon in one last desperate attempt to see the elusive boat. Minutes passed, when caught in the moonlight, he saw the shape again.

"IT IS A BOAT, HEY! HEY! OVER HERE". "TOM, I'VE SEEN IT, THERE IS A BOAT OUT THERE", Chopper was screaming and waving his arms frantically in the air. "It's turning, it's turning.....they've seen us...they've bloody seen us".

Tom and the others turned and raced back along the beach to where Chopper was standing and through weary eyes being strained to their limits, they realised it was a boat they could see. It was no more than five hundred yards from the shore and slowly but surely, it was turning and heading towards them. In the stiff breeze blowing from the sea, Tom could see the boat rising and falling with the rhythm of the waves.

"It's a fishing smack", he exclaimed, as if he was in a state of shock at actually seeing it, "it's a two-masted fishing smack". The reassuring *chug...chug* of a Gardner diesel engine could now be clearly heard despite the noise of the relentless waves crashing on the shore.

"Come on lads, we haven't got all day to sit out here". It was the sound of a welcoming English voice they could hear over the noise of the wind and the waves, "if Jerry comes over now, we'll all be bloody goners".

The men didn't need telling twice and with a cheer, they held their rifles over their heads and with Arthur leading the way, they stumbled and staggered deeper into the cold sea. The relentless tide washed away the sand from under their water-filled boots as the elated soldiers waded through the wild sea towards the fishing smack and freedom.

"It's not very big", Chopper observed as he got closer to the thirty-foot long boat bobbing up and down on the swell. Tom moved up alongside Chopper to get a closer look at it and despite the waves thrashing against the weathered, over-lapping oak planks which ran along its length, he could clearly read the name painted on its bow.

"The Brown Duck". As Tom said the name, a broad smile spread across his face and his olive green eyes looked brighter than they had looked for many hours.

A ruddy brown sail flapped against the smack's mizzen mast whilst another one of similar colour was rolled up waiting to be hoisted from its main mast. Tom and Chopper reached the rest of the men who were standing almost neck deep in the water, waiting patiently to be hauled onto the rolling deck by the two man crew. Tom noticed that the older of the men appeared to be the captain. He was about sixty, with a shock of white hair and was chewing a pipe, clamped between his discoloured teeth. Despite the gloom of the descending night, Tom could see nicotine stains running down the man's thick white beard and guessed the pipe had probably been more or less a permanent fixture in the man's mouth for most of his adult years. Despite the stiff breeze blowing, the boat's skipper was only wearing a thick navy blue jersey, its sleeves pulled high up his muscled arms. The other man was younger, perhaps thirty or forty at the most and like the older man, his face was as ruddy as the sails on the boat, a complexion which had been fashioned by years of searching the sea for its rich harvest.

"Come on lad", the older man said, in a calm and friendly voice.

Both men had a twinkle in their eyes and a smile on their faces as they hauled Chopper over the edge of the boat, no doubt imagining the bedraggled man was like a net full of the silver herrings they would be catching in a few months time, before letting him fall onto the pine planking of the deck in a like-wise fashion.

The fishermen reached down for Tom but he hesitated and looked back towards the shore. Had they really escaped from the Germans.... where were the Germans? he thought as he took one last look at the towering sand dunes to check nobody had been left behind. It was then the remorse hit him again. No, nobody was left behind, that was apart from Len and the other thirty-one men whose remains were probably still lying amongst the burnt out wreckage of their trucks and guns.

The moon was rising high in the inky sky as Tom turned away from the land that had once again become the graveyard for so many brave men, and although he didn't think about it at the time, it was somewhere, deep within the rich, dark soil of this foreign country, his own dear father was buried.

"Come on lad, don't dawdle, I told my missus I wouldn't be back late and she is going to do something special for my supper tonight", the white haired captain said seriously.

"That'll be fish then", his mate replied, before the two of them roared with laughter.

Tom smiled at the weak joke and suspected it was not the first time the men had told it but nevertheless and despite the tiredness which was beginning to overwhelm him, he marvelled at these two brave men. Men of iron in a wooden boat, he thought as their strong horny hands plucked him from the sea and dropped him in a similar fashion to the rest of the men into the bottom of the boat. Tom groaned as his injured arm hit one of the ribs of the heavy frame of the boat. He lay there with Chopper at his side, amongst the foul smelling fishing nets and rusty trawling heads. It was then he heard the diesel engine in the stern burst into life and the noise of the main sail being hoisted beside them.

"So far so good", Tom heard Chopper say, but before he could answer, he heard the mate calling them.

"Come on lads, we ain't got much left but come down into the galley and get some grub....bit tight for space down there…. mind how you go, there's a bit of a swell running".

Tom turned his head and saw the man disappearing through an open hatch at the bow of the smack and down a metal ladder. Tom had not accounted for the rolling of the boat as he started to raise his aching body from the deck he fell back knocking, Chopper down like a ball hitting a pub skittle.

"Sorry mate", Tom said apologetically to his fallen friend.

"Bit of a swell running, this bloody thing is bobbing about like a cork in a piss pot", Chopper murmured, as he attempted to get to his feet for the second time.

Tom grasped the side of the boat and looked towards the rapidly disappearing shore which was now almost swallowed up in the darkness of the night. Raising his eyes up into the clear night sky, he quietly said, "Thank God".

The sky was clear apart from a sprinkling of early stars and even the relentless sound of the German bombers seemed far away. He looked back towards the wheelhouse and through the small window coated in sea spray, he could make out the bearded face of the skipper, sucking contentedly on his briar pipe.

"Come on, mate", Chopper said, as he noticed the sense of relief which was clearly showing on Tom's face. "We're on our way home, let's get some food".

Slowly, the pair of them, each trying to support the other, made their way along the slippery deck to the galley hatch and climbed down the ladder into the small space below. The galley smelt of hot oil and in the flickering light of a hurricane lamp which was swinging on a hook banged into the underside of the deck, Tom saw Percy and Arthur sitting on a small bunk bed drinking from chipped, white enamel mugs.

"Come on, lads, squeeze yourselves in and I'll get you some tea", the mate said cheerfully, as he made his way to a large teapot perched precariously on a small pot-bellied stove in the corner. "Sorry, no milk", he said apologetically, "it ran out yesterday", as Chopper peered ungratefully into the mug of steaming black liquid.

"The bread's a bit stale too", the mate said, as he hacked off four door-step sized slices and began to spread them thickly with butter, before filling them with equally thick, rectangular slices of corned beef. "You're lucky buggers, we've been at Dunkirk for two days, picking men up from the beach and ferrying them back to the ships in the deeper water, it's bloody carnage........never seen anything like it, bloody Nazis". The man handed Tom and Chopper the sandwiches he had just made, "Anyway", he continued, "we couldn't do anymore, so the skipper said he'd sail up the coast for a bit before heading for home. Just in case there were any more poor buggers waiting to get off and there you were, hollering your bloody heads off".

Tom bit into the sandwich and found a place to sit on the floor amongst the rest of the men.

He watched as the mate made another sandwich with the remains of the bread and corned beef and marvelled at the bravery of the two fishermen. Not once had they mentioned the dangers they had faced and even when they could do no more at Dunkirk, rather than heading for home as quickly as they could, they had chosen to sail along the coast and risk the murderous Stukas once again.

"There's more tea in the pot lads, if you want some", the red faced mate said cheerfully, as he started to carry, with practised ease, a mug of tea and the sandwich up the ladder to the skipper in the wheelhouse. "He'll be keeping his eyes peeled for mines, there's more of them floating out there than there is 'errings in the sea", he said earnestly. "A cockle boat hit one, week before last, just off Dover and went down taking everyone with her".

Tom winced at hearing the grim warning and shuddered at the thought of being trapped in a sinking ship. It was his worst nightmare and he immediately decided to follow the mate up onto the deck and into the fresh air.

The galley was too small and cramped for his liking, he needed space and to feel the cool night breeze on his face. He looked back at the rest of the men and it came as a great relief to him when he saw, to a man, they were all in the land of nod. The only sounds Tom heard as he poked his head through the open hatch were those of the waves hitting the ship-lapped planks of the smack's hull and the now familiar chugging of its diesel engine. It felt as peaceful as heaven. Tom sat down on the wet deck and leant back against the ribs of the hull and after pulling some netting over him, he shut his eyes and he to, fell asleep.

It may have been the scream of the seagulls overhead or the change in the vibrations reverberating through the smacks' timbers as its gardener engine slowed down or it could have been the main sail had stopped flapping as the mate hauled it down. Whatever it was, it woke Tom who had been dozing wearily, trussed up in the bottom of the boat amongst the fishing nets and the dead crabs and starfish, trapped in the tangled mesh.

Tom slowly raised his head from his hard, make-shift pillow and looked back at the puffs of black smoke rising from the exhaust pipe which had rattled loose from its iron fixing bolts and was on the point of falling off completely. He sat up and slowly rotated his head from side to side in an attempt to bring some life back into the muscles at the base of his aching neck. Pain raced through every bone in Tom's body as he stood up and stretched his arms and legs with a satisfied groan, before cautiously making his way along the gently rolling deck to the small wheelhouse at the boat's stern.

"Where are we?" Tom asked the skipper, who had just climbed the ladder out of the engine room and up into the wheelhouse.

Wiping his hands on an oily rag, he took control of the wheel from the mate and then said with a satisfied smile on his face, "Ramsgate, lad.......the royal harbour of Ramsgate, courtesy of good old King George the fourth".

Tom didn't notice the way the old fisherman had emphasised the word *royal* and instead just repeated with evident astonishment, *"Ramsgate"*.

His eyes were staring at the welcoming white chalk cliffs in the distance when he heard Chopper's voice behind him, saying with obvious relief, "We made it mate, we bloody well made it".

The two men moved to the side of the smack and looked across the harbour where boats of every shape and size were bobbing up and down on the incoming tide. Moonbeams were dancing on the roofs of the Victorian houses which were crowded round the small harbour of this Kentish town. The fishing smack chugged past the subdued green light at the end of the concrete harbour arm and weaved its way through the lines of boats tugging impatiently at their rusty anchor chains.

"Most of them were at Dunkirk". Tom recognised the voice of the mate behind him. "The lifeboat and that big old girl over there, the Sundowner", Tom peered through the darkness to look in the direction where the mate was pointing, "they've saved 'undreds, they have", he said in a matter of fact way.

Through the dark night sky, Tom could make out a line of men who were crowded on the quayside, "Look at that lot over there", he said to Chopper. He motioned towards the silhouetted figures which were making their way towards a small church framed against a towering red brick wall curving in a sweep round the waterfront.

"Mind your backs lads", the mate shouted, as he rushed across the deck to sling the rope ball fenders over the side of the smack in preparation for mooring.

As the boat edged closer to the quayside, Tom could see the line of dishevelled men, who like him, were in full army battledress. The mate had started coiling the mooring ropes which had been lying in a tangled heap on the deck.

"It looks as if that lot by the Fishermans Church beat us to it", he said laughingly, "probably the lifeboat brought them back, either that or it was one of the other smacks".

The skipper was leaning out of the wheelhouse with his pipe clamped in his mouth as he brought the boat alongside the seaweed encrusted wall with a practised ease. Tom watched as the mate threaded the mooring ropes through the heavy rusty rings hanging from the sea wall and made the boat fast.

"Well mate", said Chopper, grinning like a Cheshire cat, "home sweet home" and then, as an after-thought, he added, "maybe we'll get some leave when we get back and unwrap some of those girls in the toffee factory again.

Tom didn't say anything and smiled, remembering what an opportunist his friend was when it came to women. As for him, he was just pleased to be back and thought a bath would be the best idea.

One by one, the men, supported by the strong arm of the mate and with one foot on the side of the gently rocking boat, they stepped onto the safety of the quayside. Tom was the last to disembark and as he passed the wheelhouse, he paused to thank the man whose bravery had saved them from a certain death. Neither man said a word as they stood facing each other. Perhaps it was the bravery they saw in each other's eyes, why they knew that words were unnecessary.

Tom put his hand on the skipper's shoulder and the old man grinned in acknowledgement and said with a wink of his eye, "Time to see if the missus has cooked some fish for my supper".

Tom smiled back and said simply, "You saved our lives" and then, before stepping off the smack and onto English soil again, he took the mate's outstretched hand and shook it with heart -felt gratitude.

Chopper's familiar smile had returned as he pointed at the name on the front of the derelict red brick building next to the little fisherman's church. Tom looked up at the time weathered letters which carved into a stone slab by the Victorian builders, "The School for Smack Boys", he read out loudly.

"Shame it's closed", Chopper replied, "It would have been better than being in the bloody army".

Tom turned when he heard the familiar sound of heavy army boots approaching. "Take the weight of your feet lads while I sort that lot out over there", barked a smartly dressed NCO, his eyes obscured by the polished peak of his cap. "I'll come back for you later".

Percy and the rest of the soaking wet men squelched their way along the quay and sat down by some fisherman's sheds built into curved brick arches which bordered the stone quayside. Within minutes they were eagerly taking the sandwiches and quaffing the mugs of tea being offered by two portly Red Cross women. Tom could smell the fishing nets hanging high in the lofts above them and thought they could have found a better place than this to have some grub.

"Would you like a cup of tea, my dear?" enquired one of the ladies. Tom shook his head as he sat down and leant against the damp brick wall. "Or a sandwich or a postcard to write a message back home. I can get you a meat pie if you would like one", the kindly woman pressed on.

"A postcard please", Tom replied quickly, "and a pencil if you have one". Tom watched as the woman searched in a large black bag that was on the bottom shelf of the tea trolley.

"Ah, here they are", she said triumphantly as she handed Tom one of the white cards.

He took it gratefully and noticed it had already been stamped.

As he started writing, *Mrs E Kealey, Lavender Cottage, White Horse Lane, Pentbury, Kent*, he noticed for the first time since they had encountered the Panzers how dirty and bloody his hands were. Holding the card by it's edges, he turned it over and wrote,

Dear Mother, I hope you are well. I am safe and back in England. I will see you when I get my next leave. Your loving son, Tom

"I'll post it for you dear", said the woman, who Tom noticed had been hovering over him as he had been writing and as she took the card from him she adjusted her spectacles and without a hint of embarrassment, began to read what he had written. "Your mother will be so pleased to get this", she said warmly, "my youngest son is over there......I haven't heard from him...." Her voice trailed away as she took off her glasses to wipe an escaping tear from her eye, "Now dear, have a cup of tea and a sandwich", she said, as she regained her composure, "you'll never know when you'll get the next one". Tom took the cup and the sandwich gratefully and looking up at the kind woman he felt sorry for her and said softly, "I'm sure your son will be alright, things are in such a mess over there, it will take weeks to sort things out".

"Thank you my dear", said the lady with the large black bag, "it's comforting to hear that".

It was some hours later and the morning sun was beginning to break through the thick sea mist when Tom and Chopper, together with Percy, Taff, Arthur and Dusty, fell in behind a column of similarly bedraggled soldiers and marched to the town's station and boarded the troop train which would take them back to the Aldershot Command camp in Hampshire.

6

Flying Fish and Silver Pennies

The little town of Thompson nestling amongst the pine covered hills and the volcanic mountains of northern Arizona had become civilised. The rowdy saloons which, thirty or forty years previously would have been full of cowboys, prospectors and loggers, had been tamed and were no longer the havens of vice they once had been. Of course, cowboys still drove their herds of longhorn cattle down the main street which in fact was the only street in the town, to the stockyards at the back of the railroad station. There, the bellowing steers would be loaded on the Sante Fé train for the long journey north to the slaughter houses. The lumberjacks and loggers still frequented one of the four saloons which remained in Thompson and played poker and drank with the men from the huge sawmill which was located just outside of the town's limits. Respectable people had also come in growing numbers to the town, where they would take a buckboard ride to see the sight of the Grand Canyon less than one hour's bumpy ride away.

Skip Krisner had lived here since he was born, eighteen years previously and as he sat in his father's rocking chair on the porch of the family's white painted, boarded house, he was thinking how much he would miss the little town. Although the sun was setting behind the mountains and in the distance Skip could see the silhouettes of the towering saguaro cactus looking like giant fingers pointing upwards in the reddening sky, it was still hot and Skip was grateful of the cool shade of the porch. He knew he would miss walking through the miles of trials which criss-crossed the pine forests, fishing in the lakes and watching the wild mustangs and elk which roamed across the cattle ranches to the east of the town. Most of all, he would miss his parents and he knew they would miss him, their only child. He closed his eyes as doubt began to enter his head. Everything a young man could want was here in Thompson. He suddenly realised how lucky he was to live here but his mind was made up. Tomorrow he would board the train to Phoenix and to the college where he would study to become a doctor.

Skip pushed back the tousle of blonde hair which had fallen across his eyes and continued with the memories of his young life in Thompson. The chair was rocking gently as he finally resolved that once he was qualified he would return to the place he loved and set up a medical practice there.

"I'll tell you one thing", Chopper said earnestly, "Scotland can't be as bad as having to be stuck in a damp, cold hole like this for six bloody months".

Tom smiled. Chopper had been complaining ever since they had returned from France and had been stationed in the gun emplacement which was part of the coastal defences that had hastily been erected around the country to repel the expected Nazi invasion.

"One of the men in the Home Guard was telling me the other day, this bloody thing and all the other pill boxes that are dotted around the coast, are part of what they are calling *Operation Sealion*", Chopper said, as he started swinging his arms round in circular motions to free up his stiffened joints. "If I had to stay here much longer, I'd begin to look like a bloody sea lion", he said with a smile returning to his face.

Tom didn't reply and walked across the concrete emplacement to look out of the rectangular gun slot towards the sea. Either side of the emplacement, he could see smaller circular concrete pill boxes which commanded a good field of fire across the narrow inlet for the machine gun nests they housed. The inlet had been formed over many centuries by the meandering river cutting its way through the towering white cliffs of the South Downs, provided the enemy with an ideal place to land huge numbers of their forces should their invasion of England take place. The gun emplacement which Tom and Chopper, together with Percy, Arthur and Taff had called home for nearly a year was large enough to house their anti-tank gun. The massive concrete bunker had been dug into the gorse covered hillside and half hidden in thick undergrowth was about twenty feet square, with shell proof walls which were nearly four feet thick. The two-pounder gun had been manoeuvred into the flat roofed structure through a large entrance at the rear with its barrel protruding through a wide, narrow aperture overlooking the inlet, enabling the men to traverse the gun through sixty degrees. As Tom looked out towards the sea he could see the lines of the so-called dragon's teeth and anti-tank ditches positioned in such a way to direct any armoured vehicles into the direct line of his anti-tank gun. In the event of an invasion, Tom's orders had been clear and simple. If Jerry arrived, they were to be given a bloody nose and to delay them for long enough to enable mobile infantry to build up and form a stop line behind him.

"What are you looking at Tom?" Chopper shouted, as he continued to exercise his shoulder joints. "Is Jerry on his way?" he joked.

Tom stood and watched some large, black winged seagulls wheeling high up in the wide expanse of grey sky in front of him, realising, that unlike Chopper, he would miss the peace and solitude of the concrete bunker. He knew the threat of any German invasion had passed and the 85th Anti-Tank regiment was being deployed to Scotland for further training before being posted overseas, presumably for more combat duties.

The train was already waiting forlornly on the tracks of the granite-block station which was looking particularly drab in the Scottish winter's drizzle, when the troops marched in.

Smiling, Tom turned to Chopper and said, "I've reserved two seats in first class for us".

The words had hardly left Tom's lips as the two men were swept aboard the train by the sheer force of the dozens of men behind them, everyone of them desperate to grab a seat.

"Never mind", Chopper quipped back, "we'll try and get a table in the restaurant car".

 The carriages stank of an odour, not unlike that of a wet dog, as they became crammed full of men in their damp, worsted uniforms.

Although the order had been given not to open the windows, the men who were either sitting or standing by them, wiped away the condensation which had already formed on the glass, in the hope they would see where they were being taken. Tom noticed that as soon as the men wiped the wet mist away with the palms of their hands, it formed again within minutes, as the warm air in the carriages came into contact with the cold glass, chilled by the cold November air.

The pair of men were squeezing and pushing their way up the train's corridor in the forlorn hope of finding somewhere to sit down when they saw a soldier leaving a carriage, presumably to find the lavatory.

"There may be seat in there", Tom said quickly.

"That will do", replied Chopper, as they barged their way into a carriage, beating off the challenge from two other men who had the same idea. Chopper seized the vacant seat eagerly by stamping his boot on it and before sitting down, he rammed his kit bag and helmet into a space which remained on the woven string luggage rack above the seats.

Tom, who was standing in front of Chopper, suddenly had to grasp the front rail of the rack to keep his balance when the train lurched forward as it started on its way to the unknown destination. Tom casually looked around the gently rocking carriage, as the train gradually picked up speed with every shovel of coal the fireman heaved into the flames roaring in the engine's firebox. Opposite Chopper was a short chap wedged between four other men, all of whom were considerably larger than him and as a result he was being squeezed like a woollen sock going through a mangle. Tom looked at the badges on the berets of the larger men and saw they were wearing the "Christmas tree" cap badge of the Reconnaissance Corps, whilst the round cap badge on the small chap showed he was in the Northumberland Fusiliers.

The Recce Corps, as the Reconnaissance regiment was known, was an elite unit in the army whose job it was to provide the mobile spearhead of the infantry. Tom knew these boys would be required to probe ahead of the main advance to gather any tactical information they could pick up. He guessed the men would form the crew of a scout car, armed only with a single Bren gun mounted on its bonnet. It was a dangerous job and every man in the unit was hand-picked and it was this, as Chopper eloquently put it some days later, which made them "a cocky load of bleeders".

The Recce men had obviously been having some fun at the expense of the little chap who they had named, Bantam, no doubt due his short stature.

"Shouldn't your mum be with you?" one of them laughed.

The Bantam said nothing and carried on reading his newspaper.

"Did you bring your colouring book and crayons?" another one asked, sarcastically.

"He'd only go over the lines", interrupted the one who was sitting close to where Tom was standing.

"You should have joined the Boy Scouts" said the fourth man, "not the bloody army".

Tom and Chopper grinned at each other as they enjoyed the banter.

"If you need to go to the little boy's room, let me know and I'll lift you up onto the seat", said the one who had started things off.

By now, all four of the Recce men were laughing their heads off at the little man's expense.

Putting his newspaper down, Bantam turned round to face the man on his right before saying almost absentmindedly, in a broad Geordie accent, "I've been reading in here your lot have been involved in some action behind enemy lines in France".

All four of the "Recce" men stopped laughing and were obviously anxious to hear more, as were the other occupants in the carriage.

Bantam picked up his newspaper and pretending to read from it, said, "The headline is, *Only the enemy in front*".

"That's our motto" said one of the soldiers. Tom could detect that there was a hint of pride in the man's voice.

"A unit of the Reconnaissance Corp comprising of one officer and twelve men, whilst operating behind enemy lines, came up against."... Bantam paused for effect.

"Get on with it", said one of the Recces, impatient to hear the news of the outcome.

"Came up against", Bantam repeated, as he continued reading the paper but now in a more serious tone. ..*"They came up against an elderly German soldier who was pushing a bicycle. After a quick briefing, the units' officer decided to attack the German on all fronts".*

Bantam paused briefly before continuing to read. *"After a fierce fight lasting two hours the unit reported that three of its men had been injured but it had managed to capture the front wheel of the German soldier's bicycle together with its saddle. It is thought that the battle is continuing in an attempt to capture the elderly German but we have been warned not to expect good news coming from the Reconnaissance Corps".*

Chopper and Tom burst out laughing.

"Well done Bantam", Chopper said to the little man who was sitting opposite him.

Tom looked down at the Recce's and saw they were all smiling. They had been outflanked by the short fusilier whose regiment's motto was *the old and the bold*. "After all lads", he would tell them many times later, "it was my lot that guarded the Duke of Wellington at Waterloo".

Bantam later told Tom and Chopper his name was Joe Kettlewell and he was in the 9th Machine Gun Battalion of the "Royals". Tom liked the little Geordie immediately and learnt that most of his regiment had departed some weeks earlier but as they were all part of the 85th Division, Bantam assumed they would all meet up again, whenever and wherever that was to be.

Eventually, the rhythm of the train changed. At first Tom thought it may be going up an incline, knowing with the hundreds of men onboard even a gradual slope would slow it down. He raised his head and listened. The puffs of steam being pushed out of the train's smoke-blackened stack were becoming louder and slower. Then, Tom heard the unmistakeable squeal of brakes being applied.

"This is it", he said, "It looks like we're arriving at the transit station".

Throughout the train men started moving. Those who had been fortunate enough to find somewhere to sleep started to wake up when somebody who was close to a window in the corridor, shouted, "Pierhead Station, lads, Greenock".

"Thank Christ for that" blasphemed Chopper, as he jumped down from the carriage and, as was his habit, started stretching every limb in his aching body.

The station platform was quickly packed with ranks of rifle carrying soldiers who were being lined up, prior to marching to the docks. Sergeants, with their voices raised above the general din and hubbub, were shouting orders thirteen to the dozen. The last of the men to leave the train were picking up their kit-bags and rifles and racing up the platform, looking frantically to find their units. Within minutes, the station seemed to be a seething mass of khaki uniforms and steel helmets, as hundreds of soldiers organised themselves into their units.

Tom and Chopper, together with the other gunners, joined the lines of troops marching out of the station when Tom heard a familiar sound. "Hear that", he said to Chopper who was alongside him, "Seagulls............it looks as if we're going on a boat ride again".

"If we are, I just hope there's more space on the bloody thing than the last tub we were on. If not, I'm not staying, I'll get off and will bloody well walk", Chopper moaned with humour in his voice.

Tom smiled and knew, that like him, Chopper was remembering how they had laid amongst the fishing nets on the deck of the Brown Duck as it bobbed about in the English Channel , wondering if they would ever see home again.

"Have yee got any sweeties, mister?"

Tom looked down and smiled at the scruffy looking children who were running alongside the marching troops, begging sweets in their broad Glaswegian accents.

"Or chocolate", a boy with a mop of ginger hair asked hopefully. Tom shook his head and put his hand into his pocket and pulled out a couple of coppers. "Thanks mister", the boy shouted, when Tom dropped them into his grubby outstretched hand, before the lad ran off to try his luck elsewhere.

"Look over there", Chopper said, with a broad smile spreading over his face.

Tom could see a group of the soldiers laughing, as one in their midst was blowing up what appeared to be a large sausage balloon. Several of the children had weaved their way into the centre of the column and were clambering around the man with their hands held high, all anxious to claim the balloon.

"There you are laddie", said the grinning man, as he tied a knot in the largest sausage balloon the boy had ever seen in his young life. "Take that home and show your mother", the soldier said, as he handed the inflated French letter to the wide-eyed youngster, who couldn't believe his luck in being given such a prize.

"I live with my old granny", the innocent boy said, before he ran off from the group of laughing men.

Tom looked at the innocent boy's face and smiled as he recalled the face of a slightly older boy who worked at Bridge Works and who had suffered similar horse play. Tom had been waiting at the counter of the main stores for the newly recruited lad to finish finding the items on his requisition from the rows and rows of the tall wooden racks which held everything from humble nuts and bolts to larger and more complex engine components. One of the brown coated store-men, a portly chap called George Greenaway, on seeing the look of frustration on Tom's face whilst he waited for the hapless youngster to search the labyrinth of bins, walked up to him with a broad grin on his face.

"He's particularly wet behind the ears, is that one". George nodded his head towards the spotty youngster, as he explained, "Only been with us for a week".

The genial man was used to having to work with awkward looking adolescents as the company took on a number of school leavers each year and they all started their working lives in the stores until they were indentured into a trade, if, as they were reminded on a daily basis, they lasted that long!.

"I'll finish serving you, Tom, otherwise you'll be here all day", George said, as he sucked on his pipe and then winking his eye, he shouted to the boy, who was still walking up and down the rows of the racks with an even more vacant look on his gormless face, "Hey lad, do you know where the tobacconists shop is, the one on the corner of the bridge".

As the slow witted boy approached the two men, George said quietly to Tom, as he looked the boy up and down, "God preserve us, he doesn't have a bloody clue. It makes me feel sorry for his mother having a thing like that...... it's only a mother who could love it". Tom smiled, knowing that despite what George was saying about the youngster, he was a kind man who didn't have a bad bone in his body.

"Yes, Mr Greenery".

The lad stood in front of the two men. He had outgrown his jacket by at least two years and his skinny arms protruded from its frayed sleeves not unlike those on a scarecrow in a cornfield and on his face was a soppy, idiotic grin.

George exploded. "Mr Greenaway, not bloody Greenery, you stupid little sod".

Tom sensed with some justification that the store-keeper was becoming exacerbated with his nemesis.

"Go to the tobacconists on the corner of the bridge and get half an ounce of roadside mixture on my account and don't bloody come back without it, you bloody half wit". George rattled his instructions to the nervous youngster.

The boy looked vacantly at the store-man and repeated the instruction, "Half an ounce of roadside mixture".

The two men roared with laughter as they heard the boy repeating, "Half an ounce of roadside mixture, half an ounce of roadside mixture", as he walked away.

"Half an ounce of roadside mixture please", the lad said confidently to the tobacconist.

The man nodded his head, as he had done so many times before when he had been presented with the same request and said sharply, "Is that rolling you want or pipe?" He fought to keep a straight face as he saw a look of horror spread over the boy's face.

"He didn't say", the boy stuttered, as his confidence disappeared like summer rain on a hot pavement.

"You better go back and ask him".

Ten minutes had passed when the boy returned to the tobacconist but he didn't mention what he had been told by George Greenaway, "If you had opened your bloody eyes, you would've seen that I smoke a bloody pipe".

The returning youngster said to the grinning tobacconist, "Pipe, please".

"Did he say if he wanted blended?" the man casually enquired. He watched with growing amusement as he the look of horror returned to the lads face when he realised he would have to go back and face his tormentor once again.

The dim-witted lad returned to the shop after getting further instructions and said mournfully, "Blended pipe, please".

The tobacconist didn't reply and turned from the counter and started to look behind him at the paper labels on the rows of the glass jars which were full of every variety of tobacco imaginable. "Black Shag, Brown Shag", he started saying to himself. "Grand Sport, Prince Albert", he continued reading the labels, "Prince Albert's Cherry Vanilla, Burleys, Golden Virginia, Captain Blacks.....

"Sorry lad, everything but blended roadside. Right out of that at the moment", the tobacconist said flatly, trying desperately to hide his smile, "best try the shop at the top of the town, the one near the old cannon".

George had finished collecting the parts which had been on Tom's requisition and the two men stood laughing at the counter as the storeman recited what would be happening to the lad.

"Old Jim, who has the shop by the bridge, will tell him that he had run out of blended roadside and send him up to the shop by the cannon", George explained. "They will tell him the same story and by the time he has finished, he'll have been sent to every tobacconists shop in the town". George re-lit his pipe and said with a wicked grin, "The poor little sod will be shitting his pants when he eventually returns, empty bloody handed".

Hanging over the dark stormy ocean, the sky was heavy with a mantle of brooding clouds as the troops started arriving at the quayside.

Chopper turned to Tom and grinning, said chirpily "Organised chaos this is my old Tom, organised bloody chaos".

Tom didn't reply but sensing his friend's mood had lightened, he got the feeling Chopper was distinctly looking forward to whatever was ahead of them.

"Christ Almighty", Chopper exclaimed, when he saw the ship towering above the hundreds of men milling about on the quayside, "it's a big bugger. That's the biggest bloody boat I've ever seen", he continued, clearly amazed at the sight in front of them and giving the impression it was just one of many *boats* he'd seen in his lifetime

Although he didn't answer his friend, Tom was also thinking it was also the biggest ship he had ever seen and his head began to nod from side to side, as he began to count the long line of lifeboats, with their vivid red tarpaulin covers, hanging like toys from their hook shaped davits.

He next turned his attention to the rows and rows of the countless portholes which ran in lines along each of the decks of the enormous ship.

Clearly impressed with the proportions of the enormous ship in front of them, he said, like a breathless schoolboy, "It's got seven decks".

The three tall funnels were standing proudly in the centre of the top deck painted a dull battleship grey and Tom smiled, as he saw some bright yellow paint showing through the grey paint on one of the funnels. They missed a bit there, probably in a hurry, he thought.

Looking along the length of the ship, he read out the name which was proudly painted on its graceful, curving bow, "The Empress of Japan". "Look at that", he said to Chopper, "I thought we were at war with that lot".

"It's over six hundred and fifty feet long" said a bespectacled, soft-looking soldier, who was standing next to the two men and who had overheard their conversation. "I've been talking to a sailor and he told me", the soldier continued knowingly, "she's a twenty six thousand tonner and will be carrying two thousand of us, as well as all the cargo. Before the war she was a luxurious ocean-going liner, carrying wealthy passengers from Canada to Japan, that's how she got her name".

The man brimmed with enthusiasm and second-hand knowledge.

A depraved grin spread across Chopper's face as he nudged the man in the ribs and asked optimistically, "Any women on board?"

The humourless man ignored him and edged away slightly.

Tom noticed how uncomfortable the smart-arsed soldier had become with Chopper's remark and winking at his friend, said, "They don't need to be pretty, desperate men can't be too choosy. Can they?"

Once again he man ignored the laughing men and edging even further away he continued to watch the scene around him, clearly anxious not to miss anything he would be able to recount later.

"What does he know?" Tom said, smiling at the joke he was about to deliver, "he wouldn't know how long his cock is, even if it was in his hand".

"More like in some other bloke's hand, bloody nancy boy", Chopper countered.

Tom smiled at his friend's blunt assessment of the man.

The quay was a hive of activity and as they waited patiently in line for the order to embark, Tom could see lines of Royal Engineers were already walking up one of the gangways with their kit bags slung over one shoulder and their rifles hanging off the other. The jibs of the blue-painted dockside cranes were hoisting enormous wooden crates onto the deck of the cavernous ship, with lines of trucks and armoured vehicles all waiting until it was their turn to be slung and lifted up before being swung in a wide arc, onto the decks.

Tom turned to Chopper and said, "Look at that lot going up the first gangway".

Chopper looked at the different cap badges and recognised amongst the sea of heads were Northumberland Fusiliers, Hertfordshire Yeomanry, Norfolks, Suffolks, and men from the North Lancashires. All infantry, he thought.

The man with the wire rimmed glasses came alongside them again and Chopper asked him casually, "Do you know what's in the crates?"

"Hurricanes".The pan-faced man didn't disappoint and added, "There's about ten of them, apparently a number of RAF squadrons are coming with us".

"Do you know where we are going?" Chopper enquired speculatively but already he knew what the answer would be.

The font of all knowledge shook his head in obvious disappointment, "No idea. It's all under wraps, as usual".

Slowly, as the men moved forward with the rest of their unit, Tom turned to Chopper and said, as he beckoned out to sea, "Wherever we're off to, it's going to be a big one. Look at that lot out there".

The drizzle had stopped and through the descending grey mist the two men looked beyond the Empress and out to sea.

"Christ", Chopper said with evident amazement, "this is going to be one hell of a bloody convoy".

The two men stopped in their tracks and with their heads nodding up and down like shepherds counting their flocks, they tried to calculate the number of ships in front of them.

"I make it about twenty in all", said Chopper.

Tom nodded in agreement, "Yep", he said, "maybe more", not knowing what else to say.

"There's an aircraft carrier out there and some minesweepers". Tom recognised the voice. It was the owl-eyed soldier again. "Five or six destroyers and over a dozen transporters as big as this one", he said. "There must be over twenty-thousand men onboard these ships".

Orders were being barked out to keep moving forward as they passed the fourth of the wide gangways before being ordered by one of the embarkation officers to board the ship.

They were walking up the fifth gangway, when they heard a rather posh voice shout out, "I say chaps".

The men turned to see where the voice was coming from.

"Yes, you two fellows, when you get onboard, can you order me a double pink gin. I'll be in my cabin, first class of course". It was Bantam, standing on the quayside with a wide smile over his face.

There were cries of "All aboard the Daffodil", as the troops moved eight abreast up the gangway. As Tom and Chopper reached the top, an NCO threw a rolled-up hammock to each of them, saying, "Follow the man in front". At a brisk pace, they found themselves, along with some others from the 85th walking towards the stern of the ship. Like sheep, they followed the line of men in front of them, through double wooden doors, along a corridor and up a wide staircase. The men were running as they went along another corridor, through more doors and then up another staircase, until eventually they found themselves in a section of the ship which was to become their home for the duration of the voyage.

"I hope somebody's remembered the bloody way", one of their fellow gunners joked, "or else it will take us a fucking month to find our fucking way out".

"This must have been some boat before it was gutted", Chopper said, as he surveyed the huge space they found themselves in.

In front of them was a row of long mess tables which had been bolted to the floor. At the far end of the cavernous chamber was a small mess room with a row of racks, where already, kit and rifles was being stowed. Chopper looked at the emptiness around him. All the ships luxurious fixtures and fittings had been removed to turn, what had been a beautiful swan, into an ugly troop ship, fit to accommodate two thousand men and their weapons of war.

"Right lads". It was the authoritative voice of an NCO who had been standing near the kit racks, barking out his orders, as if he was on his parade ground back home. "Hang your hammocks either side of the line of mess tables and make sure they're taken down, rolled and stowed every morning". He started to march towards where Tom and Chopper were standing, before adding with a grin, "There are going to be a hundred and fifty of you lot living, sleeping, eating and farting in this billet, so it'll be nice and cosy when we get everybody on-board".

Tom looked at Chopper and raised his eyes towards a handwritten sign which was fixed to the wall. Chopper read out the words on the sign, "B Deck/Aft 4" and said, "B deck. It looks as though we are one deck down from the top".

Tom grunted, remembering his fear of enclosed spaces, "Not much of an address to have" before adding ominously, "I wonder how long we are going to be stuck in this floating prison".

Chopper didn't reply, he knew of Tom's phobia and had already rolled out his hammock and was attaching it to some hooks which had been welded to the steel girders just above his head. Tom smiled as Chopper attempted to climb onto the canvass sling which was barely two foot wide and six feet long. All around them, men were attempting to defy the laws of gravity and tame the swinging hammocks. Some of them were jumping up, and then, once they were in mid air, attempting to land their backsides on the narrow canvas, whilst others, were using a different approach. They were lifting a leg, as Chopper noted, like dogs pissing up a lamppost, and then, balancing on one leg, they were endeavouring to sit astride the swinging hammocks. Once this manoeuvre had been completed, they carefully and very slowly, stretched out until a laying position had been achieved. Tom, who had yet to decide which method he would use, heard the sound of somebody crashing to the ground.

"Fuck it", groaned a familiar voice behind him, "I'll never sleep in this bloody thing". It was the voice of Percy Gorringe.

Night fell and once the men had eaten, they gradually retired to their hammocks and with tiredness overcoming them, one by one they began to tame their swinging beds and began to drift into sleep.

Tom had hardly been asleep before he was woken by the sound of a loud thud followed by someone letting forth a string of profanities. Gradually, the men of the 85th were learning the only way to stay in their hammocks, was to remain lying on their backs, as still as a week-old corpse.

As it had been in the fishing smack eighteen months earlier, it was the sound and the vibration of the ship's engines which woke Tom from his sleep and peering at his watch, he saw that it was just before midnight. He remembered the date. It was the 12th November 1941. Leaning cautiously to one side of his hammock, Tom reached out and woke Chopper.

"We're underway", he said quietly.

Under the cover of darkness the convoy was silently making its way out of the Scottish harbour and towards the cold waters of the Atlantic Ocean.

"What time is it?" Chopper groaned.

"Just before midnight".

"Strange bloody time to get moving, isn't it", Chopper, who was now wide awake, whispered back.

"Superstition I guess. They didn't want to move the convoy out on the thirteenth", Tom said in a slightly louder voice as he noticed most of the men in the hammocks around him had also woken up. "It would be unlucky".

"I bloody well hope they're right", boomed a voice from the darkness.

With the ship ploughing through the white-topped waves, life on-board the Empress of Japan began to settle into one of familiar routine. Each morning the men would go up on deck for their drills and physical training exercise. Sometimes the order "boat stations" would be called, meaning that every man on board the troopship would be required to make for the promenade deck at the double, for lifeboat drill. Over seventeen-hundred men were standing shoulder to shoulder on the single deck, all struggling to put on their cork-filled life jackets and as tightly packed as sardines in a tin when Tom heard a Sapper morbidly remark, "If a U-Boat does sink us, we'll all go down in one bloody great lump".

With the lifeboat drill over, Tom wandered around the deck looking at the convoy as it stretched out across the ocean. It was a clear December morning with a bitterly cold wind blowing from the north, but he loved being out on the deck. He shuddered at the thought of the claustrophobia he felt when he was below deck and relished the salty smell of the sea and the cry of the seagulls. He enjoyed watching the fearless birds as they dived into the frothy wake which followed the ship searching for any fish in the watery turbulence. The war seemed to be a distant memory and Tom's mind was miles away as he turned his gaze away from the birds and watched the black smoke belching from the ship's three funnels being gusted away by the wind which was blowing in his face. It was when he realised the convoy was following a zig-zag pattern as it steamed onwards, he was brought back to reality. He thought this was probably standard procedure to reduce the chance of a successful German U-Boat attack and as he stood looking out to sea, he saw the escort ships had positioned themselves between each of the troopships with the exception of a minesweeper, which was now sailing quite close of the Empress's port side.

"Ha'way pet". It was the cheerful Geordie voice of Bantam which greeted Tom.

"Morning Joe, it's a nice cold morning", Tom replied, pleased at seeing the short man again. Although he had only known Joe

Kettlewell for less than a week, he had grown to like him and they walked along the deck enjoying each other's company before sitting down on a coil of thick rope, bleached white by the spray of the sea.

"Have you got a family back home", Bantam asked Tom by means of conversation.

Tom laughed, "I live in a small village in Kent called Pentbury", he replied. "No family, just two brothers and a sister who are all married and my mother, who lives by herself now. What about you, Joe?"

Bantam reached in his pocket and pulled out a folded photograph which he handed to Tom, saying proudly, "My wife, Annie and my wee bairns back in Tyneside and my ma and da".

Tom smoothed out the creases and looked at the image of the attractive woman and the two young girls sitting on her lap, with an older couple proudly standing behind and nodding approvingly, he asked, "Were you conscripted into the army?"

Bantam shook his head. "My da was the winderman at the pit, as was his da before him. My family have been coal miners for generations and I should have followed my da into the wheelhoose". Bantam's eyes looked earnestly at Tom as he continued, "but the job is a lonely one. You're on your own all day long, sending the cages full of men down the shaft to start their shifts underground and bringing up the half ton trucks full of the black stuff that had been hacked from the face".

Bantam looked down at his boots before continuing.

"I didn't want that. Anyway, coal mining is bloody dangerous. Just before the last war, over a hundred men were killed at the Stanley Pit, so I swapped the miner's black bonnet for the tin hat of a soldier. What about you, Tom?"

Tom told Bantam of his love of the countryside and of his job as a gamekeeper and how he had met Chopper at the Bridge Works in Maidstone. He decided not to say anything about the reason why he had left the woods. It seemed so futile now.

"Shall we stretch our legs?" Tom asked as he started getting up from their unyielding rope seat. The two men moved towards the ship's rail and stood there for a few moments in silent thought, looking down at the dark water far below them, when Tom suddenly said, "Joe, any idea where we are going?"

Everyone was now calling Joe, "Bantam", the name the *recce's* had given him on the troop train but he didn't seem to mind. In fact, he seemed to prefer it to the name his parents had given him, twenty eight years earlier.

"One of the fusiliers down in the billet, thinks we're going to make a landing in Northern France and start to push Jerry back to where he came from. The chap said he had been told another big convoy had sailed just before this one with two battalions of Suffolks, Cambridgeshires and Norfolks onboard. They're all part of the 85th Division and if it's true, that makes it a bloody big Infantry division. Ha'way man".

Tom smiled at the way the little Geordie sprinkled his sentences with *Ha'way* and thought for a few moments before replying, "That's still not enough to make a bridgehead. The Jerries are well and truly dug in and they'll take some getting out now".

"Alreet pet", Joe said, as he continued to stare down into the deep water below, "but there will be other convoys meeting up with ours and I daresay there would be a lot more troops coming from the south coast".

Tom didn't answer. He knew the top brass in the convoy would be the only ones who would know the answer and they wouldn't be telling anyone. Little did he realise at the time that trying to guess where the convoy was bound for, would become one of the main topics of conversation amongst the troops for the duration of the voyage.

It was the wild swinging of his hammock which woke Chopper and as he raised his head and looked around the gloomy billet he saw he was not the only one whose canvas bed was swinging to and fro like the pendulum of a clock.

"The sea's got a bit choppy" observed the gunner in the hammock alongside him, "I don't mind it myself but I bet a few will be looking a bit green before this blows itself out".

Chopper nodded and listened to the force of the sea crashing against the steel plates on the ship's side. He rolled out of his hammock and quickly pulled on his clothes and made his way up to the rolling deck. Already a stream of men were frantically making their way to the heads, all hoping they would not heave up before they reached them. Chopper glanced down and saw the foul smelling evidence which meant some of the men had already failed to reach their destination. The huge ship was being lifted up and down like a toy boat as it's steam engines relentlessly pushed it through the gigantic waves of the Atlantic Ocean. Salt-laden spray was being driven into Chopper's face as he walked onto the open deck and peered through the haze. He could just about make out the shape of one of the escorting destroyers as it disappeared into the foaming sea and then moments later was lifted by a huge wave, rising twenty or thirty feet above the Empress. Chopper watched almost mesmerised, as the ship plunged down once again into the trough of the following wave.

"BEST GET BELOW", a sailor shouted through the noise of storm, "this is going to be a bad one".

Chopper made his way back along the water-washed deck before gratefully disappearing down the first set of stairs he came to. By the time he had managed to haul himself down the stairs and along the never ending corridors back to the billet, the scene before his eyes was one of mayhem. Only the mess tables remained bolted in their original position, everything else was being thrown about on the floor in a sea of vomit.

"Bloody hell, it's like a bloody skating rink", he gasped as he desperately tried to keep his balance in the havoc the raging sea was causing. It was when the smell reached his nostrils he succumbed. All over the ship it was the same, hundreds of men were being sick and were clinging onto anything which was solid enough to prevent them being thrown about like rag dolls, by the violent rolling of the ship. Everyone on board had the same thought on their mind. How long would the storm last?.

Eventually, Chopper reached Tom who was lying motionless in his swinging hammock. He was as white as a ghost and Chopper winced as he put his face closer to Tom's face, he could smell his friend had been sick.

"Tom, can I do anything for you?" he asked. His concern was evident in his voice. "Christ, you look like bloody death", he exclaimed thoughtlessly.

It was well into the following day when the storm finally blew itself out and life on the ship gradually began to return to a semblance of normality. Tom had not moved from his hammock since the storm began and was barely conscious. Chopper and Bantam had taken turns to nurse him the best they could but for all their bravado, they could not hide the concern they felt for the motionless gunner. From time to time, they would gently raise Tom's head from the soiled hammock and gently get him to sip some tepid water from the lid of a borrowed billycan. Occasionally they tried to persuade him to eat some of the small pieces of dry toast which Bantam had scrounged from one of the sailors.

Not once did Bantam mention what the sailor had told him, "Calm seas never made a good mariner". He guessed after this, Tom would never want to be a mariner, good, bad or otherwise.

It was a hot and sticky night when Tom, who was now fully recovered, together with Percy and Chopper were up on deck relishing the cool and refreshing breeze which was blowing. It had been nearly two weeks since they had left behind the cold November air of Scotland and were now somewhere in the Tropics.

It was Percy who noticed them first. "Look out there", he said to Tom and Chopper, pointing out into the ink-black darkness, "that looks like lights".

The men gazed across the night sky towards the twinkling lights which Percy was pointing to. It was Chopper who concluded what he thought they were, "Stars", he said dismissively. "I'm going to get some shut eye" and with that said, the three men made their way back to the billet.

The next morning Tom was awoken by somebody crashing into his hammock as he ran by. "What is it?" Tom shouted, concerned at what the panic was, immediately fearing the convoy had been attacked.

"Land", the man shouted back, "the ship has anchored and somebody said they can see land".

Tom immediately woke Chopper and Percy and after pulling on some clothes, the men ran onto the deck. In the distance, across the rippling waves they could see rolling green hills shrouded in a heavy, early morning mist.

"Where are we?" Percy asked a fellow soldier, who was standing next to him.

"Freetown", the soldier said and then, on seeing the puzzled look on Percy's face, expanded his reply, "Sierra Leone". The puzzled look remained fixed on Percy's face. The soldier took a deep breath and said in exasperation, "Africa, that's the coast of bloody Africa you're looking at".

"Africa!" Percy repeated in surprise, as he walked across to the rail to get a closer look at the country he had only seen on a tattered page in a world atlas.

Chopper's practical attitude came to the fore when he turned and asked the soldier, "Does this mean we're getting off this bloody boat?"

"No, I don't think so. There's not much happening here. It probably means they're just stopping to pick up some more coal and supplies".

Each one of the ships' seven decks was crowded with hundreds of men as the hot tropical sun began to burn off the morning mist revealing a rich blue, cloudless sky. Despite the daily exercise routines and the constant training and lifeboat drills, there probably wasn't a man onboard who wasn't relieved to find that the monotony of being at sea was being replaced by seeing something different, other than miles and miles of relentless ocean. "Bugger all to do and all bloody day to do it in", Chopper had observed on almost a daily basis.

Tom spent most of the morning watching in amazement at the speed of the re-equipping the convoy. Against a background of tall coconut palms and the velvet green mountains in the distance, dozens of boats all of different shapes and sizes were ferrying supplies from the dockside to the ships of the convoy. Collier ships, black with the dust of the coal they were carrying, bobbed to and fro with their precious cargos of fuel for the ships' boilers. Smaller, fresh water tenders wove in and out of the other boats which were dashing about in the race to get the convoy re-supplied and underway again. Tom was thinking how the scurrying of the ships reminded him of the frantic activity of the wood ants back home, when he had probed into their nest with a stick, when the howl of two Skuas from the Fleet Air Arm roared overhead and swept low over the convoy, hunting for any enemy submarine, skulking low in the blue-green water, that would threaten the ships.

"Look at this lot coming towards us", Chopper exclaimed, as three small bum boats being paddled furiously by some natives, approached the ship.

"The buggers have come to trade with us", he laughed, as he looked over the rail and saw some of the small boats loaded with piles of oranges and bananas had already nestled against the side of the huge ship which was towering over them.

"MONEY, MONEY", one of the black skinned men shouted, holding a bunch of bananas aloft.

Tom smiled, as some of the soldiers began to lower their steel helmets containing a handful of coins to the natives below and then hauling them back with the fruit nestling in the bowl of their hats. He could see the quantity of the fruit the soldiers had been given depended of the value the native had placed on the coins or, as Tom suspected, the honesty of the native who was doing the trading.

"BLANKETS, BLANKETS", one of the natives started shouting. "FRUIT...BLANKETS", he continued.

"Christ", exclaimed Percy, "the cheeky buggers want us to give them our bloody blankets".

A loud cheer went up from the soldiers crowding the decks when they saw a couple of coarsely woven army blankets which had been thrown overboard were floating gently down to the small bum boats below. More traders had arrived after frantically paddling their small boats from some of the other ships in the convoy, anxious to barter fresh fruit for anything they considered of value. Some of the smiling black men had arrived with palm-leaf baskets which were already laden with fruit and they were trying to throw the ropes they had tied to them, up to the men on the lower deck in an effort to encourage further trade.

The stifling air below decks had become so insufferably hot it continuously scorched the men's lungs as they reluctantly inhaled it and Tom was thankful to be out in the cool, sweet air and watching the antics of the natives was a pleasure he would not miss. Whilst he watched some children who were heading towards the ship in roughly hewn canoes, he noticed a shoal of flying fish which were being chased by a school of blue dolphins. Tom felt a sense of awe when he saw the pink bellies of the giant fish flashing in the bright sunlight as they leapt out of the water after strange looking flying fish, but it was the sound of laughter which caused Tom to look behind him. To the amusement of the troops, three grim-faced military policemen were trying to deter the youngsters in the canoes from approaching the ship by squirting a jet of water onto them from an ineffective hose pipe.

"Look at the little buggers", Percy laughed as they watched the children stop their canoes some yards short of ship and dive effortlessly into the crystal clear water.

"I could piss further than that", Chopper said, as the men watched in amusement at the water dribbling out of the end of the military policemen's hose pipe.

"MONEY, MONEY", one of the older boys started shouting, as he pointed into the water.

Just as Percy was saying, "The cheeky little sods want us to throw some money down to them", a shower of copper coins hit the water, sending out ever widening ripples around the youngsters canoes. The men watched in amazement as the boys dived from the canoes and swam like fish, down into the deep water searching the sea bed for the elusive coins.

"NO, NO", the boys shouted, as they surfaced like corks from a bottle, each holding a handful of the wet, sandy coins. "SILVER ONES", they started to demand from the soldiers standing high above them.

"If they want silver coins then the little buggers shall have them", growled one of the Redcaps who had been attempting to thwart the youngsters with the water jet.

Tom watched with growing amusement, as the man searched his pockets for some pennies and halfpennies before wrapping them in some silver foil he had taken from a block of fortified chocolate.

"Hey presto", the Redcap said with evident satisfaction, as he held up the coins for his friends approval, before throwing the shining coins overboard to the unsuspecting curly haired boys below.

Tom had noticed the mood of the men onboard the Empress had lifted considerably during the days the convoy had been moored off Freetown and he was one of many who were sorry when they heard the blast of the ship's horn as it up anchored and steamed out into the ocean. After six days at sea since leaving Freetown, the convoy crossed the equator and then weathered the mountainous seas as it rounded the Cape of Good Hope before finally docking in the sweeping natural harbour of Durban. It was during the afternoon in mid-December 1941 when the Empress dropped anchor again, only this time word had gone round the ship that the men were to be given shore leave. They had been cooped up in the cramped conditions on-board for over four weeks and the next day, Tom and Chopper, together with Percy, Taff and Dusty Miller gratefully stepped onto the soil of South Africa to enjoy five days of glorious shore leave.

"Seems funny to have firm ground under our bloody feet", Percy said, as he took a few wobbly steps onto the quay.

When the convoy had left Greenock, Britain had been war for over a year and the weather had been cold, wet and gloomy. The drab, grey cloak of the war had descended over the country and had enveloped the population like a London fog but as soon as the men walked ashore, they felt the cloak of war had been lifted by the warmth and vibrant colours which suddenly surrounded them. Everything was so much brighter than it had been at home. The men marvelled at the sweeps of orange and white daisies carpeting the distant hillsides and the vibrant green of the mangrove swamps which swept down to the sea. Tom stared in amazement at the multi-coloured butterflies fluttering in and out of the huge red and yellow trumpet shaped flowers which hung from the vines trailing round the verandas of the white painted houses. Tropical birds flashed like precious jewels in the bright sunlight dazzling Tom with the iridescence of the colours in their delicate plumage. He felt he had landed in paradise.

It wasn't just the spectrum of colour which amazed the men but it was also the people of Durban. They welcomed the soldiers with open arms and unstinted generosity. There were army canteens on the corners of every street where food and drink was made freely available to them and for Tom, Percy and Dusty, it had been the first time in their lives they had tasted wine. Christmas was only days away and before the convoy left, many of the men cabled their Christmas greetings to their loved ones at home. Tom was amongst them.

"Dear Mother", he wrote, *"this is to wish you a very happy Christmas and to hope you are well.*

Your loving son

Tom.

The war seemed so far away and had almost been forgotten. There had been such joy and happiness during the five days in Durban that the five men felt they had been walking on sunshine but now they were back on the rolling decks of the Empress and once again, heading into the unknown where only God and the top brass knew what awaited them.

Bantam was returning from the quartermaster's stores which were tucked down on one of the lower decks with his newly issued desert kit when he saw walking towards him were two of the men from the Reconnaissance Corps who had sat next to him on the troop train.

"Ha'way man", Bantam said cheerfully. "Do you lads know where we are going?" He held his desert kit aloft to make the point.

The men immediately recognised the little man and looked genuinely pleased to see him. "Hello Bantam", the taller of the two men greeted him warmly. "We're off to stop the Jerries getting their hands on the oil supplies in Iraq", he said, with an air of superiority.

The second man winked at his friend and said with a familiar mocking tone in his voice, "Once we get there, you lot can leave us to do the man's work. You had better go back to the stores and get yourself a little bucket and spade so you can keep yourself amused by making sandcastles".

It was not for the first time that the two men roared with laughter at Bantam's expense but the little man just smiled and walked on content in the knowledge he now knew where the convoy was going.

Gradually, the news spread amongst the men onboard the ship that they were being sent to the never ending deserts of Iraq. Tom and his fellow gunners were sitting high up on the promenade deck as they grimly discussed the prospect of matching their small anti-tank guns against the heavily armoured tanks of the German Africa Corps. There was a mood of apprehension as Chopper reminded them that stopping the Panzers in the vast openness of the desert would be more difficult than it had been in the dense forests of France.

"There aren't many trees in all that bloody sand for us to conceal the guns", he said, stating the blinding obvious before adding ominously, "and can you image the speed the bastards will be travelling towards us".

The air was sultry and the men were grateful of the refreshing wind which had arrived as the setting sun began to send finger-like copper streaks across the evening sky when one of the sailors came along to cadge a cigarette from Chopper.

Chopper opened the outer flap on the woodbines packet, saving the sailor from asking for one. "How much longer have we got to sit on this tub before we get to Iraq?" he asked the sailor, whom he called Jack.

The sailor didn't bother to correct Chopper as he knew all the Tommies on-board called the sailors either Jack or just AB, which was short for their rank of able seaman.

The sailor cupped his hands round the flame of a burning match and gratefully drew in a lung-full of cigarette smoke before saying, almost in a whisper, "I've just heard that the convoy is being diverted to Bombay. On Mr Churchill's personal orders apparently".

Despite the noise of laughter and conversation of the soldiers around them, the sound of a pin dropping would have been deafening amongst this group of men as a result of the bombshell the sailor had just dropped.

"India, not Iraq! Why are they sending us to bloody India?" Chopper exclaimed, clearly astonished at the sudden change of plan.

"If we keep going round in circles, sooner or later we'll all disappear up our own bloody arseholes", Percy observed drily.

Tom didn't say a word. Instead he turned to watch an Arab dhow, with its triangular white sail billowing in the gentle wind as it turned on the tide and began make its way into the wide mouth of the Persian Gulf.

He knew why they were being sent to Bombay. It was to stop the Japanese army from invading India.

Once again, the ship's rails were crowded with hundreds of troops as the Empress of Japan reduced her speed as she began to enter the wide harbour of Bombay. Tom had joined up with Percy, Chopper, Taff and Dusty who were all hoping they would be able to disembark together when the order was given. The Empress was still about a mile from shore when it sailed past two huge troop ships which were moored in the outer anchorage of the harbour.

"It looks like the Yanks have arrived", Percy observed dryly, as he read out the names painted on the sides of the ships. "USS Wakefield and the USS West Point", he said slowly.

"Do you think they were expecting to be sunk", Chopper said, as he pointed at the rows of rubber life-rafts which were hanging ominously from the sides of the camouflaged ships.

Whilst the rest of the group laughed at Chopper's sarcasm, Tom raised his hand to shield his eyes from the glare of the blazing sun and looked across at the drab grey and black ships. Dozens of men were climbing down the ship's scrambling nets and jumping into the barges which had arrived to ferry them to the shore. The sun was shining directly into Tom's eyes and he squinted to try to get a better look at the uniforms of the soldiers who were hanging from the nets like monkeys.

"They're Tommies", Tom exclaimed, as he recognised the desert uniforms they were wearing.

"Whoever they are, they're lucky buggers", Chopper said, "it looks like they've been given shore leave".

Tom looked back towards the shore as the Empress, with tugs, fore and aft, was now slowly being nudged into the harbour entrance channel towards one of the huge concrete piers in the docking area. Instead of the velvet green mountains he had seen in Freetown or the flower strewn hillsides which had lifted his spirits in Durban, all he could see here, scattered amongst the shamble of huts, were clusters of Victorian red-brick buildings and a huge, towering gateway which was standing on the water's edge. He looked past the strange, yellowish coloured arch with a round turret on each of its four corners and saw a converted passenger ship, looking not dissimilar to the Empress was already discharging its troops onto a nearby pier.

Meanwhile, Chopper was staring down at the foul smelling water being stirred up by the ship's propellers and said wryly, "No one is going to be diving for any coins in this shithole".

"What do they mean, twelve hours before we set sail again? That's not what I call bloody shore leave". Percy complained, as the five men walked down the wide gangway and onto the quayside. Tom was quiet. If they had been diverted to India to stop the Japs, why was the convoy sailing again, he was thinking?.

The men's boots had hardly touched terra firma before they were surrounded by a mob of dusky-skinned beggars, all pleading for money or food. Chopper scowled at the mob and his face became contorted as the stench of the place invaded his senses.

"Take my word for it Percy, that'll be eleven hours too long", he grunted, answering the question.

The men pushed their way through the sea of thrusting, open-palmed hands, noticing some of them belonged to dirty faced children whom Tom guessed were no more than six or seven years old. The soldiers walked briskly on but the beggars would not be shaken off and continued to cluster around them. Suddenly a frail old woman, who was leaning on a makeshift crutch, thrust a wooden bowl forward. Her eyes, half hidden by a dirty yellow sari, were sunk deep in her wrinkled, leather coloured face. The old woman stumbled and fell as the jostling rabble pushed her to one side. Immediately, her place was taken by a barefooted young girl who was balancing a howling baby on her hip.

Tom grinned at Chopper's linguistic skills as his friend told the beggars to "Sod off".

 He had never experienced poverty like this before and as he was about to search in his pockets for some coins, the beggars seemed to take Chopper's advice and flitted off to find richer pickings elsewhere, amongst the hundreds of soldiers crowding the dockside. Tom and his gun crew moved on and were sitting by the huge gateway they had seen from the ship watching some black-coloured hawks swarming overhead, when they were joined by another group from the 85th Anti-Tank.

"Shitehawks", said one of the other gunners succinctly.

Tom looked at the man in surprise.

"Shitehawks", the man repeated. "Those black birds, that's what they're called... they're scavengers...there's hundreds of 'em round here".

Tom shrugged his shoulders in a couldn't-care-less fashion and then asked the man, "Do you know where we're going?"

"No idea, I thought we would be staying here to stop the Japs until they told us we had to return to the ship".

Tom's brow furrowed as he attempted to understand the situation. If they weren't staying in India, where were they going? As a child he loved the geography lessons in the village school and he tried to visualize the large map of the world which was always pinned to the blackboard in the icy-cold classroom. The noise around him dissolved into silence as he tried to delve into the recesses of his mind. Where could they be heading, he thought, but try as he might, the picture from the map wouldn't return?.

The hammocks in the billet began to swing slightly as the ship cast off and through the portholes the men could see it was a bright moonlit sky as the Empress of Japan pulled away from the concrete piers of Bombay harbour. It was in mid January 1942, as the ship, together with another converted passenger liner, the Duchess of Bedford, together with the Empire Star and the two American transporters, accompanied by the cruiser HMS Exeter, steamed into the Indian Ocean. There wasn't a man amongst the seventeen-thousand soldiers onboard the convoy, who wasn't wondering where exactly they were heading?.

Tom was uneasy as he lay awake in his canvas sling staring at the black ceiling. It had only been when the ships had been anchored in the harbours of Freetown, Durban and Bombay did he feel they were in a relatively safe havens. He knew there had always been a high risk of a submarine attack when they were at sea but now things seemed different and he wasn't the only one who could feel the increased apprehension and tension onboard.

In the days which followed, the banter in the billets was more subdued than it had been since they had left blighty and for some strange reason, when the men were on deck, they were talking to each other in voices not much louder than whispers.

It was a few days later, Tom and Chopper were walking towards the stern of the ship when Bantam came running up to them. "Ha'way lads", he said breathlessly, "we going to the naval base in Singapore".

A shiver ran down Tom's spine and his blood suddenly ran cold. "Singapore" he blurted out, "bloody hell". Then as an after-thought, he added, "How do you know?"

"An AB told me", Bantam muttered. "He said the sailors can tell by the position of the sunset and their compass readings. We're heading to the Far East and after what happened to the Repulse and the Prince of Wales, the AB said it's only common sense, we're making for Singapore".

Tom remembered hearing the two huge battleships had been sunk just off Singapore by Japanese bomber planes just before Christmas, taking nearly a thousand men to their watery graves and that the Japs had been bombing Singapore ever since, whilst their ground forces were sweeping through the jungles of Malaya.

Bantam could see the look of concern on his friend's face and said cheerfully, "At least we'll be on firm ground. I never did like bloody boats".

"Nor me", Tom replied truthfully.

"Welcome to Singapore", Tom said to his small group of friends. Their eyes were adjusting to the half light of the early morning as they pushed through the masses of soldiers who were crowding the deck to get a closer look at their final destination.

The convoy was still about a mile from Keppel Harbour on the southern tip of Singapore Island. The ships had been sailing for ten days since they had left Bombay and the men had noticed the position of the ships within the convoy was beginning to change. Tom looked starboard and saw one of their accompanying cruisers, the Exeter, was dropping back and then glancing across to the port side he saw a smaller cruiser, the HMS Durban, was beginning to take its place. The shuffling of hundreds of pairs of British army boots began to resonate throughout length of each of the ships massive seven decks. On B deck, Tom and Chopper, together with Percy, Taff and Dusty, were jammed against the rail trying to make out through the dark monsoon clouds which were hanging over the harbour, what was awaiting them.

226

As the ship edged closer, their eyes were staring in growing disbelief towards the distant harbour.

"What the hell have they brought us to?", said a soldier, whose face was already blanched white with fear and who was leaning so far over the rail that Chopper thought, if he leant any further forward, he would soon find out more quickly than he had bargained for.

Curling wisps of smoke rising from the buildings around the harbour were now clearly visible as the men realised they had arrived in the middle of an air-raid.

Straining his eyes to follow the disappearing black dots in the sky and not attempting to hide the look of growing concern on his face, Chopper turned to his friend and said, "Well my old mate, I've got a bloody horrible feeling we're going to get some real fighting after all".

"You were the one who couldn't wait to get away from the bloody gun emplacement, you said it was damp" countered Tom. Both men smiled lamely, as they stood with the driving rain running in torrents off their drenched bodies.

Above the rain clouds and out of sight of the shocked troops, the Japanese bombers were regrouping into two formations and preparing to swoop down once again for another strike.

"Bloody hell ", Chopper muttered as the anti- aircraft guns around the docks threw up a fierce barrage of fire as the returning planes were sighted. "The bastards are coming back", he growled.

Tom didn't reply.

He was almost mesmerised as he watched the flak burst from the gun emplacements and spiral into the haze laden sky, seeking out the black dots which were growing larger by the second. The Japanese bombers flew through the sea of shells being aimed at them almost as though they were being protected by a mystical cloak. The clouds of searing hot shrapnel designed to rip the planes apart did not deter the Jap pilots as they released stick after stick of bombs onto the stricken docks. It was all over within minutes and with their deadly work done and leaving behind huge columns of black and white smoke rising from far beneath them, the planes roared skywards. Until the next time, Tom thought, as he watched them disappear.

"It looks as though the Japs have got the freedom of the sky", muttered a despondent voice, hidden somewhere in the crowd of soldiers staring in a sense of disbelief towards the shore.

"What a bloody mess", Tom murmured, to nobody in particular.

Beyond the concrete arms of the harbour walls, Tom could make out the damage the Jap planes had just inflicted. Fires were raging in the rows of warehouses lined up around the inner harbour. Through the acrid black smoke billowing from huge tanks of fuel oil and latex rubber, Tom saw the ominous shapes of three ships which had already been sunk in the outer harbour. As he stood looking at the half submerged wreckage, a large sea- going tug was already on the move. It slowly pulled away from a large floating crane anchored nearby with its propellers creating large swirls in the red, oil-streaked water. The noise of the mayhem which was happening on shore was beginning to be heard on the ship as it edged closer to the harbour. Sirens were wailing their mournful screams and Tom could clearly hear the now familiar sounds of ack-ack guns pounding away somewhere in the distance.

Perhaps another Jap raid is on its way, he thought.

A cruiser, with its wartime camouflage looking the worse for wear, had already moored up, meanwhile the five troop ships which had made up the convoy were beginning to line up in preparation to enter the harbour. Wakefield, which had slowed down to a walking pace was leading the way, with its four and a half thousand British troops preparing for a quick disembarkation. The Empress would be next, followed by The Duchess of Bedford, then the West Point, with the motor transporter, Empire Star, coming in at the rear.

"Wonders never cease" said Chopper, making no attempt to hide the cynicism in his voice, as he looked towards the quayside, "it looks as if they're going to let the men off before the bloody trucks, we'll be sitting bloody ducks".

Percy looked him and said grimly, "I can't see what the rush is to get off this bloody thing".

Tom wasn't listening. He had something else on his mind. There was a look of urgency on his face as he quickly pushed his way through the banks of soldiers who were crowding around the rails. He needed to find a place where he could write a letter whilst there was still time. He knew he had a note-book and some envelopes in the breast pocket of his desert jacket but did he have something to write with? Tom hands were frantically searching deep in the pockets of his short beige trousers, in the hope he would find something.

"Yes", he exclaimed in obvious relief, as his fingers touched upon the stub of a pencil

"My dearest Mother", he scribbled quickly. His hand was shaking and he had to increase his grip on the pencil stub before he could continue. *As I write this I am thinking of you and hope you are well. Do not worry about me, everything is fine here and I am having plenty of food.*

A thin smile spread across his face, as he remembered how concerned his mother was when she received the letters from his father in the trenches of the Somme, complaining there was not enough food.

It is at times like this when I wish I was back at home, I do so miss you all.

In his mind he could see the cottage at Pentbury surrounded by the green fields and the lofty trees. The fields will soon be ploughed, he thought and despite the invasive stench of the burning buildings, he could almost smell soft deep brown earth of the furrows being turned by the plough. Hurry, Tom thought, I must hurry.

It may be some time before I get a chance to write again, I hope you got the cable I sent at Christmas, I certainly wished that I had been with you all. Never fear, I will be home next Christmas, I am sure. I love you and miss you,

Your loving son.

Tom.

Tom could hear disembarkation orders being shouted. Quickly he addressed the envelope and looking up he saw the frenzied activity which was happening around him. "SAILOR, SAILOR", he shouted, as a young AB ran past. "Do me a favour. Can you post this when you get back to Scotland?"

The sailor stopped and without saying a word, screwed the envelope up and shoved it hastily into his pocket. Tom could read the look of fear on the young man's face which was saying, "Do you really think any of us are going to get out of this alive?"

Tom pushed his way back to the rails just as three smaller tugs chugged out of the inner harbour ready to berth the Empress. Looking round, he could see an AB preparing to throw a heaving line to the leading tug.

"He's done that before", Tom murmured to himself, as the man who was oblivious to the mayhem happening around him, threw a light line with a monkey's fist knot tied on the end, to one of the tug's crew, who caught it with practised ease and attached it to a heavy towing line which he made fast.

Slowly, the ship was pulled and nudged into the berth by the two tugs, fore and aft, whilst the third one was pushing amidships. Ten long minutes passed before they finally succeeded to get the huge ship alongside the quay. This done, the crew of the Empress, desperately began to work on the mooring lines by paying out the heavy hemp ropes to the shore-crews who quickly made them fast to the row of black-painted bollards on the quayside. Meanwhile the ships' mates, each with their own small gang of sailors, started up the steam driven capstans and began to heave in and secure the mooring lines. With the ship tied up, the tugs let go and hastily made off for their next ship, the Duchess of Bedford.

The lines of gangways were immediately rigged and the troops, six abreast, started to be off-loaded with evident urgency, whilst the heavy chains hanging from the towering jibs of the dock-side cranes hovered in readiness to lift off the weapons of war from the decks and the depths of the ship's holds. Tom made his way along the deck to his disembarkation point looking for the formation badges which the soldiers had sewn on their sleeves of their jackets. His throat was dry from the swirling smoke as he looked frantically for Chopper or Percy or any of the other, all he could see was a seething mass of anonymous soldiers. NCO's were shouting orders but despite everything, it was chaos on the dockside and he had lost sight of his crew.

Christ, he thought, where the bloody hell are they?

Suddenly, Tom felt very alone and regardless of the tropical heat and the warm, driving rain of the monsoon, he shivered as if somebody had stepped on his grave and reluctantly made his way down the gangway to confront whatever fate awaited him. The dockside warehouses and oil tanks still blazed and continued to spew out black smoke which together with the offensive smell of burning rubber and tar blew through the ranks of bedraggled troops as they were being assembled and marched quickly off the quay.

Somewhere, high above him, Tom could hear the drone of more enemy planes. Other soldiers had also heard them and suddenly as Tom looked up into the threatening clouds, the men crowding around him started running in a wild, headlong panic. It was like being caught up in a herd of stampeding cattle. In the crush, Tom could feel rough, frantic hands pushing hard on his back, forcing him to run in the same direction as the dozens of scared men in front of him. What they were all trying to escape from wasn't clear to him, when, without warning, his right boot kicked into something soft. It was a discarded kit bag which sent him sprawling onto the hard concrete slabs of the quay. He winced and curled himself up, foetus like, with his arms wrapped round his head in a vain attempt to protect it from the army boots which were stamping on him from above. Other men tripped on Tom's body and started falling around him like pins in a skittle alley. Despite the noise of the screaming planes overhead, Tom could hear the men swearing at him and then, as he was struggling to get to his feet, the sudden blast of an exploding bomb hit him. The pressure wave sent him sprawling backwards and together with the cursing men around him, they fell in a tangle of arms and legs onto the slabs of the quay. Dazed and with his ears ringing, Tom raised his head and looked back towards the moored ships. Smoke and flames were spewing from the seaward side of the Wakefield and he realised the ship had been hit whilst she was in the midst of refuelling. No more than a second or two passed before two more bombs hit the ship, one aft and the other striking mid-ships. Automatically, Tom curled up into a ball again until he felt sure the raid was over. He could feel his heart racing and his breathing quickened. Getting to his feet, the shaken man waited nervously in the pouring rain until order was restored. He stood with his back pressed against one of the burnt out buildings and watched as the fire parties onboard the Wakefield gradually brought the raging flames under control.

The quay, crowded as it was with soldiers and their equipment, was also seething with panic stricken women and children who were frantically being herded along by their husbands, desperate to get their loved ones onto a ship and to safety. Even at a distance, Tom could see the fear in all their eyes. Fear of what they were escaping from and fearful of what would happen to them next. Despite the noise and confusion around him, Tom noticed an NCO was calmly shepherding the women and children into an orderly queue, getting them to wait patiently at a small gate where a solitary man was sitting at a small table, calmly taking down every person's name before they boarded the still-smoking Wakefield for their journey home.

"BEST OF BRITISH LUCK, MATE", a red-faced sailor shouted as he raced past. Before Tom could reply, he heard the man say ominously, "You'll bloody well need it", as he disappeared into the thousands of soldiers and civilians milling on the rain soaked quay.

Tom edged his way along the quay and saw some of the disembarked troops were helping sailors to complete the unloading. Tom's mind was elsewhere when he dodged a huge crate as it was lowered onto the dockside.

"Get you next time", laughed a Royal Engineer, as he steadily positioned the crate alongside a line of similar sized ones. "The local Coolie labour has been recruited to do this but they always disappear during the bombing raids", the good natured Sapper complained, before adding for good measure, "the lazy sods".

Tom was outside of the docks when he recognised some fellow gunners from the 85th Anti-tank and walked across to join them. They were drenched to the skin and as the monsoon rain streamed down their faces he realised they were all kitted out, like him, in the sand coloured uniform of the desert.

"We're not exactly dressed for the tropics, we'll stand out like pricks at a bloody wedding", Tom said to the man alongside him.

"Remember the seven p's they banged on about during our gunnery training".

Tom nodded vaguely.

"Perfect bloody planning and preparation and all that shit", the rain-soaked gunner reminded him before concluding his tirade by saying, "I wish they had told that to the brainless fucking idiot who organised this".

"You're not wrong there" said a voice behind them. "This is going to be one big bloody cock-up".

Tom turned round and much to his relief, he saw it was Chopper.

His dark, wavy hair was dripping wet and lay flat on his head but despite the chaos around them, there was the broad, familiar smile fixed firmly on his face.

7

To the Edge of Destiny- 1942

Bantam and the other fusiliers were some of the first troops to disembark and after forming up were marched at the double to the line of awaiting trucks outside the massive harbour gates.

"They're not hanging about with us, are they?" Bantam drily observed to a fellow fusilier who was already in the back of the leading truck and offering his huge, outstretched hand to pull the little man up into the battered Morris. "Thanks bonny lad", Bantam said cheerfully, as Bob Richard's muscular arm heaved him onboard without exerting an ounce of effort.

Bob's stature was the opposite to that of his friend. He was over six feet tall, with a frame honed by years of pushing coal trucks deep underground in the mines of County Durham. He was a few years older than Bantam, a fellow Geordie who had trained with the little man back home, as part of the same gun crew.

"Christ pet", exclaimed Bob, as the truck drove off and he looked out from the back and saw the chaos around them.

The road from the harbour was jammed in both directions with every kind of vehicle imaginable, mixed amongst a jumble of hundreds of panic-stricken people all trying desperately to force their way through to the dock. Many of the cars had been abandoned by their occupants, who in their haste to get away had not even the time to shut the doors and in the midst of the confusion there was a solitary military policeman who, amongst the chaos around him, was trying to get things moving.

"Look at that silly sod", Bob said sarcastically, pointing a finger towards the frustrated man, "he's waving his arms about like a bloody windmill in a storm".

"Aye, I doubt he could direct piss into a bucket", Bantam aimlessly mumbled. He wasn't really interested and although his mind was elsewhere he still managed to counter his friend's blunt humour. He knew the Redcap was doing his best trying to sort out the hundreds of civilians and natives who were all desperate to get to the docks before the last of the ships left and against the torrent of people was a rapidly increasing number of soldiers who were equally determined to push their way through in the opposite direction.

The torrential rain continued to pour down in stair-rods. Rivers of muddy brown water ran down the road and in some places, completely submerging it as the small convoy of trucks eventually drove a few miles before coming to an abrupt halt outside a bomb-damaged dispersal barracks.

"Get out", barked out the impatient and slightly hostile voice of an awaiting NCO, clearly giving the impression of the urgency of the situation.

Bantam jumped down from the cramped confines of the truck and quickly glanced around. Dozens of bedraggled soldiers were walking down the flooded road and making their way towards the barracks. They looked half dead and were so covered in mud and slime, the little Geordie could not begin to tell what regiment they were from. Some had obviously been badly wounded with the tell-tale blood red stains showing through the mud and were being half carried along, whilst others were leaning heavily on their rifles for support. In the stifling heat, most of the battle weary men were just wearing shorts and boots, with a few having Australian army slouch hats on their heads. Bantam nudged Bob with an elbow in the ribs, "Look at that lot, man" he said, nodding in the direction of the battered men. It wasn't necessary, Bob, as well as every other man jumping down from the trucks was looking at the ominous sight which greeted them.

Bantam's nose twitched, detecting the lingering smell of the earlier bombing as he entered a large room which he guessed had once been a drill hall. Charred timber roof supports were clearly visible through gaping holes blown through the plastered ceiling and a dribble of water ran obstinately from some galvanised pipes, ripped open by the blast. The clean-up had been done hastily, for although most of the rubble was shovelled up and left in piles around the edges of the large hall, odd bits had been left behind and they crunched under the men's boots as they began to form up in lines.

"At ease men, I'm Major Ferguson", said the officer in a clear well-modulated voice to the hundred or so men who were standing to attention in front of him. "I will brief you in respect of the situation here and once you are fed and armed, you will be going into action immediately".

The man was probably around thirty years of age. His sweat-soaked tunic was clinging to his body like a second skin and his deep-set sunken eyes betrayed the fact he had not enjoyed a proper night's sleep for days.

"Forget what they may have told you on the convoy about the Japs poor fighting capability. They are well practised in jungle warfare. They prefer hand to hand fighting and in short gentlemen, we are encountering a ferocious enemy".

"He's not wasting any time in giving us the good news", Bob whispered to Bantam.

"I wonder what the bad news will be".

Bantam drew a deep breath. He recalled being told during one of the lectures onboard the ship that although the Japs had marched into China and had made mincemeat of the Chinese army, when they came up against the British and Aussies they would find them to be a very different kettle of fish to the ill-disciplined Chinks. So much for that bullshit, Bantam thought.

The men watched intently as the pale-faced Major continued, "We have fought them down the mainland and now we have pulled back to form a defensive line five miles from the Straights of Jahore".

The Major turned round, pointing to at a large map of Singapore which had been hastily fixed to a smoke blackened wall and indicated the narrow strip of water which separated the Island of Singapore from the mainland of Malaya.

237

"These are the Straights of Jahore gentlemen. This is where we are and this is where the enemy is". The man's finger went from one side of the narrow strip of water to the other.

He ignored the buzz of whispered comments which filled the drill hall. This was a far worse situation than the men had imagined or indeed been led to expect.

Bantam heard a man who was standing behind him say quietly, "Jesus, the Japs have almost pushed us out of bloody Malaya and now they're sitting on the fucking doorstep and they've done that in only two bloody months".

Bantam looked at the map and then quickly glanced across at Bob. He too had seen the narrow causeway which joined Singapore to the mainland and from where he was standing it only looked nothing more than a very narrow bridge.

Major Ferguson cleared the mucous in his throat with a couple of hearty coughs before saying solemnly, "Whilst we are defending the causeway to stop the Japs walking across the Straights. We are expecting them to attempt to land on the northern shore… here". He indicated the place by banging on the map before continuing, "and you gentlemen as part of the 18th Division, are to defend this strategically important Northern Sector of the island".

The Major paused and then, with his red-ringed eyes staring directly at the line of men who were standing in front of him, raised his voice and said, "You may ask, why the Northern Sector?" Without waiting for anyone to answer, he continued quickly, "Let me tell you. Firstly, there is a large navy base there at Sembawang". He stopped and realising his error said, quickly "Of course, you chaps already know that, it's where you landed. Although it has been somewhat damaged by the Emperors' bloody bombers, it is the biggest one we have in the Empire and we are not going to give it away easily".

The men shuffled uneasily on the rubble strewn floor as they began to realise the seriousness of the situation they found themselves in.

"Secondly, we have an airfield close by and although thanks to the Jap bombers it is no longer operational, we don't have the slightest intention of letting the buggers use it".

238

The officer paused. Bantam looked at the man's drawn face and could see, despite the occasional weak smile on his face and bravado in his voice, they could not hide the concern and anxiety which showed in his tired, bloodshot eyes.

"However", the officer turned and faced the soldiers directly as he raised his voice slightly, "We now have over eighty thousand extremely well trained British, Australian and Indian troops to defend the island, and that is exactly what we will do".

Bantam looked at the man's sweat soaked uniform and noticed how hot and humid it had become in the bomb damaged hall. So this is what it is like in the tropics, he thought.

"As I said", the Major continued, "The 18th Division, together with your 53rd Infantry Brigade are, as I speak, beginning to move into the northern sector. Should the Japs attempt a naval assault, we have fifteen inch guns at the Jahore and Buona Vista batteries to beat them back. These, together with the other large guns at Connaught, Siloso, Changi and Serapong, will stop them in their tracks". He leant back and perched his backside on the empty table in front of the map and visibly relaxed, he said with a slightly raised voice, "I can assure you gentlemen, with the task you are here to do, the Japanese forces will not step foot on this island".

"Question saar", boomed a voice far behind where Bantam and Bob were standing. Bantam did not need to turn round to see who had spoken. He knew from the crisp tone of the man's voice it belonged to somebody who was used to bawling out orders on a parade ground.

The Major, smiled and indicated he was prepared to answer the man.

"What about the air force, sir? Will we get air support?"

Clearing his throat once more, the officer replied, only this time with a slightly lowered voice, "We have had remorseless air attacks on our airfields which caught many of our planes on the ground". He hesitated before saying gravely, "We do not have any planes in the air at the moment".

A hushed silence descended on the room for what seemed to be lasting for an eternity. Somewhere in the building a clock was ticking.

"Another question saar". The voice emphasised the word, saar.

This time, Bantam turned his head to the direction where the voice had come from. It belonged to a tall, upright man, who was sporting a neatly clipped moustache on his impassive face. The three chevrons on his arm symbolised his rank.

Once more the Major nodded his head in approval.

"Saar, when will it stop bloody raining?"

A huge roar of laughter followed and a feeling of relief broke out amongst the assembled men. Major Ferguson joined in with the joke. Good man, he thought. Here was a man who had read the situation and felt the need to lift the air of gloom which had pervaded the room.

Visibly relaxed, he replied, "You've got another two months of this, Sergeant. This is the north-east monsoon which we get between November and March".

He waited as a good humoured groan came from the soldiers. He held his hand up for silence, "I forgot to say", he paused theatrically, "we get two monsoons a year. This one will be followed by another one which starts in June and finishes in September".

The men cheered.

The Major knew he had them in the palm of his hand. The mood in the room had changed and his experience told him that they were ready for action but he hadn't finished with them yet and he held up the palm of his hand for silence. "It's very heavy rain as you are beginning to find out, we usually get between ninety and hundred inches a year".

"If I am correct Saar", responded the tall Sergeant from the back of the hall, "that's nearly nine foot of the fucking stuff".

A huge cheer went up which filled the room.

"Good luck men" the Major shouted. "Go and do your best".

After some speedily eaten food and the issue of weapons, the men started to move forward to the northern sector, ready to dig in and form a defensive line to protect the flanks of the infantry who were already there and holding the position.

"I hardly had time to have a piss", Bob complained, as he shifted the weight of the ammunition box from one shoulder to another.

At first, Bantam didn't answer. He wasn't even thinking about the weight of the Vickers machine gun on his shoulder. He had not become accustomed to the noise of war and his ears were ringing with the thunder of the relentless shelling coming from the Japanese artillery.

"At least you had one, pet", he eventually replied with a thin smile on his face.

He heard his friend laugh despite the clamour of battle around them.

In the distance Bantam could make out where the majority of the shells were landing and after ten minutes or so of hard slog, he, together with the rest of the reinforcements, he began to see yellow balls of fire and the plumes of rich tropical earth which were being thrown skywards as the enemy artillery fire pounded the forward lines. Bantam shuddered at the thought of the havoc they would be causing and looked at Bob. The two men could now feel the vibration of the exploding shells through the leather soles of their heavy boots. As they approached their infantry lines they could smell the burnt cordite hanging heavy in the air. Bob stopped and cocked his head to one side and listened.

Despite the din of the desperate battle which was being fought in front of them, it was the shrill wailing sound of the pipes which Bob heard and as the noise became louder, the two men realised that they were heading towards them. Within a few minutes, the remnants of a Scottish regiment, led by three kilted pipers came into sight and moved slowly through the outer flanks of the infantry lines. Bantam and Bob looked at the column of exhausted men as they passed by. Although their heads were held high, the two men knew the soldiers had the look of beaten men about them.

"Ha'way, Jock", Bantam said to one of the weary men as he passed by, "have you come from the mainland?"

The grim-faced man stopped and looked grateful for the short rest, "The bastards have pushed us all the way down the bloody mainland.........this is all that's left of us". Bantam looked at the rest of the column and did a quick count...no more than a hundred, he thought.

"We have just made it across the causeway before the Sappers blew it up... it will slow the bastards down for a few days and then it will be your turn", the soldier said chillingly. "It's the speed they are moving", he continued, "they are brutal bastards, they like close combat.......the poor sods they capture or those who are wounded, they bayonet.....no prisoners".

With that, the dejected man took off his flat, beige beret, with its red pom-pom and wiped his face before trudging off. Bantam and Bob didn't say a word. Shocked with what they had just been told, they turned and watched as the line of battle weary Highlanders walked, heavy-footed, rearwards through the lines, desperate for some rest from the bloody nightmare they had survived.

Both men stood there, momentarily rooted to the spot, until Bantam broke the deafening silence. "At least pet", he said to Bob with his usual sardonic humour, "we haven't had a wasted journey".

"The bloody Japs didn't waste any time in getting here", Bob said through gritted teeth as he watched the Vickers machine gun draw in yet another ammunition belt and pull out the rounds with lightning speed before dropping them into the weapon's breech. The nervousness he felt during the first days of the fighting on the island had disappeared and now his dirt-streaked face showed nothing but determination. His head was drumming with the noise of the gun as Bantam, once again sprayed its murderous fire towards the enemy positions. It had only been three days since the sappers had blown up the causeway before the Japanese transport ships started landing huge numbers of their infantry on Singapore's eastern shore.

Bantam gritted his teeth and pressed his thumbs on the gun's firing lever. The enemy had outflanked them and had been pushing towards them ever since. For the past two hours, the fighting had been hard and bloody and much to his consternation, the cooling water in the gun's barrel was beginning to boil. He touched it lightly and winced as his fingers made contact with the hot metal casing. At least, he thought, as he stopped firing, the Japs hadn't broken through this time and thankfully they had been spared the close quarter fighting the bastards relished. His head ached and his ears still screamed with the sounds of the slaughter they had witnessed during the fierce fighting of the past two days. The Geordies had counter attacked and had recaptured the vital ground around the naval base and now, with luck, they should be able to get some rest before the next onslaught started.

Bantam's face was tense but resolute as he looked at a slime-filled shallow depression in the waterlogged ground at their new position.

"This will do", he murmured, as he thankfully lowered his heavy gun to the ground.

He was exhausted by the ferocity of the fighting of the past week and was relieved to get the weight off his aching shoulders. Bantam knew the gun backwards thanks to the training they had been given on the firing ranges hidden deep in the wild hills of the Cheviots. He could dismantle and re-assemble every one of its hundred parts blindfolded. He was hungry and thirsty and had not slept properly for days and was grateful to have reached the forward gun position which was to the left flank of the infantry who like him, were beginning to dig in. Whilst the next attack was not expected to come until nightfall, Bantam felt naked without the gun in position and was relieved when Bob arrived minutes later with the tripod and a box of ammunition.

"Thanks pet", he said, as Bob handed him the tripod. He never ceased to be surprised by man's strength. Bob carried the tripod and the ammo box with ease although their combined weight was heavier than a large sack of Durham coal. In turn, Bantam quickly stamped his muddy boot on the spade feet of the tripod and then, when it was firm, he attached the gun. In the meantime, Bob, with equal speed, was taking a two-hundred round ammunition belt from the green painted box he had been carrying. With the gun assembled and checked, Bantam, with the precision of a surgeon's eyes, studied the thick clumps of tropical vegetation growing profusely to one side of them. Whilst he was grateful for the cover it would give them, he also knew that when the Japs came, they might use the lush green growth for their own concealment. He took a deep breath and grabbed one of the rope handles of the ammo box and started to drag it across the glutinous mud. Its flat base became stuck in the wet mud and Bantam had to give it a quick heave to break the suction before he could get it into a position where he could sit on it behind the gun. His eyes were level with the rangefinder and he grunted with satisfaction of the height his makeshift seat gave him. He gave Bob, who was squatting to his right, a quick nod of his head which was the signal to starting threading the cloth ammo belt into the feed block of the gun. With his fingers grasped round the guns traversing handles, Bantam raised the safety catch and rested his thumbs lightly on the centre thumb piece. He looked across at Bob and grinned. Both men felt happier now that the gun was ready for firing. Bantam knew that once he pressed his thumbs down the gun would fire five hundred rounds per minute although he generally preferred accuracy over quantity and normally fired bursts of ten to twenty rounds every two seconds or so. He had developed such a light touch he could also fire a single round and finish if need be.

Carefully, as they had done so many times before during the past few days, the two men laid their rifles, with bayonets firmly attached, alongside the gun and checked that the grenades were tucked snugly in the pouches on their belts. Bantam looked at the fading twilight and knew the next attack would be starting soon. Recently, there had been some heavy fighting during the daylight hours but he knew the enemy favoured fighting at night. Although Bantam's body yearned for sleep, every nerve end was tingling and he was wide awake as he looked along the lines of grim-faced infantrymen, who like him and Bob, were waiting for the inevitable bloody chaos to begin.

I must have a drink, Bantam thought, as he subconsciously ran his tongue along his dry lips.

He took the water bottle from the pocket on his belt. It felt empty and he shook it, relieved there was still some left in the bottom. He took a sip of the tepid liquid and handed what was left to Bob.

Fat, green jungle frogs were singing duets in the mud pools when Bantam's ears caught the first sound of gunfire. He quickly straightened his cramped legs as the battle orders were rattled out by the NCO's. The crack of the enemy rifle fire gradually increased and was followed by the sound of phat, phat, phat as a volley of bullets smacked into the wet ground around them. Bantam knew the Jap snipers would try to pick off the officers and the NCO's in an attempt to cause confusion and panic amongst the troops, before their light infantry groups, armed with machine guns would attempt to draw the British fire to them. Bantam looked across at Bob and saw his friend was clenching his teeth with the growing tension of the imminent attack. Bantam knew his friend's courage was beyond doubt and hoped his own would not desert him now. Both men were well aware the Jap rifle groups would probably be already moving silently towards them, using whatever cover they could find to conceal themselves from sight.

"Bob", Bantam said crisply, for once the humour in his voice had disappeared, "make sure the bastards don't come out of those bamboos".

He tipped his head urgently towards the tall clumps of vegetation to his left but before Bob could reply, the Japanese attack began on the right flank. Volleys of machine gun fire opened up as the enemy started to run forward. Out of the corner of his eye, Bantam could see them as they charged forward on the flank, intent on overwhelming the defending lines of grim faced men. He felt his tongue sticking to the roof of his mouth, which was still crust dry. He blinked away the perspiration which was running in his eyes and beginning to blur his vision. Suddenly, in the half light, he saw the ghostly shapes of more Japs beginning to break cover in front of him. At first, Bantam thought the green shapes was just vegetation being blown about by the mortar shells and grenades which were exploding around him. He quickly realised the Japs had camouflaged themselves with the small branches and leaves they had snatched from the jungle's margins. Looking quickly through the eye sight fixed firmly on top of the gun's barrel casing, he pressed down hard on the thumb piece and watched the rapid fire of the .303 sharp-nosed bullets churn into the ground around the approaching enemy. All around him, bursts of light were illuminating the smoke-filled and rapidly darkening sky. Bantam screwed up his eyes against the glare of exploding munitions and the ear splitting explosions. The NCO's had stopped shouting their orders as some of the screaming Japs broke through the lines and the brutal, vicious hand to hand fighting had begun. It was now going to be every man for himself and nobody was in any doubt what they had to do now.

The controlled bursts of rapid fire spitting from the barrel of the Vickers was sending the spent brass shell cases up into the air like grains of rice at a wedding. The guns deadly fire started tearing into the Japanese front line preventing them from starting a bayonet charge on Bantam's flank. He knew at a rate of five-hundred rounds per minute, the gun would soon over-heat and without cooling water in its barrel casing, it would only fire another thousand rounds or so before it gave up the ghost. A look of concern spread across his blackened face as he quickly felt the breech of the gun and found it was already hot and sticky with black, burnt carbon. He could feel his shallow breathing. Soaked in sweat, the little man licked his lips and took aim once again, before pressing his thumbs so hard down on the gun's firing piece the blood began to drain from them.

It was a grin so wide that his top lip hardly touched the row of white, tombstone teeth beneath it, which spread across the Japanese Corporal's face when his Sergeant motioned that he wanted the man to detach himself from the main body of the front line. The man didn't need any further orders and he immediately began to collect together a small party of conscripts from the rifle company of the Japanese Imperial Division. They all knew what was expected of them and they immediately started moving towards the flank of the British lines where most of the machine gun fire was now coming from. The soldiers had been trained in jungle fighting and had spent as much time on bayonet practice as they could when they had been on the rifle ranges.

The words of their instructor were still ringing in their ears. "Show no mercy to the enemy and every time you kill one of them, it will lighten your heart".

They had lost count of the number of times their hearts had been lightened since they had entered the mangrove swamps of Malaya. Silently, the small group of men moved through outer fringes of the jungle, grateful for the concealment its emerald and brown hues gave them as they carefully pushed aside the thick bamboo stems with the points of the bayonets firmly fixed to their heavy Arisaka rifles.

Soon, when the Corporal gave the signal, the leading two of the grim faced privates would begin to crawl towards the machine gun nest and hurl the grenades which were hanging from their belts.

"BANTAM", Bob screamed out a warning, as he instinctively grabbed his rifle from the ground and fired a shot into the clump of bamboos where he thought he heard the noise and had seen the thick stems moving.

It had not been much more than a rustle but with the big man's frayed nerves he was not taking any chances and fired just in case.

Bantam's head spun round in time to see a green clad body falling backwards into the undergrowth. Bob had reacted quickly but not before the camouflaged man had detonated the grenade he was carrying by hitting its fuse against the hard wooden butt of his rifle and throwing it towards the two startled men. The small ribbed canister landed behind Bob who was still facing the clump of bamboos with his eyes fixed on the falling assailant.

The blast of the explosion hurled Bob towards Bantam in a shower of red hot debris. In the split second which followed, Bantam glimpsed his friend's outstretched arms as if as if they were preparing for a final embrace and heard the scream escaping from his blood filled mouth. Instantly, Bob's body hit Bantam, knocking him off the ammunition box and sending him sprawling into the mud. With the noise of the explosion ringing in his ears and the flash of the grenade disappearing into the night sky, Bantam frantically scrambled across to where his friend was laying. As he gently touched Bob's pain wracked face he heard the rattle of death escape from his friend's throat as his lifeless body slumped into the ground.

The noise of the battle being fought around him was echoing in Bantam's head as he instinctively collected his senses and desperately grabbed his rifle. Despite his quick-silver reactions, his blood soaked hands had not reached the gun when, looking up, he saw a Japanese soldier charging towards him. The cold steel blade of the man's bayonet glistened in the illuminated sky. Time was frozen as Bantam stared wide eyed at his assailant. He saw the man's sadistic eyes were blinking and filled with hate. Bantam's mouth was gaping wide open and with empty lungs, he emitted a silent scream as the Japanese corporal thrust the deadly blade on his rifle forward. Bantam never felt the point of the bayonet as it was plunged through his combat blouse and into his soft belly. All he could feel was the warmth of the blood gushing from the gaping wound it had made and watched, almost spell-bound, as the grinning man with tombstone teeth stamped a muddy boot on his chest, before finally, with a vicious twist, wrenching the bayonet out of the limp body.

Slowly, as if in a dream, the world around Bantam went quiet as he sank back motionless onto the wet, rich earth of the jungle. A dark veil descended and as it gradually turned black, the brave little man entered the next world.

"Bloody hell", Tom exclaimed in amazement as he watched the armour piercing shell of the QF anti-tank gun slice through the Japanese tank like a hot knife going through a pat of butter.

Chopper had already loaded another shell into the gun's breech and stood up to watch the plume of smoke which was already coming out of the tank's turret.

"GET DOWN", Tom screamed at his friend, knowing the machine gun mounted to the side of the tank's hull could still pose a threat, as could the Japanese infantry who might be following the tank.

During the past two weeks, ever since they had arrived in Singapore, the gunners had been held in reserve in the barracks to the east of the island but they were now part of a defensive force to prevent the enemy from coming down the Yong Pang road. The Japanese forces had floated their lightly armoured tanks across the narrow Straights of Jahore and although Tom had been told the tanks nearly always travelled ahead of the infantry foot soldiers, he had no intention to take any chances that this one was travelling alone. Chopper sat down quickly on the towing arm behind the gun's metal shield and watched as two Japs jumped from burning tank only to be dispatched by a volley of .303 bullets hastily fired from the Lee Enfields of some soldiers positioned in a nearby ditch. Tom's eyes remained focused on the road for any signs of more enemy approaching, when he heard explosions and hisses, almost like fireworks on Guy Fawkes night coming from inside the burning tank. As the men watched, the ammunition in the tank's magazine exploded, opening the light tank's hull like a tin of Fray Bentos corned beef.

"What do you think Tom?" Chopper asked anxiously, as he wiped off the ever-present sweat running down his forehead and into his eyes, "was this the only one?"

"No idea, but I bet Percy and the others would have liked to have seen the way we hit it".

Chopper laughed and then fell silent when it occurred to him they had not seen or heard of the others since they had been separated when they had left the barracks.

"Destroy your gun and fall back at the double men, at the double". The swirling smoke coming from the burning tank obscured the NCO who was shouting the order but there was no doubting of the urgency in his voice now. "FALL BACK....FALL BACK".

It was not for the first time Chopper had thought what a bloody mess this was and it was no different now. The retreating men around him had been cobbled together from different units and had never met before, let alone been trained together, it was no wonder they were falling back, once again from the on-coming enemy.

Tom snatched a grenade from the side pouch on his webbing belt and quickly wrenched out the pin.

"RUN", he shouted superfluously, as he quickly nestled the primed grenade on the gun's breech and followed the heels of his fleeing friend.

In the distance Tom could hear the enemy's artillery shells pounding other positions to the left and right of them and knew it wouldn't be long before the shells were directed at their position. It seemed as though every part of the city was being bombarded by the Japanese artillery and as he raced to catch up with the rest of the retreating troops, the full impact of the danger they were now in, struck him. It was now a case of every man for himself as he ran towards the comparative safety of the city.

"TOM, TOM", it was sound of Chopper's voice piercing through the din of the battle that Tom could hear.

"TOM. OVER HERE". Somehow, Chopper had managed to stop a three-ton truck crammed full of exhausted soldiers and was holding it's door open for his friend to climb in.

"For Christ's sake get a bloody move on", the agitated driver spat out the words, as Tom clambered in alongside him". "The bastards are directing their fire from a spotter they've got in that bloody air balloon and we haven't got a single plane in the sky to shoot the fucking thing down".

Tom didn't reply but glanced up through the smoke and saw the spherical shape in the sky, he had noticed it before but never realised it was being used for observation by the Japs.

"Where are we going?" Chopper asked the driver, as if he was on a Sunday afternoon outing.

The wide-eyed man looked past Tom, who was squeezed between the two men, and stared at Chopper as if he was mad. "Where the fuck do you think?"..........."We're all falling back to form a defensive position around the city centre", the man shouted as he tried to make himself heard over the noise of the trucks screaming engine. "We'll try and get there and dig in with the rest of them, if we can".

The crash seemed imminent as the driver's eyes returned back to the road. The truck swerved across the road, narrowly missing the group of civilians who were fleeing in panic from the wave of terror which was threatening to overwhelm everything and everybody in its path. As the truck raced on, Tom heard the sound of low flying planes overhead and he automatically ducked and raised his arm in an attempt to shield his head as a string of bombs struck a three-story building to his left. Showers of masonry and debris cascaded down almost blocking the road ahead of them.

The driver reacted quickly and wrenched the steering wheel round to miss the smoking pile of bricks. The truck bounced as its wheels hit the rubble which had landed further out in the road. The driver swore and glanced in his mirror at the civilians they had just passed and muttered, "Poor sods, they're terrified, especially the Chinese. The Japs are bayoneting them on sight.....if they're lucky".

Tom didn't bother to ask the man what he meant by saying "If they're lucky".

The beleaguered city was bathed in brilliant, tropical moonlight when Tom and Chopper took up their positions as part of the defensive ring which had been set up around the battered and besieged city. In front of them, out in the darkness, they could hear the blood-chilling sounds of the hand to hand fighting which was still raging further out in the city streets and the cries of the hundreds of civilians who were still trapped there. As dawn broke, the orders were passed down the line they were to continue to fight until the last man. Chopper looked at Tom but did not say anything. There was a lump in his dry throat and he swallowed hard in an attempt to shift it.

A feeling of dread permeated through every nerve in Chopper's body as he finally questioned in astonishment, "Down to the last man?"

It was Tom's turn to remain silent but in the half-light he noticed his friend's face was drawn and battle-weary. Chopper had lost weight which Tom thought was hardly surprising after what they had been through during the last few days.

Chopper looked back at him and said in a low voice, "There are eighty-thousand of us trying to defend the place with hardly any bloody food and water and sod all ammo. It won't be much longer before we are all well and truly fucked".

Two days and nights of unremitting fighting had passed and the din of a battle lost had ceased as an uneasy quiet had now descended on the shattered city.

Chopper shook his head in despair and said darkly, "How the fuck could we have been beaten by this fucking lot?" He felt nothing but despair and dejection as he looked grimly at the grinning Japanese soldiers who were cycling past with their rifles slung across their backs.

"Beaten by Nips on bloody bikes", his words tailed off as he looked across at Tom who was looking equally grim. The smell of the burning city mingled with the putrid stench of death.

The two men sat amongst a hundred or so other defeated soldiers on what had been, until a few hours previously, the perfectly manicured lawn of a government building. As part of the surrender terms imposed on the Allied forces, they all had to remain in position until the Japanese high command decided what to do with them. Devastation was all around the defeated army. Burnt out cars and army vehicles littered the streets. Bombed and burning buildings lined, what had once been wide streets full of a multitude of jostling people. It was now replaced with countless rotting corpses.

"They outflanked us", said a soldier who was sitting next to Tom. "The top brass had all the big guns pointing out to bloody sea. We couldn't even turn them round after the bastards had landed".

A small convoy of enemy trucks, so heavily camouflaged with branches of foliage they appeared at first sight to be a line of trees on the move, drove by as the men continued to give their views to one another for the reason of the defeat.

"Our defences were concentrated on the northern area at Sembawang, whilst their forward troops landed on the eastern and western shores", said another dejected voice.

"We were fucked once they had taken Bukat Tinah and captured the ammo and food supplies along with the fucking pumping station", added a dejected looking soldier from the Suffolk regiment, who it seemed had been fighting there.

A number of heads nodded in agreement. The hunger pains in their stomachs and their parched throats verified what the soldier from the Suffolks had just said about the shortage of food and water.

During the next few days the hoarse voices of British NCO's resounded across the streets of the city as they shouted commands to assembled ranks of prisoners. With the tropical sun relentlessly beating down on them, thousands of the British soldiers were being drilled and marched up and down the shell and bomb ravaged streets and on the few remaining patches of grass, without respite. Tom felt naked without a rifle hanging from his shoulder as he marched with the rest of the men, occasionally glancing to his left in a vain and pointless attempt to keep the line straight.

A feeling of repulsion gripped him, when out of the corner of his eye he saw a group of Japanese soldiers, sneering and laughing at the dishevelled and beaten troops, being marched for hours on end by their own officers.

"Halt"......"At ease"....."At rest".... Tom sighed with relief when the pointless drilling had finished and he set off to find Chopper, who had already found a place in the shade under the few remaining branches of a bomb shattered tree, away from the scorching rays of the sun.

Tom joined his friend and found he was already embroiled in a heated discussion with a small group of soldiers who were clearly angry with the situation they had found themselves in.

"I can't believe it", complained one of soldiers, whose shirt was soaked in sweat despite the fact it was wide open to his waist. "Our own bloody officers marching us up and down just for the bloody sake of it and our own bloody military police ordering their own men, what to do and what not to do......you'd think we were *their* bloody prisoners".

Tom remained silent, knowing the officers were trying to maintain discipline amongst the thousands of demoralised troops who were already bored and growing angrier by the day. He suspected the Japanese command had been overwhelmed by the colossal numbers of prisoners and needed time to get the prison camps organised.

"Those vicious bastards would like to kill every one of us", said one of the other soldiers. Have you heard what they did to those poor buggers in the hospital?"

Heads nodded but nobody said a word. A grim silence descended over the group of men. They had all heard how the Japanese infantry had stormed through one of the city's hospitals a few days earlier and had bayoneted the patients in their beds, before executing the doctors and nurses".

"Over three hundred innocent sods slaughtered in minutes....one of them was even on the operating table when they killed him", said another solemn voice.

It was Tom who spoke next. "There's a rumour that we're being moved to the prisons at Changi in the next few days. Perhaps things will get better then and we'll get a bit more to eat", he said optimistically.

Chopper looked at Tom as if had gone mad and tilting his head towards the sky he looked up at the ominous black clouds gathering overhead.

A week of unrelenting misery followed. Tom was bored and hungry and after staring meaninglessly at his boots for what seemed hours, looked behind him and saw what appeared to be a swirling storm cloud. It was the dust being thrown up by hundreds of pairs of marching boots.

"Look at that lot behind us", he said to Chopper, who was limping alongside.

Chopper winced and looked over his shoulder. For as far as he could see, there were lines of men marching out of the dead and shattered city to a place they called Changi on the northern tip of the island. Although they had only been marching for about six miles, the huge pus-filled blister on Chopper's heel had burst and now the pain became more intense with every step he took, as the raw flesh rubbed against the hard leather of his boot.

He had no intention of telling Tom of his predicament, instead he just asked, "How much further?"

"Fourteen miles or so", came back the breathless reply.

It was always in the early hours of the morning when Tom would lie awake and relish the relative tranquillity of the prison hut they had been moved to and this particular morning was no different. Dawn had not yet broken over the rows of squalid huts which made up the River Valley Road camp and the tropical birds had not yet signalled the arrival of another day from the branches of the trees which surrounded the camp. Somewhere in the distance, Tom could hear the unmistakable howl of a small troop of monkeys as they took an early breakfast of the succulent fruit hanging from the wild fig trees which still grew in the patches of jungle which remained. He pulled the lice-ridden rice sack over his hunger-wracked body and closed his eyes. The hum of the ever present mosquitoes reverberated in his ears, as the blood-sucking creatures searched for their next meal from amongst the sixty or seventy men who were sleeping on the bamboo platforms which lined the make-shift hut. Soon, when the first rays of sunlight burst through the gaps in the huts corrugated- iron roof, Tom would be able to move off the top tier of the platform and line up for the first of the day's roll calls. His stomach ached and rumbled as the stabbing pangs reminded him how hungry he was. He turned over on the hard bamboo platform and pushed his clenched fist into the pit of his empty stomach. During the past months, as the amount of food became less and less, Tom had discovered by doing this it helped to relieve the effects of starvation in his empty belly.

After roll call and before the prisoners were formed into working parties under the command of British officers, they would be given their first meal of the day. Tom smiled wryly to himself as he thought of the predictability of the small bowl of boiled rice and vegetable water they would be given. Somewhere in the darkness he heard somebody groan as they quickly stumbled outside before their bowels made the decision before them. There was hardly a man left in the prison camp who wasn't suffering from the gallops and, as Tom's senses became fully awake, the unmistakable smell coming from the overflowing latrines confirmed the fact.

As Tom lifted the bowl to his mouth he once again became aware of the drone from the hoards of insects which spent their short lives in the swamps on which the huts had been hastily built. His thoughts drifted back to something one of the regimental cooks had told him whilst he had waited for his evening bowl of rice. The surrender had happened seven months ago and ever since, the whole of the Changi peninsular had become a hot bed of rumours which circulated amongst the prisoners and at the time, Tom had suspected what the cook had told him, was just one of them.

Whilst he sat listening to the hum of insects, Tom's mind began to fill with the awful images he saw on the streets when he was marched out of the camp as part of one of the hundreds of working parties which were being made to labour in the docks or anywhere else their captors decreed. Although the Japs initially treated the prisoners with contempt, which was bad enough, Tom noticed they were becoming increasingly unpredictable and violent towards their captives. The lack of adequate food and clean water was taking its toll and with the absence of medical supplies, it was only a matter of time before the prisoners would start to die like flies.

Tom thought once more what the cook had said and it suddenly occurred to him that perhaps the man had been right. Perhaps they were going to be transported to build a railway through the jungle, where, as the cook had assured him, there would be hospitals to treat the sick and injured and above all else, where there would be plenty to eat and drink.

8

A Warm Welcome Awaits You

Tom sat on the steel floor of the box car which in its previous life had been a rice wagon and as he leant against its side he could feel the heat of the metal burning through his saturated shirt. He was one of over thirty men who had been mercilessly crammed in the stinking box but felt fortunate he was not one of the poor sods who had no choice but to try to stand and keep their balance, on legs so weak they hardly supported them on solid ground, let alone in the swaying railway truck. Already the tropical sun had transformed it into an oven and Tom knew sooner or later he would have to move and try to squat over the edge of the moving wagon to relieve himself when his relished place would be quickly taken but at least he was grateful of the rest whilst it lasted. The thick growth on his chin was jolting on his knees and beginning to make them sore as he listened to the noise of the train's squeaking wheels as they rumbled over the gaps in the rails. As Tom listened to the familiar sounds, his thoughts drifted back to the train journey he had made when the family had moved from Chartham to Pentbury. How long ago it was and how far away it seemed. He sighed at the thought but was thankful he had at least escaped from his awful captivity for a few glorious moments. They had been travelling in the wagon for four days now, sweltering by day and freezing at night. It was only when the train stopped briefly at night to take on water, the metal boxes cooled down and Tom and the others were allowed off to fill their water bottles and gulp down some thin rice soup.

At first, some of the men had been swearing about the conditions they were being forced to endure and their hatred of their captors, whilst others had been almost excitable, talking loudly to each other about where they were being taken and what they would have to do. But now it was quiet, the conditions in the train's twenty wagons had seen to that. Occasionally, Tom heard the screech of parrots as they claimed their territory in the thick jungle growing in abundance on either side of the track. Every time the noise of the rumbling train disturbed them they had to fly deeper in the jungle to seek new roosts and safety from the eagles flying overhead. Whenever he heard the parrots' calls Tom would crane his neck in the hope of seeing the brightly coloured birds. How he envied their freedom.

At first, Tom didn't take any notice when the rhythm of the train changed but as he listened, he was sure it was not the same as it had been for days. The noise of the steam gushing from the rusty engine's funnel was different, slower perhaps, he thought. The rumbling of the wheels on the tracks was also slowing. Tom became alert. He sat up.

Others had noticed it too and somebody shouted, almost excitedly, "We're here lads".

Another prisoner muttered weakly, "Thank Christ for that".

Men jostled each other in the haste to get out, anxious to fill their lungs with fresh air. Those on the floor struggled to stand up and Tom found himself being squashed against the unforgiving side of the steel wagon. The brakes squealed painfully, as they were slowly clamped onto the steel rims of the locomotive's huge wheels. The pulsing noise of the steam being pushed from the funnel was replaced with an occasional single "*chuff*". It sounded as if the engine was dying, punished for bringing its' dirty and squalid passengers one step closer to hell. The train stopped with an untidy jolt and Tom could hear the sound of Japanese boots as they ran past the wagon and then the scraping of the sliding doors as they were pulled open.

"*SPEEDO, SPEEDO*" a guard started hollering, as he thrust his arm into the wagon and grabbed the nearest prisoner, whom he had decided was not getting out quickly enough.

Tom had pressed himself flat against the side of the wagon as the groping hand came in and watched in horror as the unfortunate man was hurled in a heap onto the platform, joining those who had been removed from other wagons in a similar fashion. He paused as two of the guards rushed towards the man who was now on his knees and catching his breath. But before the gasping man had the chance to get up, they started to deliver a series of ferocious kicks of encouragement. Tom winced as he heard a sickening crunch as one of the guards brought his rifle butt down on the man's unprotected head.

Somebody gripped Tom's arm and he heard it was Chopper's voice that whispered in his ear, "Keep moving", as he stopped to watch the beating.

"You vicious bastards, you bloody bastards", some of prisoners were shouting at the guards. Tom glanced back and saw two of them were so furious at what was happening their noses were nearly touching those of their adversaries.

"Stupid buggers", Chopper said as they walked along the mud strewn platform, "they are asking for trouble".

Overhead, grim looking clouds had bunched together bringing with them the rain which had started to beat down and pour off the palm-thatched roofs of the scruffy huts which lined the platform. Tom let out a groan of pleasure as he pulled his shoulders back and stretched his aching spine. Every limb ached in his pain-wracked body and the relief of being freed from the steel box flooded through him as he repeated the exercises on his arms and his legs.

Glancing back to look at the train, Chopper, who was doing the same thing, said, "I hope we won't be doing that again".

Tom nodded his head and as he looked at his old friend he realised how thin he had become. Tom knew there wasn't a man amongst them who hadn't lost weight during their seven months in the camp at Changi and virtually everyone was suffering from sap draining fevers and the runs but Chopper, he thought, looked thinner than most.

The tropical downpour was relentless as the men were formed into ranks. Tom noticed behind the small, scruffy station was a small village which one of the prisoners had said was called Ban Pong. It was deserted apart from a few pathetic looking jungle fowl searching the muddy streets for something to eat. The rickety bamboo houses which lined the street were side-less and appeared to be empty.

However, a number of the native men had heard the arrival of the train and were shouting and running up to meet the prisoners, trying to trade anything of value the exhausted men had left on them. Orders were being bawled out and the compliant lines of prisoners moved forward with the natives following on behind, but before the men were scarcely out of the station yard, another order was given to halt. Tom stared at the sight in front of him and his stomach knotted with dread. This was not what he had been expecting. To one side of the column of men were lines of huts, standing as if marooned in a sea of muddy, stinking water. The huts looked like the ones in the village but this time, Tom could see hundreds of emaciated prisoners, many just wearing loincloths made from rice sacks, whilst others were in what appeared to be large nappies.

"Bloody hell" he groaned, as the smell from the nearby latrines invaded his nostrils and as he looked towards the foul-smelling buildings he could see swarms of large blue bottle flies which obviously enjoyed their brief, degraded lives there.

Tom felt sick.

"At ease", a British NCO barked.

Most of the men sank to the ground unconcerned about the mud. Tom and Chopper found a place as far as they could from the stinking reek of the latrines and watched as some of the natives, who were wearing long, skirt-like sarongs, made their way towards them offering to trade. Chopper pulled out some coins from his pocket and bartered them for some chunks of dry rice bread and fruit which the two friends devoured whilst waiting for what was to come. Their attention was drawn towards two Japanese officers who were in animated conversation. One of them started giving orders to some of their lower ranks and as he did so more grim-faced soldiers arrived, wearing rucksacks with bed- rolls hanging beneath them.

The two friends had finished their bread and fruit when Chopper nudged Tom and said under his breath, "Look what's heading this way. Just our fucking luck, it's the Gunzoku, the so-called bloody watch soldiers".

Marching towards them was a group of Korean guards. Both Chopper and Tom already knew the justifiable reputation the brutish looking men had.

"Christ", Tom said, without any emotion in his voice, as the guards rapidly approached them. He felt weak and wondered what more horrors would confront them.

"Scruffy looking sods, aren't they?" Chopper said, trying to lighten the mood, as he looked at the men. "No wonder the Japs consider them to be nothing more than bloody vermin".

"The Japs think all the people they conquer are bloody vermin...including us", Tom replied contemptuously.

The tropical uniforms of the Gunzoku guards had been made from a cheap, coarse woven cloth and were quite shabby compared with those of the Japanese soldiers. They didn't wear any regimental insignia other than a white cloth disc, with a red five pointed star in the centre which had been roughly sewn onto the left shoulder of their dull green tunics. Hanging from the men's necks, were square haversacks, which as they swung from side to side and banged against their chests reminding Tom of the nose-bags which hung from the heads of the dray horses back home.

"They may be scruffy but compared with us", Tom mumbled, "I would say they're almost fucking Saville Row"

Chopper laughed and replied, "Tom, my old mate, something tells me we are going to be taken for a walk through the jungle". The chirpy tone in Chopper's voice lifted Toms' spirits slightly.

"MARCHEE, MARCHEE", screamed out the shrill voice of a Japanese officer.

Gathering their meagre belongings together, the prisoners reluctantly and in most cases, painfully, got to their feet and with the sun sinking behind them, started marching out of Ban Pong.

For the first few miles Tom noticed that although the lush undergrowth had been cut away, the jungle was already growing back and a few small trees had begun to fight their way for a place in the sun. The unremitting march continued and with dusk falling, Tom noticed the trees were now much taller than any of those he had seen elsewhere. He guessed some of the giants were over a hundred feet tall but they didn't have the round trunks of the trees back home, instead they had star-shaped trunks, with roots hanging down like enormous spiders reaching down to feed on the wet jungle floor. High up and growing out of the strange monsters were huge spreading branches, heavy with the biggest leaves Tom had ever seen in his life. The monsoon rain was still dropping from the heavy black clouds overhead and he noticed the foliage of the trees was so thick that only a light spray was reaching the forest floor below. Tom realised he was not the only one who was looking from side to side at the jungle noticing the men in front of him were doing the same. There was a strange fascination about this wet tropical world. In the distance were the haunting calls of the jungle creatures moving out of their daytime hides as the veil of darkness fell. These unseen animals and birds were starting to call to each other and the wet, steaming world around the exhausted men was beginning to come alive. Then, without any warning, there was a sudden eruption of noise and movement in one of the tall trees which towered over the track in front of the column. Instinctively some of the battle hardened men threw themselves to the ground, sensing they were coming under attack.

The column of men was suddenly in disarray and the guards started shouting at the men, "*MARCHEE, MARCHEE*"; in an attempt to restore order.

Tom and Chopper had dropped to their knees and were staring up at the tree where the commotion was coming from. It seemed as though its topmost branches had come alive and as the two men stared into gloom, the noise in midst of the tree became louder and louder...

"IT'S BIRDS, it's bloody birds", somebody shouted, who was further up the column nearer to the source of the noise.

Tom could see them now. They were huge, black creatures. Hundreds of them were using their enormous wings to lift themselves from the tree and like a threatening thunder cloud they quickly began to rise high up into night sky.

"They're not birds, they're bloody bats.....bloody big bats", exclaimed another voice, almost in disbelief at what his eyes were seeing.

Tom and Chopper, realising there was no danger, stood up and stared in amazement as the cloud of the winged creatures rose silhouetted against the evening sky. Chopper pursed his lips before nodding his agreement that they were indeed bats, saying, "I've never seen bats that bloody big. They look like dogs with bloody great wings", he concluded as the prisoners were forced with the points of Japanese bayonets to get in line and begin their weary march into the darkness again.

"Yamero.......Yamero.... Stop....Stop", shrieked the high pitched voice of Warrant Officer Ito Sasaki whom some of the prisoners had already named, *Slimey*.

He was short, squat and repugnant. No more five feet tall with a mouthful of protruding teeth, most of which were in differing stages of decay. The tropical heat was brutal. Hotter and wetter than being in a Turkish bath and sweating in these conditions was nothing unusual for anyone but for this particular man, it was different. Sweat constantly poured from every pore in his bloated body and as he wiped the giant beads of perspiration away, it appeared his face was covered in a layer of slime. It was not unlike the slimy film of mucous on a garden slug, hence the name the prisoners had given him. Tom watched the loathsome looking man as he screamed out his orders and could see there was not a hint of compassion in the man's cold, black eyes. The only emotion his eyes displayed was that of utter contempt for the prisoners. Ever since their capture Tom had seen and experienced the scorn and cruelty the Japanese showed towards their prisoners but for this man, it was different. His eyes were full of hatred and spite. A black, pencil thin moustache danced on the top lip of his grinning face as he looked up and down the bedraggled line of prisoners. The man had already shown displays of uncontrolled anger towards the Gunzoku and Tom was in no doubt if he was given the slightest provocation, Warrant Officer Sasaki would be more than capable of causing very considerable pain and suffering to the POW's. The prisoners needed no further command from the vicious man to stop.

"Neru.....neru... yamero". Slimey's shrill voice was sounding more like a scream as the column came to an unorganised halt and some of the men ran towards the jungle's edge to relieve themselves. Chopper

263

was amongst the men who were already squatting with relief, as a consequence of the dysentery they were suffering from.

"It seems as if the fat little prick is going to let us rest at last", Chopper, who had joined Tom again, said thankfully.

"Thank Christ for that", Tom sighed with exhaustion as he slumped to the ground.

Every muscle in his body was silently screaming for rest and as he lay on the soft, wet ground unable to move, his eyelids slowly closed and at last his aching body found the rest it so desperately yearned.

It was the sound of gunfire which woke Tom with a start. His heart was pounding like a drum buried deep in his chest and his body shook in the same way a child shakes when woken by a nightmare. Japanese voices were shouting. He could hear more gunfire and the sound of English voices shouting. He was confused and could not comprehend what was happening as he started to struggle to his feet. Pandemonium had broken out. Tom didn't have time to collect his thoughts any further, when, without warning or provocation, the well aimed boot of a Korean guard embedded itself in his stomach. He fell back to the ground, winded and wincing with pain. Looking up he saw the grinning face of the Gunsoku. Two Japanese soldiers ran past him and he could hear Slimey's high pitched voice frantically bellowing orders.

"*Ryuushutsu, Ryuushusu*, escape attempt, escape attempt" and in the black moonless night Tom could see all the prisoners around him were awake. Many of them were already standing up and were craning their necks to see what was going on, whilst a few had left the track and had moved to the edge of the jungle.

"RUN, RUN", they were shouting.

Tom peered through the darkness and saw Chopper was amongst them. As he watched, the Gunzoku started to push the shouting men back into the ranks, bringing their rifle butts down in a rain of savage blows on the prisoners who were slow in doing so. Tempers were rising and there was a sense of malice in the air. As the ranks of men started to be bought to order, some of the Japanese soldiers joined the Korean guards and started brutally using their fists and boots to

264

push the ranks of prisoners more tightly together until subdued, they were encircled by their captors.

Without being seen, Tom slowly edged down the line to where Chopper was now standing.

"What's happening?" he whispered, touching Chopper's arm.

"It look like a couple of the lads thought the coast was clear and decided to make a run for it", Chopper replied in an equally low voice.

"Have they been caught?"

"Not yet". Choppers' expression was grim as he said darkly. "Some of the Japs went running in after them... I hope they don't catch them, if they do, I don't fancy the chances of the poor sods. Look at Slimey's face, he's bloody fuming this has happened".

Tom glanced across at the warrant officer's face and saw exactly what Chopper meant.

Unnoticed, the night had turned cold and now most of the men were shivering. About ten long minutes had passed when Tom heard Japanese voices coming from the jungle. After a few moments, these were followed by the sound of men crashing quite close to the place where he was standing and then, emerging through the thick tropical vegetation, he saw the dreadful reality. Two badly beaten prisoners were being dragged out by the Japanese soldiers. The men's faces were already swollen and bruised. Blood was streaming from the nose of one of them and although the beaten men were covered in the mud of the jungle floor, Tom could see their bodies were also blooded. The smaller of the two men was barely conscious, whilst the other one had a defiant look on his face as they were thrown down at the feet of the grinning Slimey. He shouted something in Japanese and then stepped forward and proceeded to give each of the unfortunate men a volley of meaningful kicks to their heads and groins. The men instinctively brought their knees up to their chests and wrapped their hands around their heads in a vain attempt to protect themselves from the kicking and were lying curled up and groaning on the ground. Some of the soldiers in the ranks of men who were being forced to watch the sickening spectacle started shouting obscenities at Slimey, giving their views on him and what they thought of the Imperial

Japanese army. Major Harris, the commanding officer of the prisoners immediately marched from the front of the assembled men and directly facing Slimey, demanded he should adhere to the Geneva Convention, reminding him about the treatment of prisoners of war. Without the need of any command from Slimey, one of the Japanese soldiers who had dragged the beaten prisoners from the jungle strutted forward and immediately clubbed the British officer to the ground with the butt of his rifle.

With the kicking of the two men completed, Slimey's mood seemed visibly improved. Tom watched as two of the Korean guards wound a thin strand of wire round the necks of the two prisoners, taking it down their backs to bind their wrists behind their backs and then, forcing the men to kneel, they wound the end of the wire round their ankles so that any movement the men made tightened the wire strand round their necks. One of the bound captives contemptuously spat a mouthful of blood onto the ground at the feet of the guards.

"The poor sods are trussed up like turkeys", Chopper said silently under his breath.

Tom remained silent, trying to subdue the anger which was rising from deep inside and the hatred he felt towards their captors. Ringed round and menaced by the grinning guards, the soldiers continued to be forced to stand in ranks to watch the sickening scene which was unfolding. Tom looked towards the bound prisoners and he was in no doubt this was to teach them all a lesson and to show what would happen if they ever tried to escape.

Daylight eventually broke and the soldiers still stood silently in line trying to avert their sleep deprived eyes from the sight of the two unfortunate men lying in front of them. The grave-like silence which had only been broken by the noises of the night was now being replaced by the sound a flock of birds, no doubt breakfasting on the nuts and fruit which grew in this unforgiving place. Neither of the bound prisoners had made a sound since they were beaten and the smaller man had fallen on his side and appeared to be dead.

Ito Sasaki appeared and looked down contemptuously at Major Harris, who had regained consciousness during the night but was being forced to lie where he had fallen by the point of a Japanese bayonet being held at his throat. Accompanied by a fellow officer who

Tom had not seen before, Slimey beckoned that Major Harris should be taken back to the ranks before addressing the watching prisoners in his usual high pitched voice.

The odious looking man waited before he started to speak, his eyes raking up and down the lines of assembled men. The Japanese officer at his side stood patiently until it was time to start his translation, "You are prisoners of the Imperial Japanese army".

Slimey paused for the translator to catch up before continuing.

The man interpreted Slimey's rant with obvious relish, "The commanding officers of your army surrendered, you do not have any rights".

Slimey was now beginning to scream at the troops and his translator raised his voice in unison.

"The punishment for trying to escape is death. The punishment for disobeying the orders of our officers is death and the punishment for showing any sign of disobedience is death". Fat beads of sweat ran down his face.

The translator turned to the Warrant Officer, saluted and marched away. Tom noticed that although the man was himself a Japanese officer, he was clearly nervous of Slimey and seemed to be relieved to be leaving his presence.

"*Shobun, Shobun*, Dispose of them", Slimey suddenly screamed and Tom knew the worst was about to happen.

Slimey barked out more orders, upon which four lower rank Japanese soldiers moved forward and started to drag the two bound prisoners into the jungle.

Tom watched in horror. He could see that one of the men was still limp and lifeless and Tom silently hoped he was already dead but the other one shouted profanities at the two Jap soldiers who were dragging him to his death. Men in the ranks, shocked at what they were witnessing, started shouting but their raised voices could not mask the dreadful screams of the two men as they were being killed. The ranks fell silent as the grinning Japanese soldiers returned from the jungle with the blood of the two brave men running down the polished steel of their bayonets. There wasn't a single man standing in the shocked lines of prisoners who was left in any doubt of the brutality they faced from their savage captors.

"Bastards", Tom said quietly as the march to the railway camp resumed in virtual silence.

Tom and Chopper had said little to each other since the killings, preferring to be alone with their thoughts. Tom was thinking how the men around him reacted differently to their Japanese captors. Some, like the defiant soldier who had been killed, did not accept their captivity and the inhumane treatment they were being subjected to. They fought back at every opportunity and would probably die in the process. Then, there were others, who like him, clung to the hope that one day whenever that would be, would return home, if only they could survive the hell they had been brought to. Yes, he silently contemplated, surviving and going home would be his objective from now on and he would not drown in this hell which threatened to engulf them.

As the seemingly, never ending march continued, Tom embraced the tropical jungle around him. By doing so, he could escape from the horror and could feel normal again, even if it was for only short periods of time. In a strange way, the jungle reminded him of the first time he had walked through Bell Woods and how he had marvelled at the nature around him with poor old George Saunders at his side.

As Tom continued to slog behind the row of men in front of him, rivulets of sweat poured down his face and curled round his rib cage which was clearly visible through his open shirt. The un-remitting heat was making him breathless and light-headed. Once again he let his mind drift back to the countryside he had left. He remembered how the woods at home were cool, so deliciously cool. So different, so very different, he thought to the jungle around him where high up in the trees, huge clumps of ferns were growing, together with brightly coloured mosses and lichens. In other trees, he could see orchids, similar to the ones which grew in the hot houses in the walled garden of Parkington Hall. There were huge, clambering vines looking like thick ropes, weaving from tree to tree. He remembered sitting on the coil of bleached white rope with Bantam on the ship which brought them here. He smiled at the thought of the little man and could almost feel the cool sea spray on his face. Sometimes, as he marched and drenched in sweat, he tried to imagine the early autumn frosts back home which covered the fields with a crisp white coat and the croaking of the cock pheasants hiding in the ice encrusted bracken.

Occasionally, Tom caught glimpses of the creatures which lived amongst the thickets of bamboo growing in profusion at the base of the jungle giants. In the dark shade, brown snakes, some thicker than his arm, would slither amongst the rotting trees on the wet forest floor and disappear silently, other than a soft rustle. It was the grunting of a family of wild pigs as they ran deep into the jungle, disturbed by approaching sound of marching boots which snapped Tom out of his daydream. The front of the column of prisoners had reached the banks of a wide, fast flowing river and had halted at its edge which was thick with an expanse of green, sedge-like plants. Tom looked up and down the river and guessed when it was in flood its margins would be completely under water. Even now, there were wide ranging swamps with reeds and wild rice plants growing in their boggy outreaches.

"*Yasumi, yasumi*", the grim-faced guards screamed at the growing clusters of exhausted men who were arriving at the water's edge.

"Thank Christ for that", Chopper said, as he sank down onto the damp grass, grateful for the rest.

Tom followed him, saying, "They'll make us wait here until the rest of the column catches up and then I reckon we'll be crossing that". He indicated towards the wide expanse of water with a noticeable lack of enthusiasm.

Twenty minutes of heaven-sent rest followed before the familiar sound of the guards shouting, *"Okiru, Okiru"*, get up, get up", reverberated up and down the long column of worn out men.

Tom was first to rise and he hauled his exhausted friend to his feet. The two men looked apprehensively at each other before they began to reluctantly follow the leading group of prisoners. Those at the front didn't need directions; instead they automatically followed a muddy track which had once been part of the river's bank. It was a place where the ribbon of reeds along the edge had been stamped away and had instead become a wide, slippery slope. Chopper turned and stared at Tom. He didn't say anything. He didn't need to. Tom was thinking the same thing. Other men had been marched this way......and a lot of them.

Tom looked across the river to the steaming jungle on the other side. Whilst he relished the feel of the cool water on his body, he wondered how strong the current would be and if any of the weakened men would drown. As the men started to wade across the river, Tom put a protective arm round Chopper's waist and glancing downriver, he could see dozens of other men, who he assumed were fellow prisoners, beginning to build a bridge across the wide expanse of water.

"Do you think that's being built for the railway?" Chopper asked, as swirls of the murky brown water seeped over the top of his boots and the wet slime of the river bed began to invade the spaces between his blistered toes.

Tom squinted and looked again and although they were some way from the structure, he could make out dozens of half-naked men clambering amongst hundreds of wooden piles which had been driven into the stony river bed and amongst the prisoners, were the familiar green-clad figures with guns at the ready.

"It's a job to see at this distance but it looks like it".

Meanwhile, the men at the front of the line of wading men were more than half way across the fast flowing water and Tom who was supporting his friend was beginning to feel the power of the current was hacking at his strength. Chopper to his friend and said with a grin, "Do you realise Tom, this is the first bath we've had in months".

Tom laughed and replied cheerfully, "By the way you smell, I thought this is the first one you've had for bloody years".

The two men laughed together as they finally crossed the river and clawed their way up the well- trodden bank on the other side.

They had been force-marched for over ninety miles since leaving Ban Pong and another two days had passed since they had crossed the wide Kwai Yai river when they heard the faint but unmistakable sound of English voices. Tom, who still had an arm of support round Chopper's waist, lifted his head in an attempt to hear them more clearly.

"I hope this is it", Chopper said weakly, "I don't think I can go much further".

Tom nodded his head in agreement. He had been half carrying his friend for some time now and he too was about all in. It was as though the exhausted men were sleepwalking rather than marching. For the last twenty miles or so, the flat terrain of the soft jungle floor had been replaced with sharp-edged rocks and gravel, which to Tom's concern, had began to cut into the soldier's boots. Tom noticed some of the other men were hobbling along, the victims of twisted ankles and bleeding feet. It was when the hot, tropical sun finally blasted it's way through a gap in the trees he saw the bleached stack of rock reaching for the sky in front of him. Then, as he looked towards the front of the column and he saw nailed to a tree, was a wooden board on which somebody had roughly painted, *CHONG KAO CAMP.*

"Look at that", he said, pointing at a small sign underneath. The two men paused to read the cryptic message which had been scrawled on it by a would-be comedian, *A Warm Welcome Awaits You!*

"If wit was shit, whoever wrote that would be bloody constipated", Chopper said, without a trace of any humour in his voice.

"He probably wishes he was", Tom replied wryly, but it wasn't the sign he was looking at.

In the distance, where the land sloped away, groups of skeletal prisoners were working under the watchful eyes of their armed captors.

"Look at that lot down there", said Chopper, grateful for the slowing pace of the column, "there's bloody hundreds of the poor sods".

Tom smiled at his friend's exaggeration as he looked at the sight in front of them and guessed there were about a hundred or so prisoners making a clearing in the jungle. Some of the men were hacking away at the dense tropical undergrowth at the edges of the clearing with the blades of their pangas. Others were cutting down huge thickets of bamboo and tying the stems into bundles and carrying them to an area where the ground had been completely cleared and levelled. As Tom watched, he heard the cry of "timber". Even from a distance, he could hear a loud creaking sound as the sinews of wood which the men's saws and axes had not yet parted, stretched and suddenly parted, sending a huge teak tree crashing to the jungle floor.

Most of the prisoners looked like the men in the column. Their emaciated bodies were clad only in sweat drenched shorts. On their feet they were wearing their army issue boots and on their heads was a hotchpotch of headwear protecting them from the scorching, oven-hot sun. Suddenly, Tom became conscious of the heat from the accursed planet overhead as he paused to watch the various work-parties being worked just like the slaves they had become. Not being allowed to stop or even rest in the body-sapping heat and for those who did, they were being struck and beaten by the ever watchful Gunzoku guards.

"God help us", a voice from the column uttered.

On seeing the bedraggled line of men entering the camp, some of the prisoners in the clearing, dropped their tools and started shouting and running towards those who were trudging down the slope towards them.

"SHIGOTO, SHIGOTO".

Japanese and Korean voices suddenly filled the air as the guards screamed at the prisoners to get back to work, beating an unfortunate individual who was leading the race to the ground and kicking him into submission.

"Welcome to Chong Kao camp, whatever that bloody means", a Brummie sounding voice alongside Tom, said sarcastically.

Tom's mind was elsewhere. He was thinking what the cook had said back at Changi. Where were the hospitals to treat the sick and injured? Where was all the plentiful food they had promised?

"Bastards", he said, not for the first time, nor the last!

The column was brought to attention and ordered to wait for a small group of Japanese soldiers who were marching up the slope towards the waiting men. Leading the group was an officer, who Tom noticed was unusually tall for his race and on either side of him were two shorter officers, who it appeared to be of lesser rank with green-peaked caps perched on their heads. The tall man sported a cork-lined pith helmet and a noticeable crisp white shirt with its pressed collar neatly opened on the outside of his beige-coloured tunic. Trailing some way behind the group was a heavily sweating soldier, clearly of an even lower rank, struggling to carry a set of heavy wooden steps.

Major Harris, accompanied by four of his NCO's, stepped forward from the ranks ready to salute the oncoming party. Tom noticed the officer's face was still heavily bruised and his left eye was shut tight from his earlier beating. The tall Japanese officer ignored them and slowly and deliberately made his way up the steps and studied the rows of prisoners who were now lined up in front of him. Tom's olive green eyes narrowed to slits of hatred when he noticed Ito Sasaki was making his way to the front of the standing ranks.

"I hope he's not bloody staying", Tom whispered to Chopper, whose head had already turned in the man's direction.

"You are prisoners of the conquering Imperial Japanese Army", the tall officer began in faltering English.

"Same old shit", murmured a bored voice further back, having heard it so many times before.

The Japanese officer continued, his voice was much softer than Tom was expecting. "I am the camp commander and your commanding officer. My name is Captain Kamodo. You have the honour of constructing a railway which has been designed by Japanese engineers. When it is completed it will be over four hundred miles long and it will travel from Bangkok in the south to Rangoon in the north. It will transport the materials which the illustrious homeland of Japan requires to defeat its' enemies".

"Thieving bastards" muttered the same voice behind Tom and Chopper.

"Nothing will delay the construction of the railway. The penalty for anyone attempting to escape is death. You will obey all the commands of the Japanese forces. You will salute all Japanese forces. You are the prisoners of the Japanese forces. Today you can rest and tomorrow you will work".

Tom watched, as the man's eyes roved up and down the lines of men. His cold gaze was taking in every detail.

"No work, no food", he concluded briskly.

Tom glanced at the men around him. Nobody was listening to what the man was saying. Most of them had their heads bowed, staring at their aching, bloody feet. After all, Tom thought, agreeing with the man behind, they had heard it all before.

Major Harris stepped once pace forward and with a high lift of his knee, stamped his right boot hard on the ground. Looking up at the Japanese officer who was still standing on the wooden steps, he said in his clipped, privileged accent which Tom assumed had taken generations to perfect, "Captain, my name is Major Harris and I am the commanding officer of these men".

Tom noticed how he had emphasised the words, *"I am"*.

"My men require a longer rest. They have marched over one hundred miles. They need food and water and some need medical treatment. I must insist that these things are made available before anybody starts work".

The Japanese officer held up his hand to silence Major Harris and said firmly, "No Major. I am the commanding officer of all the men in this camp. They will rest and eat today and tomorrow they will work". The man's words were softly spoken but nobody could escape seeing the coldness in his grey eyes and hearing the menace in his voice.

"Sir, I must insist". Major Harris ignored him and continued with growing authority in his voice. "May I remind you of the Geneva Convention and what it says about the treatment of prisoners".

Tom could now see the anger welling in the Japanese officer's cold eyes.

"...it is clear. At all times the wounded and the sick must be cared for and treated humanely", Major Harris continued.

Without saying a word, Captain Kamodo signalled with a slight turn of his head to one of the junior officers standing at his side. The man immediately stepped forward and struck the British officer's face with the back of his hand and as the officer fell to the ground, he delivered two hefty kicks to his stomach. The prisoners stood and watched in silence as the other Jap officer joined in and then, with one either side of the groaning man, started to drag him across the clearing before finally tying him to a post which had been driven into the ground for the purpose.

"He's a brave bugger", Tom heard the man to the left of him, mutter.

"If he continues to upset them, he'll soon be a dead bugger", replied another.

"Lesson one over with", the first man concluded.

"What do you mean?" Chopper said in astonishment. "If there aren't any huts here, where will we bloody sleep?"

Chopper and Tom were sitting with their backs against a large stack of bamboo poles talking to a fellow prisoner, who had been part of the first contingent who had arrived at the camp, a week previously. The two newcomers hungrily finished their meagre bowls of rice and thin pumpkin soup, whilst the other man was continuing to eat much more slowly and deliberately from his bowl. He had already found out that the rations of food in this God forsaken place bordered on starvation level and had found out the more slowly you ate, the more food there seemed to be.

The soldier was a Royal Engineer, whose name the men later learnt. was Sam Goodale, finished his food before answering Chopper's question.

"Before we can start on their precious railway we've got to get the materials to build the huts. That's what this lot is for", he said, pushing his back against the stack of bamboo. "For the past week we have been clearing and cutting the stuff and soon we can start on the huts.

The problem is, the first huts to be built are for the Nips and then, if we are lucky we can build some for ourselves".

"What happens until then?" Chopper enquired, already sensing what the answer would be.

"The Nips are in those tents over there", Sam beckoned to a small encampment on the far side of the clearing. "We're sleeping under the stars.........and in the pissing rain", he added with pause and a wry smile on his face. "The Japs are vicious bastards. Last week one of them nearly beat one of the men who were cutting bamboos to death, just because he didn't salute him properly".

Chopper closed his eyes. After what he had seen and experienced since the surrender, he was in no doubt about the cruelty of their captors. After a few moments deep in thought, he said, "What do you mean, he didn't salute him properly?"

"The Nips are hot about that, almost paranoid. They treat it as lack of respect from people they regard as sub-human", Sam smiled grimly as he continued. "If you're wearing a hat and you walk past a Nip or he passes you, you must turn and face him and salute the bastard. If you're not wearing a hat, you have to stop and face him but instead of saluting, you have to bow down to your waist". Sam turned to Tom and said, "If I was you, I'd get a hat, saluting them doesn't seem as bad as having to bow to the bastards ......in any case, you'll need a hat now the dry monsoon has arrived, if not, the sun will cook you to a bloody frazzle".

Sam thought for a moment before adding solemnly, "You'll find there are already some spare hats... if you know what I mean".

Tom knew exactly what the Sapper meant.

He turned to speak to Chopper but saw his friends' eyes had closed and he was fast asleep. The man was physically and mentally exhausted and nothing would wake him now. With the tenderness a mother would give to a sick child, Tom leant forward and gently removed the mud encrusted boots from Chopper's swollen and blistered feet.

Something suddenly troubled Tom. It was what he had seen in Chopper's eyes. They were mournful, but it was not that. There was something else that he had seen. Chopper had always been a fighter, standing up for what he thought was right. Is that what he was seeing, Tom thought? Had the fight disappeared from his friend's eyes? Tom was reminded of an incident which had happened years ago, soon after he had met Chopper at the Bridge Engineering Works in Maidstone.

One morning the two men had been walking through the electrical shop one when they noticed a group of electricians clustered around one of their apprentices who they were initiating into what they referred to as *the rites*. Tom could see the unfortunate lad had his arms forced apart, with each sleeve of his overalls securely gripped between the jaws of the vices bolted to the work benches. His legs were also spread wide open and his ankles tied to the legs of the benches with strips of electrical cable, thus the lad had been spread-eagled in a standing position, unable to move.

Chopper grabbed Tom's sleeve causing him to stop as one of the electricians plunged his hand into young lad's overalls and after ripping open the fly-buttons on the boy's trousers, he pulled out the youngsters quivering willy. A round of laughter followed. Another man who Chopper recognised to be the foreman electrician stepped forward and, with a practised hand, held the boy's pink appendage before clipping its soft skin to a small electrical dynamo he was holding.

The heavily-built electrician grinned luridly at Chopper and said with a sneer in his voice, "Watch the little sods' balls dance when I turn the handle".

Chopper reacted immediately. Looking straight into the man's face, he said angrily, "If you turn that bloody handle it will be the last thing you will be able to turn for a day or two".

Holding his ground Chopper unceremoniously shoved the man aside and began to release the apprentice from his torment. Tom watched as the electrician tried to intervene only to be pushed away with even more force by Chopper. He could see the anger blazing in Chopper's eyes. So could the foreman electrician.

Once released, Chopper said to the boy, "If they touch you again, come and find me... don't forget".

The white-faced lad nodded gratefully, thankful for his reprieve.

"You bloody vicious bastard". Chopper was now face to face with the sadistic aggressor, whose eyes had narrowed with resentment at the unwelcomed intervention. Chopper had not finished with him. His nose was now almost touching the bully's face and he could smell the man's bad breath as he spat out, "There's nothing funny about torturing a defenceless lad. If you ever do it again, I will come and find you and do it to you, then we'll see how funny you fucking find it". The tone in his voice was unyielding.

He moved back slightly but his eyes remained fixed on the man's face. Neither man spoke but Tom noticed a nerve had started twitching in the side of the electrician's blue veined face.

The man standing next to the foreman stared at Chopper for a moment and then relented. "You're right", he said, "we shouldn't have done it", and remorsefully he put a protective arm around the narrow shoulders of the young apprentice.

Tom and Chopper walked away. Words didn't pass between them but Tom had seen a side of his friend he hadn't seen before, and as a result, the two men's friendship had been further strengthened.

Tom studied his sleeping, bootless friend with concern, don't give up mate, he thought, don't give up. Tom relaxed slightly as he remembered Chopper's fighting spirit, concluding his friend, whatever the odds, would make it through.

Sam, who had already noticed the close bond between the two men, continued with his warnings of the brutality they could expect at the camp.

"Tom, there are three more things to remember". The tone of the Sapper's voice was grave, "Never ignore an order from the Nips and never leave a working party without their permission and go off by yourself". Sam Goodale looked at Chopper who was sleeping like a baby. "If you or your friend need a squat, do it at the edge of the cleared land where they can see you". The Sapper grinned slightly as he said, "Finally Tom, don't let them hear you calling them Japs. They don't mind being called Nips but they get nasty when they hear the word, *Jap*".

Sam started to get up and realising how grim he had sounded, said optimistically, "Once we start work on the railway, things should get a bit better".

Tom liked Sam immediately. He had a happy and cheerful disposition and Tom reckoned, despite everything that was thrown at him, he was the type of man who would ever be optimistic, no matter what.

Tom watched as the sun sank behind a towering teak tree in the distance. The blue-grey sky slowly turned into a hundred shades of red and as the light began to fade, a dark feeling of foreboding overcame him. Perhaps, he thought, they were wrong in thinking that building a railway would be better than suffering imprisonment in the Changi camp. Tom closed his eyes. He could hear the loud chorus of frogs and crickets calling from the surrounding forest floor. The ever present parrots screeched their final calls as the day slowly turned to night and somewhere deep in the lightless jungle, he thought he could hear monkeys howling as they searched for a safe place to sleep. If only, Tom thought wistfully, if only we were free and could find a safe place to sleep. Gradually his mind drifted back to the warnings the Royal Engineer had given him. Whatever happened, he vowed, no matter how much suffering he would have to endure, he would not die at the hands of his captors and nor would Chopper.

Tom could already feel the tropical sun burning his back through his sweat soaked shirt. He had been given a bowl of thin rice soup at daybreak and had filled his canteen from a wooden water barrel when he discovered that together with Chopper, they were to be one of the working parties whose task it would be, was to carry the bundles of bamboo down from the hillside.

The soil on the hillside was thin and in some places non-existent and it was not long before Tom and the rest of the men who were carrying the huge bundles of bamboo down the steep slopes found it difficult to get a foothold. As the day progressed Tom could feel some of the sharper stones were already cutting into the thin, worn soles of his boots and wondered what would happen when they gave up the ghost. Then he remembered what Sam Goodale had told him.

After two gruelling days on the hillside, Tom could see the frame-work of a hut was already beginning to rise from the flat ground far below. The sappers had started to build the main framework of the hut by using thick bamboo stems and from his vantage point, Tom could hear the sound of the men's axes as they notched each of the poles before fitting them into their allotted place. Watching the sappers working on the bamboo stems reminded Tom of the old woodman who coppiced the chestnut woods back home but his daydreaming was brought to an abrupt end by the blow of a punishment stick across his bare back. As Tom turned round a punch in his stomach sent him reeling forward and he fell to his knees gasping for breath.

"*Speedo, Speedo*", the Korean guard, who had wielded the blows, was shouting at him.

Tom struggled to get to his feet but the Gunzoku's stick continued to deliver a series of savage blows and he fell back on his knees.

"*Speedo, Speedo*", the tormentor was screaming. No prisoner would be taking a rest whilst he was guarding them.

"Are you alright?" Chopper asked, as he picked up the front end of bundle of bamboo they had been carrying and hoisted it onto his reddening shoulder.

Wincing with the pain which was still racing through his body, Tom got to his feet and replied grimly, "I'll live".

Slowly, Tom shouldered his end of the bundle and with Chopper leading the way, the two men carefully made their way down the rock strewn slope under the pitiless eyes of the guard.

"Bastard", Tom thought, half expecting another blow from the grinning man behind them.

The two men had been working for over six hours in the burning sun before they were allowed to rest and they gratefully made their way to find a place to sit in the shade and eat their mid-day rice soup and drink the scoops of water which their parched mouths and throats had been yearning for. For ten glorious minutes the pair sat there but glorious as it was, it did not satisfy the pangs of hunger which ripped through their stomachs nor the need for rest their weak and damaged bodies were demanding.

For the hours which followed, they continued to toil in the burning sun. Carrying the bundles of bamboo down the rocky slopes and then after reaching the clearing, dumping the load from their aching shoulders before making their way back up the hillside where the bamboo cutters were at work.

"Why is it that this bloody hill always seems to be twice as high when we go up it than it does when we come down?" Chopper joked thinly.

Tom smiled and looked at the lines of men going up and down the rocky slopes and from a distance they looked like the enormous army ants he had seen moving in thick lines across the jungle floor as they carried leaves and twigs to build their cavernous nests.

The long, shrill blast of a whistle was the sound the exhausted men had been longing for, signalling the end of another twelve hours of hard labour. From the slopes of the hillside and the clearing where the engineers were building the huts, men were throwing down the bundles of bamboos and the tools they had been using and started trudging back to the camp their captors had called Chong Kao. Tom and Chopper gratefully joined a group of men who were patiently queuing for their evening meal.

"There's a surprise", said a voice at head of the line of men, "we've got rice tonight!"

A groan went up from the hungry men, followed by someone saying, "I'm so bloody hungry, I could eat a bloody donkey".

"That's no way to speak about your wife's new boyfriend", somebody shouted back.

A few of the exhausted soldiers cheered, laughing at the man's black humour.

"Tom", said Chopper cheerfully as he looked down at his bowl of rice, "we've struck lucky, there's some fish in this".

The two men sat down and made the most of the extra nourishment, before walking round to fill their water canteens from an old tank the Sappers had liberated from a deserted native village .Presently they were joined by Sam, "Why are the Japs working us so bloody hard?" Chopper asked him.

"Apart from fact they think we deserve all the contempt they obviously enjoy dishing out, they need the railway to be up and running as soon possible. Their higher command won't accept any excuses for delays, whatever the reason, even if that means working us and their own men to death", Sam said solemnly.

Neither Chopper nor Tom said anything, as they removed their boots and laid their heads on the old rice sacks Sam had found and had just given them.

"The thing is", he continued. "This place is like a bloody big warehouse for the Nips. It's full of all the goodies they need for the war. Tin ore, rubber, timber, rice ....that's why they're in such a bloody hurry to get things done".

Chopper nodded his head, acknowledging the Sapper's summary of the situation they found themselves in.

"When the Sappers have finished the huts and we start building their precious railway, what direction will it go?" Chopper enquired.

Tom lifted his head from his makeshift pillow, suddenly becoming interested in hearing Sam's reply.

Sam laughed at the question. His laughter was infectious and tired as they were, Chopper and Tom joined in even though they had no idea what he was laughing at.

"Straight through a cutting in that bloody rock over there", he said, pointing a blistered finger at the towering rock face in the distance.

Tom was now sitting up and looking in the direction Sam was pointing to. In the fading light, he could just about see the dark shadow of a massive escarpment of rock, rising from the ground to a height of around a hundred feet.

Sam laughed again, "Chong Kao, it's the name of this bloody camp. Chong Kao is the native lingo for mountain cutting".

Chopper looked confused. "I can't see the cutting in this light", he said, squinting through the dusk in an attempt to get a better look.

"You won't see it in any bloody light", Sam laughed heartily. "It's not there. That's why poor sods like us have been brought to this God forsaken hole. We're here to hack a way through that lump of bloody rock for over a quarter of a mile, so the Nips can take the trains through it, loaded with loot and back to their bloody empire".

"Bloody hell", the two friends said in unison.

The days of doing the back breaking work turned into weeks and as Tom slowly made his way up the slope to collect yet another bundle of bamboo, he stopped and turned round to see Chopper, who had fallen some way behind, squatting with his shorts around his bony ankles. Tom's anxiety for his friend was growing daily. The effects of dysentery was common amongst the men in the camp but Choppers' condition was worse than most and he was now having to stop much more frequently, to let the foul smelling waste flood from his body.

After a few minutes, Chopper managed to catch up with his friend and said with a weak smile, "Do you think we will ever get to like it here?"

Tom watched the beads of sweat run down Choppers gaunt face and smiled back at him. He was pleased, weak as his friend was he still had his sense of humour.

Clouds of mosquitoes rose into the air with each blow of their pangas as Tom and Chopper hacked at base of a clump of huge bamboos. They had swopped their carrying role with two men who had been cutting the bamboo in the damp thickets where the insects flourished in their thousands. At first, Tom and Chopper would swat the loathsome things as soon as they tried to feed on the warm blood in the men's bodies but they soon realised the mosquitoes relentless attacks on them could not be stopped and it was just another thing to be added to their long list of suffering. Despite this and the backbreaking work of cutting through the stems of bamboo, some of which were thicker than a man's arm and towered up more than forty or fifty feet into the bright blue sky, Tom preferred working at the top of the slopes. He could see the brightly coloured butterflies with wings bigger than some of the birds back home. He marvelled how the beautiful creatures could flutter in and out of the blooms growing amongst the vegetation without making the slightest of sound. He relished the fragrance of the strange looking flowers which the butterflies sought out, so different he thought, so different to the.......

"Look at poor sods down there", Chopper said, interrupting Toms brief moment of respite.

Tom turned and half way down the slope he saw the Gunzoku guards shouting and pushing two of the bamboo carriers. The men were sliding and falling down the slope, trying to hold on to the bundle of bamboo they had been struggling to carry. Every time they tripped over the tree stumps which littered the hillside and dropped the bundle, the guards clubbed them with their rifle butts. Tom turned away. He could see this was a sick game the guards were playing and he feared the subjects of their game would be lucky to reach the bottom of the slope alive.

There was unmistakable venom in Chopper's voice as he said, "One day those bastards will get what's coming to them".

"I bloody hope so", Tom replied as he released his bottled-up anger by severing a huge bamboo with a single blow of his axe.

Each day as they hacked at the bamboos, Tom and Chopper looked down towards the clearing where the sappers were constructing the accommodation huts. Sam Goodale had already told them the first of these would be for the Japanese soldiers and engineers, the next would accommodate the Gunzoku and then finally the last huts to be built would be for the long suffering prisoners. At first, the Sappers had sunk four lines of the huge bamboo posts into the earth floor to form the skeleton of the huts. Once the vertical poles had been positioned, bamboo cross braces were lashed to them with ropes made from the creepers which flourished in the bamboo thickets. A day or two later, Tom and Chopper watched as the Sappers crawled over the roof framing, attaching the attap roof covering of dry grass and fan shaped palm leaves, baked dry by the burning tropical sun overhead.

"Hardly the bloody Ritz", Tom said wryly to Chopper, "but at least we'll get some shelter from the worst of the weather".

Chopper nodded his head, not wishing to waste what little breath he had left but he too was grateful that although the huts didn't have any sides, at least, the roof would protect them from the monsoon torrents and the sun's scorching rays.

The huts were about a hundred yards long and when six of them had been completed, the Sappers started constructing the raised, split bamboo staging which ran down each side of the huts.

"I hope they're going to put mattresses on them", Tom joked thinly, knowing the roughly trimmed platforms would become the communal beds for the three hundred or so men who would be crammed together on them. He didn't relish sleeping on the unforgiving platforms but he knew however uncomfortable they were, it would be better than sleeping out in the open.

"It looks as though we're in for another pep talk...joy of bloody joys", Chopper scowled weakly, when after the morning roll call, the prisoners were marched to the towering rock escarpment and lined up to face the familiar set of wooden steps.

Watched over by the ever present Japanese soldiers, the rows of prisoners stood staring at the empty steps whilst their half empty stomachs ached to be filled. When they had first been ordered to line up, the early morning sun had been low in the sky but as the hours passed it had now risen, and was beating down remorselessly on the men, unforgiving and unhindered by any shade. Tom watched as a man in front of him started swaying. At least half a dozen had already fallen heavily to the ground and lay where they fell. The combined effects of ill treatment and tropical disease were taking their toll and despite the sweltering heat, Tom could see others were shivering. He looked at Chopper and whilst he was worried about his friend's condition, he was relieved to see he appeared to be holding up.

Bastards, Tom thought.

Captain Kamodo started to walk up the wooden steps. His feet paused as he slowly and deliberately moved up the steps. Upon reaching the top step and without saying a word, he stood there surveying the five hundred prisoners standing to attention in front of him. Tom wondered what the man could see through his cold grey eyes. Did he see lines of half starved, bone protruding men? Some half naked, just wearing loin cloths pulled up at the crutch like baby's nappies, others standing on the baking hot ground wearing worn-out boots. Did he see they were all slowly dying as a result of the inhuman treatment he was inflicting upon them or did he just he see the miserable collection of men in front of him as expendable resources of war, there only to build the imperial fucking railway?

Bastards, Tom thought once again.

The deceivably, softly spoken man, attired in a freshly laundered shirt brought the heels of his highly polished brown boots together with a resounding click. "Today you will have the honour to start the task of building the Chung Kao cutting", he said decisively.

"No wonder the bastard looks happy", Tom heard Chopper mutter.

"Nothing will delay it. Every prisoner in this camp will work. No man will be too ill to work on this momentous Japanese achievement", he continued in faltering English. "Every man will remove a cubic yard of rock from the outcrop each day until the railway line is finished. Any man who fails to do this will be severely punished".

There wasn't a man standing in the ranks who was in any doubt of the evil intent which lay behind the softly spoken words coming from Kamodo's mouth. They remembered the Jap's brutality towards Captain Harris when they had first arrived at the camp, when the officer had dared to challenge his authority.

A shiver ran down Tom's spine as he watched the tall, immaculately dressed man surveying the lines of slave labour in front of him and then, with an almost imperceptible nod of his head, two junior officers who were standing either side of him like a pair of grinning bookends, started shouting the orders for the prisoners to be marched off towards the towering rock face.

Tom and Chopper reached the foot of the escarpment and looked up.

"Christ", Chopper uttered.

Slowly the two men struggled up the steep, scree strewn sides of the brutal mini-mountain. They were relieved to be released from the hillside and its resident mosquitoes but concerned what the future held for them. Upon reaching its relatively flat top, a breathless Tom noticed some of the Sappers, who were working with two Japanese engineers, had started smearing two parallel lines of black paint along the length of the outcrop, indicating where the rock had to be cut.

Chopper looked at the ominous lines with disbelief, "We're over a hundred feet from the bloody ground", he said in astonishment. "Surely to Christ they don't expect us to cut through this lot with these", he spat the words out as he shook the tools out of the rice sack they had been given.

The two men stared at the hammer and chisel which were lying at their feet astonished at what was happening. The lines of black paint were thirty feet apart and stretched for more than five-hundred feet from one end of the limestone ridge to the other. Tom glanced around at the other prisoners in the work party and almost to a man, they too were looking down at the thousands of tons of rock beneath their feet, not believing what they had been brought here to do.

Tom screwed up his eyes and squinted up at the blazing sun which never stopped robbing them of the little energy they had left. "It's going to be much hotter on this bloody lump of rock than it was on the slopes ...if that's bloody possible", he said, almost despairingly. He could have saved his breath. Chopper was thinking the same thing.

"I think we've probably got about two months left before the monsoons start and it starts pissing down again", Chopper said, not quite sure whether it would be better than it was at that precise moment.

Suddenly a Japanese officer started to shout rapid orders to the bayonet carrying guards, who in turn, screamed out commands to the prisoners.

"I suppose that's Japanese lingo for, 'don't just stand there looking at it, get fucking digging'", observed a fellow member of the 85th, who was standing next to Tom. Tom recognised him as being on the Empress of Japan, the regrettable name of the ship which had brought them to the hell-hole.

287

Instantly the Japanese soldiers and the Gunzokus moved through the men, roughly dividing some to the right and others to the left. Chopper slipped and fell but at least he was still with Tom and the other gunner. Tom turned to the man and asked him if he knew what was happening.

"They're sorting out which lucky bastards will cut through the rock and which ones will have the pleasure of carrying the fucking stuff away", he replied. The man stamped his boot on the hard rock which had lain undisturbed since the beginning of time. "It aint going to be easy, that's for sure", he said understating the obvious, "nor will it be taking it away".

From a distance the accursed rock had looked like the gleaming white hills of the North Downs which Tom had seen so many times from his bedroom window in Lavender Cottage. But instead of the soft pliable chalk, this pile of stone was as hard as iron and would leave the hands of those who were about to work on it, cut and blistered. Instead of the wild thyme and marjoram which released their sweet smelling scent when Tom had wandered over the downs to watch the little blue butterflies which skipped from plant to plant or to hear the skylarks singing their sweet song high above him, this hard, unforgiving stack of rock would soon be covered with the blood, sweat and lives of the men who were about to labour on it.

Tom and Chopper reluctantly joined the swarm of prisoners who had already started attacking the rock, bleached by the relentless tropical sun and washed by centuries of tropical rain storms. Some of the men were already being made to hack at the unyielding rock face from the ground with large, eight pound hammers and long pointed chisels the Sappers called tap drills. High above them, others were beginning to smash into the top of the outcrop with little more than brute force and picks and shovels. In the searing heat, Tom and Chopper started at the face using one of the tap drills driven into the rock by strength-sapping hammer blows. Chopper was not robust enough now to lift the weight of the hammer and instead held the chisel onto the rock whilst Tom hit it with the hammer. Every time Tom struck the chisel, razor sharp fragments of rock were sent skywards. He glanced anxiously down at Chopper who was on his knees holding the tap drill onto the rock and could see tiny trickles of blood were beginning to run down his friends, dust covered face and arms.

Sweat seeped out of every pore in the men's bodies, leaving multitudes of stripes as the salty liquid cut its way through the layers of white dust which covered them. Their throats were so parched they hardly spoke to each other and as the day wore on, they craved for water to satisfy a thirst that even in this hell hole, they had not felt with such intensity before.

Tom, spat out a mouthful of dust and cast his grit laden eyes over the pile of excavated rock which had begun to pile up behind them, "That doesn't look like two bloody cubic yards to me", he croaked.

A fellow prisoner arrived carrying a large, woven cane basket over his shoulders before dropping it, without care and consideration, then laboriously loading it with the lumps of rock the two men had dug out.

Looking at Tom, the man said despondently, "For every yard of rock the Japs want out of you lads, it means poor buggers like me, will have to carry a ton of it away, every fucking day". Under the watchful gaze of the guards, the man hoisted the basket of stone onto his scrawny back. His knees were buckling under the weight and he staggered off towards the camp where they were beginning to build a causeway over the marshy ground which lay between the towering escarpment and the prison camp. Tom watched him go off. The poor sod was so pitifully thin, Tom wondered how long he would survive and a shudder went down his spine.

The sun was setting when Tom and the rest of the men who had been hacking the rock, finally stopped working and looked down apprehensively at the pile of stones which had been laboriously dumped on the embryonic causeway. Hundreds of pairs of tired eyes watched as one of the Japanese engineers began to calculate the amount of rock which had been removed from the outcrop. The insignificant looking man peered through his wire rimmed spectacles into a battered notebook he was holding. His head moved up and down as he compared the morning headcount of prisoners with his estimation of the material they had removed.

"I hope to Christ we have met the little bastard's requirement", Chopper said grimly, knowing if they hadn't, the shift wouldn't be over until they had.

Tom watched as the inconsequential engineer ran his finger up and down the columns and along the lines of figures he had pencilled in his book and wondered if he was as harmless as he looked, before replying bitterly, "I don't trust the sod".

Neither Tom nor Chopper realised, the man, who found himself far from his family and the comforts of his home, had his own targets to meet or suffer the consequences. Nor, did they know that he would need to increase the daily amount of stone each man took from the barren rock as the number of prisoners gradually declined. They would find this out in the days, weeks and months to come.

"Bastard", Tom and Chopper said in unison, as the weed of a man shook his head and ordered the waiting prisoners to be herded back to work for another two hours at the rock face, in order to meet his required quota.

The weather was particularly humid one day and the ever constant beads of sweat were leaving visible trails as they ran down Tom and Choppers dust-covered bodies. As was their routine, Chopper, with his blistered hands, carefully wrapped a piece of rag round the top shaft of the tap drill and closing his eyes, waited for Tom to strike it with his heavy hammer.

"Look at these buggers", Chopper exclaimed, as the point of the tap drill suddenly cut through an unusually soft section of stone on the side of the rock face.

Tom knelt down and looked at the lines of creatures which were already swarming over the broken rock. "They're army ants", he said knowledgeably. They'll eat any living thing which gets in their way".

"Including us by the bloody look of it", Chopper said as he started stamping on the aggressive insects before they had the chance to crawl up his legs and take what little flesh was left on them.

Tom carefully lifted up a large, flat stone and revealed a huge nest the insects had made in a natural fissure of the rock, amazed at the size of it and the thousands of ant's eggs it contained. He watched in fascination as hundreds of the huge ants were already frantically picking up their fat, white eggs with their scissor-like jaws and carrying them to safety, away from the men's prying eyes. The ants and their eggs were five or six times larger than the ones Tom had seen in the woods at Pentbury and the scurrying creatures were certainly more vicious and could cause a lot more damage than their gentle English cousins.

"We'll leave them in peace", he said, as he replaced the triangular-shaped stone and picked up his hammer before the hovering Gunzoku noticed they had stopped working.

Over the days which followed, ominous black clouds began to swirl in the darkening sky overhead and rumbles of thunder rolled across the distant hills. The prisoners began to realise the monsoon would soon be sending its deluge onto the camp and as the men returned to camp there was more than the usual look of relief on their faces at the sight of the rows of thatched huts which would provide them with some shelter from the predictable monsoon rains.

The rain fell in torrents and the small stream which trickled down the hillside became a raging torrent, constantly flooding the camp and as a result, the filth in the latrines was washed everywhere. Day by day the work on the cutting continued in the driving rain and ankle deep mud. With the constant metallic ringing of hammers striking steel and the dull thud of tap drills being driven into rock the cutting began to take shape, like a gaping wound running through virgin stone. Men were dying daily and the lines of the newly dug graves at the back of the huts, with their crude wooden crosses driven into what had earlier been sun baked ground, verified it.

The weather was sultry and the exhausted men working at the rock face were counting the minutes until the morning shift came to an end. Over the past months, Tom had seen the strength sap from his friend's body and now Chopper was so weak he stayed slumped on the ground, hardly able to hold the tap hammer. Tom paused and looked round to make sure there were no guards close by, before he passed his water bottle to his friend but as Chopper took a replenishing slug of the life-giving liquid Tom heard the chilling sound of a shrieking Japanese voice. Although the two men had become accustomed to this, somehow this particular voice seemed strangely familiar. Looking towards the causeway, the men saw an emaciated prisoner, whose rib cage was protruding through his taunt yellow skin, had fallen to the ground under the impossible weight of the rock-filled basket on his back. One of his feet was wrapped in a protective bundle of rag and a guard was hovering over him, screaming at him to stand up. Tom and Chopper watched as the desperate man attempted to get to his feet and then, after a few wobbly steps, falling back to the ground. Even though they were at least twenty yards away, the two men heard the sickening sound of the guard's canvas boot make contact with the hapless prisoner as he attempted to crawl away, dragging the basket the best way he could. It was Tom who first recognised the familiar, high-pitched voice and just beyond the prisoner he saw the squat figure of Ito Sasaki screaming instructions to the guard.

"Look at that", Tom said to Chopper with disgust in his voice. "The bastard's back and he's ordering that bloody guard to beat the bloke senseless.

Chopper watched as the guard raised his stick....... he had seen enough and turned his face away.

 "What makes them do it? Tom asked.

 Chopper shook his head and remained silent. He was already thinking he might be next.

Tom was still thinking about Slimey as he wrapped his arm round Chopper's waist and holding him under his arm pit, he half-carried his weak friend back to camp. He knew Chopper did not have the strength to make it back on his own and thought, if he fell, it would probably be all over for him. They had not seen Ito Sasaki since they had arrived at the camp and everyone assumed he had gone to a another camp further up the line but seeing the sadist again, filled Tom with growing anxiety for his friend. On reaching the camp, instead of the rest and a thirst quenching drink they needed, predictably, the men had to line up and wait for the evening roll call to be concluded. Tom breathed a sigh of relief when it was over and was confirmed everyone was present and the order was given to stand down. With Chopper at his side, he limped towards the cook house where some of the men had already started to queue for their last meagre meal of the day.

Eventually Tom and Chopper joined a group of men who were sitting under the shade of the attap roof of the cook house, their hands clutching their bowls of rice as if they contained their tickets to freedom. Tom chased the few bits of meat he had seen hiding in the foul tasting rice with his spoon and put them into Chopper's bowl. He knew Chopper desperately needed the sustenance and although the tiny pieces meat would hardly suffice, at least, he thought, they would help until he could find something else.

It was during the early hours of the morning when Tom was sleeping restlessly on the bamboo platform in the crowded hut his mind strayed into the strange world which inhabits the space between sleep and consciousness. This had happened before when people from the past appeared from within the recesses of his mind and this time it was no different. He was with George Saunders and the old gamekeeper was telling him where to find some food.

Tom woke up with a start. His heart was racing and his mind was alert and functioning.

"Can you manage to get back by yourself?" Tom anxiously asked Chopper, as the Japanese engineer approved the amount of rock the prisoners had removed and the whistle blew at the end of the next day's shift.

Chopper looked at his friend as if an explanation was needed but instead he just weakly mouthed the word, "Yes".

Tom noticed the enquiring look on Chopper's face and said as vaguely as he could, "I'm just going back to get something".

The two men nodded to each other and started to go their separate ways and as he anxiously looked back, Tom breathed a sigh of relief when he saw a fellow prisoner put his arm round Chopper's waist and started to support the faltering man back to camp.

 Taking a deep intake of breath, Tom nervously started walking in the opposite direction in the hope, perhaps the impossibility, of finding the place where they had been working before the monsoon had arrived. He knew it would be like finding a needle in a haystack and it was likely it had been washed away by now but it was the only hope there was. He also knew if he was caught, at the very least he would be beaten but more probably, he would be killed. Walking quickly against the flow of the main body of men who were making their way back to camp, he silently prayed he would not be noticed by the ever present guards. It was a huge risk but he had to take it. His eyes were fixed on the ground as he retraced his steps back along the cutting, searching desperately for one particular stone he hoped was still lying there amongst all the others. Doubt was beginning to seep into his mind. His chin was pressed tightly against his chest and his eyes were frantically darting from side to side when somebody suddenly crashed heavily into him. Tom's weak legs were not strong enough to withstand the force of the impact and he fell backwards, hitting the ground so hard it knocked the air out of his lungs. As he lay there trying to catch his breath, he heard the man he had crashed into swearing at him before extending his arm downwards to haul Tom up back onto his feet.

"Are you bloody mad?" the soldier exclaimed in astonishment "If you're trying to escape, you haven't got a hope in bloody hell".

Tom muttered a mixture of thanks and apologies to the man and ignoring his warning, continued on his way. His heart was pounding so fiercely now it felt if it would burst through his chest. Half walking and half running, he continued to make his way back through the cutting in his desperate search.

"There it is", he said to himself, almost in disbelief.

He glanced round furtively to see if any of the guards had seen him. No, thank God. With a sense of relief washing over him, Tom took a deep breath and dropped down onto his hands and knees. His heart was in his mouth as he carefully lifted the large flat, triangular stone.

"Please let them be there", he whispered.

Immediately, the huge ants started fleeing from the disturbance Tom had caused and he could feel their unstoppable progress on the back of his hand. Without wasting any time and not thinking of the risk in doing so, Tom plunged his hand deep into the ant's nest. He could feel the insects biting his bare arm with their gaping pincers. Pain seared through his flesh like plunging red hot needles but he ignored it and pulled out a handful of the plump white eggs he had been searching for. With his free hand he snatched off his hat and dumped the precious, gooseberry sized eggs into it.

The earlier dream had taken him back in the woods at Pentbury, mixing ant's eggs with the pheasant's food and being told by the old gamekeeper, "They will build those birds up". Tom hoped when the ant's eggs were mixed with Chopper's meagre rice ration, they would do the same and the extra nourishment would save his friend's life. One more handful and then I must get going, he thought.

As he scooped out the last handful of eggs through the layers of marauding ants, a heavy boot crashed down on his arm with such force it made him shout out with pain. He froze, not daring to move a muscle. Any moment the butt of a Japanese rifle would be brought down on his bare head or the point of a bayonet would be thrust between his ribs. The blood in Tom's veins ran cold and the nerves in his face winced with expectation. He lay motionless with the side of his face pressed hard against the stony ground waiting for the inevitable to happen. He could feel the ants running over his face and the thought of Slimey standing over him with his boot pressed hard down on his wrist was making his heart thump wildly against his rib cage.

It seemed minutes had passed before he dared to open his eyes and when he did he saw the hob nails on the sole of the dirty leather boot which was pinning his wrist to the ground. The steel hobs had cut into his flesh and red droplets of blood were trickling down the side of his hand. Was this going to be the way he was to die, trussed up with wire and impaled on the end of a Japanese bayonet? Slowly, Tom raised his head slightly from the ground and noticed that above the short boot which was still pressing down on his wrist, was a canvas puttee wrapped tightly round the assailant's leg. A thought suddenly flashed through Tom's mind. The boot was dirty and not the highly polished boot of a Japanese officer. Tom's taunt body relaxed slightly as he realised the boot could not be Slimey's. It must belong to a Japanese guard or a Gunzoku. He twisted his head round and cautiously looked up at the face of the man who was staring down at him. As he did so, he felt the pressure being slowly released from his wrist as the man eased his boot.

"*Okiru, Okiru*, get up, get up", the soldier ordered.

Cautiously, Tom rose to his feet and looked at the man whom he had not seen at the camp before. The soldier was quite young, probably no more than twenty years old. A conscript perhaps, Tom thought. The man's eyes did not have the contempt burnt into them which he had seen so many times before and were looking down at the hat, full of ant's eggs. Tom stood still, not daring to move as the young soldier's eyes roved up and down the skinny body standing in front of him. Tom picked up some of the white eggs and put them into his mouth. The young soldier looked at him, emotionless, and nodded his head to show his understanding. Tom held his breath and was wondering what would happen next. Nothing, Tom continued to hold his breath and waited.

Then, without warning the young solder suddenly waved him away with a flourish of his hand and the words, "*Atchi ike*, go away".

Relief flooded through Tom's thin body and he stared into the young man's face and nodded his head in gratitude.

He mumbled a heart -felt, "Thank you".

It was then he noticed the smile on the soldier's young face.

Tom was surprised to see the expression on the man's face had changed. It had softened and was now one of warmth and compassion. It did not have the brutality he had become used to. Tom looked quickly around before bending down to pick up his cap full of ants' eggs and hurrying back to camp.

Tom visited Chopper in the so-called hospital hut whenever he could in the days which followed but despite everything he did, Chopper remained almost lifeless on the hard bamboo platform. At first, his health seemed to improve after he had been fed with the ant's eggs but he needed proper medical care and like so many of the others in the camp, Tom knew his friend was slowly dying.

It was some days later when Chopper managed a weak smile as Tom lifted the battered army water bottle to his dry mouth and gently poured a trickle of water into it.

Chopper slowly raised his hand and held Tom's wrist. Tom noticed his friend's strength had gone. "Thanks mate", Chopper mouthed softly, as he licked the moisture from his lips with his swollen tongue.

His voice was so weak now, Tom could hardly hear what he was saying and had to press his ear to Chopper's ghostly white face. Tom reached down and took his friends limp hand into his own.

"Tom", Chopper's voice was now just a whisper. "Tom", he said weakly, "tell my sister".

Tom's eyes filled with tears which gathered in the corners until they trickled down his cheeks. He desperately tried to blink them away but they welled up again, unstoppable, as he looked down at his friend. Chopper's mouth was agape and his once, bright brown eyes were devoid of life and were already becoming opaque. Even in the final moments the brave man had held onto life until the last, but when death came, it came quickly and released him from his torment.

Tom continued to stare down at his friend, shaking his head in disbelief at what had just happened, until a wave of grief and self pity overwhelmed him and he started sobbing uncontrollably. He cried for the loss of a fine friend. He cried for the way the man suffered and died and he cried for the profound loneliness he now felt. He had vowed they would survive this hell together and he banged his fist on the mud floor of the hut in disbelief that such a thing could happen. How could a good man like Chopper meet such a squalid death at the hands of these monsters? Tom thought angrily.

Some hours passed before his sorrow was replaced by a blind rage which swept over him like a wild-fire. Tom vowed vengeance. He wanted vengeance against every bloody Japanese soldier and every bloody guard in the camp but in particular he wanted vengeance against the man they called Slimey.

Tom waited as Chopper's body was carried to the burial ground behind the huts.

No flags flew or bugles played amongst the forest of wooden crosses as the weightless corpse was lowered gently to the ground.

Beneath the top layer of mud the ground was hard and stony but with all the strength left in his body, Tom had managed to scrape out a shallow grave with a mattock borrowed from the Sappers. Its long wooden handle was split and the curved steel blade hanging on the end was blunt from months of hacking into the rock face. As he laid the mattock down, Tom wondered how many more graves it would be able to dig.

Gently, like a mother laying her baby into its cot, he lowered his friend's thin and frail body into the grave. Then, as he was about to cover it, he reached down to touch the two dog tags which were fastened around Chopper's neck. Tom gently rubbed the green, six-sided tag between his thumb and forefinger as if in a final gesture of goodbye. He could see his friend's name stamped on it and hoped that when the war was over the tag would be found and Chopper could be identified and moved to his final resting place. Carefully Tom removed the red circular tag from the thin leather thong and put it deep into his pocket. "When I get home, I'll give it to your sister", he murmured to his dead friend.

His mind had become blank with blur of grief and hate and a feeling of panic suddenly washed over him. Perhaps he should say something, just a few words ...but what? Chopper had not been particularly religious but he deserved more than just being left in a hole in the ground in this God forsaken place with no words of goodbye. Tom's mind went blank with despair. A sense of panic set in. Too much had happened to think clearly.

And then, somewhere from the deep recesses of his mind, something he had said as a child at Sunday school returned to him.

Kneeling by the graveside, Tom said quietly, "I am the living one, I was dead but now I am alive" and he looked at his friend's face for the last time before whispering a final, "Amen".

9

Hell and High Water- 1944

He was oblivious to the heat and noise of the train. Tom had lain in the corner of the rice wagon during most of the four day journey back from Bang Pong to Singapore railway station. Frail as he was, a small flame of hope flickered in his heart. He had survived and was on his way back from the hell of Chong Kao. Perhaps, just perhaps he would not die at the hands of the enemy he had grown to hate with so much venom and would be returning home after all. The heat and the stench in the steel box had been remorseless and Tom's body, like every one of the other emaciated prisoners who had survived and were returning from building the accursed railway of death, was racked with disease and starvation.

Tom shifted his body on the unyeilding steel floor. He had forgotten how small the box cars were, only eight feet wide and less than twenty feet long. There were nearly forty men jammed in around him and the only break from the relentless journey was once a day when the train stopped and the prisoners were given something to eat and drink and for those who hadn't already succumbed, the chance to release their groaning bowels. It didn't seem to matter now.

Tom knew what to expect.

There had been some talk that the railway line, further up from the camp, had been bombed by American planes. Surely going back to the prison camp at Changi couldn't be as bad as what he had just suffered, Tom thought, and possibly, just possibly, the war would soon end and they all would all be rid of this accursed place.

He slowly raised his bony arm and tucked it behind his head to form a pillow and closed his eyes. Sleep came quickly this time, helped by the rhythmic sound of the train.

Within minutes Tom's mind was back in the machine shop at the Bridge Engineering Works in Maidstone and he was feeling particularly pensive as he sat on a small stool with his back resting against the side of a lathe, eating a sandwich.

Subconsciously, Tom's swollen tongue licked his cracked lips as he tasted the sandwich in his dream. Through a small gap in the layers of dirt which lined the machine shops' windows he could see the blue sky of the summer day outside, and reflected how many years had passed since he had left the woods.

The men always ate their lunch by their machines and whilst most of them would bring in a flask of something hot, some still retained the old practice of bringing a lemonade bottle full of cold tea. It was always quiet in the machine shop at this time of day. There was stillness in the air. Most of the men were either reading newspapers or a sitting quietly playing cards.

Tom watched aimlessly as one of the card players calculated his score and moved a matchstick along the row of holes in the cribbage board.

The machines had been turned off and their drive belts had stopped making their familiar flapping noises. The rest of the factory had also stopped for lunch and not a soul was moving throughout huge building. Even the youthful apprentices were silent. It was thirty minutes of peace and tranquillity and Tom suddenly realised how much he relished it.

Chopper was on holiday with his sister and her family. Tom smiled as he remembered Chopper complaining that "he would only be the wet nurse and he would rather be at work", but they both knew he was looking forward to the week at Margate. In any case, he loved being with his two young nephews.

His dream continued and in it Tom was staring through the dirt encrusted window and realising how much he missed seeing the clear blue sky and hearing the cacophony of bird songs in the woods. Looking up at the machine shop's dusty black ceiling with its criss-cross of belts and pulleys he felt trapped and could feel his heart racing. He took a deep breath and filled his lungs. The ceiling seemed to be slowly descending like a black cloud, trapping him in its oppressive gloom. He suddenly felt the urge to leave it before it overwhelmed him.

It was a something he had not felt before and compared with the freedom and the open space of the woods, the workshop had suddenly begun to feel like a prison cell. He stood up and shook his shoulders in an attempt to shake off the claustrophobia and took another deep intake of breath. Instead of the deliciously sweet scent of the bluebells which hung in the spring air by the spinney or the smell of summer rain on the long, curling fonds of the ferns growing by the old quarry. All he could smell now was the offensive stench of the cutting fluid. Its repulsive smell clogged his nostrils. His lungs suddenly yearned for the fresh air of the countryside. He needed to feel the wind on his face and once again to see the ever changing colours of the sky. He needed a different job.

The steel floor of the box car was un-yielding and Tom was becoming restless in his sleep. He twisted and turned, first from one side then to the other, before he slept on as his dream of the machine shop continued.

He was leaning against the lathe and absentmindedly took a cigarette from the packet he fished out from the top pocket of his overalls and put it to his lips. His mind was made up. He needed to get away from the place. Perhaps, he would go back to game keeping.... no, not that, he thought, definitely not that, but what?

He lit a cigarette and as he watched the swirling patterns of its smoke, he came to the conclusion he would talk to Chopper about it when his friend got back from Margate and then decide what to do next.

Tom woke up with a start. He was in the stinking rice wagon and somewhere in the distance he could hear the cackling laugh of a hornbill as if it was mocking the suffering of the men in their swaying metal cages. Yet, despite his discomfort, he somehow felt relieved the work on the railway had finished and was grateful of the rest the journey gave him as the train rumbled back to the prison camp in Singapore. It was then the reality of his dream hit him.

It was his own fault he was here. It was his fault Chopper was dead. If only, he thought remorsefully.

"Home sweet bloody home", a voice said sarcastically, as the line of returning prisoners was marched through the familiar gates of the River Valley Road prison camp, the same one they had left eighteen months earlier. Tom raised his head and weak as he was, he managed a feeble smile as he looked up with wry amusement at the rows of barbed wire which now lined the top of the wire fences around the camp. Where could you go, he thought grimly and even if you did manage to escape, you wouldn't get very far with the Nips controlling every inch of the island. The nightmare images of the way escaping prisoners had met their end returned to his tortured mind.

Familiar swarms of mosquitoes, their bodies were fat with the blood of captives and captors alike rose from the swamps surrounding the rows of the wooden huts of the camp as the prisoners were marched into the next stage of their incarceration. Virtually all of the sixty men who crowded into the hut with Tom were suffering from chronic dysentery and it wasn't long before the human filth from the maggot-filled latrines soaked into the nearby, sluggish, foul smelling river.

"No bloody peace for the wicked, we only got here yesterday", said the stooped figure of a Sapper, who was being pushed past Tom in the opposite direction. Tom realised the man was already part of a work party which had been formed to load the Jap freighters, moored at the docks with the inexhaustible booty of war.

Six weeks of forced labour in the docks and the putrid smell of the hut passed and Tom was almost pleased to be on the move again. His hooded eyelids blinked rapidly over his cold-lifeless eyes as he stood in the bright sunlight. Their bright, olive green colour had disappeared long ago and they were now as pallid as the skin which hung from his bone-protruding body. He doubted whether he weighed much more than six stones now, much the same as the other prisoners who had been herded out of the hut in readiness for another forced march. Tom lifted his bowed head and glanced around. They were being formed up in a group of about two-hundred men. Already, lined up in front of his group, were about four or five other groups of similar numbers. The searing tropical sun beat down as they all stood there, waiting for the Jap soldiers and the Gunzokus to assemble the remaining groups. Even now some of the Korean guards were already moving amongst the prisoners stealing anything of value they could find amongst the last few items some of the prisoners had managed to keep during their years of incarceration.

"Here were go again", said the round-shouldered man who was standing next to Tom. "Look at those bastards", he nodded his head towards the lines of Japanese soldiers who were standing each side of the mass of prisoners and nursing their machine guns with a familiar menace.

Tom did as the man had instructed and saw there was also a separate detachment at work, ready to deal with any prisoners who fell out during the impending march. Anybody who was too sick or too weak to make this particular journey would be making one of a different kind.

Tom felt wretched and looked at the man. Names didn't matter anymore but he could see by the man's faded cap badge he had been with the Norfolks.

"They won't march us until they've got about two-thousand, that's what went two weeks ago", the man said, without looking up.

Tom suddenly became more alert on hearing what the man was saying and asked in surprise, "Where are they taking us?"

"The docks", Norfolk said, in a flat, emotionless voice.

"The docks", croaked Tom. His throat was dry and he was not confident he would make the march to the docks, remembering they were about twenty miles away. "Then where?" he enquired, in bewilderment.

"Japan!"

"Japan!" Tom was thunder-struck and his senses were instantly awoken as he repeated the word. He collected his thoughts quickly and asked, "What for.......How long will it take to get to bloody Japan?"

"We've made it so far", Norfolk said vaguely and then added, "The bastards are going to use us as bloody slaves in their fucking coal mines and steel mills".

Tom's mind was in a daze with what the man had said and almost in a state of shock, his eyes drifted at the rows and rows of suffering men standing around him. They had been starved, worked and beaten until they had become bags of bones. How on earth will they make it to Japan....and then what?" he thought, as he waited nervously for the order to move on.

"Least I've got a pair of boots and these fucking shorts out of the callous bastards" said Norfolk as he let out a cynical laugh. "Wouldn't do for us to arrive at the gates to their shitty Empire, stark bollock naked... how would it look?"

Tom managed a weak smile and remembered they had not been given any clothing since their capture two years earlier. He looked down at the tattered shorts which were bunched together around his scrawny waist and he tightened the string which was keeping them up.

"PRISONERS... MARCH", yelled out the Japanese officer in charge.

Contempt was burning in Tom's eyes when he looked up at the man, as he stood there in his spotless uniform. A band of white silk was carefully wrapped around the tropical pith helmet set square on his head and on his feet were the familiar polished brown knee length boots of an officer, which gleamed in the bright sunlight.

Ever since his capture, Tom had been repulsed by the arrogance of the enemy officers and the contempt and brutality they displayed towards the prisoners and their own lower ranks. This and the sight of them in their clean and spotless uniforms always angered Tom and he said quietly to Norfolk as they began reluctantly to shuffle forward, "Bit of a difference between how he looks and how us lot are looking".

"SPEEDO. SPEEDO", the soldiers screamed at the prisoners. The words spat out of their mouths like bullets and carried a similar menace.

"Bastards", Norfolk swore, as he dragged his ulcerated foot along the dusty ground, desperately trying to keep up with the line of men in front of him, "next stop, the shit hole they call Japan".

The march to the docks took most of the day and with only two short stops for a small gulp of water and a handful of black-grained rice, it was no surprise when Tom let out a sigh of relief as they approached their destination.

Thick black smoke was already belching from the rusty funnels of the cargo ships moored up alongside the quayside. A handful of Japanese navy vessels, which Tom thought were probably waiting to escort a convoy once the human cargos had been loaded onto it. Small clouds of dust were being blown off the heaps of coal piled high on the quayside and Tom could see native prisoners shovelling the black-stuff into trucks. Those poor buggers are in worse condition than we are, he thought wistfully, as he watched the starved and beaten wretches being forced to push the trucks of coal along the quay before loading it on a ship which was moored further along quay.

The long-awaited order was given for the POW's to stop. The weather was oppressively hot and sultry and Tom was relieved he had made it so far.

"Look at that bloody rust bucket, surely we are not going on that load of shit", croaked Norfolk who was now in a worse state than he was when they started the march.

Tom looked at the old cargo ship moored up in front of them. "Hofuku Maru" he said aloud, as he read the name on the ship's bow.

Norfolk didn't reply. His thoughts were elsewhere. "How far is the land of the bloody rising sun?" he asked, already concerned about the seaworthiness of the rusty freighter moored in front of them.

Tom shrugged his shoulders, "Three thousand miles, give or take some" he replied, not really knowing or caring.

He looked ominously at the ship. A black cloud of smoke was already coming out of its tall, soot covered, single funnel. The freighter was considerably smaller than the "Empress of Japan" which had brought them to this place of hell, probably about six-thousand tons, Tom guessed at its size.

Norfolk pointed towards the stern of the ship where a small makeshift shelter had been built on the deck. "There won't be much room in that little hut for all of us lot", he joked thinly.

Tom didn't answer. He was already thinking how the two-thousand men who were standing on the dockside could be transported in such a relatively small ship.

"*CHUMOKU... CHUMOKU*" screamed the rasping voice of the Jap officer with the polished boots. "Attention, Attention".

The first few rows of POW's wearily raised their bowed heads, whilst the main body of the huge group just stood waiting. They couldn't hear what was being said and they couldn't care less. It didn't matter. They would learn what was going to happen to them soon enough.

"ATTENTION..... Prisoners disobeying the following orders will be punished with immediate death,......For disobeying any orders......For showing any sign of disobedience......For talking without permission......For walking or moving without permission... ...", the staccato voice droned on.

Tom cautiously looked around, the POW's had become accustomed to being made to stand in the blazing sun but he knew despite clenching their buttocks tightly together, some of the poor devils would succumb to the effects of tropic diseases and their bomb bays would open and the resultant hot flow would start running down their legs.

The Jap officer continued with his incessant list of orders, "The navy of the great Japanese empire will try not to punish you with death....those obeying all the rules....."

Tom distinctly heard Norfolk, who had his chin tucked tightly on his bony chest respond by saying "Bollocks to your bloody rules".

"The great Japanese empire will rise and govern the world", the officer concluded his tirade to the relief of the weary prisoners.

"Bollocks to the Japanese bloody empire", Norfolk's voice croaked again, heavy with contempt.

Tom stood silent. Will there be no respite from this hell, he thought?

Tom and Norfolk watched as those who had been nearest to the ship were herded up the gangway and down into the first of the two cargo holds. The thought of nearly two-thousand men being forced into the bowels of such a small ship caused Tom's heart to race as the familiar feeling of claustrophobia began to grip him like a vice.

.He had nearly reached the gangway when he heard a high pitched voice screaming at the prisoners. Immediately he looked up and saw the unmistakable squat figure of Slimey standing at the top of the gangway. Tom froze in his tracks. He had not seen the man since leaving Chong Kao camp and seeing him again ignited the rage which had smouldered deep inside ever since Chopper's death. The anger boiling within him was more intense than anything he had ever felt before. It had been buried deep and now it welled up as he realised the man whom he held responsible for so many deaths, was travelling back to Japan and would escape retribution for his evil crimes. It had been Tom's overwhelming need for revenge which had kept the weak flame of life alive in him and he knew he must not lose it now.

He took another quick look and silently vowed that one day he would see to it that the grinning man with the rotten teeth would pay for what he had done. Tom lowered his head and kept his mouth tightly clamped as he passed by the odious man and stepped onto the ship's deck.

Tom winced when he felt the hot metal of the deck plates through the holes in the soles of his boots as he walked unsteadily towards the vertical ladder which led down into the hold. When he joined the line of men waiting to descend into the depths of the hold, he could smell it was already reeking of vomit and body waste. Slowly Tom climbed down the ladder. His grip was weak and he breathed a sigh of relief on reaching the bottom rung without falling off. Blinking to re-adjust his vision to the murk which confronted him, he could make out vague silhouettes. Then to his horror, he realised there was already hardly any room left to move. Probably, four or five hundred men were already pressed together in the hell hole and many more were on the deck waiting to be forced down the ladder and crammed into the dark hold. When would this stream of human misery stop coming? Tom thought.

The gut wrenching feeling of claustrophobia gripped him again.

As he was jostled deeper into the mass of men being crammed into the hold, a wall of heat hit him. Surely nobody can survive down here, he thought. He could feel the searing heat radiating from the metal sides of the ship as he began to push his way back through the banks of men who had now been driven further into the tomb-like hold by their grinning captors. I must try to keep close to the open hatch, he thought, there will be more air there. Others had the same idea but somehow, Tom managed to shoulder his way through until he saw the open hatch high above his head. Standing there but being jostled on all sides by desperate men, all anxious to breathe some clean air, Tom heard the grating sound of metal and looking up, he saw two grinning Japanese sailors pulling up the ladder from the hold. The hatch cover was slammed shut with a resounding bang and as the inside of the hold became almost pitch black, some of the prisoners began shouting at the now, invisible men above them...

"Bastards, you bloody bastards", a chorus of voices screamed, each engulfed in growing despair.

"You callous vicious sods". The voice was angry and calculated.

Other prisoners joined in with their own frank opinions of their captors. "You inhuman bastards, open the bloody hatch".

"Let us out, for the love of God, let us out", sobbed a delirious man, who was already on his knees close to Tom.

Poor sod, Tom thought, knowing the man was on the edge of losing his sanity. He stooped down and gripping the weeping man under his armpits, lifted him to his feet and propped him against one of the steel girders which were riveted down the sides of the hold.

"God help me", the man babbled. His voice croaked with anguish.

Tom scoffed. I don't think God seems so inclined, he thought to himself.

"Like rats in a bloody trap, that's what we are, rats in a bloody, shit-filled trap", another voice said as he gulped the stifling, bitter air.

Somewhere in the gloom another man had started crying. He sounded like someone who had suffered long enough and had now resigned himself to death, Tom thought, as the man's wailing continued. As Tom listened, he heard the man's crying was turning into helpless sobs, like those of an innocent man being led to the gallows.

Tom's eyes were gradually becoming accustomed to his dark prison. There was a solitary light bulb hanging down from a support girder welded to the metal roof of the hold and as he looked around, he could make out the features of a man who was being squashed against him. Even in the gloom, Tom could see the man was dying. He had seen this look hundreds of times since his capture and he put his arm round the man's waist knowing that if he didn't, the poor devil would fall. The man tried to speak through his swollen lips but no words came from them, just pitiful sounds. Tom could smell the foulness of the doomed man's breath. He could see the man more clearly now and saw his gaunt face and hollow cheeks. His rib cage was clearly visible and he was naked, apart from a beret and a soiled jappy nappy. Would this poor sod be the first one to die in this hell-hole? Tom thought as the man slipped from his weak grasp.

Through the thick, metal plates of the ship, Tom could hear the metallic sound of clanking chains and the faint shouts of voices coming from the deck above him and then, as he listened, the increased thudding of the Hofuku Maru's revving engine. Without warning, the ship suddenly rocked as it left the relative safety of the docks and turned out into the open sea. The rising swell was crashing against the freighter's starboard bow, sending vibrations which reverberated through every part of the aging ship.

"That's it then", said a grime covered man, who was grimly holding on to an iron girder in an attempt to keep his balance, "we are on our way to fucking Japan". Somebody towards the other end of the hold started howling.

The thud of the engines had been relentless and it was difficult for Tom and the other two-thousand prisoners to calculate how long they had been travelling, other than once a day the grim monotony of survival was broken by a grating sound as the guards slid back the metal bolts which secured the hatch covers to the deck. Once or twice when Tom had been able to gulp some fresh air he had seen Japanese soldiers with machine guns at the ready, standing behind the grinning guards. He had no doubt the bastards would dearly love to let loose a couple of bursts down into the writhing mass of prisoners below. If for no other reason than to break the monotony of being at sea or purely for amusement, it didn't matter to them. This time, as the hatch cover was slid back, all hell broke loose. It was now becoming a case of everyman for himself.

It was self survival.

Tom was lucky this time. With the hatch open, he could feel the fresh sea air on his face and he breathed in the delicious elixir until his lungs nearly burst.

"God" he gasped through lips that were black and cracked as a result of his unrelenting thirst.

His swollen eyes blinked as the darkness of his prison was briefly replaced with the narrow shaft of sunlight which shone in. For a few glorious moments the smell of the cesspit was replaced with the scent of the sea. His lungs demanded more of the sweet air. Seagulls were screeching overhead and Tom could hear the noise of the sea as it crashed against the rusty bow of the ship. He could almost taste the fine spray in the air and for those precious few seconds he entered a world he had almost forgotten and one he was beginning to think he would never see again.

He watched as the buckets of water were lowered down into the hold by one of the grinning captors above and wondered if he would be one of the lucky ones who managed to scoop some of the precious life-giving liquid. If not this time, perhaps the next, he thought. As he desperately fought his way through the jostling prisoners to reach one of the buckets, he noticed how they were becoming fewer, as were the buckets of thin soup, since they had left the dock at Singapore.

Every time the hatches were opened, some of the men incarcerated in the gloom screamed obscenities at their captors whilst others cried out for air and water. Down in the dark and from the scrum of desperate men, someone stumbled into Tom. "Sorry mate" the man said quite cheerfully, given his circumstances, "my bloody leg has swollen, it's a job standing up … hope it's not gangrene".

"Any idea how long we have been in here?" Tom said, deliberately not enquiring further into the man's condition. He sensed they both knew what the outcome would be if the leg was gangrenous and the fetid smell coming from it wasn't good.

"A Dutchman I was talking to, told me he had counted the number of times night had fallen through the gaps in the hold's hatch cover and he thought it was probably about fourteen days although it seems a lot longer to me".

"Any idea how long it will take to get there?" Tom asked.

"The chap said he thought it would be about twenty-five days", replied the man with the gangrenous leg.

Tom didn't reply. He was doing the calculation in his head. Twenty five minus fifteen, that's ten. Ten days left. Bloody hell, he thought, I'm sure I can last that long. Suddenly he was feeling much better.

"Have you noticed this bucket of shit is slowing down?" the man with the gangrenous leg enquired.

"No", Tom said, surprised at what he had just been told.

"The Dutch bloke I'd been talking to, thought the engines were conking out".

"Blimey", Tom said, clearly interested at the prospect, "perhaps we will be getting out of here before we get to Japan".

There was no doubt, the ship was crippled and unknown to the men as they listened to the changes in the sound of the engine, the ship had started to limp into the dock at Manila. A loud cheer echoed round the hold, when sometime later, the ship banged against the solid quayside and the men heard the welcome noises of it was being tied up. Their hopes rose for their suffering to end.

It was not to be. With the engines being repaired and hatches tightly shut, the men, most of which were completely naked by now, were left wallowing in their own filth. The sun continued to beat down on the ship and the temperature inside the hold was suffocating. Almost constantly there was a chorus of voices pleading for air and water. The men were literally dying of thirst and somewhere in the midst of them, Tom heard somebody shout "For the love of God, let us out, we're dying down here".

"Sod all chance of that", Tom said quietly to himself.

Some of the imprisoned men had given up and were lying in the debris which swirled about the floor of the tomb-like hold. A few were silently crying, whilst others howled, afraid of their impending journey into the jaws of death.

Tom briefly opened his eyes. He had been closing them frequently now, attempting to shut his mind from the hell around him and dreamt of the green fields and woods he had left so long ago.

Then, in the gloom in front of him, he saw some figures attempting to form a human tower.

"What are you doing?" he asked the man at the bottom of the three man tower. His voice was weak.

"Trying to get to those pipes up there" gasped the man. Tom could see the man was struggling to withstand the weight of the men above him on his bony shoulders.

"What for?", Tom asked, intrigued by the men's efforts and becoming more interested by the minute.

The man was beginning to tire of Toms' persistence and snapped back at him, "To get some bloody water"

"Water!", Tom exclaimed. Was this the sign of hope, even life, he had prayed for?

Tom couldn't disguise the incredulous sound of his croaking voice. His dry mouth and swollen tongue desperately craved for moisture, not just moisture but water! He could hardly believe what the man was saying. Tom's senses suddenly become alive as a result of what he had just heard.

"Is there water up there?" he asked anxiously.

"On the steam pipes coming from the engine, they cooled down when the engine was buggered and it left drops of condensation hanging along them".

Tom looked up and like heavy dew on curving blades of grass were rows of droplets of water, waiting to fall.

Without being asked, Tom joined the group. Perhaps the lush green fields of Pentbury wouldn't just be in his dreams.

The repairs to the ships' engines had taken two long months. During this time, the hatch covers had been kept mostly shut and only opened for when the meagre buckets of water and rice to be lowered down and just once, when it was decided to remove the bodies of the dead and those who were obviously on the point of death.

"Do you think we'll ever leave here?" Tom asked one of the 'fortunate' prisoners who had been part of the contingent who had hauled the dead from the holds onto the quayside and had taken the opportunity to breathe some fresh air.

Conversation between the prisoners had virtually ceased now and the man replied sparingly, "The Japs think there may be cholera on-board and if there is, they don't want to take it back to their beloved homeland".

Tom remembered what Norfolk had told him. The Japs didn't want the prisoners to cause any problems or offence when they reached the land of the rising sun. No wonder the ship remained moored tight to the quayside.

"Wonder what happened to Norfolk", Tom said to himself as his mind drifted to the fate of some of the others. Taff, Percy, Dusty Miller, Sam

Goodale, Bantam. More names continued to race through his head as he reflected on their fate. Surely they can't all be dead, he thought.

It was then he remembered Chopper and the vengeance he sought for his friend's death brought the faint glimmer of life back into his body.

The hatches remained firmly closed. Tom had heard somebody say there were still six or seven hundred men crammed into the hold with a similar number battened down in the aft hold. Most of the prisoners, including Tom, were now beginning to despair they would ever see their loved ones again as others continued to die of disease, thirst and starvation.

It was some days later when Tom asked the man laying on one of the soiled platforms next to him, if he knew how long they had been incarcerated in the hold.

"I think it must be about two months but..." The man stopped in mid sentence and suddenly raised his head, saying weakly, "Listen".

Tom had already heard the clanking of mooring chains and the unmistakable sound of the ship's engines being started. "Thank Christ", he managed to say through his swollen lips, "at last we're finally on the move".

"Do you know Skip, the size of this deck is equal to two acres of land", Pete O'Brian said absentmindedly to his fellow pilot, Skip Krisner, as he looked out onto the enormous flight deck of the aircraft carrier, the USS Hornet, as it steamed towards the Philippines?.

"You don't say", Skip said sleepily.

The pair had been having some precious sack time, having lost count of the number of combat missions they had flown during the past six months, ever since they had left the naval base in Virginia. Skip sighed, any rest, no matter how short, had become an unaccustomed luxury. He closed his eyes again.

"I sure do", continued Pete earnestly, still thinking about the size of the carrier's deck. "Back in Kansas, my old papa could grow over one hundred bushels of corn on that amount of land".

"That's a lot of bread", said Skip Krisner, who was now fully awake and surveying the scene spread out in front of them. His tousled blond hair had fallen across his young face and a broad smile spread across his face as he thought that the particular two acres they were sitting on would be a lot more productive than the patch of land in Kansas.

Skip looked across at the deep blue ocean as it sparkled and shimmered. The unrelenting rays of the sun reflected on the Pacific's surface like thin sheets of beaten silver. He gazed in awe at the immense armada of ships which made up the Task Force as it stretched out for as far as he could see. Skip remembered the first time he had looked down on it from the solitude of his F6F Hellcat fighter plane and how its sheer scale had taken his breath away. The Task Force was made up of six separate Task Groups. The Groups comprised of four or five huge aircraft carriers. Every one of these vast, lumbering, floating airfields was surrounded by their own defensive ring of cruisers, destroyers, fast battleships and radar pickets. Each Group was deployed in a circle of about six miles, which meant the total formation covered an area of sea over twenty-five square miles. Skip never tired of looking at such a magnificent sight and despite its tremendous fighting power. All he saw was a picture of beauty and splendour.

Pete watched his fellow naval aviator looking out to sea. "That sure is a sight to see, Skip. I feel much safer with that lot around us, much safer than I do when I'm up in the sky".

"It's not that bad up there". Skip laughed and motioned to one of the Hellcats that were giving the Fleet aerial cover in the cloudless sky overhead. "We've already obliterated the Jap air power and now we're sweeping their warships and merchant fleets from the sea", he said confidently.

"We sure have got the firepower to do the job", replied Pete, in his mid-west American accent, "did you know there are over ninety-five thousand men on-board all of these ships?"

Skip laughed again. He knew his friend, who came from a small farming town just outside of Kansas City would never get used to the enormity of the fleet. "Yep", he teased Pete's knowledge and emphasising the word *you*, said, "and do *you* know that the carriers have got nearly a thousand planes in their hangar decks".

"And only two very able pilots to fly them", Pete responded, putting his arm round his friend's shoulder as they walked off laughing from the flight deck to get a cup of black coffee and a club sandwich from the wardroom buffet.

Huge festering sores covered Tom's feet making any movement difficult. The engaging smile which had once been a constant feature on his face almost since birth had been replaced long ago, by hollow, sunken cheeks with black gaps in his bleeding gums where his teeth had once been. He felt faint with dysentery and although his legs were trembling, something in his mind was telling him that he must not fall down. He closed his eyes and leant against the flakes of a rusting girder. His mind was becoming confused by the lack of food and water and from the effects of beriberi he was also suffering from.

He closed his eyes and drifted mercifully once again into sleep. Reality waned away and his mind became haunted with dreams of his past. He began to hear the birds singing in the woods again. Something was screeching overhead. He listened. There it was again, a loud screech. That's a jay calling, he thought. The old woodman was there too and was shouting at Tom. "Stop shouting", Tom screamed as he felt himself fall into the water at the bottom of the old quarry. He kept falling and falling until the cold water splashed on his face and he could feel the elixir of life on his lips. Jim Colegate was still shouting. The jays were screeching louder. Tom called out, "Mother, mother, help me.....please help me". He could see his mother, her arms out-stretched, running to help him.....

Tom opened his eyes but his vision was blurred and he slipped back and forth into his dream. He did not realise his brain was slowly being starved of oxygen.

Skip and Pete made their way down into the hangar deck of the USS Hornet and although it was dimly lit, they could see the rows of planes with their wings folded, all waiting to be elevated onto the flight deck ready for the next offensive. Although some planes were on the flight deck ready for the order to take off, Skip could make out the rows of Hellcats, over fifty of them altogether, with a lesser number of the larger Avengers. Some of the deckhands were snatching a few minutes of sleep amongst the piles of rope which were stacked against rows of red oil drums, whilst others were wheeling bombs and rockets, already primed and fused, to the planes using little one-handled barrows. Skip took a deep breath to take in the smell of oil and aviation fuel which was ever present on this hanger. He could hear the noise of planes preparing to take off above him and waited in anticipation for the deafening roar of the Hellcats when they raced down the flight deck for take-off.

"It must be like living inside a bass drum if you have to work down here", Skip shouted to his fellow aviator, hearing a deafening drone overhead followed by a huge thump which vibrated through the steel frame around them almost down to its last dome headed rivet.

"That's an Avenger being launched by the catapult", Pete shouted rather unnecessarily to Skip, who had heard the sound a thousand times before.

It was just after breakfast of ham and eggs, sunny side up, when Skip strapped on his harness and after carrying out pre-flight checks, sat in the cockpit of his Hellcat waiting for the signal to take off. The canopy was still slid open and his eyes were on the deckhand with the chequered launch flag. He took a deep breath and tasted the salty sea air and waited. The waiting was always the worst part.

The spotter planes had found a fleet of almost forty Japanese supply vessels anchored off Manila in Subic Bay and there was also a small convoy of enemy freighters on the move just off Luzon Island.

"It will be like shooting fish in a barrel", one of his fellow pilots had quipped at the briefing in the Ops room.

Skip glanced down at the instrument panel as he nervously waited to climb into the never-ending blue sky over the Pacific and back into action once more. He knew that once he was in the air the knot in his stomach would disappear and the adrenaline would kick in.

Whilst he was waiting, he mused that it was less than five years ago when he had been in Phoenix studying to be a doctor, to save lives and now here he was, taking lives by the dozen.

He looked around him. He was in the second row of the planes which were already warming their engines and twisting his head round, he could see Pete's plane was in the row behind. Whilst Skip waited for take-off he counted the waiting planes. There were over twenty of them. He looked down from his lofty perch at the deckhands in their bright yellow linen flash clothes and tight fitting caps as they manoeuvred the last of the planes into position, ready for take-off. The elevator from the hangar had done its work and now all the planes were on the flight deck, prepared for the path of destruction which lay ahead of them.

Skip pressed the engine start button and gave the Gruman Hellcat full throttle. He felt it shudder as the accelerating thrust from its powerful Pratt Whitney engine propelled it along the wooden deck of the carrier. Skip knew the single propeller plane did not need the nine-hundred feet of deck and felt the nose begin to lift off the deck as the plane started its steep climb. Immediately, the Hellcat was caught in a cross wind causing Skip to hold it steady as he continued to climb. He looked down at his instrument panel and saw the needle on the vertical speed indicator was rising quickly. Skip smiled, knowing the climb rate of the plane could max at over three-thousand feet per minute and he gently nudged the joy stick again to let it climb before levelling out at thirteen -thousand feet. The Hellcats were powerful fighting machines, with their fat fuselages and broad square ended wings which each had three Browning guns and six rockets slung snugly underneath them which nestled under the plane's belly was a five-hundred pound bomb.

Skip looked around at the other Hellcats which were buzzing around him like bees swarming on a sultry summer's day and far below him he could see the Carrier Task Force spread out across the sun spangled ocean. He glanced down again and saw the protective screen of ships around each of the groups of carriers and he was in no doubt that somewhere, lurking beneath the armada, were submarines which were giving the Task Force even more protection from enemy attack.

"What a magnificent sight", Skip said to himself, tucked snugly in his cockpit, mounted high on the plane's fuselage, as more Hellcats and Avengers were taking off from the other carriers.

Wow, this is going to be some party, he thought, as his radio crackled into life. "Jap convoy sighted, repeat Jap convoy sighted".

Skip pulled back on the joystick and felt the plane rise quickly and he felt the familiar tightness in his throat. Around him were other Hellcats and now for the first time, he could see they had been joined by some lumbering Avenger bombers. The Avengers are big old birds, he thought, with their crew of three and the two, one-thousand torpedo bomb tucked against the plane's bellies.

Skip stole a quick glance at his watch and noted it was 10.30 hours. He checked again. It was September 11th 1944.

The voice of the lead pilot shouting the co-ordinates for the attack rattled in Skip's headphones and the planes began to peel off into two waves. Skip watched over his port wing as the first wave of twenty five aircraft moved off to attack the ships that had been seen anchored in Subic Bay. He throttled the plane's two-thousand horse-power engine back and dipped the nose down so he could join the second wave which would attack the Japanese convoy of freighters steaming off Luzon Island. Skip felt confident in his armoured cockpit, knowing the plane could easily out-perform the Japanese Zeros. In any case, he thought if a Nip pilot did get lucky, he knew his plane could withstand significant damage, if in the unlikely event he was hit. He looked out at the point fifty calibre machine gun and the even more reassuringly high velocity rockets which were mounted under the wing tips. He smiled when he thought that these boys were equal to a destroyer's broadside.

"Christ", he murmured to himself, "this sure is going to be some turkey shoot".

A hoarse voice bellowed in his headphones, "Enemy convoy sighted".

Skip's head whipped around anxiously for any Nip interceptors which may be protecting the convoy and was relieved there was no cloud cover for an enemy plane to lurk in. In any case, if they did arrive, he was ready to splash them down.

He watched as wave after wave of Hellcats were going in and as he looked down, Skip saw they had singled out a large ship, like a swarm of killer bees attacking a dying beast. He pushed hard on the joystick and felt the rapid descent of the plane. The sensation made him take a deep breath. It was like being on a roller-coaster back home, only worse and he wondered if he would ever get used to it. Skip leaned forward in his seat and could clearly see the ship the planes were attacking was travelling slowly at about ten knots. The first of their rockets hit the slow moving vessel, scoring direct hits to its mid-ships and immediately setting its bridge superstructure ablaze. The beast is doomed, he thought with satisfaction on seeing its bow was already sinking into the cold water of the Pacific Ocean. Skip glanced back and saw two other ships in the convoy were being attacked and decided to lay off to wait for another opportunity. He could see plumes of water rising from the foaming sea around the stricken vessels. One had already been hit below the water-line and was sinking and as he watched, there was a massive explosion in its stern. On seeing the flames coming from the ship, Skip realised it was probably a diesel tub and not one of the old Jap steam ships.

An excited voice yapped from the radio, "Gee.... gee, this is too easy guys".

About a mile ahead, Skip suddenly saw an old freighter which was making slow headway as it steamed ahead of the main convoy, leaving a trail of black smoke belching from its single funnel.

"My turn", he said to himself as he turned and dived low towards the target he had singled out. His eyes were straining to read the name on the side of the freighter's rusting hull. "Hofuku Maru", he read out loud, "nice name for a ship". Skip smiled as he steadied the plane in readiness to begin his attack. "Ho fuck you too", he said, with a broad grin across his young face.

He inhaled deeply and pressed the now familiar trigger on the joystick and watched as the 0.50 calibre bullets from the wing-mounted guns danced their deadly way down, before they ripped open the freighter's deck. He could see some of the ship's crew running along the deck towards the stern in the futile attempt to find somewhere safe to hide from the hell that was descending upon them. Skip's eyes focused on one of them in particular. A heavyset man was pushing the others aside so that he could be the first to find a place to take cover. There were some optimistic blasts of anti aircraft fire coming up from a gun that was mounted on the bow of the rust bucket but Skip ignored them. He wanted to take a closer look before letting the rockets loose, so he throttled back and banked the plane round again. He could see the short, fat man more clearly now and noticed he was wearing the uniform of a Japanese army officer. The man had stopped running and his narrow, cold eyes seemed to be looking directly up at Skip, sending a shudder down the pilot's spine. He had never experienced this feeling before and although the glimpse had been almost as quick as the flap of a butterfly's wing, instinctively, he knew there was something very evil about the man. Quickly Skip steadied the plane before pressing his gloved thumb down hard on the stick button.

"First rocket away", he said to himself. It was a habit which he had acquired since leaving the naval base at Virginia and now it was something he did subconsciously.

The guy at briefing was right, he thought, this is like shooting fish in a barrel as the five-inch, hard-pointed rocket smashed into starboard side of the Hofuku Maru. Skip's eyes were as sharp as any predator when the vivid streak of fire hit the ship and then, a split second later, he watched almost spellbound, as fingers of orange flames reached up towards him, as if they were vainly trying to grasp the plane which had conceived them. At first, the ship seemed to resist the attack like an ancient tree confronting the force of a Mid-West tornado but then it yielded with a massive bow explosion, hurtling debris in all directions. Skip's eyes were transfixed on the stricken ship as his thumb searched once more for the button on the stick. The ship shuddered as the second rocket hit it and as he watched, Skip could see another Hellcat was beginning to attack the freighter's port-side. The plane's wing dipped and as Skip began to peel away, he saw with satisfaction, all that was left of the place where the fat Jap with the bloated, sweaty face and the pencil thin moustache had been standing, was now a large, jagged burning hole in the steel deck plates and as Skip looked again, the ship was beginning to slip under the waves.

Skip levelled the plane and yelled into his radio, "HOFUKU MARU IS SINKING, I repeat Hofuku ….Maru....sinking...... out".

He could hear other voices shouting from the radio, "Ogura Maru unable to make way and sinking...... out"...... "Surakarute Maru has sunk...... out".

Tom Kealey had been amongst a group of men in the centre of the rusting freighter's aft hold and still clinging to a spark of life when he heard the low pitched roar of planes overhead. He raised his head and listened. The men around him had heard them and were shouting. Every man imprisoned deep in the hold was thinking the same thing. Could this be the release from hell they had been praying for?

Tom held his breath and listened again. Yes, he was right. The sound of the freighter's engine was changing and it felt like the ship was increasing its speed.

Yes, Tom realised, the ship was going faster. Was it trying to outrun the planes? It was then he felt the vibrations rumbling down the length of the freighter's rusting hull, immediately followed by a massive jolt which shook every bone in Tom's taut body.

"HIT US, HIT US" someone had started shouting, "For Christ's sake hit us".

Hundreds of the prisoners suddenly came to life and joined in. Was this the chance to escape from their long years of captivity and suffering? Men who moments before lay huddled together and almost lifeless, suddenly clambered to their feet as feelings of hope and salvation surged through their weak bodies.

It was as if the men's prayers were being answered, when, without warning, there was an ear-bursting explosion and the ship seemed to shudder down to its last rivet. Tom could feel men sliding and falling around him as the freighter rolled from side to side. He was like a drunken man and instinctively reached out for something to hold on to. Nothing. There was not even time for him to feel a sense of panic before another explosion hit the ship. A blinding flash illuminated the hold as the aging ship's stern seemed to rise from the sea like a harpooned whale.

Tom fell and started sliding through the filth covering the floor plates. Men were shouting and screaming in desperation as they began to fall headlong towards the freighter's sinking bow. Frantically Tom spread-eagled his arms and legs hoping to find something to arrest his downward slide. His descent seemed unstoppable until he became embedded into a knot of panic-stricken men desperately hanging onto a floor girder. In the darkness which followed he could hear men shouting, each fighting for survival.

His mind had become alert, he was alive.

Tom blinked. The flashes of light burst into blinding intensity driving out the blackness which had seeped into Tom's mind and instantly awakened his consciousness.

Quickly extracting himself from the melee, Tom frantically hauled himself up the floor girder which, as the ship's bow slipped into the depths, was now almost vertical. He reached a point where girder was braced to an upright stanchion. Gripping the side plates, Tom hung on for grim death. His olive green eyes had come to life and a smile slowly spread across his face.

Weak as he was, and with his feet against a girder, he pushed off into the water, flooding into the hold. A long-lost grin returned to his face, as he said quietly, "Thank God".

The navigator in one of the lumbering Avengers was giving the position of the attack, "Co-ordinates, fourteen degrees, twenty-five north. One hundred and nineteen degrees, fifty east.. I repeat. One four degrees, two five north,... One, one, nine degrees, five zero east...

A broad smile spread across Skip's young face as he watched the Hofuku Maru slowly sink. Job well done, he thought, knowing there would soon be over a hundred planes seeking out the rest of the Japanese convoy hungry to destroy it.

Another voice was shouting from the radio, "SURVIVORS IN THE WATER..... I repeat, THERE ARE SURVIVORS IN THE WATER....OUT"

10

A Polished Boot on the Door-Step

The warbling tones of the Andrew sisters was coming from the Phillips wireless set, when without warning, the music suddenly stopped and Emily heard a crackling voice announce the war had ended. She gasped and dropped the potato she was peeling into the sink. Did it say the war has ended, she thought to herself as she shuffled her way across the room as quickly as she could. Her slippers had seen better days and in her haste they nearly left her feet. There was interference on the signal as Emily put her ear against the cold Bakelite casing and she wondered if the accumulator needed recharging. Thankfully the crackling stopped and despite her poor hearing, Emily recognised the low, gravelly voice of Winston Churchill. She listened as the Prime Minister continued to say the Germans had signed the act of unconditional surrender and was thanking all those who had fought valiantly on the land, sea and air. Emily's heart was beating quickly and the blue veins protruded on the back of her shaking hand as she pulled up one of the old wooden chairs which clustered round the table and sat down.

"The war has ended", she murmured in disbelief to the wireless. Talking to the wireless was a habit the old lady had acquired during her years of solitude. "The war has ended", Emily repeated as the sound of the church bells hanging high in the wooden belfry began to ring out in the distance. This was the news she had been waiting for and her heart suddenly flooded with joy and relief. "Tom will be home soon", she cried, as tears rolled from her eyes and coursed down the deep lines on her wrinkled face.

Three long months of waiting slowly passed.

It was late in August when the blue Fordson tractor chugged into the field opposite the cottage to start harvesting the golden heads of corn, ripened by the late summer's sun. Emily sat in her favourite chair by the window and watched as the tractor with a binder in tow began to drive through the yellow sea of corn.

She closed her eyes and thought how things had changed since she was a child when the harvest was cut by men with their long-handled scythes.

A reel of wooden boards on the side of the binder was turning effortlessly like a silent water wheel as it swept the gently waving corn stalks towards a row of moving blades. The old lady was almost spellbound as the cut stalks dropped onto a small canvas belt before being bundled up and tied with twine into sheaves. Emily watched as the tractor and binder made its way through the corn dropping the sheaves onto the freshly cut stubble as it went. The farm men who were following the machine picked up and trussed six or seven of the sheaves together and stood them up into stooks.

The next few weeks were dry and warm and the heads of corn ripened in the stooks as they stood in the field like lines of soldiers on a parade ground but it wasn't only the warmth of the late summer sun which lifted Emily's spirits. It was her unremitting joy of Tom's imminent homecoming.

She was continuing her daily vigil at the window one warm day in September when a horse-drawn cart appeared in the field and the waggoner started loading the stooks of corn onto the cart to take them to the stack yard, ready for the threshing machine to do its work. Grains of corn were always mixed amongst the chaff left behind on the wagon's wooden floor and Emily knew the waggoner would scoop them up and bring a small sack of the golden grains across the lane, for her chickens.

"Ah", Emily said to herself as she suddenly remembered she must get a cup of cocoa and a slice of fruit cake ready for the arrival of the kindly old man. She seldom had visitors these days and looked forward to seeing him again and hearing the news from the village.

Eventually the chill of autumn arrived and the rain Emily had heard beating on her bedroom window had stopped with the coming of the dawn. As she drew back the curtains, she saw a group of pheasants feeding on the grain which lay hidden in the rain-soaked field and her thoughts drifted back to the time when Tom had been a gamekeeper.

Thankfully all the men from the village who had fought in the war had now returned, save two. One had been a young airman named Alan Tong whose body had been found close to the wreckage of his spotter plane in the dense forests of Germany and the other was her own dear Tom. As she continued to watch the birds, her gaze was broken by a blackbird swirling in the cold autumn wind. Emily's thoughts returned to the present and she wondered, as she had so many times before, where her son was. She had heard he had been captured with the fall of Singapore and thankfully he had not been amongst the thousands who had died there. In her heart she knew he was alive, but where was he? Her eyes strayed across the room to her late husband's bronze memorial plaque, standing on its edge on the sideboard and trusted that God would answer her nightly prayers and Tom would be home, safe and well before Christmas.

The first frosts of the winter were exceptionally late when they came in December bringing with them some early flurries of light snow blowing in from the east. The cottage began to feel cold once again and Emily spent most of her time huddled in front of the small fire burning in the range. The war in the Far-East had been over for nearly four months and Tom had not returned but with Christmas approaching Emily busied herself in preparation to welcome him when he did arrive. She knew he would be home then, just as he had said in his letter.

The sky had darkened to the faint violet hue typical of a late December day and once Emily had fed the chicken with the remains of the waggoner's corn, she made her way to the bottom of the overgrown garden to find some holly. It was Christmas Eve and at her age, her bones were stiff and she found it was a struggle to clamber into the woods to search for the festive branches. Eventually she managed to find the tree she was looking for and after avoiding its needle sharp leaves, she carefully broke off a few of the lower branches. She was surprised to see they still had clusters of red berries clinging to them because normally, the redwings and the fieldfares would have eagerly devoured them but as snowflakes driven by a biting wind, swirled around the old lady, she knew the berries wouldn't last long now. Back inside the house, she managed to climb on a chair and put the sprigs of the holly round the picture frames and over the large, mahogany framed mirror which hung over the fireplace. The house began to look Christmassy again.

Emily felt a sense of excitement as she laid two places at the table, confident Tom would be home soon and at last, they would enjoy another Christmas meal together. There was sufficient food in the larder and she had saved the four large oranges Harry had given her, knowing these would be a treat for Tom when he arrived. Two quart bottles of Fremlins pale ale stood on the sideboard alongside the packet of twenty woodbines Emily had bought specially for the occasion. Finally, she laid the fire in the front room, making sure there was sufficient coal and logs in the small cupboards, either side of the fireplace. All was ready.

As night fell, Emily put a match to the crumpled balls of newspaper in the fire-grate. The flame caught and licked the kindling and as it grew, Emily carefully added a small shovel of coal. That done, she made her way up the narrow stairs to light the solitary wax candle which was already standing on the window sill in her bedroom. It flickered as it found the flame of Emily's match and started to cast eerie shadows round the cold room. Carefully she made her way back down the dark stairs. She didn't want to fall, tonight of all nights. With the important jobs done, the old lady carefully wrapped an old blanket round her shoulders before falling asleep in the Windsor chair in front of the fire. Old age had crept up on Emily in the same way as the inevitable bitter winter weather had crept up on the countryside outside.

There was a crisp white frost sparkling on the corn stubble like a million tiny stars as the old dog fox walked out of the wood to begin his nights hunting. His lean face was pinched against the cold as he raised his head and looked across the field towards the old cottage and noticed there was the flame of a candle flickering in the window.

Emily woke with a start and immediately cried out her son's name as she realised it was Christmas morning. "Tom, she exclaimed". The wire-rimmed spectacles which had been clinging to the tip of her nose fell to the floor un-noticed.

"Where is he?" she asked despairingly as she looked round the cold room hoping to see him.

He's upstairs, she thought, as she gripped the arms of the chair and tried to heave herself up. "He didn't want to wake me up and went straight up to bed", she muttered.

Her legs were weak and her body was not awake as she sank back heavily onto the chair's hard wooden seat with a groan. She was in a hurry to greet her son and tried again, only more slowly this time. Grimacing with the effort, she rose slowly from the chair. Her old bones creaked and it was difficult these days to get her body moving but grasping the handrail, she pulled herself up the draughty flight of narrow stairs as quickly as she could and hobbling along the dark landing, she made her way into Tom's room.

Empty!

She stood staring in disbelief at the empty bed and her face dropped with disappointment as her eyes frantically searched the room. She stood shocked not knowing what to think. Slowly and despondently she made her way back down the stairs. At first, she sat in the lonely cold room staring vacantly at the garland of holly decorating the mirror, still shocked Tom had not come home. Gradually, her mood lifted and she became convinced he would arrive later and she began to feel better. She re-laid and lit the fire and sat by the window watching and waiting for him to walk up the road through the drifted snow which had been whipped up during the night. At times her nose was almost pressed against the ice-cold glass of the window pane and as the long hours ticked by, another Christmas Day passed without her son coming home. Whilst Emily sat forlornly watching the shadows of the flames of the fire dancing on the walls, her spirits sank and once again she became ensnared in the web of loneliness which had become woven around her ever since Tom had said goodbye so long ago.

The weeks lengthened into months and the spring morning had broken, bringing with it the promise of the season's warmth. Even though Emily lived alone, she always woke at daybreak and this bright March morning was no different. She had been awakened by the sound of the dawn chorus and this was the first time for many cold months she had heard the joyful sound. Although the wind outside was beginning to lose its snarling bite, inside the cottage was still cold and damp after the bleak winter's weather. Emily rose from her bed and took a blanket off the lumpy horse-hair mattress and draped it round her shoulders. She shivered as she pulled back the thin curtains and looked out of the small bedroom window. At least there was no ice on the inside of the glass or even on the window ledge where earlier it had covered the solidified pool of red candle wax which was left there since Christmas. There had been so many mornings during the winter when the ice on the window panes had left intricate patterns of leaves and ferns which had prevented her from looking out across the field to the line of majestic elm trees and the warren beyond.

It had been nearly twenty eight years since dear Edwin had died and Emily was now over seventy. For all of her life she had risen early, ever since she went into service as a scullery maid when she was a young girl of thirteen. The work had been hard and unrewarding. Scrubbing floors and washing dishes and scrubbing more floors and washing more dishes. The images flashed through her mind and as she thought about those early days, her mind drifted back to the nights she had spent in the draughty attic bedroom at Chartham Grange crying herself to sleep with sore hands and an aching back, wishing she was back in Uxbridge with her beloved parents and siblings.

Emily shivered with the cold and pulled the blanket around her and despite the sounds of spring outside, she felt old and lonely and as she made her way downstairs, a warm tear trickled down her cold cheek.

Another of Emily's habits was to light the fire to get some heat into the room and boil the kettle before she got dressed. When Edwin had been alive, he needed hot water to shave with and to make a cup of tea before he went to work and then as the boys grew up, they needed the same. Slowly, conscious of the rheumatism in her old bones, she knelt down and scraped out the soft grey ash from the cold fire. She sighed with relief when she saw the flicker of a small embryonic flame burst into life setting fire to the thin sticks of kindling wood. Emily lifted the tongs from the hearth and carefully balanced a few knobs of coal on the burning wood and anxiously watched the smoking fire.

"Good", she said to herself when she saw through the billowing white smoke, the welcome orange flames of burning coals.

After filling the old blackened kettle with fresh water, the old lady stood it on the narrow iron shelf in front of the fire grid, safe in the knowledge it would not be too long before it boiled. She pulled her chair closer to the heat of the fire and thought how nice it will be when the warmer weather returned. She had not always been a country person. Her father had been a miller and as a child, her mother had sailed to America with her parents. Emily poked the fire absentmindedly, as she remembered her mother telling her that when the family reached America, there had been an outbreak of plague which killed Emily's grandfather and being told how her grandmother had turned around and found her way back to England. If her kith and kin had the fortitude all those years ago to return from America, there was no reason, Emily mused as she looked at the dancing flames, why Tom would not be able to come home from wherever he was.

Emily lifted the sagging gate with a practised ease as she went into the back garden to feed the few remaining chicken with some potato peelings and a handful of layers mash. Ever since Tom had left home, this had become a daily ritual and she never failed to enjoy the greeting her feathered friends gave her, grateful to them for breaking the loneliness she felt.

"Chicken, come and get your breakfast", Emily called, as she emptied the sweet smelling mash into their trough before looking into the nest box. Her face lit up with delight when she saw one of the hens had rewarded her with an egg. "Good girls", Emily said to the chickens clucking around her feet, as she carefully removed the warm egg.

She was washing her hands in the stone sink in the scullery when she heard the sound of a car stopping in the lane outside of the cottage. Visitors were such a rarity now and in curiosity she made her way across the room to look out of the window. The old lady gasped in disbelief when she caught sight of the man's khaki uniform as he slammed the car door and started walking towards the front door.

When she caught a glimpse of the badge on the man's peaked cap she clasped her hand over her mouth in shock. She recognised the badge immediately and as the soldier removed his cap she watched motionless, frozen to the spot, as he smoothed out his chestnut brown hair with a leather-gloved hand. A cold tingle ran down her spine and suddenly it became difficult for her to breathe. Her short breaths were in such quick succession it felt as if her lungs were filled with cotton wool. The old lady was fighting to control the tears which were filling her eyes as the realization dawned. Her son had returned home. At last Tom had come home from the war.

"TOM", she screamed with relief, through the unopened door.

Emily's thin, wrinkled fingers desperately grasped the brass door knob. She pulled the door open with such speed, she saw him standing statue-like with a clenched fist, raised in readiness to announce his arrival on the door.

I'll cook him the egg, Emily was already thinking, and I can make some scones.

The morning sun flooded into the room through the open door and searched out every crack and crevice on the old woman's face. He was wearing the uniform of an officer in the Royal Artillery Corps. His tunic was immaculately cut. Pulled in at the waist by a shining leather belt with a sword frog hanging from it and diagonally across his broad chest was another belt, the shade matching to perfection his gleaming high boots. Emily could see his hair had been so immaculately cut it looked as though each hair had been individually put into place. The tears of joy in her eyes blurred her vision and she stood in shock, totally unaware she was staring at her son. There was a melancholy look on his thin face and the old lady could see, almost hidden from view, there was a hint of sadness in his olive green eyes.

"TOM", Emily cried out in recognition. Her voice quivered with years of pent-up emotion as she stumbled forward to embrace her long-lost son. She had waited so long for this moment and had never once given up hope that he would return home one day and here he was, an officer, standing like a stranger on the door step.

"Tom, Tom", she gasped as she reached out and took him into her open arms.

There was a look of surprise on the man's face as he gently extricated himself from the old lady's embrace and quickly stepped back, retreating from the doorstep onto the brick path. For a moment, neither Emily nor the soldier uttered a word, until the visitor broke the silence.

"Mrs Kealey?" he said softly.

A sharp breath came out of her almost like a groan. Emily's mind was in a spin of confusion as stared at the man's lips as if they had mimed the words. She did not want to hear what the stranger was saying and stood with a scream trapped somewhere deep down inside her frail body.

Her body convulsed with shock and it felt as though her flesh was being ripped from the bones.

"No, no", she muttered at last.

Suddenly Emily felt faint and everything started going round. She reached out to grip the door frame to stop her from falling. Her grip tightened on the wooden frame as her heart sank and tears of bitter disappointment began to flow freely from behind her wire rimmed glasses and down her furrowed face. She stood staring at the man for almost a minute without speaking.

She had realised the man standing in front of her was not Tom.

The soldier coughed and cleared his throat before saying her name again. "Mrs Kealey", he repeated slightly more loudly this time and with growing authority in his voice.

This time she heard him and could see he was an officer. A captain perhaps, Emily thought as she stared once again at the badge on the peaked cap the man was holding. It was the badge of her son's regiment and looking at the gold coloured insignia she could hear Tom's voice ringing in her ears, "Once a gunner always a gunner". A shiver ran down her spine as she remembered how she had hated hearing those words coming from his mouth and how she had resented the army from stealing both her son and her husband from her.

The officer gently took her arm and helped her back inside the cottage. He was surprised how thin and frail the old lady was. She was trembling and she felt afraid as she turned to look once more at the man, whom she could see was of a similar age to Tom. Emily's mind was in turmoil as she felt his hand release its firm grip on her arm as she slumped into the chair by the dying fire. She watched silently as the man pulled out one of chairs which had been pushed under the table and sat down close beside her. The softness she had seen in his olive green eyes had become veiled with a grey hue of sadness.

He reached out and gently took her hand before looking directly into her eyes and saying gently, "I am very sorry to have to tell you that your son, Tom, has been listed as missing". He paused before saying, "Presumed dead".

The old lady's hand was cold and lifeless and a look of shock was frozen on her face. The man stared down at his polished brown boots waiting for the woman's grief and despair to burst forth. It was something over the past year he had witnessed so many times before but this time it did not happen. Instead she just sat there, staring into his downcast eyes.

"Mrs Kealey", the officer said tenderly, as he raised his head, "You must not give up hope that your son is still alive".

He paused to collect his thoughts before saying, "The nature of the war in the Far-East meant many men became separated from their regiments". "Some of them were transported to Japan after their capture. Perhaps Tom was one of them", he added as an after-thought, hoping to soften the news he had just delivered.

"We are, of course, doing everything we can to discover what happened to all of the missing men but there will be a lot whom we will never know what...how....", he hesitated awkwardly before deciding to say no more.

The young officer could see the old lady wasn't listening to him. Her mind was elsewhere. My God, he thought, this is bloody difficult. He had been in so many houses and had sat in so many different chairs. His eyes wandered round the small room whilst he waited for the woman to say something. They were drawn to the polished bronze medallion on the sideboard. Dead man's penny ......husband, he thought, or perhaps a son. Two photographs stood either side of it . One of them was a wedding group. His eyes roamed to the pretty young bride in the photo, laughing...happy. She was wearing a wide brimmed hat ringed with flowers....her tiny waist held by a wide belt clasped together with a large silver buckle. His mind strayed. Was he holding the hand of the slim young woman in the photograph.... her husband dead....killed in the Great War, he wondered, before glancing back at the old lady? Poor woman, she looks so vulnerable. He looked at the other photograph. It was a soldier wearing the uniform of a gunner...... laughing ....carefree with his cap perched at an angle on the back of his head. That's him, the young officer suddenly realised...... that's Tom Kealey. But where the bloody hell, are you now? Are you dead or just bloody missing?

He lit a cigarette and drew in the smoke, waiting for what he considered to be a respectable length of time before breaking the silence and finally saying, "We will keep you informed as soon as we hear anything....... have any information".

He remained sitting on the hard chair with his head bowed, trying to avoid looking directly at Emily's white face, drained of blood. It never gets any easier, the officer thought to himself as he fiddled with the peak of his cap waiting for the old lady to say something. He had been in this situation countless times since the end of the war and knew after waiting for suitable period of time to elapse, it was best to leave the person to grieve alone.

He declined the cup of tea Emily finally offered and after asking if there was anything he could do, the soldier expressed his condolences, clicked his heels together and left. He had seen himself out and Emily heard the soft click of the latch as the man closed the front door behind him.

She sat staring at the fire which was long dead in the grate and when she eventually rose from her chair, she realised the daylight had gone and it was quite dark in the cottage. Alone, with only her thoughts to comfort her, Emily sobbed quietly, as she stared out of the window into the blackness beyond. Her heart was empty, stricken with something that tears alone would not comfort. Her hopes dashed and her dreams destroyed.

The minutes passed by and the ticking clock was the only sound in the room until Emily suddenly exclaimed, "Missing presumed dead, the officer had said, not dead, just missing. Missing, presumed dead...... not dead", she kept repeating to herself. "Presumed dead, just presumed"

"Yes", she said with growing conviction as she collected her thoughts. Tom was alive.

"He's alive", Emily suddenly said, as if she was confirming what she had been thinking.

Somewhere he was alive and he would come back. Yes, he would come home. Tom would come back, perhaps in time for next Christmas and it was these thoughts racing through her mind which lifted her spirit. Yes, she thought, she would wait for him.

It was sometime later when Emily remembered the letter, Tom's letter. The last letter he had written to her. Slowly she rose from the hard chair. Her knees creaked as she made her way carefully across the pitch black room and groped for the mantelpiece over the cold fire, searching for the box of matches she kept there. With the small box safely in her hand, she slowly slid her hand further along the wooden shelf to find the oil lamp.

"Ah", she said, as her fingers touched its cold brass base.

Emily's hands were gnarled with rheumatism and it took her three attempts before she was able to strike the small match. Its tiny flame flickered and she carefully lifted the glass chimney of the lamp which had stood on the dusty mantle for more years than the old lady could remember and with a shaking hand, she held the burning match against the oily wick of the lamp.

"Good", she muttered, as the wick reluctantly yielded to the flame.

Slowly and carefully Emily replaced the lamp's glass chimney and watched as the black smoke from the burning wick curled upwards into the room. In time, the light such as it was, settled and spread across the room.

She knew exactly where to find the precious letter. After all, she had read it so many times since it had dropped on the door-mat four years ago. With the feeble yellow light of the lamp lifting the gloom of the room, Emily shuffled across and took the grubby envelope from the sideboard drawer before making her way back to the fireplace and the flickering light. With a shaking hand she carefully took out the precious sheet of paper and read the words once again. Her brow furrowed and a quizzical expression spread across the old lady's face as she looked at the envelope. She had often wondered why it was so dirty and crumpled and why the postmark showed it had been posted in Scotland.

Was he in Scotland, she pondered? Had he already come back from Singapore? A hint of a smile returned to her face as she carefully removed the letter and read it in the flickering light of the lamp.

My dearest Mother

As I write this I am thinking of you and hope you are well.

Do not worry about me, everything is fine here and I am having plenty of food.

It may be some time before I get a chance to write again, I hope you got the cable I sent at Christmas, I certainly wished that I had been with you all

Never fear, I will be home next Christmas, I am sure.

Your loving son

Tom.

There was the look of a mother's joy on the old lady's face as she folded the precious letter and carefully tucked it back into its envelope. It was a pity Tom couldn't have found a bit more time to write a longer letter, she thought. Perhaps he had been busy but then, he was never much of a letter writer.

The light from the candle which Emily carried illuminated the narrow staircase as she made her way up to bed. Her mind was so full of thoughts of her son she doubted whether she would sleep but it didn't matter. Next Christmas, or even before, Tom would be able to answer all of the questions which were racing inside her head but best of all, when he returned, she would be able to embrace the son she so desperately missed.

The old lady was smiling as she blew out the candle and laid her head on the goose down pillow and closed her eyes.

11

Journey's End

Speeding cars splashed through the water which lay deep in the pot holes along the Street. The impatient drivers were more interested in reaching their destinations in the shortest time possible than to notice the elderly couple who were huddled under a leafless horse chestnut tree on the rain lashed village green. The November morning was cold and wet as Tom Kealey's nephew, grey haired Eddie Kealey and Susan, his wife of forty-five years sheltered from the rain. Under the couple's feet and buried deep in the wet grass were a few of the glossy coated conkers which had fallen from the tree in the autumn. There was a distinct chill in the air and the light, early morning drizzle had given way to heavy rain. On the opposite side of the green, large puddles of water lay like small ponds on the saturated ground around the goal posts. The north wind was signalling the start of winter as it blew from the Downs, obscuring the familiar white chalk cliffs from sight by a thick descending mist. Eddie dismissed the thought of how unpleasant Pentbury was in the pouring rain and instead thought about what was to come.

Susan cast an envious look at a couple who were walking towards them, each sheltering under a large umbrella and she turned to her husband and said with a hint of recrimination in her voice, "I told you we should have brought an umbrella".

Eddie watched curiously as the couple approached and holding out his umbrella, the genial looking man said, "Filthy weather, would you like to borrow this, we can manage with just the one?"

As Eddie thanked him, he suddenly remembered they were the couple who lived in the converted oast house up the lane. He and Sue had once visited their huge landscaped garden when the couple had opened it for a charity day and he recalled how they had been told it had once been a hop garden, one of the many which years ago had surrounded the village. No sooner had Eddie and Sue gratefully huddled under the borrowed umbrella, a gust of wind caught it and turned it inside out. Eddie uttered an unseemly oath under his breath and then battled with the elements as he tried in vain to return the umbrella to its original shape. Whilst Eddie struggled with the wayward brolly, the horizontal rain continued relentlessly, soaking the two couples as they waited for a bedraggled pack of Cub Scouts and Brownies to walk up the lane to join them, together with small groups of other people who had also arrived.

The date was the 11th November 2011 and it was Remembrance Sunday.

Twenty or so men and women had now started to gather on the edge of the green around the stone War Memorial which had been built to commemorate the men from the village who had given their lives during the Great War. The youngsters stood and shivered and wished they were at home playing their computer games instead of getting wet on the village green. The elderly vicar walked slowly from his car and stood bare headed in the driving rain. A red poppy was pinned to his flowing white surplus, made almost translucent by the inclement weather.

"The poor man is soaked to the skin", whispered the voice of a concerned female parishioner from under one of the large coloured umbrellas that now hid the faces of most of the assembled congregation.

The vicar coughed and a respectful silence followed.

"We have come together to worship Almighty God", he said in a loud, clear voice.

Gradually, one by one, some more of the umbrellas were lifted and the vicar smiled with pleasure as he saw familiar faces appearing from underneath them.

He continued with the service, "To recall in our minds those through death, injury or bereavement, suffered to bring peace and freedom to our world".

"We will now sing the hymn, O God our help in ages past", he said, "you will find the words on the sheets you have been given". His eyes searched for the young Brownie who had handed the sheets round and he smiled when they alighted on the young girl.

Some of the large multi-coloured golf umbrellas clashed with others as they were quickly lowered as the owners tried to retrieve the sodden hymn sheets from their pockets and handbags.

The vicar didn't wait for them.

"O God our help in ages past, our help in years to come", he sung with considerable gusto.

The villagers, at last started to catch up with him. "Our shelter from the stormy blast and our eternal home", they sung together. The rain had nearly stopped as the singing of the hymn was coming to an end and Eddie lowered the borrowed umbrella   "... Be thou our guide while life shall last and our eternal home", he sang

"Let us remember the men from this village who gave their lives in time of war", the rain soaked vicar said solemnly, as he fumbled to find the list of names from the pocket of his black trousers which was partially covered by his clinging surplus.

"He's forgotten the list", laughed one of the Cub Scouts.

Some of the others joined in and giggled before a meaningful glare from their leader stopped their youthful mirth, his irritation showing.

"Allard... Brown...Hubert Day... Lawrence Day... Chesson... Goodwin", the tone of the vicar's voice was becoming more sombre as he read from the list.

The rain had stopped and two young Brownies emerged from under the hoods of their brightly coloured anoraks and together were searching for the names which were carved in the stone cross, as the vicar read them out.

Their excitement increasingly grew, as they pointed out the name before the next one was read out, "Cyril Spartell....Micheal Spartell...Tong...Walters...

Edwin Kealey," and the vicar paused before finally saying, "Tom Kealey".

"That's sixteen men from the First World War and two from the Second", a be-medalled old soldier whispered rather too loudly into the ear of his elderly wife. Eddie glanced at the man's eyes and noticed they were welling with tears.

The vicar continued with the service, his deep, slow voice rolled out, "They shall not grow old, as we that are left grow old, age shall not weary them, nor the years condemn".

A short man in a long grey raincoat who had been standing next to the vicar put his hand under his coat and like a rabbit from a magician's hat he pulled out a battered silver bugle, tightly wrapped up in a remnant of yellow cloth. The man had been waiting for the vicar to say the words, "Nor do the years condemn". This was his signal to be ready and he raised the bugle to his lips in preparation.

"At the going down of the sun and in the morning, we will remember them", the vicar continued.

The assembled crowd repeated the words, saying loudly and together with conviction, "We will remember them".

The man with the bugle puckered his lips around the mouth piece and his cheeks bulged and turned the colour of the poppy on his chest as he sounded the start of the two minutes of silence with a splutter. He gave the bugle another blast realising with embarrassment the cloth he had wrapped it with had not worked. The rain had got into his instrument.

The young Cub Scout laughed again.

People were wondering what on earth it would sound like when the flustered man tried to play the Last Post. Eddie smiled when he thought how amused his Uncle Tom would have found the situation. He stifled the smile and looked towards the newly carved tablet of white stone which had been recently inserted into of the base of cross and a sense of satisfaction came over him.

Two by two, the Brownies and the Cubs carefully walked up the slippery, moss-covered stone steps to lay their wreaths of red poppies. The village had remembered its dead for another year and at last, glimmers of blue sky were beginning to peep out from behind the dark clouds of the November day.

A number of the villagers were now looking at the newly installed tablet of stone and were pointing at Tom Kealey's name which had been carved deeply into it only a few months before.

"Did you know him?" a young voice inquired.

Eddie saw it was the Cub Scout who had laughed at the vicar and was now inspecting the name on the tablet.

"He was my uncle", he replied.

"Was he shot by the Germans?" asked the bright-eyed boy, whose imagination was beginning to grow by the minute, imagining the exciting sounds of battles being fought and the rattle of machine guns.

Grinning at the young lad, Eddie replied, "No, he was on a ship that was sunk".

"Oh" said the boy, "he wasn't really a soldier" and with an evident display of disappointment, he ran off to play with the others in the puddles on the village green.

The old soldier with the red rimmed eyes and the row of newly polished medals hanging from his chest turned to Eddie and with his voice breaking with emotion, he asked, "What kind of man was he?"

"I never knew him", Eddie replied, "Tom died over seventy years ago when I was a baby. He is remembered as a good-natured man, cheerful, always quick to joke and with a great sense of humour".

There was a pause before Eddie continued, "In every photograph that was taken of him, even as a young boy, he was laughing. Not just smiling at the camera but really laughing. I was told he was somebody

who just enjoyed life and was liked by everybody who knew him……..
It was just a terrible pity that he died".

The old soldier didn't say anything but Eddie could see the tears which were streaming down the man's blue veined cheeks as he slowly limped away with painful memories of his own war seeping back.

Eddie looked down once more at the crisply carved inscription of Tom's name and turned to his wife and said, "It took a long time but I feel he has come home at last".

"If you hadn't found the old Japanese record card, you would have never known what happened to him", Sue replied.

Eddie remembered how they had sifted through the stack of boxes of Japanese prisoner of war record cards at the National Records Office, each one yellow with age. Thousands of cards had filled the desk in front of them, so many they spilled onto the floor before they found Tom's card which, like so many of the others, had a red diagonal line drawn across it. He recalled Sue asking him what the red lines were for and he had told her that it meant the prisoner had died in captivity. Wide eyed in astonishment she had exclaimed, "What every one of them?"

The memory of seeing all the red lines scrawled across the piles of cards came flooding back and Eddie knelt down on the wet ground and using his handkerchief, he sponged away the rain drops which were running down the stone cross and filling the newly-cut letters spelling out his uncle's name. Turning to his wife he said rather abruptly, "Come on, let's go and find the car".

They had parked their car opposite the Green in the old farmyard, alongside its row of derelict cowsheds and as they headed for home, they drove up the narrow lane called the Street. Past the old timbered houses with their red tiled roofs and past a huddle of large-windowed cottages which stood close to the road. Eddie knew these had once been the village shops but they had been converted into houses long ago, when the villagers started to drive to the superstores to buy their bread and meat.

Leaning forward in his seat he wiped off the condensation which had formed on the inside of the windscreen with the back of his hand. "It's going to take some time to clear", he said to his wife, who was frantically searching for a yellow duster which had been buried somewhere in the glove box.

Sue found the elusive duster under an assortment of maps and sweet papers and began leaning across Eddie's line of vision trying to wipe away the water which was continuing to run in beads down the misted glass.

"Once the heater comes on and the heat begins to dry our clothes, the screen will start to clear", Eddie explained, thinking it would be easier to see where he was going through a misted screen than trying to look through the duster his wife was yielding with such vigour.

"Look, Eddie", Sue said, as she cleared a small mist free patch on the windscreen, "look to your right, it's the village church".

Quickly wiping the condensation from his side window, Eddie saw the top of a wooden spire standing high above the roofs of the houses and the trees beyond. "That's where my grandmother is buried, he said, "now we are here, shall we see if we can find her grave?"

Sue peered through the small circular patch her husband had cleared on the side window and saw the rain was just beginning to start again and said with an air of resignation, "I suppose we can't get any wetter than we are now".

Eddie eased the car off of the narrow lane and onto, what would have been a grass verge, had it not been churned into a sea of mud by the tyres of the faithful parishioner's cars.

Standing next to the old church was an ancient yew tree. The biting cold wind was whipping its rain laden branches back and forth, deluging the couple as they walked into the graveyard hoping to find Emily Kealey's resting place. At the first glance the task seemed impossible. Many of the headstones were leaning over, stubbornly refusing to fall down, whilst others stood proudly, as if they were imploring the couple to read their ancient inscriptions. Eddie and Sue began their search starting with the stones nearest to the church and then gradually working their way outwards to where the solemnity of the graveyard gently merged with the orchards and where the odd, unpicked apple still clung grimly to the old trees. The rain soaked couple tried not to tread on the fallen grass-wrapped headstones which had capitulated to time, stepping over each stone, reading what inscriptions they could. Occasionally they paused to scrape off the moss and lichen which had formed with the passage of time when some promising inscription was spotted and passed by those which were too eroded to see.

It was Eddie who found it first. They were on the point of giving up and returning to the car, when in an isolated, overgrown corner of the graveyard, he saw the name they had been searching for.

"SUSAN, I'VE FOUND IT", he shouted.

He tore a tussock of grass from alongside the grave's edging stones and quickly used it to wipe off the green slime covering the base of the small, black granite cross and read the inscription which was still carved clearly on it.

"Emily Kealey, beloved mother and grandmother, died 15th July 1955, aged 79 years, In Gods care"

"There she is".

Eddie took his wife's cold, wet hand into his own and holding it gently, said sadly, "Strange isn't it, she was lonely for so much of her life and here she is, in her final resting place.... laying in solitude.

"You once told me her husband, your grandfather Edwin, died at the Somme", Sue murmured.

After a few moments of respectful silence, Sue watched as her husband unpinned the red poppy from the lapel of his rain-soaked coat and laid it down gently at the base of cross. Turning to her, he said, "I think we should find a stone mason to add the names of Tom and Edwin to the cross and then all three of them will be together again and Tom's long journey home will be over".

Sue nodded her head in agreement.

The Vauxhall's engine roared into life as Eddie twisted the ignition key on the car's dashboard and put the muddy sole of his shoe slightly too hard on the accelerator pedal.

As the car slid away from the mud splattered verge, he turned to Sue and said, "I think the cottage where they lived is just up the lane, we'll have a look at it when we drive by".

The day-light was failing fast and heavy rain was hammering on the windscreen. The sweeping wiper blades were only just managing to beat the deluge away and Eddie flicked the switch on the steering column to speed them up.

"It's up here on the right", Eddie said, as he eased his foot off the throttle slightly and peered through the falling rain as they approached the old family cottage.

The sign over the door still read Lavender Cottage but there was now a large grey plastic satellite dish fixed to the chimney stack. The old water pump on the side wall had gone and a garage had been built where the wash house had once stood.

"**LOOK OUT**", Sue screamed, as she instinctively reached out and pushed her hands hard against the car's padded dashboard, preparing herself for the crash which she feared was inevitable.

Eddie cursed.

He had been looking across at the old cottage and his mind had been elsewhere.

It came into his vision as it was about to cross the lane and automatically he stamped down hard on the brakes. He felt the pedal judder as the car's anti-lock braking system came on, sending vibrations up his leg. Eddie's heart was in his mouth and the skin on his knuckles had turned white as he gripped the steering wheel trying desperately to keep control of the car as it slewed and snaked across the wet road.

Instinctively, he frantically pulled down hard left on the steering wheel. "Shit", he mouthed. He had over-steered and his right hand yanked at the wheel to compensate as he attempted to check the path of the wayward car.

He heard Sue let out a scream and out of the corner of his eye he saw she was already braced for the impending impact.

Despite Eddie's efforts the car was seconds away from hitting the creature that was standing its ground in the middle of the road.

Eddie's heart was racing even faster as the car's front off-side wheel started to plough a deep furrow along the sodden grass verge scattering dollops of mud skywards. It seemed as if time had stood still before Eddie finally brought the vehicle back under control and to a sliding halt a hundred yards past the old cottage.

Slowly, he relaxed his vice-like grip from the steering wheel and taking a deep breath, turned to his trembling wife and said, "Are you alright?" before adding rather meekly, "I never saw it".

The old dog fox which had run into the lane from the woods at the side of the cottage was still standing in the middle of the road looking at the shaken couple in the steaming car. Its wet, copper-brown coat was matted and clinging to its long, lean body. After a few moments and a slight nod of the head, the creature made a quick exit through the thin hawthorn and maple hedge. Eddie and Sue watched in silence as the white tip of its bushy tail disappeared into the distance as the noble animal raced across the field towards the warren.

Foxes were still catching rabbits in the field in front of Lavender Cottage.

"Tom Kealey"

Born at Chartham, Kent on 27th December 1907

Died on-board the Hofuku Maru on 21th September 1944

Printed in Great Britain
by Amazon